THE

Mark Urban was educat........ .....g s College School
and graduated from the London School of Economics with First Class Honours. Between school and
university he served as an officer in the 4th Royal
Tank Regiment, subsequently joining the Territorial
Army. He was Defence Correspondent of *The Independent* for more than three years, and as a foreign
affairs and defence specialist for BBC2's *Newsnight*
he covered the Gulf War and the collapse of Soviet
communism. During 1993–4 he worked as BBC
TV's Middle East Correspondent based in Jerusalem
before returning to *Newsnight*. He presents *Levia-
than*, Radio 4's programme about history and current
affairs and is the author of several non-fiction books
including the bestselling *Big Boys' Rules: the Secret
Struggle Against the IRA*. Working as a reporter in
many of the world's recent conflicts he has come to
know the world of espionage and special operations.
THE ILLEGAL is his first novel.

The Illegal

Mark Urban

First published in Great Britain in 1996
by HEADLINE BOOK PUBLISHING

First published in paperback in 1997
by HEADLINE BOOK PUBLISHING

A HEADLINE FEATURE paperback

10 9 8 7 6 5 4 3 2 1

ISBN 0 7472 5470 2

Typeset by Palimpsest Book Production Limited,
Polmont, Stirlingshire
Printed and bound in Great Britain by
Mackays of Chatham PLC, Chatham, Kent

HEADLINE BOOK PUBLISHING
A division of Hodder Headline PLC
338 Euston Road
London NW1 3BH

For my beloved Hilary

Chapter One

Driving a Met Police Astra at 90 m.p.h. in pursuit of a BMW 525, albeit one with four armed robbers on board, requires skill and a good deal of luck. Detective Sergeant Lee Johnson and Detective Constable David MacFadyen couldn't believe theirs when the BMW slewed right across the Uxbridge Road and into Frithville Gardens.

'Fucking magic!' shouted MacFadyen 'straight into a cul-de-sac.'

'Control, this is Kilo Six Two; suspects have entered Frithville Gardens; send Armed Response Vehicles to this location immediately—' Johnson had not managed the 'Over' before the Astra, failing to make the same corner, hit the kerb at 65 m.p.h. The deep kerbstone took the front axle off clean, the rest of the car continuing in a shower of sparks through the window of 'One-Hour Snaps' on the corner. For a fraction of a second as they skidded across the pavement, Johnson experienced that curious silence, a feeling of detachment, which is the last thing many people feel. As the car came to rest inside the shop, its bonnet no more than two feet from a dumbstruck school leaver behind the counter, Johnson and MacFadyen cracked open the doors and stumbled out.

The BMW had already been to the dead end of the road, turned, and was on its way back, as Johnson and MacFadyen rushed to block its escape. Johnson drew his Smith and Wesson, signed out four hours earlier barely five hundred yards away at Shepherds Bush police station. To his surprise the BMW came to a halt and its occupants jumped out. Four men, one Uzi, two shotguns and four mail bags moving across the pavement towards the door of Number 26. Balaclava or not, Johnson recognised the figure of 'Sancho' Doherty, the Scouser who led this gang, hunching into firing position, pointing his shotgun straight towards them.

'Back off or I'll drop you bastards!'

Johnson kept going, Doherty gave him both barrels, but at nearly a hundred yards with a sawn-off weapon, he didn't have much chance of stopping the CID man. The pellets went hissing over Johnson's head. Doherty turned, making his way up the path and through the smashed front door of the house. Inside, the screams of its tenant, Hortense Villiers, had begun in earnest.

Johnson and MacFadyen were making their way gingerly towards the house, using parked cars as cover, when another of the villains appeared at an upstairs window, took aim with the Uzi and fired off at least twenty rounds in their direction. This was more serious. Both policemen dropped to the street as the cars in front of them shuddered from the 9mm parabellum striking home.

'Jesus Christ! Are you all right, Jock?'

'Yeah boss,' MacFadyen replied, swallowing the words as the rush of adrenalin and naked fear made him take short, stabbing breaths. Johnson spotted a woman, apparently oblivious, manoeuvring a push-chair out of the front gate of a house almost opposite Number 26 and shouted, 'Stay inside! Police! Go inside!' His breathing was erratic too, enough to mean he almost swallowed the words and had to repeat them twice before the woman turned on her heels and went back indoors.

Johnson had been shot at before, but this was not good. Any attempt to move from behind the flimsy cover offered by an already riddled Renault would expose them to the full firepower at the disposal of Doherty and the others. How long before the armed backup arrived? If Doherty had any sense, he would be over the garden wall behind the house by now. Johnson recognised the possibility that the gang he had pursued for almost two years might get away.

'Sancho!' he shouted. After a brief moment, Doherty came to the window.

'You realise you're surrounded. You should have stayed in bed this morning you daft Scouse bastard!'

'Suck my dick, Johnson! We've got a hostage, we're walking out of here.'

Johnson could happily be verbally abused all afternoon so long as a) he wasn't being shot at, b) Doherty was staying put and c) the backup was getting closer. A few moments and insults later he looked down beyond his polished DMs to see uniformed officers rounding the corner. Even the useless desk sergeant at Shepherds Bush had heard the machine-gun fire and it hadn't taken him long to dispatch every available body.

'Stay back! Cordon the area and wait for the Armed Response Vehicle!'

MacCready, another of Doherty's Scouse mafia squeezed off another couple of rounds from the Uzi, apparently to underline the point.

The siren from the unmarked Range Rover could be heard long before the vehicle appeared at the bottom of Frithville Gardens. As the uniforms were already evacuating residents at the end of the road, a couple of moustachioed hard men from SO19 sauntered up the road. The Range Rover had been followed by an Armed Response Vehicle with more SO19 types in uniform. They had removed two Steyr assault rifles from the padlocked metal locker on the back seat and joined their plainclothes partners inching up the bottom of the road. They reminded Johnson of many of the Special Forces types he had known in the Army: the plainclothes ones always seemed to be in an unofficial uniform with their moustaches, jeans and trainers. The two uniformed SO19 types had donned their dark blue berets and flak jackets. Johnson found the firearms types a little odd – they always took great care in their appearance, a lot of them were ex-Army and just couldn't let go of the whole macho business of toting weapons.

The SO19 foursome got the Uzi welcome too and went rushing back towards their wagon.

'So much for the fucking Village People!' MacFadyen muttered, as the SO19 men disappeared around the corner. 'What do we do now? Run for it?'

'We wait here until the hundreds of arseholes who will soon be on the scene can figure a way to get us out. They'll cut us down if we make a run for it.'

Inside, there was pandemonium. MacCready, like a caged beast, had set about smashing the bedroom furniture.

'Are you alone?' Doherty shouted in Mrs Villers's face.

'All alone since my husband died, God rest his soul.'

Doherty turned to one of the others. 'Take her into the kitchen and tie her to a chair. She might get us out of this shithole.'

Johnson and MacFadyen were to spend another hour and twenty minutes lying in the gutter. After a while their body heat began to drop – the ground draws it out. Johnson found himself shivering. His nose was pressed close to the surface, his eyes de-focused for a moment and he began to daydream. He wondered whether his wife knew what was going on. Probably not. Then he remembered the first time he saw her, in the King's Head in Bristol. He had gone there on a weekend to get away from the boredom of his course at Swynnerton. It was a student bar, and soldiers' folklore maintained those were the best for pickups. He remembered gazing across for hours, transfixed by her pale skin, blue eyes and her broad, deep mouth. She had worn a curious pair of pink dungarees, which hadn't put him off at all. As he had finally plucked up the courage to offer her a drink, she had looked up at him with her big eyes and he had felt like one of those cartoon characters with steam coming out of his ears and eyes rolling like the drums on a fruit machine. He had known he was falling fast.

When it started, Jane was not bothered by the fact he was a soldier. In fact, she was so delighted by the appalled reactions of some of her right-on student friends, that he had realised it was all part of his appeal. But after she graduated with her 2:1 in law she had moved from a tolerant student community into a profession with its own rules and self-image. Things had never been quite the same. Still, he smiled at the memory of the King's Head and the UB-40 playing on the juke box, and hoped she wasn't worrying about him. 'I got you babe,' he remembered the song.

Eventually Superintendent Farmer, the second in command of SO19, arrived to take personal control of the incident. By then, sixteen of his officers were already in the area. After the undignified retreat which had ended their first foray, the SO19 boys were leaving nothing to chance. They had kitted up to the hilt, clad in dark blue jump suits, flak jackets and helmets and brandishing Heckler and Koch sub-machine guns and snipers' rifles.

Farmer appeared and gave his men their first orders: 'I want two sniper teams established. One front, one rear. Gibson, Grenville, see if you can put yourself on the first floor of one of the houses opposite. You'll have to enter through their back gardens. MacMichael and Stevens, you'll take the rear, we're liaising with the Transport Police to get you along the tube line behind Number 26. The embankment should give you a good vantage point.' The superintendent turned to address his remaining men. 'We'll form two groups of six, one in reserve by my wagon please, the other about halfway up Frithville ready for immediate action to break the front door down if things start getting lively in there.'

Inside Number 26 the phone was ringing and Doherty and the others were arguing about whether to pick it up.

'Shut it, I'm still thinking,' Doherty said. He stood beside Mrs Villiers in the kitchen. MacCready was upstairs, the other two returned to the living room at the front of the house. Mrs Villiers's face was grey. Even to Doherty, it was apparent that her heart was not good.

Superintendent Farmer had devised a bold plan to rescue the two detectives, involving an armoured Land Rover which had just arrived from Heathrow airport and several of his officers.

As time passed, MacFadyen's mind turned from self-preservation to the cups of tea he had drunk at the nick before that morning's stakeout of the Majestic safe deposit box company in South Kensington.

'Chief?'

'Yeah?'

'I'm desperate for a piss.'

'Do what? You must be joking.'

A few moments' silence.

'I can't take my mind of it,' MacFadyen said plaintively.

'Well have one then.'

'I don't want to piss my trousers.'

'Well piss away from yourself then . . . Jesus.'

MacFadyen was just about to, when the armoured Land Rover came roaring up Frithville Gardens.

'Put your dick away mate, I think we're leaving.' Johnson felt a moment's panic, wondering whether the villains would think they were about to be stormed, but things happened very swiftly.

The Land Rover drew level, halted and three officers with bulletproof shields jumped out. They held the protective cover over Johnson first and then MacFadyen as they scrambled off the road and into the back of the Rover. With the two CID men on board, the Rover reversed back towards the Goldhawk Road.

Johnson made his way to Superintendent Farmer at the incident control point, hobbling slightly on legs made cold by the street.

'All right my son?'

'Yes sir. Thank you sir. What happens now?'

'We get chummy to the phone and we give him things straight. We wave gun at chummy and moments later, I promise you, chummy will be coming out of the front door with his hands up.'

'I don't think it's going to be that simple, sir. That villain your blokes shot at the filling station blag in Chigwell last year was in the same gang. They bear a grudge. It won't be easy. Quite honestly, they're plant life, sir.'

Farmer nodded and walked away. More SO19 officers had arrived in another van. They had scaling ladders, ropes and searchlights. One sniper team had already made it into a house in front of Number 26. Other police were moving up Frithville Gardens itself.

As they were standing about, the owner of the One-Hour Snaps shop had arrived and almost fainted at the sight of the Police Astra in his premises. Johnson and MacFadyen had enjoyed a boyish giggle from a distance, but eventually he had caught them up.

'What do you think you're playing at? the Keystone-fucking-cops?'

'I'm very sorry, sir—'

Johnson was interrupted by MacFadyen, who said: 'You see, I was in a hurry to pick up my enlargements.' The owner shot him a poison glance.

'We were in pursuit of armed criminals,' Johnson continued po-faced. 'I'm sure the damage will be covered.'

'I'll believe it when I see it,' the shopkeeper said before his mood apparently lightened and he added: 'I suppose I might get a better shopfront out of all this.'

As the man walked away, MacFadyen muttered so that only Johnson heard him. 'But what about my enlargements and free Fuji-chrome beach bag?' As Johnson shook his head in mock disapproval, they noticed something was happening.

'Sir, they've answered the phone,' said one of the constables in the back of the incident control vehicle.

A handset was rushed into Farmer's grasp. With his other hand, he put down the ACPO guidelines and ran his fingers through his white hair, contemplating his next move. 'Mr Doherty—'

'Shut your mouth and listen,' the villain interrupted.

As Farmer digested what Doherty was saying he looked around nervously and bit his lip. The conversation ended abruptly. The superintendent turned to a uniformed inspector from Shepherds Bush who had leant into the back of the vehicle and told him: 'They want a getaway car and they say they're going to start carving up the lady in the house if it's not on its way in fifteen minutes.' Then he added, 'They say they're going to chop her up bit by bit.'

Doherty ran a hand down the black moustache which had earned him his nickname. His forearm was tattooed 'LFC'. Despite the manner in which he had put his ultimatum, he knew the chances of escape were minimal. Instead of making him despair, that thought simply fed his rage. He began kicking in the units around the kitchen. Tears streamed down Mrs Villiers's cheeks.

~on and MacFadyen stood surveying the scene from the

end of the road. One written-off Astra, a few shot-up cars. Nobody walking the street and policemen with sub-machine guns crouching in front gardens. After Doherty's threat, Farmer had put several more teams of police in and around the street.

'Well my old china, it was a good tip,' reflected the detective sergeant.

'We should have had a proper stakeout at Majestic,' added MacFadyen.

'I don't know. You can't blame the head shed. How often does a low-grade tout deliver up a gang like Doherty's?' Johnson replied with the generosity of the hunter who knows long-pursued prey is almost in the bag.

Inside Number 26 events were moving quickly.

'Jacko, get in here,' barked Doherty.

'Hold her hand out. Put it down on the bread board.' Jacko did it without apparent thought.

'Oh no, please no,' sobbed Mrs Villers, 'have mercy on me.'

Doherty picked up the phone.

'You've had your time, where is our car you bastard?'

'I've just been speaking to the Commissioner and—'

'Quiet. I'm going to take off a couple of fingers.'

Jacko looked away, as Doherty leaned over, beads of sweat on his brow. There was a crunch of blade on bone.

Johnson and MacFadyen heard the screams from the end of the Gardens.

Superintendent Farmer put the receiver down and picked up a microphone.

'All units move now. I say again, move now. Hostage under attack.'

Two SO19 men vaulted over the back fence and kicked in

the kitchen door. The first fired a three-round burst, hitting Jacko in the chest. Doherty dropped to his knees with his arms in the air.

'Don't shoot! Don't shoot!'

At the front, four more heavily armed officers had gone through the front door. MacCready came down the stairs, squeezing off the Uzi. The first officer fell as the round hit the ceramic plate in the front of his flak jacket, producing a cloud of brown powder. Two others opened fire and MacCready fell forwards, bouncing down the stairs. The other villain came out of the front room with his hands raised; the siege was over.

Johnson and MacFadyen rushed foward, ducking the police tape at the bottom of the road, towards Number 26.

Two SO19 men came bounding out of the house holding Doherty by the shoulders. Sancho's hands were held behind his back with plasticuffs. He was pushed against a parked car and a third SO19 man flicked Doherty's head down repeatedly, hitting his face against the roof. Blood seeped from his shattered nose.

'Anything you want to say to this fucking toerag, sarge?'

Johnson surveyed Doherty's bleeding face. 'No. I'll have plenty of time with him in the interview room.'

An ambulance crew pushed past the two plainclothes men. Mrs Villiers was led out, her mouth still open in a silent scream, blood speckled on her pink carpet slippers.

In the living room of Number 26, the two detectives surveyed the spoils of the raid on Majestic. Four sacks full of the contents of seventy-three deposit boxes emptied earlier that day in South Kensington. Jewels, money and papers.

'I suppose we'd better get these back to the nick.'

'And down to the Club?'

'Only to be sociable, you understand.' For the first time Johnson's face broke into a smile.

Chapter Two

It was 4.50 at Gower Street. 'GWS' as it is known in the Service. Charles Denton's day at work was coming to an end. Everything was coming to an end.

Denton worked in K2 Section on the fourth floor. He began to collect the papers on his desk. They were intercepts of conversations. Denton's job involved sifting them and all other reports relating to three Arabs. They were diplomats at the Algerian embassy. It used to be Russians and Poles, but K Branch – Counter-Espionage – had redeployed its staff in keeping with the changed realities. In as much as Whitehall, or anybody else, understood them. Some of the papers were marked:

TOP SECRET – UMBRA – UK EYES ONLY

Which meant: property of the secret state – very sensitive material gathered by intercepting somebody's signal traffic – don't show this to foreigners, allies included. Others were headed:

TOP SECRET – AZURE – SS EYES ONLY

That meant: ditto – material gathered by letting yourself into somebody's flat and bugging it – don't show it to people outside the Security Service.

It was a very elaborate way of protecting papers ninety-nine percent of which were about: video camcorders, and where on the Edgeware Road to buy them; why the children hang out with those no-good Kuwaitis at the cinema in Whiteleys and when is Ahmed going to tell those timeservers in Algiers that he needs a raise? The other one percent concerned the Service's suspicions that the Algerians were helping the Iraqis keep an intelligence network in London.

Still, the use of those codewords meant Denton could not leave the papers on his desk overnight. Secret paperwork was Denton's pet subject, not that he let on to his colleagues that he could massage virtually anything out of Registry. He placed them into folders and got up. His head was light and he put a hand onto the table to steady himself. Fifty-nine years old and not likely to see sixty. He put the folders into a cupboard-sized safe, closed it and spun the combination lock.

'Goodnight Shirley.'

'Good night Mr Denton – see you tomorrow.'

Denton walked into the corridor and towards the lift. 4.54. He got into the lift. It travelled down one floor. The DG and one of her deputies got in without a word. A coat from Jaeger and a scent from France. She eyed Denton briefly, without recognition, and then looked at her watch.

Denton thought, 'So, I'm six minutes early, you bitch.'

'We'll have to hurry,' the Director General said to her companion.

Denton got out at the ground floor. The DG and DDG (A), as Mr Pestlethwaite is properly referred to in Service correspondence, continued down to the basement, where the DG's Daimler awaited in the underground garage.

Denton walked onto Gower Street, his spirits lifted momentarily by the summer sun, turned right and travelled the short distance to Euston Square tube where his optimism evaporated. There was the usual herd on the platform.

'Good evening, this is Circle Line information . . .' The herd shuddered in anticipation, 'owing to a man on the track at Victoria, all services are suffering severe disruption this evening'.

'What a shitty country this is', Denton thought – but this time aloud. The young woman beside him smiled meekly and pretended to be interested in her paper.

For Jane Johnson it was also a day of tedious routine. As a junior solicitor, paper blighted her life too. Like many people who have succeeded in scaling the first rungs of a professional life, she had become alarmed at how little the future she had craved through so many years of education actually amounted to. All of the great dilemmas of law and natural justice which had fuelled the debate in her tutorials at Bristol now just seemed like some vain intellectual game. In the cramped quarters of the law offices where she worked, her thoughts often strayed to something else at the centre of her life. She worried about Lee and whether she still loved him. Often she lay awake at night thinking about this. She would watch him sleep and feel herself torn by feelings of love frustration. His lack of ambition for them and his daughter worried her deeply. It was like he didn't want anything more than to be a low-level CID man living in shitty Hammersmith. She had realised that she wanted more than that.

In that inner sanctum where couples conceal their private thoughts, Jane could not stop the most poisonous of doubts from gnawing away at her self-confidence. Did she still really love him? Was their sex an act of love any more or simply one of domestic routine? Was he her equal intellectually?

Recently the girls in the office had enjoyed talking about Damien, a young cycle messenger. Jane felt guilty that she had found herself joining in. These days, when she made love with her husband, Jane could not stop her mind wandering – not to Damien or anybody specific; just away from Lee. Sometimes it still worked for her, more often she found herself pretending that their lovemaking had given her pleasure. Damien noticed her as she went to pick up a mug of coffee from the little kitchen at the other end of the office.

'All right love?' he said, winking.

She didn't answer, although she marvelled at his confidence for somebody of his age. Many men still considered Jane a highly attractive woman, no matter that she had had a child and her backside, in her view, had never been the same again. She had been the centre of her small-town world when she was growing up in Lake, on the Isle of Wight. So many tongue-tied, acned young lads had beaten a path to her front door to ask her out, or just to see whether she was in for a chat.

Jane's mother and father still lived in that house – a bungalow to be more accurate. They had the convenience of living in a retirement belt; they were not looking to spend their last years anywhere else. Jane occasionally alluded to her listless worries and her mum believed that the answer was for her and Lee to have another child. Jane could see the logic of this, since the birth of Gemma, their first, had been a revelation for both of them. Perhaps they needed another one to keep them from worrying about their own lives too much. Lee had been non-committal about the idea and she suspected that his reservations were mainly financial. He was not good at compromise, and his desire to give the best to Gemma might have to be modified in order to have another child on a detective sergeant's salary. Lee had been deeply protective towards his daughter since an incident in the playground at Brook Green earlier that year. Jane knew a man had exposed himself at their girl and touched her too. Lee felt guilty about the incident, and became angry whenever she brought it up, so they had agreed never to talk to Gemma about it again unless she raised the subject.

'It's Lee,' Karen, one of the secretaries, said, breaking Jane's anxious introspection.

'Yes', she said, picking up the phone receiver.

14

'Are you all right?' he asked.

'Yes, why shouldn't I be?'

'We had a bit of drama today. We cornered Sancho Doherty and his mates, I thought you might have heard about it.'

'Should I have?'

'Well it got a bit noisy, a lot of brass flying around. Jock crashed the Astra into this shop, but we were close enough still to corner them. The car didn't look too happy though.'

'Oh,' she said.

'One of our boys stopped a round, but he's fine, un-scratched, they didn't look so smart afterwards, though they're all alive too.'

As he recounted the episode, her irritation began to grow. He sounded like one of those adolescent boys trying to horrify his mother with gleefully recounted details of a near-death scrape.

'You don't sound too thrilled?' he enquired at last.

'I just wish you'd do something less dangerous.'

'It's my living, love,' he replied, a little crestfallen.

'I know, that's the problem sometimes.' Jane could tell that he was performing to some other detectives in the room, particularly when he said he was going for 'a sherbert with the lads'. At the moment she put the phone down she felt contempt for the lot of them, but her contempt turned to guilt as she realised that she should feel more relieved that her husband had not been killed.

Charles Denton was home at Blackheath soon enough. He switched on the television: the national news was ending. A familiar tune began and then:

'On London Tonight, two robbers and one policeman are shot in a London siege . . .'

Denton went into the kitchen and put the kettle on. He had no interest in what he called 'pretend news'. International first, then national; that was all the news he wanted. The words drifted into the kitchen: 'policeman's lucky escape' . . . 'elderly West Indian woman, whose identity has not yet been disclosed.' Denton put some digestives onto the tray with the tea and some pain killers.

'The drama began at eleven this morning when thieves forced their way into a safe deposit box centre in Kensington . . .' He walked into the sitting room. After thirty years in which he had prided himself on the ability to disguise his emotions and fears from others, the effect of seeing the television pictures of the Majestic building was devastating. The tea tray dropped to the floor with a crash.

Chapter Three

Johnson awoke by instinct just before 7.30. It had been a heavy night at the Club. Too much lager and too many glassy-eyed coppers lurching a few inches from his face telling him he was 'the best DS in the Met' and 'the fuckin' bizzo'. Pearls of wisdom, pissed away with the Tennents and remembered only by him. After a couple of hours in the sack he didn't want to get up, but Johnson had always believed that life involved daily triumph over what you didn't want to do. It was the rule that he made breakfast, and Johnson anchored his life in such discipline. It was what had made him a good soldier and what made him a good detective. That was Lee, he did what others found too difficult.

He tiptoed downstairs and put the kettle on. The paper said nothing about the raid. A lot about Yugoslavia and Maastricht but nothing about the raid. In a few moments his wife and daughter would be down. He set the things on the breakfast table, pausing to inspect his running shoes on the doormat. Almost dry.

Johnson heard the thumping of five-year-old feet on the stairs and looked up to see Gemma. She was in her dressing gown and slippers with plastic Minnie Mouse heads on the toes. A shy smile cracked across her round face and she looked down to avert her father's gaze. Lee walked across the kitchen and picked her up. 'You're getting heavy, little one,' he said and then let out an exaggerated groan.

'Why?' she asked.

'Too much cement for breakfast. Why do you eat so much cement?'

'I don't!' she replied, looking down again.

Since the incident with the stranger, Lee was always on the lookout for signs of anxiety in his daughter, always trying to amuse and delight her.

Jane arrived in the kitchen without saying anything and begun busying herself with the toaster.

'You're not very talkative this morning.'

'I've got to get into work,' she replied brusquely. 'What time did you get back last night?'

'Late,' he replied, giving Gemma a conspiratorial sheepish grin. They ate in silence; Lee perused the sports pages.

'Gemma, run upstairs and brush your teeth, I'll be up in a minute to get you dressed,' said Jane. Her daughter scurried up the stairs singing to herself.

'Don't be pissed off with me, I'm sorry about last night,' Lee offered.

'I'm not pissed off. Well, no more than usual when you get up to one of your capers.'

'It wasn't a caper. We arrested four violent blokes. It was a result. It was what we do the job for.'

'It wouldn't have been worth getting killed for, would it?'

'What is?' Lee replied, 'Working in a solicitor's office?'

'Don't be cheap.'

'I'm sorry. Look, let's get a sitter tonight and go out and celebrate. Where do you fancy?'

'I don't know. Find somewhere you like.' Jane stood up and headed for the door.

'Don't go in this mood, then we'll both be pissed off all day.'

'I haven't got time,' she said.

'Just kiss me goodbye then.'

Jane turned, obliged, and then left.

★　　★　　★

Johnson and MacFadyen surveyed the four bags. Locked overnight in a secure room, the time had come to sort out the gang's takings. With a theatrical flourish, MacFadyen emptied the first onto the floor. The others followed. A mass of paper studded with jewellery, rolls of banknotes, the odd item of lewd lingerie, one very motheaten teddy bear and a bundle of FA Cup Final tickets.

Johnson left to find a message that a Mr Oswald Pew was waiting to see him. Pew was the managing director of Majestic. He wore a striped shirt and pinstripe suit, fortyish, with a narrow face not unlike Prince Charles and a voice to match.

'Good morning Mr Pew.'

'Good morning, officer. I've come to expedite the return of the stolen property.'

'We'll have to take statements Mr Pew. You know, I last saw my necklace on such and such a date when I put it in my box number so and so. We'll need a list of who was renting each box. They'll have to be interviewed and they may have to appear in court.'

'I'm afraid that might not be possible.'

Johnson remained silent.

'Some, I'm sure, will be willing to help in the way you describe. In fact several of our clients have already contacted me. Of course they want matters resolved as quickly as possible. I can give you their names.'

'And the others?'

'Confidentiality is a very important part of our business, Mr Johnson. Many of our clients would not want their names connected with our establishment, let alone a robbery.'

'What are we talking about Mr Pew? Things hidden from the Inland Revenue, things hidden from their wives?' Johnson had allowed irritation to sour his voice and regretted it almost at once. It was unprofessional.

'I do not question them and, frankly, neither should you. The privacy of the deposit box is sacrosanct.'

'Well, let's do a deal, Mr Pew. You provide me with half a dozen willing helpers and that should be more than enough for our court case. But if there's something in there that we really have to ask further questions about then you promise to show us the box holders' list.'

Pew looked out of the window. He fiddled with his tiepin, avoiding eye contact.

'The alternative is that we would have to get a court order—'

'Mr Johnson. Don't threaten me. There should be no difficulty providing you with clients prepared to help. In fact I have a list with me. That should be more than enough for your case.' He handed an envelope across the table. 'All items which are not claimed by the people named on it will be returned to their rightful owners by our management. We shall arrange collection as soon as possible. Why push it any further?' Pew stood up to leave.

'I'm sure there won't be any problem. But who knows, Mr Pew, where a criminal investigation may lead?'

Pew walked towards the door, placing a brown trilby onto his slicked-back hair. He paused.

'Mr Johnson. People put their most private things into our care. Things which could destroy other people's happiness, the reputations of companies, perhaps even things which could bring down governments. I learned long ago that, in my business, prying into that secret world is the fastest way to personal ruin.'

Pew turned and was gone.

Johnson went back upstairs to find MacFadyen pushing the stolen goods to one side of the floor with a broom. There was a pile of evidence bags, a typewriter and a stack of forms. MacFadyen unbuttoned his navy blazer. Johnson's partner was portly and several inches shorter than him. They had worked together for two years and they had built up a good rapport. Humour oiled their relationship and kept them sane in the face of the daily stupidities handed down by their bosses, who they referred to as the 'headshed'.

MacFadyen ran a hand across his ginger beard, inserted a sheet of paper and turned to Johnson. 'I might as well take the first stretch.'

'We'll be here for days Badyun. The fruits of victory,' Lee quipped.

'Badyun' was his partner's nickname from his days in the Strathclyde force. Only Lee used it in the Met, it being 'Bad One' in Glaswegian. Its origin lay in an old Billy Connolly newspaper strip cartoon which contained a character called 'Badyun MacFadyen, Corporation Bus Driver'.

'Aye, well I asked the boss for some help but he told me there was nobody who could be spared.'

Johnson walked across to the heap of valuables, picked a bracelet at random, put it in an evidence bag and wrote across the top: 'Item MSD 1, white gold bracelet with inlaid diamonds'. MacFadyen bashed away on the typewriter.

And so it went throughout the day. By late afternoon they had worked their way through the jewels, banknotes – including many thousands of dollars and pounds – to the papers, which they were dreading because they looked so boring. The bag holding each item was tagged so that the evidence could not be tampered with.

'Item MSD 342. Certificate for seven hundred shares in the Maxwell Communication Corporation' – it was MacFadyen's turn on the bags.

'Somewhat unfortunate them being stolen, think what they must be worth,' Johnson remarked sourly.

'Chief, I'm losing the will to live. It's time I either had another cabby on the typing or we went down the Club.'

'Badyun, we'll do twenty more. I can't make the Club, mate. I've promised Jane . . .' Johnson stood up and stretched. As he got up, MacFadyen threw a thick sealed envelope at him, which split as it hit the floor. Johnson had not been ready for a catch.

The detective sergeant picked up the package. Through the torn cover he saw the words:

Operation RACETRACK
Summary of Results on Termination
TOP SECRET – FOR DIRECTOR GENERAL'S EYES ONLY

written on a folder. There was some other information. It was the only copy of the document and it had a ticket on top, like library books used to have. The ticket was headed 'Registry Record' and appeared to be a list of people who had handled the paper.

'Item MSD 343, when you're ready, sarge.'

Johnson put the papers down and picked up a bundle of what appeared to be love letters.

'Item MSD 343. Personal correspondence, addressed to one Vulnavia de Barry, 23 Bedford Mansions, Old Brompton Road, London.'

'Wait a minute, what about the other thing, the split envelope?'

'We'll do that tomorrow, I want to have a closer look at it.'

'Something particularly smutty, is it?' MacFadyen's eyebrows did a Mexican wave.

'No it's just odd. We'll do it tomorrow.'

Soon enough they were finished. Johnson put the split envelope into the small backpack which he carried to and from work.

It was not a long walk to his home in Hammersmith. Their

home was in an area the estate agents called Brackenbury Village in an attempt to draw in the yuppies. They had failed, which wasn't surprising, as most of the houses were small, two-bedroom terrace numbers.

Jane was not back yet.

The child minder was upstairs giving Gemma a bath. He drifted through the steam to kiss her blond curls before leaving the bathroom. He wondered whether he felt less comfortable with his daughter's nakedness since what had happened at Brook Green. It was one February afternoon. It wasn't late but it was already beginning to get dark and the usual crowd of parents and children had thinned out considerably. He had left Gemma on a swing. There had been other children playing with her and their mother was watching them. Like a fool, Lee had dashed off to the newsagent on Shepherds Bush Road for a couple of minutes. He came come back to see her next to a man sitting on a bench by the swings. The other children and their mother were nowhere to be seen. As Lee ran towards Gemma, he realised that the man was masturbating. Gemma turned towards her father and the man realised what was happening, giving him the chance to escape. Lee looked into his long face and heavy eyes for a moment before he ran off. He wanted to chase the molester, but surrendered instead to the desire to gather his daughter into his arms. Many times Lee had fantasised about protecting his girl from harm, but when the moment had come, where had he been?

He had told Jane a partial version of what happened, saying he had only turned his back for a few moments. There was no mention of the newsagent, or of the fact that he had only gone there to buy a *Hello!* magazine for his wife. He had thrown it away as he walked Gemma silently home.

Johnson snapped out of his gloomy daydream and walked down the stairs, sitting down to study the files from the split envelope. All seemed to relate to this Operation RACE-TRACK. All appeared highly classified and dated from the early 1970s. He opened the Director General's Eyes Only folder.

1. Operation RACETRACK was conceived as a way of providing material which might help in the recruitment of Mikhail Starodubtsev, a KGB Colonel working under cover at the Trade Delegation. Surveillance suggested that Starodubtsev had spent several hours at a house at 21 Kandahar Road, London SE16 on 16th January 1971. Subsequent inquiries established that the house was a brothel.'

The key turned in the front lock. Jane came into the sitting room. 'Hi!' Her voice was weary, but Lee felt relief at the fact that she seemed friendlier. She glanced at him sitting on the sofa. 'You're not going out looking like that?'

'No, of course not.'

'Well come on, let's get changed, look at the time.'

'I'll be up in two seconds, just give me a moment.' Johnson read on.

2. Under Operation RACETRACK, approved by Director Counter-Espionage, on 20th January 1971, a plan was devised to put the premises under surveillance. After covert entry, Special Facilities were installed in all rooms of the house. Furthermore, we were able to mount photographic surveillance from an upstairs flat of a house overlooking No 21's front door. We believed this would provide us with the necessary material to confront Colonel Starodubtsev.
3. RACETRACK continued for several months without recording another visit by the colonel. He proved

adept at counter-surveillance. However, on 3rd June 1971 a man was photographed entering the house who was recognised by O/K3, Michael Martin, as an officer of an allied intelligence service. Having identified him verbally to you, I shall refer to him here only as QUASAR.'

Once again, Jane's voice broke the spell which the paper was fast weaving in Johnson's mind.

'Come on, for heaven's sake! It's already five past eight.'

Johnson put the reading matter back into his bag and rushed upstairs. 'It's all right. You know me. I'll be ready in no time.'

Dinner at the White House was pleasant enough. Lee Johnson lost himself for a while on Jane's favourite topic: could they afford another child? The Johnsons were trapped in a house worth considerably less than, mortgaged to the hilt, they had paid for it in 1989. But Jane had spent enough years with him to know that her husband's mind was elsewhere.

'We don't get out very often, I'd have thought at least you wouldn't be miles away. What is it?'

'I'm not sure,' he said, gazing into his wine. 'I think catching Doherty's mob yesterday might just be the beginning of all sorts of problems for us rather than the end.'

'What do you mean; was it something to do with that file you were looking at?'

'Oh, I don't know.' Lee felt a pang of uncertainty about telling his wife what was in the papers. If he did, he sensed he would lose control of his discovery and he didn't want that to happen.

'Oh come on! Don't be so daft!'

'I shouldn't talk about it, it's police business and anyway it might turn out to be nothing.' As he said it, Jane blushed and her mouth sagged – a look of uncertainty and rejection.

'Thanks very much! It can't be anything that interesting then.'

Lee felt torn between shame at spurning her interest and satisfaction. Was he happy for paying her back for her turn in the morning? Or was it just that he knew she would take a discovery like this away from him?

The rest of the meal passed without incident, but it was not the kind of romantic evening that Lee had been hoping for. At one point he had remarked what a contrast this £40 meal with its bottle of Chianti was from their evenings in Bristol which had usually involved a couple of pints and a bag of chips. But Jane had known Lee long enough to see this reminiscence for what it was: his references to their courting days no longer softened her ire or lifted her spirits.

Lee's feelings had sunk during their main course when she had chided him for being a stick in the mud at a dinner party a few weeks before with a couple of her solicitor friends.

'I know you don't like Trivial Pursuits, but why couldn't you have gone along with the game for our sakes?' she had implored.

The truth was that Lee had played it before with these people and had got fed up with them showing off. Why couldn't she understand that? He began to feel that he had done the right thing not discussing the secret documents with her.

A couple of times near the end of the meal Jane had said how tired she was, and Lee understood what that meant.

As they came in, he could see the folders sitting on the coffee table, framed in a shaft of light from the hall. Jane started up the stairs. Why didn't he follow her? Three glasses of wine had sharpened rather than blunted his curiosity.

'I'll just put those papers away.'

He went into the sitting room, picked up the folders and walked towards his bag. Standing in the light from the hall he opened the first folder and began again where he had left off.

    4. Through the Special Facilities installed earlier in the brothel, QUASAR was recorded having sexual intercourse. Subsequent inquiries indicated that he had been having sex with a seven-year-old girl, Nicola Dawson.

Johnson's mouth went dry. The hairs on the back of his neck stood up. 'Oh no,' he mumbled, just audibly. Try as he might, he could not push the picture of his own daughter out of his mind. Tears welled into his eyes. He remembered the egregious Oswald Pew and his sermon on the sanctity of safety deposits: things which could destroy people's happiness, things which could bring down governments.

Lee crept into bed a little later. Jane mumbled 'good night'. Sex, though, was the last thing on his mind. He stared at the ceiling. Lee's thoughts raced to and fro. What had he got himself into? Should he just dump the papers in a dustbin somewhere or give them to his boss? The Chianti and veal parmigiana was beginning to take its toll on his stomach. It was well past two before he finally dipped into a fitful sleep.

Chapter Four

At 8.30 the following morning, Johnson found himself outside the door marked, 'DCI P. Rickett'. Rickett had spent nearly twenty years in CID and did not have long to push for retirement. As one might expect of somebody who had committed so much of his career to drinking, Rickett had acquired a heavy paunch. His head was large and ball-like, largely bald with melancholy eyes which hinted at the disappointment of a man who had spent his professional life breaching his personal principles one by one. Johnson was hardly surprised to find the detective chief inspector practising a swing with an imaginary seven iron.

'Sir. We've found something rather unusual in the haul from the Majestic job.'

'What exactly? Take a seat, DS Johnson.'

Johnson handed over the folders to Rickett, who had taken up position behind his desk. He perused the folders quickly.

'They appear to be documents belonging to the Security Service, sir.'

'Tag them up in an evidence bag and give them back,' said Rickett. For a moment Johnson was speechless. Rickett appeared ready to resume his imaginary round.

'Sir, if you look at the top folder it relates to all kinds of crimes. Prostitution, sexual abuse of a minor. It might be a matter which would require further investigation.'

Rickett read for a few moments. Johnson studied a plaque

29

on the wall: an engraving of Edgbaston with an inscription: 'To DCI P. Rickett with regards from his colleagues on Operation Cauliflower in the West Midlands Regional Crime Squad.' The grey walls of his office were decked with engraved truncheons, the badges of forces from South Yorkshire to Bavaria and other memorabilia.

'All of this is years old. We can't go picking a fight with MI5.' The DCI's patience was beginning to ebb.

'But sir, it relates to the sexual abuse of a seven-year-old girl and who knows what else. Who knows what kind of prosecutions it might lead to – and anyway if the files have been stolen MI5 would want them back.'

'DS Johnson. As a result of this Majestic job we will be bringing charges of attempted murder of a police officer, kidnap of one Hortense Villiers, GBH to same, armed robbery, possession of illegal firearms and theft of a BMW. You and DC MacFadyen will receive a commendation. Most people would call that a result.'

'I know, sir, but—'

'You cannot believe what a hail of bollocks we will come under if we post these files through the front door at Gower Street. You and I would spend the rest of our natural lives being interviewed by every smartarse from MI5, the Home Office – you name it. There would be enough paperwork to obscure all light from my windows. We don't know if these papers are genuine. Even if they are, we don't know why they were in a deposit box.' Rickett shifted his stance and adopted a more sympathetic tone. 'If somebody did something dreadful to a little girl twenty years ago, I'm sorry, but I'm afraid we can't do any more about it.'

Johnson felt robbed of any logic to counter his boss. He had turned a blind eye enough times. From the people he saw jumping red lights on his way home to the sobbing petty fraudsters he had cut loose. More than most of his colleagues, he lived his life trying to uphold the law, but even Detective

Sergeant Lee Johnson recognised that police work required flexibility. DCI Rickett fuelled his doubts.

'Consider yourself a brave copper for running that Mersey mafia to ground, send these files back where they came from and close the door on your way out.'

Johnson found himself walking and along the corridor towards the room where DC MacFadyen awaited him. He made a decision not to put the papers into an evidence bag immediately. He toyed with the idea of referring the matter to a more senior officer. He would make a decision later.

MacFadyen had gone to work tagging items from the fast diminishing pile of spoils.

'Morning, chief,' the detective constable croaked as he placed a padded envelope wrapped in sellotape into an evidence bag. His bloodshot eyes and parched voice indicated a night on the booze.

'Morning, Badyun. Christ mate, shut your eyes or you'll bleed to death.'

'I can't deny it, a few bevvies were drunk, by way of continuing celebration to mark our victory over the lawless hordes.'

Charles Denton had paused at a phone box on his way to work. He dialled a number from memory. A career in intelligence had taught him never to write down such things.

'Hello. Oswald Pew please. Yes, it's Paul Ryan.'

Pew came onto the other end of the line.

'Mr Ryan, I expect I can guess why you're ringing.'

'Yes, I expect you can. Were my boxes among those burgled?' Denton felt already he knew the answer.

'I'm sorry to say that they were sir. However I've every reason to believe that all of the material stolen has been recovered.'

'When do you think I might get my things back?'

'If you'd like to go to the police station and give a statement they will hand them back to you as soon as you like sir. Of course, if you would prefer to keep matters more confidential, I will happily recover them on your behalf.'

'I think I would prefer the latter,' Denton responded, perhaps a little too quickly.

'Very well. I shall recover them on your behalf, shall I give you a ring when I have?'

'That might be a little difficult, I'll be around and about on business,' Denton lied blithely. 'I'll call you in, say, two days?'

'Certainly Mr Ryan.'

The conversation was concluded. Denton completed his journey to Gower Street. Throughout the morning, pain and confusion gnawed at Denton as he scanned the latest intercepts of MI5's Algerian targets. The next two days would be very difficult for him. He had taken the documents out of Registry to prevent the curious learning the secrets of Operation RACETRACK, because Operation RACETRACK held clues to the identity of QUASAR and to so much else in Denton's deceitful life. He had not considered the possibility that the Majestic safety deposit box company, in the heart of smart London, would prove such an insecure resting place for them. Would the police discover their contents? Would they be on their way back to Gower Street now? His heart thumped away, his guts stirred excruciatingly.

Denton knew that keeping a cool head would probably take him through the crisis. Irene would have helped him. His wife, his partner, taken from him by cancer three years ago. Now he had to get through it alone. He considered flight. He considered destroying the papers if and when he got his hands on them. He ruled out both. The only reason he had not destroyed them earlier was in case he needed to put them back one day. Denton had to consider many things: had the stolen files already been handed back to the Service and then returned to Majestic to smoke out the person who had put them there? Too clever, perhaps – anyway he could make some checks at Gower Street.

MacFadyen had already left when Johnson tiptoed through the room of bagged treasures and went to leave the station. It was well past seven. He asked the desk sergeant for the key to the photocopying room.

'Do you want to sign the book, Lee?'

'No, if that's all right Reg, I'm not going to be a second.'

Johnson went into the room and fired up the Xerox. His face felt flushed; he felt blood pulsing through his throat. Reaching into his bag for the papers, he started work, two copies of everything. It was done soon enough. He paused, realising he had not copied the Registry Record, the list of people who had read the files. He heard sounds down the corridor. He decided to be thorough and slapped the files face down again to make the last copies. Whoever put them there would get their papers back and he would have time to study the copies and think over what should be done. Johnson comforted himself that, if it all amounted to nothing, he could destroy his copies. If he could find out who had abused young Nicola Dawson, then belatedly, he might be able to get her some kind of justice. Even if he couldn't, he knew nothing his police work would bring him during the coming months would be quite as absorbing as further study of Operation RACETRACK. So as he left for home, destroying the photocopies was the last thing on his mind.

Chapter Five

Denton had taken a morning off work to go to the Majestic company. He had told Shirley, his secretary, that it was a medical appointment, which was perfectly plausible. Denton's recent life had been peppered with meetings with medical people. They had no more hope for him and he had never had faith in them.

He walked into Oswald Pew's office. Not a confident stride, but the hesitant gait of a sick man. Denton had a brown mackintosh over his arm. His hair was mostly gone, simply wrapped around the back and sides of his head. Silver-framed spectacles sat on his nose, which had a bulbous end – a little like WC Fields but without the florid damage of drink. His face was washed out, pallid like the pages of so many ancient Registry files.

Pew looked up:

'Ah! Mr Ryan. Good to see you sir.'

'Mr Pew, how are you?'

'I'll be all the better when all this is sorted out. It's all been a most difficult time for the firm, and I expect an anxious one for you sir.'

'Indeed.'

The small talk was over without Pew returning the courtesy of asking Denton how he was. Denton found that, as his appearance got worse, fewer and fewer people asked him how he was in case, heaven forbid, he actually told them.

'Mr Ryan, as you know, the police returned the stolen

goods to us yesterday afternoon. If you could give me a rough description of what you had in your boxes, I will fetch the items concerned.'

'Well, there was one large manilla envelope containing documents. A4 size – about an inch thick and a padded envelope, you know one of those Jiffy ones, which was a little smaller.'

'Were there names on the envelopes?'

'No, they were unmarked, although the smaller one had sellotape wrapped around both ends,' Denton replied.

'Were those both in one of your boxes?'

'Yes.'

'And your other box?' asked Pew.

Denton had thought long and hard about admitting that the other box was needed to store a rather bulky sum of money – almost $280,000 to be precise – but decided against it. To claim the cash would be to provide his enemies with proof of his activities. It was not the sort of sum a junior officer in MI5 could tuck away. This whole scene in Pew's office could be a set-up, with tape recorders running and policemen waiting in the next room to arrest him.

'It was empty,' said Denton, grasping his fate.

'Yes sir,' replied Pew, seemingly unsurprised.

A few moments later, Pew came back with two sealed plastic bags. He pushed them across the red leather top of his mahogany desk.

'Are these the right ones, Mr Ryan?'

Denton hid his dismay at the sight of the split envelope inside one of the clear plastic bags. He examined it for a moment before noting with satisfaction that the other package seemed intact.

'Yes, this is it.' He wondered whether the envelope had been opened by the thieves or the police. He tucked the envelope into the inside pocket of his mac and stood up.

'Once again Mr Ryan, I do apologise for the inconvenience and hope you will continue to be our client.'

'Yes of course,' Denton replied. He would keep the boxes, for the sake of avoiding suspicion. But Oswald Pew would never see Paul Ryan again if he could help it.

'Mr Ryan, please don't think this impertinent,' Pew said as he rose to shake Denton's hand, 'but if you find that you do recall leaving something in your second box, I can assure you that it would be returned with complete discretion. There is no question of us passing that information on.'

What did he know, this man with his flattened vowels and aristocratic bearing? It was a difficult moment for Denton, his resolve was being tested. Was it a last attempt to entrap him?

'No, I'm sure I hadn't kept anything in there for some time.' Denton's last lie, like all the others he told Pew, was passed off with solid professionalism.

Late the previous evening, Friday, Denton had returned the files to Registry. He had used a skeleton key to let himself in. Registry was a little like a library. There were rows of computer terminals linked to R2, the computer which held the index records on tens of thousands of Security Service suspects. There were also banks of filing cabinets packed with cards and microfiche. Before returning the files to the special access section of Registry in Gower Street, Denton had taken some very necessary precautions. The registry tickets on each of the files showed him as the last person to book them out. Carefully and in apparently different hands he had added the names of others in that very small group who in Service-speak were 'cleared for indoctrination' into the secrets of Operation RACETRACK. He backdated these phantom withdrawals. He had kept one small record slip from among the documents and tucked it into his pocket. It was vitally important that everything else be put back as quickly as possible, so if anyone came looking, they would never know that the papers had spent the last fifteen years in a vault in South Kensington.

At home the next day, Denton did not feel particularly relaxed, despite his success in Registry. He played over in his mind the many things which could have happened to the papers. Had they been the thieves' real target? Unlikely. Had the police opened the envelope? Perhaps. If the police or MI5 had opened it, why had it been done so roughly and put back together with sellotape? Why had the files not been sent straight back to headquarters at GWS?

He began to allow himself the comfort of believing that everything would be all right. He looked at the empty plastic bag which had held the files. The tag on it said 'MSD 456', there was a date when it was recovered and it was signed by 'DS Johnson' or 'DS Johnston' – it was hard to read the writing. He had kept the other package inside its evidence bag: it might help him to pretend that he had taken it home by mistake, or didn't know the contents of the padded envelope, if the Special Branch were suddenly to break the door down.

He walked across to the window, looking out onto the grassy expanse of the heath. Three children ran along, not far from the window, trying to launch a kite. A pair of framed photographs sat on the table. One showed Denton among classmates at the Bishop Livesay School, Bulawayo, northern Rhodesia, in 1949. The other, which he picked up, showed him and Irene shortly after they came to Britain in 1960. Denton cradled the picture of the happy couple. They had been so keen, so idealistic, then. Irene had died so disillusioned. He looked at her faded likeness: 'I think everything's going to be all right, my love.'

Lee, Jane and Gemma Johnson had had a fairly predictable Saturday. He had played with his daughter. The rest of the week had passed quickly enough. Statements had been taken from several owners of stolen property. The other items had been collected by Oswald Pew while Johnson was out of the office. He had decided not to read more of the papers until he could give them his undivided attention. With Gemma and Jane upstairs, now seemed as good a moment as any. He opened the file he had started several days before.

5.. Following the identification of QUASAR as an officer of a friendly intelligence service, surveillance under Operation RACETRACK was terminated. The matter was referred to your predecessor as DG.

6. Discussions were held between him and other senior officers in the counter-espionage steering group as to whether an attempt should be made to exploit the material gathered at the brothel in 21 Kandahar Road in an attempt to recruit QUASAR as an agent of this service. SIS was not informed either of QUASAR'S existence or of this subsequent discussion.

A banging car door in the street distracted Johnson. He knew enough about the spooks to know that 'SIS' was MI6 – the people meant to carry out spying abroad on behalf of the British government. Johnson shook his head in disbelief. 'SIS was not informed' – another reason why these papers had been buried in a vault.

7. DG decided that there should be no attempt to recruit QUASAR. He was guided by the principle that running an agent in a friendly service might cause incalculable damage to relations with this vital ally, if discovered. However, DG also decided that no action should be taken against QUASAR and that his superiors should not be informed about the incident. DG felt that, under some unforeseen future

circumstance, it might prove necessary to exploit the material gathered on QUASAR.

8. Accordingly, on 6th July 1971, QUASAR was interviewed by O/K3, Michael Martin and a junior officer of his section, Charles Denton. QUASAR was told only that he had been sighted going into a brothel, not that we knew what had transpired inside. He was told to be more careful and it was stressed that his superiors would not be informed.

Johnson saw that the report was signed by Michael Martin, as director of counter-espionage some years after these events. It was apparent that it was a briefing prepared for a new Director General who did not know all the facts. At the bottom of the page, in copperplate hand, the DG had added his own note.

Action: destroy all audio tapes and photographic material relating to this operation. Unlike my predecessor, I cannot foresee a circumstance in which we would use this kind of material to compromise an intelligence officer of so close an ally.'

Johnson put down the first file. Something had caught his eye. He looked again, scanning the last few paragraphs. Charles Denton, that was it. He noticed that Charles Denton was the last name on each of the Registry records on the front of all the files. Michael Martin seemed to be on most of them too, as were the names of one or two other people. But the last one in each case was Charles Denton.

Chapter Six

Home for Harry Canning was a nineteenth-century colonial house in the wooded country near Cedar Falls. It was a short drive from there to Harry's work. Washington took longer – an hour from his stripped floors and tasteful curtains. His walls were adorned with pictures of the great and good. The literature on his shelves was mostly professional: *Operational Deception in World War Two*, *Getting Bigger: How Corporations Grow*, and the dreary memoirs of several foreign leaders. In the lavatory a little harmless literary frivolity was allowed: *101 Uses for a Dead Cat* and a stack of Larsen cartoon books. Around the house there were plenty of family photos too. His wife, Jean, their daughter Mary-Beth, her husband, their children.

Canning saw the Agency car pull up outside. He had a driver and a bodyguard. The bodyguard was unusual, even for somebody of his rank. It was felt prudent after Canning's tour in the Middle East. Canning had been station chief in Kuwait at the time that Hezbollah tortured their man in Beirut to death. An attempt on Canning's life six months later by means of a car bomb was taken as confirmation that he had been definitively compromised. But Canning found that the four kilos of TNT which had demolished his Buick also provided a considerable boost for his career. Rushed out of Kuwait City, with no post available at a similar grade, he had been promoted.

'Good morning Mr Canning, how are you today, sir?' asked the driver.

'Good. How are you, Fred?'

'Just fine, sir.'

Canning eased into the back of his car and began the fifteen-minute journey down the leafy lanes of Virginia to Langley. He scanned the *Wall Street Journal*, then the *Post*.

The main business for that day involved a conference with the other high-ranking officers to determine priorities for the year ahead. As DDI – Deputy Director for Intelligence – Canning was the Company's chief analyst, his department the Agency's brain. Clearly, his input was critical to the assessment. The meeting was chaired by Director of Central Intelligence. The top-level Agency leaders were backed up by a few staffers.

Their meeting took place in the Director's conference room, which had a fine view over the parkland which surrounded the buildings, softening the brutal lines of this concrete cathedral to the Cold War.

The agenda for the meeting, though, was very different from that which had informed the Agency at its founding. Much of the morning was given over to the threat of Russian nuclear weapons going adrift, of chemical weapons doing the same, of poor countries buying ballistic missiles to lob at their enemies. The senior officers had all doffed their jackets. Most, including Canning, had rolled up the sleeves of their Brooks Brothers and Ralph Lauren shirts. Nobody smoked: they all had the appearance of men and women who recognised that being overweight was a bar to rapid advancement.

Everybody knew the problems, but their task was to find the best means of informing the US government about them. When they reached the subject of economic intelligence gathering, their uncertainty became acute.

'As you all know, the President has ordered that the gathering of intelligence to enhance the economic position of the United States become one of our core missions,' the Director began. 'Given that we have been prioritised in this way, we must find the best way of aggressively pursuing intelligence of this kind and I think the question we must address today is whether to enhance our technical collection methods further in this respect or whether the time has come to devote more resources to human collection.'

'Hell sir, you tell me to get somebody into Mitsubishi and I'll crack that place wide open. What we need is an explicit political order behind us,' said Jim Parker. Parker was DDO – Deputy Director for Operations – a coy title given to the head of the Clandestine Service which runs spies in foreign countries. As a fiery Georgian, Parker was keen to give proceedings a no-nonsense air. Everything about him, from the ring which bore witness to his service in the Marines to the broad shoulders and face of a man who had been a keen boxer in his youth, marked Parker as an unusual person to find near the top of the Agency of the 1990s. His argument about requiring more explicit instructions ran true to a theme which anybody who knew him recognised – that of preventing the politicians from ducking the responsibility for difficult operations. Parker knew that the carve-up of the Agency in the seventies – the Church Commission – had produced some dividends at least. If the people on the Hill or in the White House wanted something tricky done now, they couldn't leave the Clandestine Service to catch it in the neck: there were Intelligence Committee minutes, presidential findings, to prove their knowledge, their complicity. Although Parker's use of such arguments was familiar, he was being disingenuous in applying it to the question of gathering economic secrets, which he privately considered in some way unworthy of his service.

'Jim, the problem has always been that the risk of getting people caught on the ground, spying on an ally, is not justified by the results we might get from them,' Canning remarked. Canning always seemed to be playing to his audience. His manner, prematurely white hair, sunlamp-flawless complexion and preference for crisp white shirts, gave him the appearance of a TV anchorman. 'I believe we can get very significant results from putting more dollars into computer analysis of the banking transactions systems which—'

'Harry, I hear you,' the Director interrupted, 'but you and I both know that the Japs have started their own intelligence service with getting ahead in economics as its primary objective. I've no doubt that the Japanese and the European Community are a greater threat to the way of life of the average American than Ghaddafi or the Shining Path . . .' the Director had once more taken over steering the meeting. 'Harry, I think the resources will be there for what your folks want to do on the banking system, but I think we all have to recognise that the time for human intelligence operations in this area is upon us. It's really a question of deciding the targets and what we should do if the play goes against us and we get caught.'

Canning had anticipated that the conversation might take this direction and produced a sheet of paper from his briefcase.

'Indeed sir. I've drawn up a wish list. These are the ten organisations we would most like to see some form of agent reports out of.' Canning passed copies to the others. 'I don't think anybody will be surprised to see the Japanese Ministry of International Trade and Industry at number one.' There were sniggers around the table.

'The German Bundesbank, the European Commission, Mitsubishi . . .' the Director read aloud.

'I suggest these priorities primarily as the best way of supporting the dollar on the international exchanges and protecting our own industries from dumping of goods by foreign corporations . . .' Canning was pleased with his coup. He had wrested the initiative from Parker.

'What about the penalty if a US political attaché is caught taking documents from some guy in a parking lot in Tokyo?' one of the staffers, a primly dressed woman in her mid-thirties, asked from behind Parker. The DDO turned his crew-cut head towards the voice.

'Miss, if you think any American is going to give a damn because we've been paying off some Jap to protect our auto workers' jobs or the value of the dollar then I suggest you book into the Company physician for a reality check.' The woman looked down at her papers, chastened.

'Obviously the benefits of getting agent reports so that we could better target our technical means – wiretaps, intercepting fax machines, you name it – would be considerable.' Canning wanted to get the meeting back onto his agenda.

The Director tried to bring matters to a conclusion: 'I think we're all agreed that we want to do this. We've got DDI's list of possible targets as a starting point. I think the time's come to ask the President to sign a finding authorising the penetration of some of these organisations indulging in hostile trade practices. As for the penalties of getting caught, I think the mood of the American public and of the Congress has changed. I think DDO, Jim Parker, is right on that.'

Parker was surprised at being credited with swinging the mood of the meeting – all he had suggested was that they needed explicit political directives. It was one of the Director's little ploys, putting words into people's mouths. Parker knew he couldn't buck the mood of the meeting now. 'Well sir, the sooner we get the presidential finding on this, the sooner we can do this in an aggressive manner. Of course, until today I would never have considered running an agent in a friendly country,' Parker's voice was heavy with irony. 'Now I guess I can call all those 'contacts', 'friends of Central Intelligence' and 'sources' what they were all along.' Canning abstained from joining the sniggers.

Parker drove himself home that night. He too had been in danger during his CIA career – in Vietnam, in Iran and elsewhere. He was the only person present at that day's meeting who carried his own gun, a .45 automatic in a shoulder holster. His home was close to Langley too, a modern built ranch house with a two-car garage. Parker had few books on display, but among those on the shelf in his den were *Leathernecks: Fighting Legends of the US Marines*, *Ten Winning Poker Hands* and *Classic American Automobiles*. There was no light reading matter in Parker's lavatory: instead there was a framed Viet Cong flag and a colour photograph of a smiling US Marine in Beirut, with the caption 'I Just Stepped in Some Shiite'.

Chapter Seven

Johnson picked up the phone and dialled the number for Majestic. 'Mr Pew please . . .' Johnson looked up to acknowledge MacFadyen's arrival in the office.

'Mr Pew, good morning, I wondered if I might ask you one or two questions about people who recovered property.'

'What exactly did you have in mind?' said Pew, warily.

'Was there a Charles Denton among them?'

'I'm afraid I can't answer that question, Sergeant Johnson; it's a matter of confidentiality.'

'Has anybody been in to collect a bag with the number MSD 456, some papers in an envelope, a split envelope held together with sellotape?'

'I'm terribly sorry, I can't answer that either,' Pew remarked uncomfortably.

Johnson sensed his awkwardness, 'can you tell me *who* collected it, Mr Pew?'

'You put me in a very difficult position, sergeant.'

'Not as difficult as the position you'd be in if we hadn't recovered your clients' property, Mr Pew.'

'I can't give you that kind of information – we have obligations to our clients. If it is so important to you, perhaps you should consider the legal route.'

'Perhaps you should save me the trouble Mr Pew. A little friendly steer in the right direction, that's all I'm after.' There was a long pause.

'There is no Charles Denton on our list of depositors.'

47

'Thank you. Who collected that envelope?'

'That's it sergeant. I can't say any more. I have a meeting which I'm late for, goodbye.'

'Goodbye Mr Pew, we'll speak again soon.'

Johnson replaced the receiver. MacFadyen had made no secret of his interest in the conversation.

'What was all that about, boss?'

Johnson had already made the decision that his partner must know about the files and their contents. As MacFadyen put the office kettle on for a brew, Johnson told him the story.

'Fuck me, boss. What are we going to do about it?'

'Well if you're in with me—'

'Fucking right!' interrupted MacFadyen. The detective knew all about Johnson's guilt over the incident with Gemma. It had all come out while boozing down by the river that summer. He wanted to support him, knowing that Lee might see the case in the files as a chance to bury his guilt.

'If you're in, I think we can track down some of these people. Perhaps we can get Nicola Dawson to press charges, perhaps we'll just have to settle for the satisfaction of finding the people responsible and seeing them squirm a bit.'

'Have you told Big Prickett?'

'He told me to leave it well alone. He said we'd have a hail of bollocks land on us if we touched it.'

'Ah, the smack of courageous leadership,' said MacFadyen.

'So we're on our own. If we can build a case to the point we could pass it on for prosecution, all well and good. Big Prickett will shuffle off quietly to the golf course, unable to do anything else. But if we fuck up . . .'

'A lifetime of traffic duty on a pushbike?'

'With no saddle,' added Johnson.

Johnson made a few more calls, which established that any further inquiries about Nicola Dawson would have to go through Child Protection Team detectives at Bermondsey police station. As he finished making a note of the conversation he looked up to see MacFadyen cradling the London phone book.

'There are only four C. Dentons in here.'

'Try them out.'

One was Caroline Denton, another subscriber a man twenty-one years old and another disconnected. The remaining listing was for a C. Denton in Blackheath and there was no answer from his phone.

'He's probably at work,' said MacFadyen after trying the number for the third time.

'Perhaps we should drive over and see him this evening,' said Johnson. Johnson had an impulsive streak, a fatalism coupled with the ability to smother too many thoughts about what might go wrong. It was what took him through the door first on raids, it was what had made him trust his life to a parachute on many occasions in the Army. 'We haven't got time for too much frigging about, mate. Let's just put some heat on him and see what happens.'

Denton had spotted the blue Astra as he walked towards his front door and was not sure what to make of it. They were plods, no doubt about that. Why were they there? Perhaps it was something to do with all the vandalised cars. Perhaps they were waiting for him. He turned the key in his front-door lock and shuffled in. He took off his brown mac and a dark brown trilby which he had also been wearing. Having picked up his mail – an Access bill and an envelope which promised him he could win a million pounds – he went up to the flat. Moments after he was in, the door buzzer went. Denton knew who they were as he picked up the handset.

'Metropolitan Police, sir. We're making some inquiries and I wondered if we might have a word?'

'Certainly, come up to the first floor.' Denton pressed the buzzer.

He opened the door, to face Johnson who, at just over six foot, was a good deal taller than him.

'Detective Sergeant Johnson—'

'Johnson?' repeated Denton.

'Yes, sir, and this is Detective Constable MacFadyen.'

'How can I help you gentlemen? Please come in.'

Johnson's voice was tight: how could he explain their presence?

'It's a rather delicate matter, sir.' Denton remained silent. Johnson walked over to the window. He looked across the heath, but his attention was soon drawn to the photographs.

'Did you grow up in Rhodesia, sir?' He looked Denton in the eye.

'Yes, my late wife and I came here thirty years ago.' Denton did not break eye contact.

'I can't think why you left the sunshine, Mr Denton.'

Denton did not provide him with an answer.

'Anyway, let me get to the point. We're investigating a child prostitution ring that was active in the Bermondsey area during the 1970s,' Johnson began.

Denton felt mixed emotions. His spirits fell first – this was all the evidence he needed that the man who signed the bag containing the RACETRACK papers had read them. But then his spirits lifted a little – why were these two men here with this story, when the first thing to have expected if the papers had been handed back to MI5 was a hostile interrogation from several senior officers of his Service?

Johnson continued: 'One of the people we have interviewed in connection with these offences has mentioned the name Charles Denton to us.'

Denton's spirits rallied a little more as Johnson elaborated a story which both of them knew was false.

'And I wondered if you might tell us any more about it?' said Johnson.

'I can't help you, officer. I don't know which Charles Denton you're looking for, but it's certainly not me.'

'Our informant told us to ask Charles Denton about what went on at 21 Kandahar Road. He said Charles Denton worked for the government. Do you, sir?'

The hairs on the back of Denton's neck had risen at the mention of Kandahar Road. Both of them might know that the papers were the real agenda, but he had not anticipated how direct Johnson's questions might be.

'Yes I do,' replied Denton.

'May I ask you what you do, sir?'

'I work for the Ministry of Defence. But I can't think that is anything more than a coincidence.'

Johnson was heartened – this was the right Charles Denton all right. MI5 officers usually pretended to work for the defence ministry. 'I don't know, Mr Denton. I must admit, even I'm not sure what the connection might be between the appalling things that went on at that house and the Ministry of Defence. Which bit do you work in?'

Denton appeared not to hear the question.

'I'm curious, Mr Denton. I used to be in the Army: which bit of MoD do you work in?'

'It's not the MoD as such. I work for the Security Service, obviously I can't say any more than that.'

'Obviously,' MacFadyen chipped in. He was waiting to see just how uncomfortable Johnson could make this man, and things looked promising.

'What can you tell us about the goings-on at 21 Kandahar Road, Mr Denton?'

'Nothing, officer.'

'We think some very evil things went on there. You won't tell or you don't know anything about it?'

'I don't know anything about it,' Denton replied mechanically.

'If you did, in connection with your work for MI5, would you tell us anything about it?'

'No, not without the relevant authority to do so. I don't think, on that basis, that this conversation can proceed any further.' Denton stood, indicating that it was time for the guests to leave.

'Well, we may have to ask for that authority.'

'Indeed,' said Denton, but he sensed that if things were that simple, they would never have had this conversation.

MacFadyen headed out of the door first and down the stairs. Denton put his hand on Johnson's shoulder. The detective sergeant turned and looked into Denton's sunken eyes.

'Mr Johnson, we're on the same side, you and me, both trying to defend the realm. Whatever you think you may have discovered from your informant . . .' Denton paused a moment and then continued. 'The Service will always protect its secrets, whatever you may think went on all those years ago. You've no chance of getting anything into court.' Johnson did not reply. Instead he turned and rushed down the stairs towards the Astra.

As they drove off, MacFadyen looked across at his sergeant.

'He sussed us out.'

'Did he?' replied Johnson, who deep down understood what had happened just as well.

'I think he knows exactly what we know.'

'He's a good liar, that's for sure. He never broke eye contact when he told his porkies.'

'Boss, if we really want to fuck him –' MacFadyen looked across – 'we've got to find something that isn't in those papers we've got. That's when I want to see his face.'

The Astra swept across the darkness of Blackheath and Johnson knew Badyun was right.

Denton replayed the conversation in his mind. He sat down, drew a biro from his jacket and tried to make the best note of what Johnson had revealed. During the following hours he came to certain conclusions. It was possible that Johnson was a Security Service plant who was baiting him to see if he did something rash – more likely that he was exactly what he made himself out to be. If he was, why pursue the sordid events in that brothel all those years ago? How many policemen would want to do that?

Denton's dispassionate analysis did not leave much room for Johnson's impulsiveness. Neither could he, as a childless widower, fully understand the emotions which the RACE-TRACK files had triggered in the policeman. He looked out of the window and said aloud, 'Dear oh dear, way out of your depth.'

He spent the next forty-five minutes studying the parked cars in the road, nearby buildings and the comings and goings of the local residents.

He did not believe his flat was under observation, but one could never be completely sure. He donned his mac and began down the stairs towards the communal front door. A spasm of pain went through his guts; he gripped the banister to prevent himself crumpling.

Denton walked through the deserted streets for well over an hour before arriving at a phone box in Greenwich by a highly circuitous route. Once more, he did not feel he was under surveillance. Beneath his raincoat, sweat drenched his shirt and the top of his trousers. It was time to speak to QUASAR. Of course Denton didn't call him QUASAR: he called him Pete. Denton inserted a phonecard and dialled Pete's number.

'Hello Pete, it's Charles.' A voice crackled on the other end of the line. 'I'm well I suppose. Listen Pete, we have a significant problem developing. We must meet soon.' Denton looked around the phone box as Pete answered. Denton resumed: 'Next week? That's excellent. Shall we say our usual London place? At what time?' While he was on the phone, Denton forgot his pain. He spoke to so few people these days outside Gower Street, and his relationship with Pete had been a long and intense one. The conversation was concluded and Denton started on his way home.

The pain didn't stop as he walked uphill towards his flat. He pushed himself up the pavement, glassy wet with rain, stepping to one side as some drunken youths piled out of a chip shop shouting and swearing. Why was he still doing this, when he might only have months to live? Because nobody else could. Although Denton's masters said they were busy training a replacement, he was the only man who could talk to Pete and that made him indispensable. This thought had strengthened him during that desperate time when Irene died and now it strengthened him in the face of his sickness. There was something else too: the desire to use Pete to get one more really good blow in at those he hated. In a few months he would retire from MI5 and this whole business could be passed on to others. As he hobbled into view of his flat, Denton allowed himself the conceit of reflecting that his had been an extraordinary career. 'Pride comes before the fall . . .' he mumbled aloud, shaking himself into his counter-surveillance drills once more. It *would* be an extraordinary career – so long as he was able to prevent those policemen prying any further.

MacFadyen had persuaded Johnson to stop at a pub on the way to Southfields, where he lived. Lee had insisted on having just a half of lager, MacFadyen ordered a double Scotch.

The detective constable raised his glass to the light. 'Aye a wee goldie from Sconnie Botland! Cheers!' He tipped it back. MacFadyen had been gliding the previous weekend and was trying to persuade Johnson to join him on a future trip.

'I don't think Jane would wear it at the moment, mate.'

'C'mon, it's fucking mental, it's like being a bird. You'd be good at that, with your beak! Maybe you could get her into it.'

'She's not like that, mate. Reading – that's her idea of

54

recreation. I've tried that many times to get her walking or running. It's just not her thing. To be honest, there are bigger problems than that at the moment.'

MacFadyen dropped his brow in concern. 'What do you mean, pal?'

'I don't know. A bit of a seven-year itch, I suppose. It's just not easy to keep the romance going. It all seems so tired.' Lee sipped his Carlsberg.

'Nobody's been playing around or anything?' MacFadyen asked with a directness born of his concern for his friend.

'No, no. Nothing like that – nothing I know about anyway,' Lee replied.

'Oh, I was going to ask to see the photos if there was . . .'

They both laughed. The conversation was largely perfunctory as they resumed their journey, until MacFadyen told him to pull in just before Southfields tube station.

'You getting out here?' Lee asked – they were still a little way from his partner's flat.

'Come with me.' MacFadyen led him to a flower stand. 'Take Jane some flowers and tell her everything's going to be fine.'

Lee didn't normally like being told what to do, but he could see this was a good idea and not one he would have come up with himself.

The flower seller looked up. 'Yes, cocker?'

Lee paused for an uncomfortable moment, before mumbling, 'I'd like about ten quid's worth please—'

MacFadyen butted in. 'What about a couple of bunches of those lilies?' Lee nodded and the flower seller turned and began gathering them. 'And some eucalyptus for a bit of greenery,' MacFadyen added.

Johnson handed over his tenner and was surprised when the flower seller gave him three pounds change. He took the elegant stems self-consciously and turned to MacFadyen. 'How come you know so much about flowers?'

'Listen, mate, when you've fucked up as many relationships as I have, you get to know which flowers to say sorry with.'

Lee smiled and patted his partner on the back as he turned to part. He felt MacFadyen's solitude as he strolled into the darkness, but then that feeling of melancholy was replaced by a childish excitement at the thought of what Jane's face would be like when he handed her the flowers.

Chapter Eight

Johnson looked across at Jane, their breakfast-table silence punctuated only by the purposeful munching of muesli. After she had extricated him from the Army, it had taken little persuasion to lure Lee away from full fries and over-stewed tea. Occasionally he reverted, taking in a 'greasy' at the café near their house. Jane rarely accompanied him on these trips down cholesterol lane. The flowers the previous evening had lightened the mood and the tension which had stifled many of their breakfasts that week was no longer there.

'Are we going to Ikea on Saturday?' She broke the calm.

'Yes, why not? I might be doing some work on –' Lee considered telling her again, but decided against it – 'another case, but I'm sure we can.'

'Don't put me off again. You know how much we need that new table.'

'Oh, desperately!' he replied.

Jane wobbled their decrepit kitchen table.

'Oh, you're saying we don't need one?'

'No, I'm not. All right, we'll do it.'

Jane's victory was not yet complete though.

'Which other case, anyway?'

Lee decided to answer, but carefully. 'It's something we came across in the safe deposit job the other day. It may not amount to anything, but we're just doing some digging.'

'In your own time?'

57

'Sort of . . .' Lee remarked uncomfortably, sensing the moment of revelation was nearing.

'You don't get enough time off anyway. We can't give up our weekends as well for something your boss doesn't even agree with. I don't know why you bother giving any extra to that job. It's not as if, well, it's not as if it gets you anywhere.'

Lee sensed that the moment to tell her about the files had slipped away again.

Denton surveyed the Gower Street throng through his grubby fourth-floor window. The morning had yielded some useful information. He had established that Detective Sergeant Lee Johnson was indeed a real CID man working in West London and not somebody from the intelligence world trying to trick him. It was also easy enough to check that Johnson had been one of the detectives on the team which had thwarted the robbers of the Majestic safe deposit box company. Denton was convinced that curiosity had led Johnson to read the documents. But who had he told? How far would he push it? There was one way of finding out.

Having gone to the combination lock cupboard, Denton had removed a form and laid it flat on his desk. It was headed 'Form H43. Permission to Intercept Communications'. This solemn bureaucratic document was better known by the wags in his Service as the 'Buggers' Charter'. Under well-established Service procedures, the form had to be authorised both by the head of counter-espionage and either a Deputy Director General or the DG herself. Denton's knowledge of Gower Street's loopholes was such that he did not anticipate much difficulty forging their signatures, by-passing their offices, and getting the form direct to the people who would place the intercepts in the relevant exchanges. But the real problem was how he would hide the cost of somebody transcribing the conversations. Under a recently introduced

Security Service costing system, his head of department now received quarterly printouts of such things. Denton concluded it would be very difficult to do, and could only be contemplated as a last resort. Somehow he would have to persuade Pete-alias-QUASAR to help him with this when they met on Monday. Explaining just why he needed foreign help to bug a British policeman would not be easy.

MacFadyen strode along the corridor through the CID section of the police station. He was carrying a black coffee from the machine on the floor below and the cheap plastic cup which held the steaming liquid did not stop it burning his fingers. As he passed Detective Chief Inspector Rickett's office, the door opened.

'MacFadyen, step in for a moment.'

The detective stood uneasily in the centre of the room. Rickett walked round behind his desk and sat down.

'There's a committal hearing for Doherty and his gang. Make a date for Thursday morning. Be in court by ten. Pass it on to DS Johnson.'

'Yes, sir.'

Rickett took a golf tee from his ashtray and fiddled with it. He was about to speak, but MacFadyen beat him to it.

'Sir, is that it? Because otherwise I've got to put this coffee down.'

'Well, there was something else,' Rickett began. MacFadyen rested the cup on the front of the DCI's desk.

'Did DS Johnson mention the contents of some documents you two found after the Majestic job?'

MacFadyen did not know where this conversation was heading. He decided to admit to some knowledge but not to let on to any more.

'The Security stuff, sir?'

'Yes.'

'Well, he told me in very general terms. He mentioned

that you were against pursuing the matter so we handed them back.'

'Good. It's best forgotten about. I explained to your sergeant that whatever case there might seem to be in those files, it's too long ago and we'd never get far with it.'

'Yes, sir, he told me that's what you said.'

'It's just I've been thinking it over. I know DS Johnson can be a bit hard headed at times . . .'

MacFadyen watched his superior's discomfort as he got to the point.

'I'm not that far off retirement. I don't need to tell you how many years I've had on this force. I don't want it all mucked up now. A decision's been made and we've all got to stick to it. So keep all of this to yourself and let me know if you think Johnson's going to stick his neck out over this.'

'Sir—'

'I know I'm asking a favour from you, MacFadyen. I know you two work well together, but I think it's best for all of us to just leave it well alone.'

'I understand, sir.' MacFadyen's stolid face concealed his contempt.

'Thank you.'

The detective constable turned to leave. As he got to the door, Rickett gave his parting shot. 'The best thing for all of us, if anyone ever comes asking, is to say we never read those files.'

He made his way to the office, where Johnson was already in. MacFadyen did not show his anger through shouting. Instead his face reddened and he spoke through tightened lips: 'Big Prickett just had me in his office.'

'Oh yeah?'

'He wanted me to grass you if you started digging on those MI5 files.'

'What?'

'What a fucking tube he is.'

'Do you think somebody's leant on him?'

'Have they fuck! He's just covering his fat fucking arse. I think he's had second thoughts about not sending them to the spooks.'

'This is great, this is!' Johnson shouted, kicking the desk before falling silent in despair.

'Well, it's got to be worth doing then.' MacFadyen winked at him.

Later that morning, Johnson finally got through to Wendy Mortimer, a detective sergeant attached to the child protection team at Bermondsey police station.

'It's DS Lee Johnson here, working over in Shepherds Bush on an armed robbery case. We've come across something which might help you to make a case on your patch.'

'Oh yes?' In the crowded corner of the child protection team room, she drew on a cigarette and reached for a notebook. Her gravelly voice betrayed her middle age and heavy smoking.

'We believe it involves child prostitution.'

'That can be very difficult to prove, I'm sure you understand that.'

'Indeed. Our problem is that our boss is completely against our pursuing the case, so our conversations have to be entirely unofficial.'

'What's his problem?'

'It involves national security.'

'I see. It sounds rather unusual. I've been dealing with sex abuse for ten years and I've heard some excuses, I can tell you! But nobody's tried 'national security' on me before as a grounds for not investigating a crime.'

Johnson pressed on: 'I'd rather say no more on the phone. If we met up we might be able to swap some intelligence at the very least – unofficially, obviously.'

'The *best* you can hope for is unofficial help from me, I'm afraid. We take the confidentiality of our cases very seriously. It may not even be worth your while coming down.'

'Can I ask you whether you know the person at the centre of what we've discovered?'

'I can't divulge who's on our registers.'

'Nicola Dawson,' Johnson said blankly, ignoring her protest. Mortimer did not respond.

'Nicola Dawson,' he repeated. 'Could you check her name on the register? You might have to go back a few years—'

'I don't need to check her name. Perhaps we should meet.'

On Saturday, Johnson went down to the bottom of the garden to the small potting shed which a previous owner had put there and which he rarely used. Saws and other tools hung from nails in the walls and there was a work bench fitted with a vice. He reached underneath the wooden surface, retrieving the plastic bag held there by masking tape. Opening it, Johnson surveyed the two photocopies of the Operation RACETRACK files. He would have to hide one of them elsewhere or there was little point having it, he decided.

So far, Johnson had only really studied the file, prepared for the Director General, summarising the operation. As he surveyed the other papers he realised that much of them contained little of interest. In one case it was a document which appeared to have been prepared for training officers in surveillance techniques. Scanning through it, one passage caught his eye:

In 1971, during Operation RACETRACK, K Branch reacted quickly when given the opportunity to attempt the entrapment of a senior Soviet intelligence officer based in London. Although the operation did not succeed in this aim it proved the Service's ability to position extensive surveillance assets in a short period of time. Six K Branch officers and eight A Branch technical officers were formed into a special team for the operation. Photographic surveillance was achieved by renting a flat overlooking a premises known to have been used by the colonel. A cover story was given to the owners that the flat was being hired by a manager for a foreign firm posted to London for an undetermined length of time.

Johnson found nothing else of interest in the eight-page dossier. There were also various forms requesting bugging devices and photographic services for the operation. Glancing at them, he came to the conclusion that the only thing which seemed to have given many of the files value in the eyes of whoever placed them in the safe deposit box was the simple fact that they referred to Operation RACETRACK. There were two other files, however, which looked more promising. One was evidently a transcript of the goings-on at 21 Kandahar Road, while the other was headed:

TOP SECRET : DG/DDG's EYES ONLY
Report on meeting of K Branch officers and QUASAR, 6th July 1971

Johnson put aside this second document and picked up the other. It was listed as a transcript of events from 3rd June 1971. There were various notes and references on the top of a covering sheet, including one which said 'Tape No: 4786K3/71'. The first two pages consisted of a couple of prostitutes gossiping away, evidently without a client in their presence. The transcript referred to one as 'Diana' and she, fairly clearly, was the madam. At 6.37 p.m., it recorded:

Unknown man *: Good Evening, Mrs Morris.
Diana: Come in, lovey, take your coat off.

Johnson followed the asterisk to the bottom of the page:

Transcriber's note: man had [deleted] accent.

The deletion had been made with a black marker pen. Above it, whoever had done so had initialled the document. It appeared to be 'MM' for Michael Martin. Johnson returned to the text:

Unknown man: Is she here?
Diana: Yes dearie, she's waiting upstairs for you. She looks a picture.
Unknown man: Good, good. This is for you.
Diana: We don't have to do that now. Don't be silly.
Unknown man: It's all there. Same as last time.

The sum was not mentioned. Johnson wondered how much somebody sold a seven-year-old girl for in 1971. He tightened his grip on the papers.

Diana: Let's go up now, shall we?
Unknown man: Yes.
Sound of stairs being climbed. Indistinct words. They arrive upstairs.
Diana: Hello, Nicola my darling, it's your Uncle John to see you again. Don't be shy, Nicky my love. What's the matter? Come and say hello. You can play with Cindy again later. Come on now, ducky.
Unknown man: Hello, honey. Look what I've brought you, isn't that lovely!
Diana: How nice! Say thank you to Uncle John.
Nicola: Thank you, Uncle John.

Johnson felt unhappy about reading on. The fact that this sordid encounter had taken place in 1971 did not make him feel any less of a voyeur. Perhaps he could find more clues to QUASAR'S identity. More likely anything really revealing would have been deleted by Martin again. He read on. The sex act was described as 'probable sexual congress' by the transcriber. Johnson wondered about the person who had sat there with headphones and a typewriter. They were mostly middle-aged women who did this sort of work for the spooks. What had she been thinking when she typed 'probable sexual congress'? Did she have a daughter? Were there tears in her eyes as there were in Johnson's now? QUASAR's words drifted through his shimmering vision:

> **Unknown man**: Don't cry. Don't cry, honey . . . Don't cry, I won't hurt you, again.

Johnson's concentration was broken by his wife's calls. He looked up through the window of the shed and saw her beckoning him from the kitchen. He put the files back into a plastic bag and sniffed away his shaken feelings. Taping the package back underneath his work bench, he started up the garden towards the house.

'Come on!' she urged him, 'you know what it's like at Ikea on Saturdays.'

Johnson drifted round the store amiably enough, although his thoughts were elsewhere. There was a range of tables being inspected by various couples evidently still in what Johnson called the nest-building phase of life.

'What do you think?' asked Jane.

'Well, it's fine I suppose.'

'That's not very helpful.'

'No, not at all,' Gemma chipped in. Johnson looked at his wife and they both laughed.

Chapter Nine

Monday came soon enough for Charles Denton. He had spent the previous afternoon checking over the agreed meeting place. He had done so as a precaution, although it was in the very nature of their rendezvous that it was too busy to spot unusual things easily. He had come away after an hour and a half's careful scrutiny, convinced that it was as safe as he could make it.

Denton had mixed feelings about the meeting. The robbery and Johnson's inquiries had made it a matter of some desperation that he and Pete fight for the sake of their continued relationship. He did not relish having to explain these things. But he felt happy anticipation about the meeting, too. His relationship with Pete, over more than twenty years, was one of the most remarkable in the history of their business. They met only two or three times a year on average, which Denton believed was the secret to their success. Denton had never pushed Pete too hard – although under pressure from his bosses to do so. QUASAR was a remarkable asset, after all – there was always interest in any material from him. But ultimately Denton was able to protect his agent – his friend too – from exploitation. 'Don't kill the golden goose,' Denton had always told them, and they had always had to accept it, because nobody else could match Denton's relationship with the man. The bosses had always kept Pete's product on the tightest possible distribution. How would they cope when he was gone? He didn't know. Somebody was being trained to replace him, they kept saying. He was sceptical. How many people had ever fully understood what was going on between him and Pete? Very few, perhaps half a dozen during those twenty-odd years, which was what had saved Pete from the molehunters and Denton from the treacherous tides of history. It was a unique relationship, he told himself once more.

He was at the agreed meeting point an hour before time. He had told the office he was going out to survey the Algerian embassy and some other points of interest. Waterloo station was moving from the mid-morning doldrums to its minor lunchtime climax. Denton surveyed the commuters. He felt no pain; he had treated himself to a temgesic before leaving the house and that was powerful stuff. It blunted his wits, but he wanted to forget the pain for the moment. He surveyed the salary men seeping to and fro across the concourse. They didn't look much different to him, but he regarded them with something bordering on contempt. How little you know, he reflected. His mind drifted to the extraordinary sacrifices he and Irene had made in their life together and he felt it had been worth it. What a tragedy that Irene had died before she could witness how it had all turned out! Denton was about to do what made him so special, and that – not the temgesic – made him high.

He spotted Pete from a long way off. They moved together into the Casey Jones fast food restaurant and their meeting was underway.

'You look like shit,' Pete said early on, and then asked, 'How much longer have you got?'

'Oh, it's not imminent,' Denton lied, knowing he had already passed some of the doctors' early predictions for what he called 'D-Day'.

'I'm sorry, anyway,' Pete said, drawing on the hot coffee he had bought.

'I won't be seeing you more than once more, though,

I'm afraid.' Denton glanced away from Pete, looking once more for any watchers. 'Somebody else is being prepared to take over.'

'I see,' Pete replied, while secretly wondering whether that might be the time to break off the relationship. 'It won't be the same with anybody else,' he said.

'I'll miss it too,' Denton replied, adding: 'There's a severe problem, as I told you on the phone. We need to gather information about this policeman, but we can't be seen to do it. It's all too difficult for the Service, legally speaking.'

'So what are you saying?'

'We need to use a freelance outfit. But we can't have payments traced to us. We never told anybody about our relationship with you: ministers don't know about it; nobody else on this side knows about it. We need to protect that.'

'I don't believe you guys. You're so cheap you want me to pay for this thing?'

'We think that would be the most . . . secure solution.' Denton tried not to show his embarrassment.

'Oh boy,' Pete said, shaking his head. 'And you guys wonder how you got the reputation as the cheapskates of the intelligence world.'

An hour and a half later Denton was on his way out of the station. It was over. The only evidence of their liaison was the Styrofoam cups cleared from the table soon after they left. Denton came away very pleased with himself. Pete had not only agreed to pay for the operation but he had also agreed to get him a 'goodbye present': a special package of material for their final meeting. Denton had only told one real lie, but that was basically the same lie which their relationship had been based on for all these years. He decided to treat himself to a taxi to Blackheath. He would have an hour to study the contents of the plastic shopping bag which Pete had given him before he had to put in an appearance at Gower Street.

He climbed the stairs to his flat. It was more than three hours since he had taken the pain killer, so it was hard work. He reached the top with a sheen of sweat on his forehead. But while the cramps in his stomach wracked his body, his mind raced in anticipation of what he would find in Pete's bag. Denton sat heavily on his sofa and slid the papers out. His eyes raced along the lines of the files. Occasionally a smile played across his mouth, or a furrow his brow. This was what he lived for – the moments of revelation in which the cherished secrets of another state flowed into him. He went to his drinks cabinet, a Korean-style mahogany chest with brass fittings. After fishing out a bottle of cognac, Denton poured himself a generous portion, reminding himself at the same time to buy a pack of mints on the way to work.

He concluded his scanning of the documents, drawing occasionally on the glass of Napoleon. He put the papers back into the shabby shopping bag before placing them in the hiding place he had used for years. He did not intend to have the papers in his flat for long. They would be passed on quickly to people who could make use of them.

As he left for Gower Street, Denton's thoughts switched to the problem of how he would frustrate Johnson's inquiries. Pete had suggested he use Panther Secure Services Ltd – PSSL. Arrangements would be put in place to pay their bills; Pete's organisation had more money than Denton's and the services required of Panther would not come cheap. Panther could not be considered among the leaders in its field. It was run by a couple of hardcase ex-Paras, commissioned from the ranks and subsequently pushed sideways. Its two founding partners customarily wore identical navy blue blazers to business meetings and exhibited an exaggerated respect for royalty. In its time, PSSL had picked up work from MI6, the CIA, the Iraqi Mukhabarat (in the times when Saddam Hussein was still considered no more than a client who paid promptly) and the Saudis – although they didn't really count, as virtually everybody on the security scene had done work for them. Panther lacked the credibility of the firms headed by ex-SAS officers or men with titles, so these governmental contracts tended to be few and far between. The firm managed instead to keep its six staff and predictably anonymous offices in Croydon on the go with a variety of private contracts. These ranged from the bugging of rival companies' boardrooms to checking the security of certain bank couriers on behalf of their insurers. It was precisely the firm's nature as small-time, basically reliable and hungry which made Pete choose them. He had told Denton to wait a few days before contacting them.

As he rattled along the Circle Line, staring into the gloom of the tunnels, Denton pondered how he would eavesdrop on Johnson. It would be easy enough to bug the detective's home. The office would be a little trickier, although it certainly wouldn't be the first time a police station had been bugged. Panther would have to set up a system for the tapes to be transcribed promptly. He hadn't forgotten what a serious inconvenience Johnson might become, but he was relishing the challenge of running the scale of surveillance operation which the bosses had never allowed him to do. Denton's 'colonial' education had always counted against him with the snobs in the higher reaches of the Service. Charles Denton, lately of Rhodesia, was not considered good enough for the GI, the General Intelligence management stream, so he had reached a professional ceiling in his forties. As he made mental notes, Denton had trouble suppressing his good spirits.

Hal Canning and Jim Parker made their way along the reflecting floors of Terminal Three towards their gate. It was unusual for Deputy Director Intelligence and Deputy Director Operations to leave America together at the same time, but the new chief of the Secret Intelligence Service – MI6 – had invited them to London for a special meeting on the threat of Soviet nuclear, chemical and biological weapons.

It had been a brief affair and the CIA had thought it best to show willing, and now its two senior deputy directors were on their way back to Washington.

Parker had found the conference thoroughly annoying. He considered it to have been a waste of time, but there was also something else growing in his mind. He had noticed that the Brits seemed more polite, more deferential, to Canning. He had seen the same signs in Washington recently, but he had not regarded them as particularly significant, chiding himself inwardly on his insecurity. In Britain, though, he had definitely noticed something. Canning had been put next to the Chief of MI6 at lunch. In general, their treatment seemed to suggest that they regarded him as the coming man, or at least one of the principal contenders. In his heart of hearts, the bulky ex-Marine recognised that Mr Blow-Dry Canning was far better at dealing with people like the Brits than he was. As the two men shuffled towards the departure gate, the Deputy Director for Operations reflected that the trip had opened his eyes to certain things about his colleague.

It is government policy that federal employees travel coach and indeed Canning and Parker had been booked economy-class tickets by their assistants. However, buying them expensive open tickets and exploiting their frequent fliers memberships meant Canning and Parker *never* travelled coach – unless you counted flights with the Air Force. As they settled into their ample business-class seats, Canning and Parker made dutiful conversation. Parker would have preferred to take a different flight – Canning's urbanity and transparent ambition made him such dull company. Parker preferred to discuss the stewardesses' legs and which one of the stewards was a fruit or not.

'He seems like an outstanding thinker,' said Canning, with Parker apparently ignoring him. 'The new man the Brits have got; he seems outstanding,' the Deputy Director for Intelligence repeated.

'Yuh,' Parker responded at last.

'Of course, I'm not sure how much the Brits count for these days. Some useful backup in the Middle East, that's about it. They're still living on Gordievsky.'

'I'd be singing that song for years if I'd run somebody that high in the KGB,' countered Parker, the field man, the agent runner.

'I know, but really . . . Compare what we can get out of the Israelis – even the Saudis. Still, I suppose their loyalty is touching.'

'Don't forget, Hal, the Brits are our window into Europe, and that's the bottom line these days.'

'Sure, the Europeans share their product with the Brits, the Brits share it with us – what they don't classify "UK Eyes".'

'Let's change the subject: here comes the fudge packer,' Parker remarked sourly. A steward with bleached-blond hair and a name tag identifying him as 'Marlon' arrived with the drinks trolley. Canning opted for Perrier, Parker – a Jack Daniels. Parker looked on as Marlon wheeled the trolley further up the aisle. The steward was in his late twenties, tanned, fit-looking – almost a parody of the Californian beach creature. 'What a geek!' Parker quipped. Canning could not contain his irritation.

'Always the redneck, Jim: why can't you give people a break sometimes? Don't be such a goddamn homophobe.'

'Relax, Hal. You can save indignation on behalf of minorities for hearings on the Hill. At thirty-five thousand feet nobody's going to hear you.'

'Fuck you!' said Canning under his breath. He fussed with his briefcase, pulling out a copy of *Newsweek* in which he feigned interest as his anger with Parker simmered away, blurring his thoughts and making his mouth sour.

'Let's get something straight,' Parker continued, knowing Canning was trying to hide his anger. 'You think you can be the next Director of Central Intelligence. Maybe. You can certainly fool Congress most of the time. But don't think I would ever let that make any difference to the way I'd run Clandestine Service.'

Canning had always prized himself on his ability to avoid confrontation, but he could not suppress his anger and contempt for this absurd southerner who had no place at the top of the modern CIA. 'Don't lose too much sleep over how you'd run Clandestine Service with me as Director, Jim. Still, it's not too late for you to think about a second career. Maybe the Marines would let you take schoolkids around the Iwo Jima monument: you could give them a talk about John Wayne and apple pie.'

'I'd be proud to, asshole. By the way, just how did you avoid going to Vietnam?'

Canning said nothing. For years mutual loathing had existed between the two men: faint praise for one another's ideas in committee, unusually close scrutiny of one another's budget proposals. Now it was out in the open and Canning did not know quite what to do about it. As the flight dragged on, he fretted away. He didn't want to apologise, but he didn't need Parker's overt opposition. The Deputy Director for Operations, on the other hand, appeared genuinely unconcerned. He buried himself in the latest Tom Clancy paperback and drank another two JD's. He felt better for having vented the feelings he now recognised had been building in him for months.

When they arrived at Dulles, the two men went to separate cars. Neither had spoken another word on the flight. Canning and Parker now knew where they stood.

Chapter Ten

MacFadyen had made his excuses and avoided going to meet DS Wendy Mortimer at the child protection team. As Johnson drove down south of the river alone, his thoughts drifted to whether MacFadyen was losing interest in the case. Had the detective chief inspector's little chat had its desired effect? As he skimmed across the black pools lying on the streets in his unmarked Astra, Johnson wondered about his partner. MacFadyen never seemed happy with his lot in life. He had worked as a fisherman and in the Clyde shipyards and now he was giving the police a try.

MacFadyen had transferred down from the Strathclyde CID – a force which prided itself on one of the highest crime clear-up rates in the country. This efficiency, he insisted whenever asked, resulted from a simple readiness to 'fucking batter' suspects. In the Metropolitan Police where it was now fashionable to refer to the public as 'customers' and the force as 'the service', such ideas were no longer expressed in front of senior officers. Johnson felt sure that MacFadyen would leave the Met sooner or later. Sometimes he talked about training to become a pilot: he liked the idea of flying crop dusters in Africa. Although advancing into his late thirties, MacFadyen had never settled down or even had a live-in girlfriend. The jock shared a sense of impulsiveness and a lack of respect for higher authority – once the two of them had taken off to Spain together for a long weekend of boozing and storytelling. Johnson forgot his partner's reluctance to come out that wet evening; instead he simply hoped that he found whatever he was looking for.

DS Mortimer had suggested that they have their 'unofficial' chat in a local pub rather than at the Bermondsey station. They met in the hallway of the station and began to walk along together. They did not talk about the case which had brought them together. Mortimer looked exactly how Johnson expected a detective involved in the battlefield of people's private and sexual lives to look. Her eyes were slightly hooded, but benign and caring. She frequently dipped into her bag for cigarettes. Her hair was closely cropped and mostly grey.

They entered a pub called the Grenadier, and Johnson was at a loss to know why Mortimer had taken him there. A fat man in a shellsuit leant over a pool table revealing an ample bottom cleavage; others sat around staring blankly at the game. The decor was horrible, and Iron Maiden was being played very loud on a juke box. As they sat down the pool player pocketed a ball, turning to his mates to shout 'fucking nice one!'

'I'll get them in, shall I? What do you fancy?' asked Johnson.

'A white wine and soda please.'

Johnson fetched the drinks as Mortimer lit up another cigarette. He sat down beside her to make himself heard although he felt vaguely embarrassed about huddling together with a stranger in this lowlife pub.

'You obviously know this Nicola Dawson then?'

'Oh yes, she's quite infamous around here.'

'I was a bit surprised that you know her name, what with all this going back so many years.' Mortimer looked uncertain, she did not reply. Johnson continued: 'Anyway, the only real chance we've got of making a case is if she agrees to press charges.'

'What do you mean exactly?' Wendy Mortimer looked uneasy.

'Well, charges relating to her abuse.'

'Her abuse?'

'Yes,' said Johnson, sensing a revelation was on its way.

'DS Johnson, I've spent months putting together a case about Nicola Dawson's two daughters and her husband – well, the man who used to live with her. He's been abusing them and she took an active part in it all.'

'What?'

'She's got two daughters – of eleven and eight. They're in care now and he's in custody, but I'm still hoping to build a case against her.'

'She's been taking an active part in it?'

'Well, the children say she encouraged them to do it and not to tell anybody about it.' Mortimer had pulled a notebook from her handbag.

Johnson sipped his lager, reflecting on what this all meant. He turned to DS Mortimer: 'Well my understanding is that Nicola Dawson was coerced or pursuaded to have sex with men at a brothel in Kandahar Road in 1971.'

'Frankly, it doesn't surprise me,' Mortimer shook her head slowly. 'One generation of abuser begets another. Some people just grow up without knowing what love really is; how to stop the emotional turning sexual.'

'Jesus, what a mess. Can I speak to her?'

'Let's be realistic, DS Johnson. It strikes me that the last thing my case needs is your case.' Her eyes were steely now: 'It would be quite a plea of mitigation for Nicola Dawson. It can't really be in my interest to put you in touch with her.'

Johnson did not respond. His spirits were ebbing. If he couldn't find the victim of this injustice, there was little point in him pursuing it. But another side of him spoke with the same cynicism which so surprised him about DS Wendy Mortimer. If Nicola Dawson was desperate to beat charges, then nailing the foreign spy at the centre of the RACETRACK files might seem like an attractive option to her.

'We've not got much to talk about now, have we?' she broke into his thoughts.

'I suppose not, we'd better drink up.' If Nicola Dawson's boyfriend had already been charged and was in jail, there was a good chance he could track her down. They stood up to leave. Johnson eyed the pool player, who was in his early thirties. He had a fat, flushed face. As the two detectives neared the door, the pool player turned and shot a glance at Johnson. 'What are you staring at, knob?' The detectives slipped out of the Grenadier.

The following day, Johnson rang around the courts. Eventually he was able to persuade one clerk to give him the address which Nicola Dawson's boyfriend had given. It appeared to be a flat in a high-rise in Stockwell. Fortunately, directory inquiries had her boyfriend, John O'Casey, listed at the address. Johnson rang it.

'Is Nicola Dawson there please?'

'Who's that?' a voice with an Irish accent replied.

'My name's Lee, we go back a long way.'

'She's not here.'

'Where's she gone?'

'The coast somewhere, a boarding house.'

'Which coast?'

'I don't know exactly. What did you say your name was?'

'Lee Johnson.'

'Brighton, I think. I think she's just trying to get away from everything.'

'Yeah.'

'Take care now. I'll mention you called if she rings.'

'Yes, thank you, you do that. Tell her I'm giving her a chance to get back at Diana from Kandahar Road.'

'What was that?'

'Tell her I can give her a chance to get back at Diana from Kandahar Road. Nicola used to work for her. I'll give you a number.' Johnson gave the Irishwoman his direct line at the station.

Charles Denton had made his way to the offices of Panther in Croydon. He did not have a car, so it was a lengthy journey from Blackheath and he didn't arrive until seven in the evening. He studied the office – nothing on the walls except a year planner and a calendar for a spark plug firm featuring a topless model. He noticed a disparate selection of magazines on a coffee table by the door: *Readers' Digest*, *Sunday* and *Majesty*, which featured a photograph of the Princess of Wales. He was greeted by Pinchman, one of the two partners. Pinchman wore his navy blue blazer with a Parachute Regiment crest on the pocket, grey flannel trousers and grey polyveld shoes. He had a moustache, thinning hair and his stomach had gone to pot. He gave Denton a firm handshake.

'Mr Ryan, nice to meet you. Our friend from overseas said you'd be running this show.' They both sat at a cheap wooden table in Pinchman's office.

'Yes.' Denton disguised his shock that Pete had told Pinchman to expect a 'Paul Ryan'. It was dangerous to use the same pseudonym that had been used to rent the safe deposit box. It was very untidy – he should never have confided it in Pete and Pete should never have used it with Pinchman.

'It's a surveillance job, I understand.'

'Yes, that's right. We need to keep tabs on one Lee Johnson.' Denton removed a sheet of paper from his briefcase and pushed it across the table. 'This is where he lives and works.'

Pinchman studied the page, trying to cover his surprise. 'He's a policeman, I take it?'

'Yes, he's a detective sergeant in the CID.'

'Bent is he?'

'Oh yes and worse. I'm afraid he's taking too close an interest in a very delicate matter of national security.'

'I see.' Pinchman didn't really see at all. He had made Ryan for MI5 or MI6: why not deal with this policeman through disciplinary channels? If he was corrupt, surely he could be pushed sideways?

'He's a loose cannon, Mr Pinchman. We don't know what he's said to whom. We need to find out. He may go to the press; he's not very stable. I'd like his home and office telephones intercepted. I'd like to be able to pick up daily reports each evening, about this time. Somewhere in central London would be more convenient.'

'I'm sure we can do something about that.' Pinchman began scribbling with a pencil in a small notebook.

'Do you want us to send somebody to have a chat with this Johnson, put him in the picture?'

'No, not yet. It might be necessary but not yet.'

Pinchman picked up a telephone, calling in 'Martin' from another office.

When Martin Dodge arrived, Denton found him vaguely comical. He was no more than five foot four. Dodge had a small, pinched face and a wispy moustache. His build was also slight; he had the frame of a boy of twelve.

'Mr Ryan, this is Martin Dodge: he's going to be doing your spadework. He's ex 1 Para. Upstanding bloke.' Denton and Dodge surveyed one another. Pinchman brought him up to date on the conversation – looking down at his notebook every now and then.

'What's the action on bumping the cops, Mr Ryan?' Dodge asked.

'I'm sorry?'

'If we're caught planting the devices or following your target what do we tell the cops? Especially if we're caught inside a cop shop – it might be a little embarrassing.' Dodge expected this wizened old spy to give him one of those discreet Whitehall telephone numbers: when an informant rings or somebody is caught doing a break-in for the Branch or MI5, a call to one of these will result in a speedy release from custody.

'I'm afraid you'd be on your own, Mr Dodge. This operation is completely deniable.'

Dodge's gaze flicked toward his boss, clearly uneasy. Pinchman nodded at him. 'It's OK, Martin. I've discussed all this. Mr Ryan and his partner expect maximum discretion and our fee has been calculated accordingly.' Shortly afterwards, Dodge made his excuses and left.

'Don't underestimate Dodge, Mr Ryan. He's fucking hard. If it comes to it.'

'Well, let's hope it doesn't.'

Dodge had a dizzying propensity for violence. There was a deep streak of malevolence within him which both earned him his living and denied him any roots or happiness. In 1 Para, Dodge had almost beaten a teenage republican to death in Newry. The youth had been 'taking the piss'. It had taken deft footwork by the Army Legal Service to fend off the police on that one. Dodge had twice been charged with GBH since leaving the Army. One of those who filed charges against him had been his wife, who left him after six years of abuse. The other plaintiff was somebody who owed somebody money, and that somebody had hired Dodge to collect it. After shattering the bad debtor's left kneecap with a claw hammer, Dodge had skipped bail and gone to Croatia to fight with the National Guard. Even some of Dodge's old mates in the Paras called him the Poisoned Dwarf. On his return from that war, in which Dodge boasted to have 'taken a few Chetnik scalps', Panther had somehow managed to persuade the Crown Prosecution Service to forget all about the misunderstanding with the hammer. Pinchman had called in a favour from a friend at Box 500 or MI5, who had blocked charges on the grounds that Dodge was 'an intelligence asset' of HMG. Panther would doubtless have to pay for that favour one day, and Pinchman wondered if Denton was the man sent to collect.

Denton looked Pinchman in the eye. 'Mr Pinchman, I can't really overstate the sensitivity of this work. Even within my organisation all knowledge about this operation is very strictly compartmented.'

'I understand. You can expect us to be discreet. We've never been in the business of publicising our contracts.'

Denton stood up. 'When can I expect the first intercepts?'

'Give us a week, Mr Ryan.'

The two men walked towards the door. Pinchman looked down at the copy of *Majesty*. 'What an asset she is to this nation.'

'I'm sorry?'

'The Princess of Wales, what an asset. She's probably worth millions every year to the balance of payments.'

'Oh yes.' Denton couldn't think of anything more to say.

'We're all defending the realm in our own way, don't you think, Mr Ryan?'

'Quite so.' Denton walked into the darkness and pondered whether Pinchman and Dodge were really up to the job.

Chapter Eleven

Johnson and MacFadyen sat studying their notebooks from the Majestic job with all the earnest concentration of a couple of undergraduates who had spent three years drinking heavily but were suddenly nearing their finals. They had been telephoned by the Crown Prosecution Service to notify them of a forthcoming hearing involving Sancho Doherty and the other armed robbers arrested in Frithville Gardens. It was going to be a quick affair. All had given statements admitting their actions in the robbery of the Majestic safety deposit box company and they were to be brought before a judge to be committed for trial. It was usually a fairly brief hearing, but it required the two detectives to refresh their memories about those dramatic events. Some smartarse lawyer might use the hearing to claim the robbers had been beaten in custody; other spanners might be thrown in the works. So they sat in their cramped station office going through files and their notebooks. At the same time, the two detectives also had other cases to worry about: the time which they could devote to their private quest into the RACETRACK files was limited.

Johnson's early excitement on reading the RACETRACK material had been replaced by a more sober appreciation of the enormity of the investigative task facing somebody trying to crack MI5 business dating back so many years. Equally, he had become convinced that the files must be investigated by somebody and he relished the challenge. He knew from both CID work and his Army days in Ireland that

83

intelligence registries were sacrosanct. Anybody who removed such sensitive files was almost certainly up to no good. MI5's own Registry was the safest place to bury any skeletons – heaven knows there must be enough in there – and this had convinced him that if Denton had put them in a deposit box, he could nail him for something pretty serious.

Lee was drawing up a list of calls to make and approaches to try. He had decided while out running that morning that this collection of hunches would represent his last attempt to deliver a result on the crimes which MI5 was so keen to hush up. Johnson usually ran about five miles a day, and he had found it was a good time to ponder his work problems – it allowed him to escape the ceaseless interruptions of home and office. Running also reminded him of his Army years: it was good self-discipline. He prided himself on it; it was one of the things which separated him from the fat, boozy, old lags which made up so much of the CID.

His plans to put aside his private investigations were interrupted by MacFadyen. 'We must know somebody in SB who could dig something out for us?'

'The Branch?' As he said it, Johnson realised there was somebody he did know, although not very well. He had met Detective Sergeant Elaine Stevens on an intelligence collation course run by Greater Manchester CID a few months before. She was a Special Branch officer working in the regional office of the Security Liaison Officer in Manchester who had given some talks on the course about anti-terrorist intelligence work. She was clearly bright, around Johnson's age, and had seemed very friendly during the coffee and biscuits before and after her spiel. Johnson was aware that the security liaison officers were MI5's ambassadors in the provinces. They worked closely with the Branch, sharing offices and much else. In one of her talks, DS Stevens had mentioned their ability to log directly into MI5's Registry database. Johnson opened one of his notebooks and flicked through until he came across the list of names which he had copied off the Registry records of the RACETRACK files. There were only six of them.

He picked up the telephone and rang GMP enquiries. Soon afterwards, the phone was ringing in the SB/SLO's office in Manchester.

'Is DS Stevens there, please?'

'Speaking.'

'Oh, hello. It's DS Lee Johnson, Met Police. You remember we met at the collation course earlier this year?'

'Oh yes, I remember you. What brings me this pleasure?'

Belatedly, Johnson remembered that Stevens had flirted shamelessly with him on the course. He tried to adopt a thoroughly professional tone. 'I need some help. Very unofficial.'

'You know SB do things by the book, DS Johnson.' There was silence from Johnson. But she was just toying with him. Before he replied, she spoke again: 'I was just being daft, what do you want?' The 'daft' reminded Johnson how thick her Lancashire accent was: not Manchester, somewhere further north.

'I've got some names. Security Service people who might be able to help with an inquiry I'm conducting. They may have witnessed a crime some years back.'

'I can't see the Met investigating something like that.'

'It's personal, but I think . . .'

'Forget it, Lee, it's none of my business. Just call it a favour in the bank – if I can help.'

'Well, I'd like to know the whereabouts of these people. Some may have retired.'

'Fire away.' Stevens pressed the phone against her ear with her shoulder and unlocked one of her desk drawers. She drew out the Security Service internal phone directory.

'C. Denton.'

'Yes.' She found the entry in the book. 'He works in Gower Street, fourth floor, directorate of counter-espionage, K2 Section. Do you want his direct line number?'

'Yes please!' Johnson enjoyed the moment. This was a choice piece of information which could be used when the time was right.

His pleasure though was shortlived. He gave four more names, none of which were in the book. Only on the last did Stevens register again.

'M. Youlton, Mrs.'

'Oh yes, I don't have to look her up. Marjorie Youlton, she's the Director General's PA, has been for more than ten years. She's an institution there.'

'Right.' Johnson did not have high hopes of getting her to talk: all experience had taught him that PAs to top managers were invariably the most loyal employees.

'Lee, I can check those others: let me ring you back. It shouldn't take long.'

Elaine Stevens walked across to her computer terminal. After logging on with a sequence of passwords she got into the B Branch database. This was quite separate to the Registry and contained all the administrative files relating to the Service. The B Branch database was well known to Security Service officers as a quick way of finding retired colleagues or looking up other administrative or financial details relating to their operations. Elaine found what she was looking for quite quickly. She wanted Johnson to know just how quickly – she could not quite contain her desire to show off.

'Johnson.'

'Lee, it's Elaine.'

'Christ, that was quick.'

'Service with a smile. Are you standing by?'

'Yep, fire away.'

'Michael Martin was Director of Counter-Espionage when he retired in 1984. He died of a heart attack in 1990.' She carried on reading from her screen.

'Roger Forbes-Hamilton – *Sir* Roger Forbes-Hamilton –

was Director General from 1965 until 1974. He died three years after he retired.'

Johnson made a mental note. This was the Director General at the time of RACETRACK.

'Mark Buchanan – no knighthood for him – was Forbes-Hamilton's successor as Director General. He packed it in in 1979. He's still alive, you'll be pleased to hear. He's living near King's Lynn in Norfolk.'

Johnson scribbled the address eagerly. 'What about the last one?'

'Mavis Stewart. She was Marjorie Youlton's predecessor-but-one as the Director General's PA. It looks like she worked with Forbes-Hamilton and for Buchanan, judging by the dates. She's still drawing her pension but we only have a PO Box number for her.'

'Elaine, that's brilliant, thank you.'

'That's all right. Promise you'll buy me a drink next time you see me.'

'Of course.' Johnson's mind raced as he looked at his notes.

'I'll be down soon enough. I'm always coming down on Irish business.'

Johnson wound up the call, distractedly. He was already thinking through their next move.

'What's the story?' asked MacFadyen.

'The DG who ran RACETRACK is dead. So is Martin, the man who appeared to know even more than Denton about the operation. Martin and Denton were the two chosen to confront the perve.'

'Check. Are all our leads brown bread?'

'No. Buchanan is still alive. He was the DG who ordered all the compromising pictures and tapes destroyed. So is the Miss Moneypenny figure who shuffled their papers, one Mavis Stewart. He's living out his retirement in Norfolk; she's got a PO Box in Cumbria.'

'Useful lady, this DS Stevens. Why was she so helpful?'

'I don't know. Maybe she just likes showing how good they are up there. She made it pretty clear she expects something back.'

'Oh yeah. Maybe she wants bothering.'

'Bollocks. You haven't seen her.'

'If she's ugly, she'd be really grateful.'

'Yeah yeah.'

'Would you though?' MacFadyen enjoyed the game.

'No, don't be daft. You know me.'

'Not even if it was medically necessary?'

Johnson smiled at last, MacFadyen was happy.

Charles Denton was at his desk, gazing occasionally through the net curtains and out onto Gower Street. He was going through UMBRA transcripts of Algerian diplomatic telexes. These were intercepted at Palmer Street and brought straight to Gower Street. The Algerians used English in their traffic: no transcription or translation was necessary. The GCHQ machines which unscrambled the Algerian cipher had been made by Marconi in the 1970s. These days they were reserved for what the GCHQ men at Palmer Street called the 'Enid Blyton States' – countries whose cryptography was so amusingly primitive that a competent maths undergraduate with a pencil and paper could break the ciphers with a few hours' work. Iraq did not fall into this category. Before the Iraqis had been kicked out of their London embassy, they had used very advanced Italian and German crypto machines. These intercepts had been taken to Cheltenham for crunching by super-computers, with varying results. Happily for GCHQ, Algeria was firmly in the Enid Blyton camp.

Denton's attention had been caught by a request for visas for three men due to travel to London via Rome. The sender of the telex in Algiers had alerted a man determined by MI5 to be the senior spook in the embassy to meet these three gentlemen off the plane. Denton had sent the three names to Registry, where a research assistant was checking them against various databases.

As he waited, Denton began worrying about a subject which he had put out of his mind for days. Should he have told anybody in the Service about Johnson's visit to the flat in Blackheath and the questions about RACETRACK? Denton still felt he was right about Johnson acting alone, and if he was acting alone then it was not very likely that his superiors in MI5 would ever find out about the detective sergeant's visit. But if he was wrong and Johnson did ever approach the Service, then what would happen? Denton's actions would then bring suspicion on him.

These thoughts were interrupted by the arrival of the assistant from Registry.

'I thought I would bring this up for you in person,' the young woman said.

Denton scanned the pages. Two of the names were unknown, but the third had rung bells. Issued in the name of an Algerian, a passport with the same name and number had been used before by a colonel in Iraqi intelligence who had visited Germany at the time of the murder of a Kurdish dissident in Frankfurt. It was the first solid evidence that the Algerians were helping the Iraqis to sustain a foothold in Britain.

Jane Johnson collected her daughter from playgroup and parked her car in the street where she and Lee shared their domestic life. As she walked with Gemma, her briefcase and some shopping she noticed a man looking through the front window of their house, into the living room. Her pace slowed. The man was very small, almost boyish, wearing bright blue overalls. He turned and saw her.

'Oh, excuse me. Do you live here, madam?'

'Yes, what are you doing?'

'Telecom. I'm an engineer; I was trying to gain access for some essential maintenance.'

'There's nothing wrong with our phone. We haven't reported anything.'

'No, it's essential maintenance. It's your main phone junction boxes. We've had a few faults and we're replacing them around here as a precaution; you should have got a letter about it.'

Jane Johnson gathered up her daughter, thinking the letter might have been part of the junk mail which Lee routinely threw away without looking at. Gemma eyed the stranger. 'What a funny little man!'

'Quiet darling, be a good girl.' Jane spotted a grey van outside the house. It had ladders on the roof and appeared much like any other repairman's van. She noticed the Telecom symbol on the man's overalls. Her concerns began to ebb a little.

'Have you got any identification?'

'Of course, yes madam.' He produced a laminated plastic card – also with the Telecom symbol on it. 'You can ring my head office in Croydon too if you like,' he offered.

'No, that's all right.' She let herself into the house. The man did not follow immediately, or help her with her child and bags.

'I'll get my tools then.'

'OK, fine.'

The man returned, walked past her and into the hallway. Jane closed the door. Martin Dodge was inside the Johnsons' house.

He went into the living room.

'The socket's behind the sofa,' she told him.

'Ta.' Things were very well laid out from his point of view. The phone socket was only a few inches from a power point. Jane went into the kitchen and Dodge could hear the sound of a kettle being filled. He unscrewed the power point first.

Most bugging equipment is limited by the life of its batteries – freelance operators who cannot tap lines at the exchange always appreciate access to mains power. Having run a small wire along the edge of the skirting board from the power socket to the phone junction box, Dodge replaced the latter with one of his own but also stamped with the Telecom 'T'. The new box contained a small transmitter which would relay telephone conversations to a recording machine away from the house. The whole job was accomplished in three minutes. The kettle boiled and Dodge began tidying away his tools as Jane entered the room.

'All done thank you, missus.'

'Finished?'

'Yes.' Dodge moved towards the door.

'What about the socket in our bedroom? Don't you have to check that one?'

'Oh yes! I'd forgotten. Sorry missus, long day.'

He climbed the stairs alone – Jane did not want to be with him. Dodge checked out the layout of the rooms. He did not use the Polaroid camera in his holdall because he was concerned that she might hear it. He didn't bother to inspect the bedroom phone socket either. But Dodge did make a mental note of the Saisho electric clock radio on the bedside table. These were easy to buy and a bugged one could be substituted for the original if they ever needed to record a little pillow talk. After a few minutes, Dodge descended the stairs. He put his head around the kitchen door, where Jane was making tea.

'All done now. Thanks very much. I must be on my way. Sorry, can't stop for tea.'

Jane turned and he was already leaving. The front door banged as she poured Earl Grey into the single mug sitting on the sideboard. 'I wasn't offering,' she thought aloud.

Chapter Twelve

Johnson's feet fell rhythmically, hitting the paving stones as he ran along the river. He passed the pubs with their happy boozers and felt a little more pious as he headed down towards Chiswick. In the Army, Johnson had run in boots, carrying a rucksack with forty pounds of bagged sand in it. In civvy street it was Nike Airs on his feet and nothing on his back.

As he pushed himself past the idling walkers and parked cars his mind turned to the problems of RACETRACK. So much of his life was spent trying to nail people who'd blagged building societies or stolen a few cars. Johnson still enjoyed putting these people away, but so many of the crimes they attended these days had absolutely no prospect of being solved. He was dealing with dozens of cases each year – clearing up only a few. Many cops talked about knowing who had done particular crimes but not being able to put them away. Johnson recognised that in most cases they simply hadn't the faintest idea who was responsible. Johnson hadn't felt the same excitement about anything he'd worked on since Ireland and his days in covert surveillance. He had packed that in after a year and a half: Jane couldn't stand it. Lee told himself for years that they had made the decision together, but slowly he had come to resent her for it. The boys in Ireland would have said he was ego-tripping on the RACETRACK files: carrying on because he thought he could crack it, not because he ever thought you could get a decent prosecution out of it. Still, he couldn't wait to make his next call or think through how he would take down Denton or find Nicola Dawson. It was always on his mind and he savoured his moments thinking about it. This business with the files was a bit like being in love.

He returned from his run decided on several things. Tracking down Nicola Dawson was a priority. Tomorrow was Saturday, though, and so he decided that he would use the day to go up to King's Lynn. It would take some front, walking in on a former boss of MI5, but Johnson felt some confidence that Buchanan was basically on the right side. After all, he had ordered all the RACETRACK photos and tapes destroyed. He had also put on record his disagreement with the predecessor's assessment that QUASAR, the spy from a friendly country, might ever serve as an agent of HMG. What would he say to Jane though?

Johnson came through the back door into the kitchen and took his trainers off, leaving them on the doormat. He was sweating heavily, a dark scarf had formed on his T-shirt. He went upstairs and began running the bath. Jane put her head around the door.

'What are we doing tomorrow, sweaty pig?'

'Oh babe, I had something planned.'

'What?'

'I've got to go up to Norfolk.'

'Why?'

'Investigation, you know.'

'No I don't know!' Her lips had tightened and her face became flushed.

'I'll try and be back by teatime . . .'

'What do you think we're meant to do while you're up there? You selfish bastard!' She walked out and banged the bathroom door.

Johnson got up and chased after her into the bedroom. 'Jane, please! It's important to me.'

'Why is it always "me" with you? You're a dad, you're a

husband. There are so many things that need doing around the house. It's months since you promised to mend the puncture on Gemma's bike . . .'

'Look, it's the thing that cropped up after the robbery – I think it could be really important . . .' Once more Lee was on the verge of telling her – he just wanted her to ask a few questions, to concede that what he did might be worthwhile or interesting.

'You're becoming so preoccupied, so uncommunicative. I don't know what you're talking about with this case. You're moody, you're asking to disappear on your own with no notice . . .' Jane seemed close to tears and close to accusing him of having an affair. 'You're changing.'

Johnson's patience gave out. 'Don't talk crap, nothing's changed!'

'Piss off to Norfolk then. Come back when you've got bored with it all. You're a selfish bastard.'

Johnson walked back into the bathroom and decided she was right about the last bit at least.

He was not quite prepared for the length and boredom of the train ride to King's Lynn. East Anglia was too flat to be interesting. He had bought the *Mail* and *Soldier* at Smiths before he left. He wasn't sure why he had bought *Soldier*, since he had never read it in the Army and considered it to be head-shed propaganda. He scanned through it and felt nothing very much until he chanced on an article headlined 'Courage of Sappers Rewarded'. It was about the activities of 32 Armoured Engineer Regiment clearing mines and other war wreckage from Kuwait after the Gulf War. They had recently been awarded medals for this work. Years ago, Johnson had served with this regiment in Germany before he went to Ireland on detachment. He still had one or two mates left in the Sappers. He scanned the piece forlornly, searching for their names. It wasn't much of an article but he felt some pride at having caught up with the activities of his old regiment. He reflected that the Gulf must have been a good caper. He resolved to get in contact with Bill Jessop, who was still serving, as soon as he could. They had been best mates together in the Sappers and it had been too long.

Johnson had taken the precaution of ringing Buchanan's telephone number before he got on the train to King's Lynn. He had rung off when the old man answered. He had detected an Ulster accent, which seemed to fit. Now he found himself taking a bus into the village where the old spook had made his retirement.

Johnson followed Lavender Lane down a gentle dip, looking for a house called 'White Gates'. Soon enough he spotted them. Highly original, he thought. Johnson paused because he could see a man pottering about in the garden. The figure emerged occasionally from behind one of the hedges. His hair had been blond or reddish, the face was heavily freckled. He had clearly been quite a big man – over six foot like Johnson – but his frame had shrunk a little as it aged inside its mottled skin. The slowness of his movements struck the detective. Buchanan was in his mid-seventies at least, but Johnson was surprised that he was not more sprightly.

Johnson sauntered up to the hedge and peered over. He knew little about gardening but decided it was as good a starting point as any.

'Excuse me,' he began, his voice a little reedy with nervousness. The old man straightened up gently and looked Johnson in the eye. 'Do you mind me asking what kind of plant that is on the front of your house?' Buchanan surveyed him as he pointed to the creeper. 'It's just I'm looking for a present for my wife and it looks like the kind of thing she'd like.'

'It's a clematis. It looks a good deal better when it flowers – in June normally,' Buchanan replied. His accent was unmistakable to Johnson.

'You've obviously put a good deal of time into it.'

'Oh yes, although it was on the house when we bought it.'

'That's a northern Irish accent, isn't it?'

'Yes, that's where my roots are.'

'North Antrim perhaps?' ventured Johnson.

'Fancy yourself as a bit of an expert?'

'Not really,' Johnson retreated.

'North Down, I'm from originally. You sound like a Londoner yourself.'

'I am, yes.'

'Did you serve over there?' Buchanan asked.

'I did,' Johnson replied with some unease.

'Good on you.' There was a moment's silence as the men examined one another. Johnson pretended to be interested in the garden.

'I hope you didn't mind the question,' said Buchanan.

'No, not at all, I had a good time in the Army – in Ireland and all. A lot of people don't like serving over there. I thought it was a good crack – as you lot would say.'

'Indeed. I only asked because I have to worry about my personal security,' Buchanan continued. 'The IRA would probably like to kill me.'

'Oh really?'

And then Buchanan fixed Johnson in his gaze. 'You understand why a man might worry, don't you?'

'Yes, I do.'

'If the phone goes and somebody hangs up, I worry that somebody might be checking to see whether I'm in or out. Which they would prefer depends on whether they're robbers or terrorists I suppose.' Johnson could feel himself blushing involuntarily as Buchanan continued. 'Then if somebody with a London accent comes and makes conversation with me four and a half hours later – about the time it would take to get here from London – I might worry a little more.'

'You've nothing to worry about, Mr Buchanan,' Johnson

used the old man's name deliberately – a defensive measure to try to slow the speed with which he was losing control of this encounter.

'How did you find me?'

'I can't say. Sorry.'

'Why can't you say? Do you want to prey on my fear?'

'No, of course not. I'm a policeman, a detective sergeant. The methods I used to find you are not open to people who would harm you.'

Buchanan put down his trowel and turned slowly towards his front door, for a few moments apparently oblivious to Johnson. He started slowly towards the house, an arthritic stumble. Then he spoke over his shoulder: 'Well, you're not a terrorist or a journalist – my two least favourite kinds of people. You might as well follow me in. No point our conducting business in front of everybody.'

Johnson moved around to the front gate and let himself into the garden. As he caught up with Buchanan, the old man was nearing his front step. Johnson noticed the copper bracelet on his wrist.

'Could you be so kind as to help me,' Buchanan placed his hand on Johnson's forearm. Slowly, and with pain, Buchanan raised his left foot to conquer the stair. Johnson noticed tears in Buchanan's eyes – evidently a lot of pain.

'My wife has gone into King's Lynn to shop. We have half an hour or so to chat. I hope that's sufficient.' Buchanan lowered himself slowly into an armchair in his living room. Johnson was surprised by the decor – he expected it to be more like a London club. Instead it was furnished with the kind of three-piece suite, lamps and TV which any retired middle manager might aspire to.

'I'm grateful for any time you can spare me.'

'Are you with the Branch? Somebody in the Branch could find me without too much difficulty.'

Johnson was thrown off balance again by the quality of

Buchanan's guesswork – if that's what it was. He decided to be as straight as possible with the former DG about what he was doing, but to be circumspect about how he had picked up his knowledge of the RACETRACK files.

'Mr Buchanan, I'm not with the Branch. I'm just a little man in the CID . . .' He flashed his Met warrant card quickly in front of the old man: 'I've come here because I want you to help me put right an injustice which happened in 1971.' Johnson could see the wheels turning already in Buchanan's mind. 'I'm doing this off my own bat. I'm stuck with a riddle and you can solve it.'

'Maybe, maybe not.'

'But please, promise me that our conversation will remain private – just between the two of us.'

'Oh, I'll be discretion itself,' Buchanan replied and winked at Johnson, much to his surprise.

'It concerns Operation RACETRACK.' Johnson studied the effect of using the codeword.

'I can't really remember what that was, I'm afraid. You've got to understand, sergeant, I knew so many operations and agents in my career. When you get to my age all those codewords just get mixed up, it's easy to forget.'

'As I understand it, it was an attempt to trap a Soviet diplomat by staking out a brothel. But your blokes ended up eyeballing somebody entirely different. Somebody who'd gone into the house to pay for sex with a little girl.'

'I think I know the operation you mean, yes,' said Buchanan, for the first time in their conversation looking a little uncomfortable.

Johnson began to feel he was getting somewhere at last. 'I'd like to nail that man, Mr Buchanan. That foreigner, I'd like you to tell me who he was.'

'Oh I see. It's very difficult for me to remember. I know that might sound a little lame.'

'As I understand it, you took a stand, Mr Buchanan. You

decided that all of the pictures and tapes relating to the op should be destroyed—'

'Yes?'

'As I understand it, you believed it was wrong to blackmail an officer of a friendly intelligence service. I suppose I can understand why you couldn't do anything at the time, but now I'm trying to back a principle: I'd like to see that paedophile in jail.'

Buchanan said nothing for a few moments. He looked down at his bent fingers and then, finally, up at Johnson. 'You're a clever fellow, sergeant. You've found out quite a lot.' Once more Buchanan looked around the room, considering how to mull over twenty-year-old secrets. Should he tell this man anything?

'There's no glory to be had in taking stands on the basis of principles, sergeant. You may be right about that operation – I may indeed have tried to put things right. My predecessor thought differently, my successor too. There were always people in a case like the one you're referring to who were prepared to do their own thing – you know, at the middle management level. I took stands on principle, so I missed out on a knighthood. Did you know that I'm the only Director General of the Service since the War not to get one?'

'No, I didn't know.'

'I took many stands on principle. I decided that our Service couldn't behave like that of a great imperialist power any more. For years my philosophy seemed fine with the Labour bunch. The other lot got in and my face didn't fit any more.'

'Did this RACETRACK business finish your career, Mr Buchanan? Did the Tories get wind of something you'd done?'

'No. It didn't, we wouldn't ever tell ministers about an operation like that one. Let's just say that there were many factors in it, and the business you're referring to may have been one.'

'Where was he from, this QUASAR bloke?' Johnson asked, and saw that Buchanan blanched visibly for the first time.

'You've picked up some dangerous knowledge, sergeant. How do you know these words like RACETRACK and QUASAR?'

'You don't expect me to tell you, do you, boss? You didn't want QUASAR recruited because he worked for such a close ally. That means he was American, doesn't it?'

'He worked for a friendly intelligence service. It may have been American. It may have been Australian, Canadian, German perhaps – even the Israelis. We had rather good relations with them at that time, helping us fight Black September.'

'Your memory seems to be recovering,' Johnson observed.

'Don't patronise me. I don't want to talk about that operation any more; there are still people who could be badly hurt by it, including you. Our Service could be damaged by your inquiries and our ally's service could certainly be damaged.' Buchanan pursed his lips, as if to underwrite his determination to say no more.

Johnson stood as if to leave. He regretted teasing Buchanan, feeling annoyed with himself for precipitating the old man's silence. He would try one more question: Johnson had observed long ago that the relief of an apparently completed interview often leads people to make their worst slips. 'Surely there wouldn't be that much damage. Or are you telling me that QUASAR is still serving?'

Buchanan was hauling himself out of the armchair, obviously in some pain. He looked up at Johnson and snapped: 'You must draw your own conclusion. We made a big mistake not turning that loathsome man over to his own side when the incident happened, and it would be far more difficult now – that's all I'll say. My predecessor didn't, and once a few years had passed it was difficult for me to because they would always have wondered why we left it all that time. Trust would have been undermined either way.'

The two men walked towards the front door. For a moment it appeared Buchanan would see Johnson out to the gate. Johnson stopped him: 'No, Mr Buchanan, you stay there: no point you doing the steps again.'

'All right, thank you, Lee Johnson.' The detective sergeant looked at him quizzically. Buchanan answered his look. 'I read your warrant card. Don't assume old people are stupid, sergeant.'

'Boss, I won't make the mistake again of taking your memory at your estimation of it –' it was Johnson's turn to wink, '– and please keep our conversation to yourself.'

'Have a pleasant trip back to London. I'm sorry it wasn't more worth your while.'

Johnson walked back up Lavender Lane towards the bus stop for the ride back into King's Lynn. He felt confident now that QUASAR was still serving, and only slightly less confident that he was an American. Then there was the implication that Buchanan's orders about the destruction of RACETRACK surveillance material might not have been followed. Perhaps in time he would come back and see Buchanan again. Johnson did not think the old man would shop him.

Buchanan dialled the telephone number from memory. 'Marjorie, good afternoon, it's Mark Buchanan . . . I'm not too bad, thank you – the joints are playing up a bit . . . I need to have a word with the DG if she's there: there's something she needs to know about quite urgently.'

Chapter Thirteen

On the train Johnson tried to make as exact a note as possible of what the former MI5 boss had said. He wanted to fill in gaps in the scribbled jottings he had made occasionally during their brief talk. It was difficult at times, and Johnson regretted not hiding a tape recorder about his person. People like Buchanan always played with words: the particular phrasing of a denial might seem straightforward at first but contain a clue if studied more closely.

At the end of his scribbling Johnson came to the conclusion that Buchanan had consummately manipulated the encounter. The old boy had given away very little but found out quite a bit about what Johnson himself knew. When he left King's Lynn he had been quite optimistic – after all he had actually got in to see the man and had a discussion, albeit brief and cryptic, about RACETRACK. Now he began to feel that the whole trip might have been an error of judgement – particularly if Buchanan passed on to his former colleagues exactly what had been learned. The detective sergeant realised he had wound his neck out a fair distance on this cheap day return to King's Lynn, not just with Buchanan but also with his own wife. He would see whether she bore a grudge later that evening. As for Buchanan, he would just have to hope for the best.

Jane had her revenge with a terse note left on the kitchen table. She had gone to the cinema with friends. Gemma sat in front of the TV with Kim, a fourteen-year-old bleached blonde with a black lycra skirt enlisted for the evening as a babysitter. Jane had come home just after nine; Lee had already helped himself to sausages and baked beans. The remainder of the evening and Sunday did not go well, despite his trying to make things better by apologising for spending the day away. They did not have sex. Lee worked out it was at least a fortnight since they had. It was all very well for Jane to go on about having another baby, but at this rate only a series of lucky breaks would allow them to make one. As he sat in front of the TV on Sunday evening Lee's anger about why things were going so badly gave way to anxiety. For the first time he felt real concern about their future together. It gripped him with fear: the fear of having committed years of his life to this woman and having brought this sweet little girl into the world, only to see it all fall apart.

On Monday, Johnson, MacFadyen, DCI Rickett and assorted lawyers made their way into court for the committal proceedings on the Majestic gang.

'All rise,' called the usher as the judge entered.

Sancho Doherty and one of the other villains were brought in in handcuffs. The two members of the gang who had taken police bullets were still in hospital. They had already given their statements and instructed their lawyers about their pleas.

Looking across the courtroom, Johnson noticed Oswald Pew, the man from the safe deposit firm. Pew had kept his overcoat on – a dark blue number with a black velvet collar. He was toying with a brown trilby hat and his glance switched now and then from the accused to his hat and then back again.

The proceedings went much as the police had hoped they would. The charges relating to each man were read in turn. The lawyers for Doherty's henchmen entered 'not guilty' pleas on some of the lesser charges. They would later claim that Doherty himself had been responsible for these mis-demeanours. However, they pleaded guilty to all the serious ones, which included attempted murder, armed robbery and GBH. The defence lawyers did not attempt to get their clients released on bail. Instead the villains were remanded in custody and committed for trial. As the warders stood up to take the accused back to their cells, Doherty turned towards Johnson and MacFadyen.

'I'll have you, you fucking woollybacks,' he shouted, and then, as one of the warders pushed him forward roughly, 'You'll rot in hell.'

Johnson smiled back at him.

'Ah, the discreet charm of the bourgeoisie,' observed MacFadyen as they stood to leave.

As the policemen walked into the corridor outside the courtroom, a small group gathered around Johnson and his partner. Detective Chief Superintendent Hacker, who was Rickett's boss, approached first.

'Well done, lads, nice clean hearing. I can't wait for the trial.'

'Thank you, sir,' Johnson responded.

'The boys have tied this one up very nicely,' added DCI Rickett.

'It must be time to ask for a bigger office,' said Johnson, smiling at his superiors. There was general laughter. The senior policemen went their own way and then Oswald Pew approached the two detectives.

'I suppose I've never thanked you two.'

'Don't thank us till the jury convicts them, Mr Pew,' Johnson replied.

Pew made small talk about the villains, the cricket and the state of the pound until MacFadyen tired of the banal banter and walked away.

'I'll see you back at the nick, boss,' he said, before striding down the corridor with a spring normally absent from his step.

'Mr Johnson, my conscience has been playing up a bit,' Pew began.

'Oh yes . . .'

'I realise I was not the most helpful of people when you asked me for assistance,' said Pew, as the detective surveyed him with growing interest. 'There was one curious thing after the robbery. Everybody claimed their possessions except for the contents of one of your bags, and we accounted for the contents of every robbed box except one.'

'So what did somebody want to leave well alone?' Johnson prompted.

'It was a very large amount of dollars, about a quarter of a million I would guess, in $100 and $50 bills.'

'And you're suggesting the renter of only one of the boxes claimed it was empty at the time of the robbery?'

'Correct.'

'And the box was rented by . . . ?'

'You can guess, can't you?' A half-smile of nervous complicity played across Pew's face.

Johnson remained impassive. 'Perhaps I can, but you tell me.'

Pew lowered his voice: 'The same gentleman who had rented another box. The box containing that torn envelope full of papers that you were interested in, and the other package.'

Johnson felt cold. 'What other package?'

'There was a jiffy bag. It was intact, wrapped in tape, no address – perhaps that's why it didn't come to your attention. Anyway, I think I've been as helpful as I can.'

'Thanks for the tip, Mr Pew,' he said but already Johnson's mind was racing. 'How do you know the money was in his box – not somebody else's – somebody who reclaimed other things from you but didn't want to own up to the money?'

'Well, one can't be completely sure . . .' Pew conceded,

causing Johnson's excitement to falter. Pew watched a barrister walk past and turned back towards Johnson. 'It's not something which would stand up in a court of law, but you could call it intuition – professional intuition. There's something else I suppose. That quantity of money is quite a bulky sum. I'd say that only seven of the robbed boxes were big enough to hold it, and it's one of those which we can't account for.'

'It's very helpful, Mr Pew, thank you. Did you ask this gentleman about the money?'

'Indirectly. I asked him whether his other box had anything in it. He said no.'

'Describe him to me, this bloke.'

'I'd rather not do that, I think I've been helpful enough to you. Perhaps our account is settled now,' Pew turned as if to leave.

Johnson had wanted Pew to describe Denton by himself, but he decided to pass this up in order to capitalise on Pew's sudden attack of candour. 'Mr Pew, was he a man of about sixty, gaunt, ill-looking?'

Pew stopped but did not turn to face Johnson when he replied, 'Yes.'

'Full head of hair or balding?' Johnson asked, hoping to make Pew fill in some of the detail.

'I won't say any more. I think you know the gentleman in question. Just remember the rules of our business, the sanctity of our clients' trust. It would finish me if I trespassed in that area and it will do you no good either.' Pew moved away, the irons in the soles of his handmade brogues clicking as he propelled himself away, down the linoleum-lined corridors of the court.

Martin Dodge had donned the uniform of a Telecom engineer once more. He had set up a small collapsible tent just off the Goldhawk Road, facing the Shepherds Bush police station.

Inside the tent he had opened one of the green iron cabinets which house telephone connections and dot the landscape of British cities. Earlier that day he had rung Metropolitan Police inquiries and obtained Johnson's direct-line number; nobody had asked him who he was. Now he was going through the bundled phone lines in the cabinet seeking out the right line. Dodge was not optimistic, since he guessed that Johnson's phone probably went through a modern PBX exchange which would give him one of several dozen lines at random when he picked up the phone to make an outside call. Tapping all those lines was not practical. It might, however, be possible to intercept incoming calls at the junction box: failing that he would have to get into the police station and successfully plant a bug in Johnson's office. Dodge's years of work with Panther and other security firms had taken him into homes, offices and once even a private yacht to plant bugging equipment, but never into a police station. It was not a challenge he relished.

Eventually Dodge did manage to isolate a bundle of lines which he believed led into the CID section of the station. He donned a headset and tried them one by one. With each answer he said, 'BT engineer checking the line.' Eventually he tried the right extension. MacFadyen, who had just returned from court, reached out for the receiver. 'DS Johnson's phone, DC MacFadyen speaking.'

'BT engineer checking the line. We're tracing a fault. Have you had any problems with it?'

'None that I know of.'

'OK, thank you.'

Dodge broke the connection. He marked the green wire with a white chinagraph pencil. Reaching into a tool kit, he fished out a small transmitter. It was one of the cleverer bits of industrial espionage equipment, designed to work with modern exchanges, but it would only allow them to intercept incoming calls. Dodge fitted the device. It was only a temporary measure, not least because it was powered by a tiny watch battery. After closing the cabinet in the street, he took down his tent and put the equipment into his grey van.

Dodge drove to a flat which had been rented in Jubilee Road, Hammersmith, midway between Johnson's home and the police station and within a mile of each. It was also a second-floor flat, which made for better radio reception than one lower down in the house. The landlady had been told that a small building company was renting it for their skilled workers: this could explain the comings and goings of the half-dozen or so individuals which Panther already had working for Charles Denton and being paid for by an allied intelligence service through a number of cut-out bank accounts.

Dodge had installed a pair of FM radio receivers in a trunk in the corner of the sitting room. There were also four special tape recorders in the box. These were voice-activated machines which could record on normal cassettes but made the tapes last twice as long as usual. There was a primary machine connected to each FM transmitter with backups also linked in. The trunk was cunningly designed. It resembled a normal metal container except for having a power socket hidden at its rear, and radio antenna sockets. It was padlocked, in case the landlady, with her spare key, ever became curious when the flat was unoccupied.

Dodge unlocked the Yale, went through to the sitting room and opened the trunk. He tuned the second receiver to the frequency pre-set on the transmitter he had just placed in the phone junction box. Then he removed a cassette from the machine connected to the receiver monitoring Johnson's home phone. It was their first material from the tapping devices. Dodge could not resist listening a little as he rewound the tape. He recognised the voice as that of Lee Johnson's wife Jane, who he had bluffed when he planted the device.

'Lee's off on some wild goose chase again, honestly, I despair of him sometimes,' Jane said.

'It's not that bad, is it? You've got to cut him some slack,' replied another female voice.

Bitches are never happy, Dodge thought. For a few moments he allowed himself to feel some sympathy for Johnson. Then he reminded himself that, in Pinchman's words, Johnson was a 'toerag'. Women are still bitches, he concluded.

After a further check on the equipment, Dodge locked the box and left the flat. He drove his van onto the Shepherds Bush Road, towards another flat rented by Panther, where a woman was waiting to transcribe the first cassette.

Chapter Fourteen

At Gower Street, Donald Travis, Legal Adviser to the Director General, went through the door marked 'Room 312 DG's Conference Room'. Inside he saw the DG, and several other senior officers including the Director of Counter-Espionage. The DG wore a dark blue suit, her hair was close-cropped and she looked over her glasses at Travis as he entered the room.

'Donald, come in. How are you?'

'Very fit thank you, DG.'

'Donald, I've already mentioned Mark Buchanan's phone call to you. James has just been bringing me up to date on Operation RACETRACK.' On the conference table in front of them lay some of the documents put back in Registry by Denton. As far as anybody in Room 312 knew though they had never left Registry. The period of activity following Buchanan's call meant that the tickets on the front of the folders now showed several different names after C. Denton, K Branch.

'It's funny how these things come out of the woodwork sometimes', Travis remarked.

'Well, there's obviously been a very serious violation of procedures somewhere along the line,' the DG remarked. 'Somebody's been talking or somebody's blown holes in our security some other way.'

'Indeed, it's very serious,' Travis chipped in unnecessarily.

'This is all so old that it may be very difficult for us to find out when exactly somebody or something went awry. James tells me most of the leading lights in on this operation are dead now. Donald, I'd like you to interview this loose cannon from the CID. He's clearly disregarded any established channels by dropping in on the former DG. The cheek of it! Could you find out what he thinks he's doing, and how on earth he came by this information?'

'Yes of course.'

'And Donald—'

'Yes, DG?'

'Frighten him, will you. It's probably the easiest way of getting him off our backs while we find out what's been going on.'

Travis ducked into his office, two doors up the corridor, and told his secretary to cancel his meetings for the morning because there was a 'fearful strop on'.

Fifteen minutes later he was on his way in a Service Daimler along the Euston Road, heading for Shepherds Bush. A bemused head of CID at the Yard had already given permission for Johnson to be interviewed. Travis studied papers as the car cut through the mid-morning traffic. He was an imposing man, physically and intellectually. He had made his name in the Army Legal Service, reaching the rank of colonel before being recruited into the Security Service in his forties. He wore a spotted silk tie, held in place with a gold pin and a Gieves and Hawkes pinstriped suit. Wedged in the back of his Daimler, Travis looked like any other captain of industry. But Travis's industry was secret intelligence, and on this particular morning he would have to deal with somebody who had no right to probe their intellectual property.

Johnson had been out on another case when he received a radio message to return to the station. Travis had said all he wanted to say to Rickett some time before the tap on the door signalled Johnson's arrival.

'Come in,' Rickett beckoned.

'Boss?'

'Sit down, Detective Sergeant Johnson, this gentleman is from the Security Service and what he's been telling me has me frankly horrified.'

Johnson knew at once that Buchanan had talked.

'I'd like to interview you, detective sergeant. I'm not doing it under caution, but if you wish you can have a Police Federation representative or lawyer present.'

'No, that's all right,' Johnson replied. He noticed Rickett had begun pacing around the office, his lips mumbling inaudible curses; sometimes looking over at him, sometimes at the ceiling or out of the window.

'I am going to tape the interview, if that's all right with you,' Travis said as he removed a small recorder from his briefcase.

Remembering his experience with Buchanan, Johnson replied: 'I'd like to tape it as well then, sir, if that's all right?'

'What are you going to do with the tape?' Travis asked.

'Well, it's for my own reference if you're suggesting disciplinary or legal proceedings might be on the cards.'

'Is that what you're expecting?'

'No, but I'll be on the safe side if you don't mind, sir. That's how we do it now, sir. A tape for the interviewing officer and a tape for the—'

'—Suspect. I know the Pace rules. Get your tape recorder if you must.' Travis was clearly unhappy but seemed to decide it was pointless arguing. Johnson popped out of the room.

Rickett looked at Travis apologetically. 'I can't believe his front, sir. Bloody nerve,' he said, then carried on moving around like a caged beast.

Even before the detective sergeant had returned, Travis realised he'd made a mistake.

'Mr Johnson, we are going to discuss matters of the highest security classification. I can't allow you to record the conversation unless I am confident that the tape will be held under tight security.'

'Have you changed your mind, sir?'

'I haven't changed my mind,' snapped Travis with an ill temper well known to inmates of Gower Street. 'Let's stop frigging about, shall we? If you make a recording it will have to be held by us.'

'I won't then, thank you, sir. I'll take written notes if that's all right?'

Travis was happier with this idea, since jottings in a notebook can always be denied – a tape constitutes better evidence altogether.

'I've no objection, but I would remind you of your obligations under the Official Secrets Act.' As he said this, Travis slid a small piece of paper with the Act written on it for Johnson to sign. Johnson did so without hesitation. As he handed it back to Travis, he remarked. 'I signed this thing so many times in the Army, sir, and a couple of times in the Met, once more isn't going to hurt me—'

'Will you pack it in and answer the man's questions, Johnson?' Rickett butted in.

'Why did you visit Mark Buchanan at his home last weekend?'

'I thought he might be able to help me with some inquiries.'

'What inquiries?'

'Inquiries into a child prostitution ring.'

'Why talk to Mr Buchanan about it?'

'I believed the Security Service may have known about what was going on.'

'What made you think that?'

'I had information that your people were staking out a house at the time the offences were committed.'

'Where did you get this information?' Travis asked briskly.

Johnson surveyed Rickett. It looked like the detective chief inspector had not told this MI5 man about the Majestic job and the Operation RACETRACK files. Johnson decided his best hope lay in sucking Rickett into the questioning.

'I'll ask you again. Where did the information come from? Do you realise there may have been a very serious security breach?'

'I believe DCI Rickett can tell you why I became interested in the case.'

Travis turned towards the hunched figure who had stopped pacing around his office.

'I can't,' Rickett said.

'Mr Rickett, I came to see you when I first became aware of the offences. I made a note after our meeting, I can tell you when it was.'

Rickett appeared not to hear him.

'Detective chief inspector?' Travis prompted.

'Are you talking about the deposit job?' Rickett asked.

'I am, sir,' Johnson let this statement hang in the air.

'Look, I'm not being interviewed: you are,' Rickett told Johnson.

'I'm just here to find out how this has happened,' Travis tried to reassert his control over the meeting. 'DS Johnson, can you make it clear to me which deposit job we are talking about?'

'The Majestic company in South Kensington. Robbed a few weeks back now. We recovered some papers.'

'What sort of papers?' Travis felt he was getting to the bottom of it at last.

'Mr Rickett read them too, sir.'

'I didn't. I didn't see any papers,' Rickett said immediately.

'I made a note of the fact that you'd read them, sir.'

'I didn't read them. Stop trying to rope me into your mess, Johnson.'

'They were classified papers, belonging to MI5 as far as

I could see,' said Johnson, who was fast giving up hope of pursuing his investigation and trying instead simply to stop himself falling deeper into trouble.

'Did you see these classified papers, Mr Rickett?'

'No, I didn't see any papers.'

'But you understood what Mr Johnson was talking about. You mentioned the safe deposit job?'

'He came to me and said he had heard some rumours about this child abuse business. It was way back: these allegations related to something years ago. I said there was no chance of building a case on this kind of matter so I told him to drop it.'

Johnson savoured the lies Rickett told as he tried to save himself. He could see that Travis was becoming confused: documents or rumours?

'Mr Rickett, I don't understand why a deposit job would prompt rumours. Are you sure you didn't see any papers?'

'I'm absolutely sure. It was around the time of the deposit job, it may not have been the job itself. I just recall that about that time, DS Johnson mentioned these rumours. He'll have to tell us where he got them from.'

'Mr Johnson?'

'I read papers which were taken in the safe deposit job. That's how I learned about this child abuse business and the involvement of the Security Service in all this.'

'Where are the papers?' Travis asked.

'We returned them to the Majestic company. Mr Rickett took a decision not to send them back—'

'That's crap!' Rickett interrupted.

'He took a decision not to send them back to you, sir. Subsequent inquiries suggested that the box holder had collected the papers from the Majestic company.'

'Did anybody sign a receipt specifically for those papers?'

'No, sir. The papers were just tagged up in a bag and given an evidence number. They were only signed for in general terms, along with a great many other items, by Mr Oswald

Pew of the company.' Johnson kept the existence of the second package and the cash to himself.

'How can you prove to me that you did acquire that knowledge from papers?'

Johnson thought hard. Was it time to admit to photo-copying the files? He decided that he could not do so. MI5 in general and this man in particular could not be trusted. Johnson decided to steer around the specifics. 'Well, I mentioned the codename Operation RACETRACK to Mr Buchanan,' he volunteered.

'Somebody could have told you that codename.'

'I read the papers before I returned them and I remember a fair amount of what was in them,' said Johnson emphatically.

'Mr Rickett. Do you know what Operation RACETRACK was?'

'No. I haven't a clue.'

Travis turned towards Johnson. 'Are you telling me that nobody told you about the operation?'

'Well, no one apart from Mr Buchanan. Obviously he told me a bit about it,' Johnson replied, now relishing implicating somebody else.

'Which of you am I meant to believe?' Travis asked rhetori-cally, 'Because if I find out I've been lied to I'll skin you alive, Johnson.'

Johnson made notes furiously.

'I can't say that this interview has been satisfactory. I intend to speak to this Mr Pew and I intend to interview the two of you again, separately.' Travis stood up to leave.

'Sir, would you mind checking my notes and signing them, if that's OK?' Johnson asked.

'What?' Travis was incredulous.

'I just want us to agree that my note of this meeting has been accurate. Just to be on the safe side.'

'Don't wind me up, Johnson. I don't play games.' Travis walked past him out of the office.

Rickett ended his pacing and fell heavily into the seat behind his desk. 'Shut the door, Johnson.' He surveyed his officer Johnson for a few moments until he could contain his resentment no longer. 'You fucking prick, Johnson. You're a fucking piece of shit dropping me in it like that.'

'With respect—'

'Fucking shut it and listen – and don't give me any of that "with respect" crap, we're both old enough to know it means that you have none. You and your empire building have dropped me deep in the shit. Why couldn't you leave it all alone? Going up to Norfolk and questioning a former head of MI5 in his rose garden? You're out of your fucking mind. Didn't you think it would end up like this?'

'I took a gamble and I lost it,' Johnson replied.

'You took a gamble? It's me you've fucked. It's my years on the force you've pissed away. You and your sacred cause. I told you there would be a hail of bollocks and you just can't believe how bad it's going to get now.'

'Why didn't you tell him the truth, sir?'

'Because I'm trying to save my fucking pension, you moron. Can't you see what you've done? I thought I wouldn't be one of those coppers who left early on "sick leave" because they'd fouled up. I'll be lucky if I get that now. As far as the rest of the world is concerned, I never saw those papers. I've made my bed and now I've got to lie in it.'

'I can't retract what I've said, sir.'

'Well you'd better start thinking about it. Chief Superintendent Hacker told me you'd be out on your ear if you hadn't got that commendation for arresting Doherty's gang. One move out of line, and he'll kick your arse out of this force. He's just waiting for you to slip up. Do you understand?'

'Yes, sir.'

'Unofficially, Johnson, you're finished in CID. You might as well put in for Traffic or Dog Section because that's about all you're ever going to get.'

'Are we off the record, sir?' Johnson was bristling now too.

'Yes.'

'Why don't you fuck off to the golf course and make room for somebody interested in catching criminals?'

Chapter Fifteen

Johnson returned to his office to find MacFadyen concerned, obviously aware that something had happened.

'Rumour is you just got your arse chewed by the man from MI5,' he began as Johnson came in and sat down.

'I'm finished, mate. I'm finished in CID, Rickett told me. He said that I'd be out now if it wasn't for the commendation.'

'Fuck!'

'The joke is that Rickett, to save his arse, told this MI5 bloke some bullshit versus bollocks about somebody telling me about the child abuse business. I just stuck to the facts – in as far as they made Big Prickett look stupid – and the MI5 geezer was totally confused by the end of it.'

'I think all that's probably best left alone now, boss.'

'Fuck 'em – I ought to carry on just to screw them up. My promotion prospects are nil now anyway. But I suppose you're right.'

MacFadyen produced a half-bottle of Whyte and Mackay from his desk and poured a generous measure into a Styrofoam coffee cup. 'Take this.'

Johnson helped himself to a good gulp of the whisky. 'Funny thing is,' he said, savouring the neat spirit, 'the MI5 bloke didn't ask me directly either whether I'd copied the papers or whether I'd spoken to Denton. He tried the hard man routine, but he's obviously bullshitting.'

'Who knows what he knows? These guys are always playing games.'

The two men sat in silence for a while. Then Johnson smiled. 'I forgot to tell you, our friend Pew finally came good outside the courtroom. He reckons that Denton—'

'Did he say it was Denton?' MacFadyen cut in.

'No, but he recognised Denton's description. He said that Denton probably had a quarter of a million dollars in another box and that he'd left it unclaimed.'

'Ouch!'

'I reckon our friend Denton may have been doing a bit of blackmail,' Johnson said.

'Maybe. Or maybe he was just keeping the money there for the spooks who don't want to own up to it all now. Denton might be completely onside, which is why MI5 are putting the frighteners on you now.'

'I'd still go with blackmail. I'll tell you something else. Pew also thinks there was a second package with the documents that we didn't spot when we were going through them. Too small for papers: who knows what was in there?'

'Lee, are we really any closer to cracking this riddle than when you first read those papers? Now we've got the second envelope to worry about, which frankly could have contained anything from uncut diamonds to a pack of condoms!' Then MacFadyen's tone changed. 'This thing's become an obsession, mate. It's going to ruin you unless you watch your step.'

For Jim Parker, the weekly sessions with the full board of CIA were onerous. He did not regard himself as a committee man. His idea of management involved flying to foreign parts, making a fuss of visiting station chiefs and generally projecting his personality on the Clandestine Service. He found himself sitting once more across the table from the unbearable Hal Canning.

'I've done some more work on our economic targets,' said Canning, once again handing out copious quantities of self-aggrandising paper. 'As you'll see,' he said, as others studied the documents, 'our main aim will be to break unfair trading practices.'

'How?' Parker challenged him.

'Well, there are the overt means – using intelligence gathered from improved eavesdropping and agent running to bring pressure to bear on the Japanese or EC through diplomatic and trade channels. And there are the covert means, which we could discuss a little further today.'

Parker studied Canning's tan, his crisp white shirt, and wondered whether the Deputy Director for Intelligence was wearing makeup. He didn't take him for a fruit, but the incident on the plane had been interesting.

'We can exploit market-sensitive information against particular companies or particular currencies,' Canning continued.

'You're saying we could use information which would allow us to screw the Yen or the Deutschmark on the foreign exchange?' Parker asked.

'Well, DDO,' Canning replied without looking at him directly, 'it's obviously not that simple.' He relished the chance to lecture Parker.

'Surely we've got to decide whether a stronger or weaker Yen is to the US advantage before we try to manipulate the market?' the Director of Central Intelligence asked.

'Indeed,' Canning replied, 'but the aim may not be to make their currency higher or lower: the aim may simply be to force their central bank to empty its pockets in defence of its own currency.'

'The Brits spent two billion bucks in a day trying to rescue sterling,' the Deputy Director for Administration said.

'Do you think the Germans roasted them on purpose?' the Director asked Canning.

'Who knows, but it was a smart move if they did.'

'If we take this money off the Japs, what are we going to

do with it?' the Director asked. 'Even the GAO would notice that much!' There was deferential laughter from his deputies and assistants.

'That's a separate decision, what we do with the money. Maybe we don't take it at all, we just give information to our Saudi or South American banking friends and they collect the profits. We could even recycle some of it into covert operations.' Canning turned to Parker, apparently offering him a financial olive branch. He had the whole board of CIA eating out of his hand and he loved it – the whole board except for the Deputy Director of Operations.

Parker tried hard to contain his annoyance with Canning.

'I don't know whether we could tiptoe round GAO and Intelligence Committee rules if we were moving around these large sums. I'm not sure that this kind of covert action, in the finance sector, is where the Agency should be at. Is this really what we do now? I'm all for protecting US industries, but really . . .'

Parker studied Canning's papers. It was apparent that more eavesdropping resources had already been switched to the economic task. There were some examples of information gathered during the previous month: a Japanese corporation trying to drive its last US competitor in the television tube industry out of business and a French firm bugging US airlines in order to undercut their transatlantic fares. The pressure would soon be on him to commit more agent runners to the job of finding people ready to betray their companies or the financial institutions they worked for.

The meeting went on for another hour without reaching firm conclusions. Nobody was surprised when the Director told Canning to set up an informal group of senior CIA officers to report on the 'possible aggressive exploitation of economic intelligence'. Parker sloped back to his office. The furniture was classic American corporate: studded leather with a picturebook window looking out onto the Virginia landscape.

He peeled off his jacket and settled his big shoulders into the high-backed leather chair then barked an order for coffee to his assistant.

'Mr Dubois is here for a quick meeting,' she replied.

'Send him in and make it two coffees.' Parker surveyed his operational chief of staff as he entered the room. Vince Dubois was a pallid easterner who knew almost as much about the Clandestine Service as Parker did. But Dubois was not an armchair intelligence officer. Parker had promoted him to his job after Dubois made the Agency's first recruitment of a Hezbollah player in the early 1980s.

'Have you read that economics shit that Canning is circulating?'

'The stuff about penetration of foreign corporations and banks?'

'Yep, well read this. More bullshit from the desk of the world's biggest expert.'

Dubois studied the paper which had been discussed at that morning's briefing.

'He's caught the spirit of the times, Jim,' Dubois concluded as he finished scanning the pages.

'Meaning?'

'We'll probably have a new president next year. All this country cares about now is recession. They don't care about Saddam any more; only the *Post* is interested in nuclear proliferation. The nation's turning inwards: protectionism, isolationism. Canning understands the way it's going.'

Two mugs of coffee were placed on the desk in front of them. Dubois had one with a Marine Corps drill sergeant on it and the words 'Death is Nature's Way of Saying You Flunked Boot Camp'. Parker's mug had an American eagle wearing headphones. Underneath the usual legend, 'In God We Trust', was written 'All Others We Monitor'.

Parker fixed Dubois in his stare and asked. 'Is that goddamn

Ivy League, sunlamp, blow-dried son of a bitch our next Director?'

'I would say he had the best chance of anybody inside the Company at the moment.'

'Jesus, he's going to have our Service hanging around the bars at auto makers' conventions trying to subvert Japanese executives. We can forget any more effort against terrorism or the former Soviet Union.'

'We've seen big changes before, Jim. That's the way it goes.'

'No, Vince, this is more serious. If Canning takes over, this service is finished.'

'Maybe.'

'Vince, we've got to fix this asshole. I want to take him down. Any slip he makes, we've got to be waiting.'

For the first time, Dubois understood just how deep the enmity between the two Deputy Directors had become. To Dubois, and to one or two others on the inside track at Langley, it was apparent that Parker and Canning were lining up for a fight to the finish.

Johnson and MacFadyen had spent much of the rest of the day working on another robbery case. Two men in Donald Duck masks had raided the Halifax building society on King Street in Hammersmith and the detectives had gone there to see if there were any clues still worth picking up. After taking details from fifteen possible witnesses they decided to go back to their office and make a few calls.

By six o'clock Johnson was warming to MacFadyen's insistent requests that they adjourn to a pub. Johnson didn't normally booze after work, but he reckoned he would need a few drinks before he could tell Jane about the showdown with Rickett.

'Come on, Batman, let's get pished,' MacFadyen said.

'All right, mate, I'll have one for the road.'

As Johnson stood and pulled on his leather jacket, the phone went.

'Leave it, it's probably somebody trying to sell insurance.' Johnson ignored his partner's request. 'Hello, Johnson.'

'Lee Johnson?' a young woman asked.

'Yes, who's that?'

'It's Nicola. I got the message from John's sister.'

'Nicola Dawson.' Johnson felt the hairs on the back of his neck stand.

'Yes. I didn't understand the message. What's it all about?'

Johnson had yanked a notepad out of his top drawer. He scrawled 'Nicola Dawson – GIRL PROSTITUTE' on it and flashed it at MacFadyen, who looked up in despair, took off his coat and sat down.

'Nicola, it's a bit of a long story,' Johnson began.

'Listen, Lee, I'm in a box. I only put 20p in, you're going to have to call me back. Have you got a pen?'

'Fire away.'

Nicola gave the number. Johnson recognised the code immediately as a Brighton one. 'What's it all about then?' she said.

'It's about what happened at Kandahar Road when you were a little girl. About the foreigner who interfered with you. I want to nail him.'

'You're a fucking copper?'

'Yes, but I want to get that bloke who messed around with you.'

'I'm not going to help you. Do you know what the pigs and the social workers have done to my family? They've taken away my children!' she shouted into the receiver.

'Please, Nicola, don't hang up. If you help me, maybe things will be better for you on the other case.'

'You must be dreaming!'

She ran out of money and Johnson put the receiver down. 'Just my luck, I get told not to touch the case on pain of dismissal and the key witness rings me up!' Johnson dialled the number quickly.

'It's no more than that, Nicola. I just want you to tell me who abused you and I want you to make a statement about it.'

'What makes you think anyone abused me? You've got some fucking nerve!'

'Nicola, I know what was going on there. I know about Diana Morris; I know she was the madam. I know you did a foreign client for her.'

Nicola was almost silent. Johnson thought she might be crying.

'I'm sorry. I don't mean to be so blunt, but it's vital to me that you help me.'

'Why should I?' she asked.

'It might help you with your case. It might get me off the hook; I've stuck my neck out over this.'

'That's what it's about, is it, your neck?' she asked, and Johnson regretted his words immediately.

'No deal. I'm not interested. I'm in enough shit anyway.'

'Nicola, please think about it. Take my home number. Ring me any time day or night if you change your mind.' Johnson gave the number, but he wasn't sure whether she had made a note of it.

'I'm going now,' she said.

'Please don't—'

She had rung off.

'Fuck,' Johnson looked down at his notes. Before MacFadyen could say anything, the detective sergeant was on the phone again, checking the Brighton number. He jotted down the address of the phonebox.

'She wouldn't help?' MacFadyen asked.

'No. Who knows, she might call back.'

'Lee. Right now you need her like a fart in a spacesuit. Let's just forget the whole thing and go to the pub.'

'All right, all right,' Johnson agreed, and the two men left their office in silence.

Lee came home after two pints of Carlsberg. 'Dr Carlsberg,' they used to call it in the sergeants' mess, when they had a glass to steady their hands and soothe their heads the day after a night on the piss. Well, he needed the doctor now.

Jane was propped up in front of the TV, watching *Brookside* avidly. Lee caught himself thinking how odd it was that somebody who considered herself such an intellectual could be so captivated by soaps. He curbed the thought. So much, lately, when his mind had wandered, he had found himself criticising her. He tried to stop himself; he knew that such thoughts were gnawing away at his love.

He knew it would be pointless trying to talk to her while *Brookside* was on – that would just get the conversation off to a lousy start. Instead he went into the kitchen and found a Carlsberg in the fridge.

'Ah doctor, I need you tonight,' he thought aloud as he popped the can.

'Sorry?' Jane said next door.

'Nothing, love.'

When the programme ended, Lee said meekly: 'Listen Jane, I've had real trouble at work today.' She did not reply.

'I was called in by Rickett today and some bloke from MI5.'

'MI5?'

'You know those papers I brought back after the Majestic job and I wouldn't tell you what was in them? Well, they were MI5 papers we found after the blag. There was all this stuff in the files about a brothel where this fella was going for sex with a little girl. It had all been hushed up by the spooks. Rickett said we should send the files back, so we did, only I thought, "why should somebody get away twice with abusing that girl?" so I photocopied them first.'

Jane groped for the TV remote without taking her eyes off him and switched off the set. She was getting distressed. 'Why didn't you tell me sooner about these bloody files?'

'I tried to, but you never seemed interested . . .' he volunteered a little lamely, knowing in truth how much he had wanted to keep the discovery to himself. 'I know I was a bit of a prat about it. I'm sorry. Anyway that Saturday I went away, I went up to Norfolk to see somebody about what was in the files. He was an old boss of MI5 and that's what brought this bloody interview down on me today. Now Rickett's told me I'm finished in CID.'

'Oh great!' she mocked, but there was a part of Jane which was pleased that this had happened. It was not the kind of thought that she could ever express aloud – except perhaps to her closest friend – but she did not mind the idea of Lee's police career being on the rocks if it meant that he would do something more worthwhile with his life. Her strongest emotion, though, was one of betrayal, that he had let things develop so far without confiding anything in her. 'Why didn't you tell me?' she repeated.

The conversation went on in a similar vein. Lee lost track of the time. Like many of their rows, it took the form of Lee attempting to offer rational answers, albeit from a weak position, and Jane telling him not to be so clinical and asking essentially the same questions over and over again. He knew he had a lot to be contrite about, so he did not react with anger, but as the conversation tailed off he found himself wondering what he could do to restore her faith in him.

Chapter Sixteen

Charles Denton had spent a good deal of time following up his discovery about the Iraqi colonel coming to Britain on an Algerian passport. A surveillance operation had been approved by the Director of Counter-Espionage and the colonel had been given the full treatment during his three-day visit to Britain. His hotel room in Bayswater had been bugged, he had been followed by a team of twelve watchers and everybody who met him had been photographed and identified for Registry files.

Operation PERICLES, as this anti-Iraqi effort was christened, was taken out of Denton's hands as soon as it had developed into something big. A thrusting thirty-six-year-old section head from the counter-espionage branch had been placed in charge and Denton had not left GWS during the entire seventy-two-hour circus which led up to the colonel's departure on a plane from Heathrow to Prague. The senior officers in his branch had excused themselves this apparent injustice by referring to Denton's health and the closeness of his retirement.

Denton had decided to go to the Patio Restaurant (absurdly named given that it was in the basement) for lunch. These days he could only manage soup or mashed potato: his guts simply couldn't cope with anything more than that. As he was standing to leave his office, the phone rang. The Director of Counter-Espionage wanted to see him. Denton shuffled out of his office and decided to take the stairs one flight up rather than the lift. He made his way to the office, the room number of which he knew well from dozens of memos but which he had in fact never entered. He looked up at the small typed sign on the door: 'Director K, Please Enter Through Room 504'. The mousy secretary ushered him through.

'Charles! Nice to see you. I hope you heard about the success of PERICLES.'

'Yes, excellent,' Denton replied.

'Listen Charles, there's something you might be interested to know about.'

'Yes?'

'Do you remember back in 1971 – well before my time in the branch of course – you were involved in an operation where we put a brothel under surveillance to catch a Russian, but caught somebody else entirely?'

'Vaguely, yes.' Denton's stomach had turned cold.

'Some policeman has been sniffing around. He actually went up to Mark Buchanan's house in Norfolk and asked him about it. What a nerve, eh?' The Director had become animated. 'DG is absolutely furious about the security leak. This plod knew codenames, the works. Anyway, the Legal Adviser is on the case: he can't work out what's going on. The policeman apparently thinks he has some chance of making a case, which is a joke because Travis would have him so tied up with Public Interest Immunity Certificates he'd never be able to take it anywhere. This detective's being put on the fast track to nowhere in the CID.'

'Really,' Denton chipped in.

'Anyway, you may be called on to tell us more about this whole business as you're virtually the only chap on the branch involved in the thing who's still here.'

'Fine.'

'Well, that's enough of that. By the way, that was really excellent work spotting that Iraqi's alias in the Algerian diplomatic traffic.'

'It was a team effort, James.'

'You played a central part. If you don't mind me saying, there are too few people like you coming into the Service these days. Anyway, well done once again, terrific work. It's the stuff diplomatic expulsions are made of.' He smiled weakly before adopting his compassionate expression. 'Charles, I've had a word with personnel, and we realise that you're really quite desperately ill. Given your exemplary service, we feel that we should let you go before you hit your planned retirement date. I know you were expecting to soldier on until December, but I think we can sort something out in the next week or two on health grounds. OK?'

'You really mustn't feel . . .' Denton panicked inwardly at the thought that it might all be over so soon.

'Well we do, Charles: we want you to have as much time in the sun as possible,' the Director looked down at his papers to indicate that the audience was at an end.

Denton left the office and made his way into the toilets and began to wash his hands. He looked in the mirror. His eyes looked sunken and jaundiced. The good news was that nobody seemed to know that Johnson had been to see him as well, but the bad news was still very bad. All sorts of senior officers were now poring over the RACETRACK files. The longer they looked, the higher the chance that they might discover that he had put the files in the safe deposit box and then the questions would really start. As he dried his hands, Denton knew he had to strike one last blow against the people he hated, using Pete's last shipment of intelligence to do it. But he hadn't counted on trying to do things so quickly.

After work, he took the tube to Parson's Green and walked from there to the flat where Panther had set up their transcribing operation. He was entirely unsurprised when a middle-class lady in her late fifties opened the door. She was wearing a maroon cardigan, and had glasses which hung by a string from her neck.

'Hello. Mr Ryan is it?'

'Yes, that's right,' Denton replied.

'Mr Pinchman sends his apologies but told me to tell you that he couldn't meet you this evening – something's come up.'

They walked into a sitting room. An electric typewriter and cassette player equipped with headphones and a stop-go pedal were the tools of her trade. Denton noticed an open Barbara Pym novel face down on the desk beside the typewriter. The flat was rather well furnished: plenty of chintz and country prints. It was the sort of place businessmen rent for their Sloane Ranger daughters when they finish their cookery courses.

'You'll want this then,' she said, handing him an envelope containing about a dozen typed pages.

'Was it just material from the house?' Denton asked, dreading another evening sifting his way through pages of Jane Johnson's complaints about her husband.

'No, there was a different place as well in today's lot. Not much recorded on that line, though.'

Denton understood that Johnson's office was now also bugged and took some satisfaction from it.

'Mr Pinchman left you this note.'

Denton took a sealed envelope with 'P. Ryan Esq.' written on it.

'I'll be off then. Thanks very much.'

'Don't mention it,' she replied.

Denton did not open either of the envelopes until he was back in Blackheath. He made himself a pot of tea and sat down at his writing table. Denton's eyes narrowed as he deciphered Pinchman's scrawl:

We are pleased to enclose the first intercept from the target's place of work. However, we are experiencing some difficulty gaining access, for reasons which I am sure you will understand. In the meantime we have intercepted the line elsewhere, which unfortunately means we are able only to record incoming calls. We hope to rectify this situation as soon as possible.

Rank amateurs, Denton thought, but his anticipation as he opened the transcripts blotted out these doubts. The domestic stuff was the usual rubbish. Johnson himself did not appear to have used the phone during the twenty-four hours in question. Seven pages of the transcript were a conversation between one 'Kim', evidently a babysitter, and 'Darren', a boyfriend of hers on a school exchange in Germany. Denton was amused by the thought of the Johnson's trying to work out why their phone bills were so big. Nevertheless, he read every word of the transcript – it was a question of professionalism. Every word – including the bits marked 'silence of about forty-five seconds', which were invariably followed by Kim asking Darren: 'What are you thinking?'

More than an hour later, he got to the second bundle of papers: three sheets held together with a paperclip. The first few seemed to relate to an armed robbery which had happened that day. Almost at once, Denton felt frustrated that he could not read either outgoing calls or internal ones at the police station. And then he got to the bottom of the third page:

Target One: Hello, Johnson.
Woman: Lee Johnson?
Target One: Yes, who's that?
Woman: It's Nicola. I got the message from John's sister. Nicola Dawson.

'Oh no,' Denton said aloud as he read the brief conversation. 'Oh, no.' He got to the last line of the transcript:

Target One: OK, I'll call you right back.

Denton found his hands shaking involuntarily. He had never thought that Johnson would ever find her. It was a Brighton number that she had rung from, he could see that straight away. Nicola had told him she wouldn't help, but what had transpired when Johnson rang her back? How had Johnson discovered her? Denton wondered whether it was really so serious if Nicola had refused to co-operate but then decided he should only assume the worst. With time slipping away before his retirement from the Service, he could now see major problems developing on two fronts.

He fretted, biting at his finger-nails, mopping his brow. Then pain gripped his bowels with such urgency that he rushed into the toilet. There was the usual sickening rush and a cold shiver across his body. He stood up and glanced down at the bloody mess in the water. In many ways Denton was psychologically adjusted to his fate, but this sight always pained him to the very core.

Cancer of the colon. That's what was killing Denton. It was inoperable and had already spread to the liver where it was taking hold. The doctors gave him a few months, but then he had already outlasted the most pessimistic initial diagnosis. Still, he had lost nearly two stone in the last few months. He had shrunk inside his clothes. Denton needed braces to keep his trousers up, the waistbands gaped open bearing witness to those happy days when he had a paunch. With his bald head, bulbous nose, sunken eyes, and these ridiculous clothes, he felt like a clown, a dying clown.

He emerged from the lavatory and walked over to a photograph of his dead wife. He clutched it to his chest; he felt he was on the verge of collapse.

'My darling Irene . . . I'm glad you can't see me like this.' Denton spoke aloud, a stream of disjointed, unsettled consciousness. 'I would be so much stronger if you were here

. . . they might get me now . . . we'll have the last laugh . . . maybe I should embrace it – when they find out what I've done, everyone at Gower Street will realise that I was twice the spy that they were . . . I just need a bit more strength . . . I just want to end it on my terms, not theirs . . .'

Denton's head was spinning. He didn't know how long he had been standing there. He glanced over at the clock on the sideboard – it was nearly eleven. Moving towards the door swiftly, he collected his mac, descended the stairs and was soon stumbling through the darkness. He reminded himself to observe counter-surveillance drills so it was after midnight before he rang Pinchman at his home in Mitcham.

'Yes!' he answered angrily.

'Mr Pinchman, it's Paul Ryan,' Denton began.

'It's a bit late, Mr Ryan.' Pinchman adopted his talking-to-difficult-clients voice.

'That's the nature of our business, I'm afraid.'

'What can I do for you?'

'We've missed the most important possible call of this operation because that absurd little man of yours couldn't gain access to Johnson's office,' Denton snapped.

'Look on the bright side, Mr Ryan. You only got what you got because he tapped the junction box in the street—'

'It's not good enough. It's slack. It's unprofessional. I asked my friend if he knew what he was doing when he engaged your company and he insisted he did. So far I'm not impressed.'

'Steady on, chief. We've delivered. It's not easy bugging a CID office – surely you understand that –' Pinchman was now sitting bolt upright in his bed and his wife had stopped snoring – 'but Martin's going to do it.'

'All right. Now listen. The intercepted call into the station shows that things are going rather worse for us than we thought could ever be possible. I'm going to talk to our mutual friend about more active measures to solve this problem.'

'What do you mean, exactly?' asked Pinchman.

'We'll have to resolve that tonight . . . this morning. I'm going to talk to our friend now.'

Denton wound up the call and popped a fresh forty-unit phonecard into the machine. He telephoned 'Pete's' home number.

'Pete? It's Charles. I'm sorry my old friend, but we've got real problems. Johnson's found the girl. The girl from 1971. Our firm is trying to gag Johnson but that's as far as we can go officially.'

Denton had always been struck by the man's composure: from the first interview with him and Michael Martin to the last time they met in the Casey Jones at Waterloo station. Now he had heard real anxiety in Pete's voice for the first time. It was hardly surprising: who else could harm Pete in quite the same way as Nicola Dawson?

'Great! So your chickenshit operation has achieved nothing and cost me a fortune,' Pete spat.

'My dear friend,' Denton drew breath, 'I think we need to think things through now. We don't know that the girl is going to tell him anything – in fact she seemed rather set against the idea. But still it's risky.'

'Yes.'

'So I think we need to move things onto a different plane. The kind of plane which our firm could never work on for all the usual boring legal reasons.'

'I need time to think things over,' said Pete.

'Well, regrettably we don't have much, my friend. And there's something else. You'll have to get that last package to me earlier than we thought. I'm afraid my health has taken a turn for the worse, and the firm is asking me to take early retirement.'

The conversation came to an end and Denton stepped onto the puddle-strewn street. Pete was on the phone to Pinchman agreeing just how much the new operation was going to cost as Denton meandered through the drizzle, scanning the street for any signs of surveillance. He went through the usual procedures before going home, so he didn't make it in until 1.30 a.m. Within twenty minutes he was lying in bed, sinking into a fitful, tortured sleep but sleep nevertheless. Denton could still hope that everything would turn out fine.

Chapter Seventeen

Jane sat at her desk, her eyes fixed on some immigration papers, but her mind miles away. She had not taken Lee's revelations about MI5's visit to Shepherds Bush police station well. He had insisted that he would not have to give up the police, but admitted that he would probably have to transfer out of CID as soon as something became available. She had never particularly liked him being in the police. Those all around her in the legal profession expressed their contempt for coppers so frequently that, although she often tried to speak up for the police, some of the prejudices had seeped into her. Of course she knew her husband was not corrupt; she knew he wouldn't beat up suspects, although she wasn't so sure about MacFadyen. But she did think the Army and the police had made him almost too sure of himself, led him to believe he was above the law – witness his trip to King's Lynn.

Lee had spoken about trying to get into the police's own surveillance teams, or perhaps joining Customs and Excise to do the same. It had always been his dream to combine his Army and police experience. She knew that this was no more than dreaming now: he would be lucky to get a job in Traffic. Although she had been dreading the day when he would come home and tell her that he had gone into surveillance, she now felt sorry for him because he could not see that his ambitions were bankrupt. She had not wanted him to go into surveillance, but now she did not want him to lose all his hopes either. There was a lot of the boy in Lee. He needed to dream, and she accepted that.

Jane's working regime varied quite a bit. She did thirty-two hours a week at the solicitors' office: sometimes four days, sometimes a couple of half days and three full ones. A lot depended on her daughter's playgroup and the times when she could get a child-minder. She was grateful to Middlebrook, Bloomfeld and Singh because she knew she would go mad without work of some kind. A couple of her friends who had given it up to raise kids had 'lost their brains', she would always say.

Jane was sitting there with the same sheaf of papers when John Middlebrook, the senior partner, asked her into his office. It wasn't really usual for him to insist on privacy, he was so passionate about the partners' equality and the absence of secrets in the practice. She had been too pre-occupied with her difficulties with Lee to anticipate what happened next.

'Jane, sit down please,' he began. 'I'm not going to beat around the bush or soft soap you.'

The thoughts about Lee fell away; she sensed bad news.

'You know what a rough time we've been having. Legal aid is being cut back all the time. Even those clients who can afford to pay are often months behind in settling their bills. As you know, our two main business clients went bust last year—'

'John, please get to the point.'

Middlebrook stroked his beard. 'We've got to cut you back to sixteen hours a week for the moment.'

'I see.'

'We're just not getting the income.'

'John, can't you manage more than sixteen? We're stuck in a mortgage trap, we really need the money and Lee's work is going really badly too.'

'He's a policeman, things can't be going badly for him.'

'What's that supposed to mean? They are going badly. We'd like another child—'

'Jane, I'm really sorry but there's nothing we can do. The firm is on the brink. It's got to be a maximum of sixteen hours for the moment.'

'Why do you say for the moment?'

'For the next couple of months, I can guarantee you that amount.'

'You mean you can't after that?' Tears were welling into her eyes.

'I can't, I'm sorry. If you want to look for something elsewhere, I'll understand entirely.'

'Maybe I should.'

'You're a bloody fine lawyer—'

'Not good enough to hold down a full-time job.'

'Of course you are, but you have to understand.'

'You really picked a good time,' she said, standing to leave. Jane had plucked a paper hankie from her pocket and blew her nose. She walked out of Middlebrook's office, with its frosted glass window. A couple of the secretaries were looking at her with pity. None of them asked why she was upset, and Jane realised that she was the last to know.

Lee didn't get home until past seven. Jane was watching the television, but not really paying attention to the news which had just started. There were more problems with sterling. Ministers were accusing the Germans of manipulating the market against them.

'Hi babe! Where's Gems?' Lee said, after banging the door.

'Upstairs playing.'

'What a day. We spent the whole day trying to check people who sold Donald Duck masks to see if there was anything unusual about the two used in the Halifax blag.'

'Really.' She stared ahead without looking at him.

'Bloody waste of time it was. We ended up talking to the supplier in Harpenden who told us they'd imported seventy thousand of these stupid masks in the last two years.' Lee was oddly ebullient for somebody in such trouble. Jane did not reply.

'Fancy a curry tonight?'

'We can't afford it.'

'Don't be daft. Twenty quid?'

'You haven't asked me about my day yet,' said Jane, her tone growing harsh.

'Sorry. What sort of day did you have?'

'I was sacked. Happy?'

Johnson lowered himself onto the arm of the sofa. She was still staring ahead.

'What happened? Baby, look at me!'

'The firm's on the brink. That's what John Middlebrook said. He said I can work two days a week for a bit and then it's probably finished.'

'What exactly did he say?' said Lee, sensing that she might be exaggerating a little.

'It's not that difficult to grasp –' she turned towards him for the first time – 'I can work two days a week if I'm lucky.'

Lee buried his hurt feelings at her sarcasm. 'I'm sorry, love.'

'I don't know what we're going to do now. My pay's cut by half. You've messed up your job. What are we going to do?'

'We'll be all right.'

'Will we? I can't see how we're going to pay the mortgage.'

'I can sell the car, I suppose,' Lee offered, hoping this sacrifice might calm her.

'A six-year-old Ford, that's going to change everything, isn't it!'

Lee's patience gave out. 'Why are you having a go at me? It's not my fault!'

'It's your fault that you've pissed away your job.'

'You never wanted me to stay in the Met anyway.'

'We haven't really got the choice now, have we? What are you going to do with your qualifications?'

'I could get a job with a force up north somewhere. Somewhere where it's cheaper to live,' he offered, though he was bewildered as to why he was becoming the object of her anger.

'Wake up and smell the coffee, Lee! What kind of reference do you think Rickett's going to write you now?'

Johnson was angry. 'Where did your qualifications get you then?' he shouted. Almost immediately he regretted it and rushed out of the room, ran upstairs and changed into his running gear.

'What do you think you're doing? Don't run away from me in the middle of a conversation!' she shouted up the stairs.

'I'm going out,' he called back.

'That's very helpful! A bit of support would be nice, but I suppose they didn't train you how to be an adequate human being!'

Johnson came down the stairs slowly. He had put a lid on his anger now and spoke to her with a hushed voice. 'Do you want to ruin things between us, on top of everything else that's going wrong? Because you're saying some really nasty things, things it's going to be difficult for me to forget.'

'I want a partner. I don't want somebody who's going to jeopardise everything on some stupid personal crusade trying in some stupid way to put right something that happened when you should have been looking after Gemma!'

Lee looked her in the eye and said nothing: he was too angry to speak. She knew she had gone too far but didn't want to apologise. He walked past her and through the back door. A few moments later he was running down towards the Thames.

*　　*　　*

When he returned half an hour later, he found Jane was calmer but still in an uncompromising mood.

'I've spoken to my mum,' she said. 'I'm going to go down to the Island for a few days with Gemma.' Jane's parents had retired to the Isle of Wight.

'I'm not invited then?'

'Just for a few days. I thought we might go tomorrow. I need to think things over, get my ideas together a bit.'

'OK, sure, if it makes you happy.' He went upstairs to get out of his sweaty clothes and to shower.

There was little conversation at dinner. Afterwards, they were both sat in front of the television on the sofa. Lee leant over and began kissing her. First just behind the ear, then on the cheek, the neck and finally on her lips. Jane hardly responded until he began kissing her lips, but even then she only did so half-heartedly. Lee, hoping this meant her mood was softening, slid his hand into her shirt and began to stroke her breasts. With this, she seemed to become stiffer rather than more relaxed. Eventually she pushed him away: 'Look, I'm sorry, I just don't want to.'

Jane went upstairs and busied herself getting things together for her trip. In truth she had enjoyed sex little for the last few months. When it happened she often did not come any more and, to her shame, she had found herself faking climaxes in the hope that he would stop. She had been confused and concerned about these feelings. At first she had simply put them down to boredom – a seven-year itch in their marriage. Now she suspected that it was all symptomatic of her deeper unhappiness with married life. In silence and sadness she readied herself for bed.

Lee came to bed eventually. There had been a little perfunctory conversation before they had switched off the light. Just as Lee was begining to doze, the phone beside the bed went. Lee struggled to focus his eyes. The clock said 00.23.

'Hello,' Johnson answered.

'What's the time on your Saisho clock radio, Lee?'

'Who's that?'

'Stop sticking your nose into ancient history, Lee. Stop trying to find out about 1971.'

Johnson was fully awake now. 'Say who you are or fuck off.' Jane was stirring now.

'You'll only get one warning, Lee.'

'Oh yeah?' Johnson was deeply angry now.

'If you don't stop, I'll wait until you're out then I'll tie up your wife, fuck her up the arse, slit your daughter's throat in front of her and then burn the pair of them.'

Martin Dodge replaced the receiver in the phone box outside the bingo hall in Shepherds Bush. It was going to be a busy evening.

Posing as an old colleague, Pinchman rang the desk sergeant at Shepherds Bush and established the office's room number on the pretext that he needed to send a card there through the Met's internal mail. Armed with this information, Dodge was going to get into the station through the rear door and attempt to bug Johnson's office phone. Dodge carried a small backpack containing several different bugging devices: the choice between them would depend on which design of telephone Johnson used. He walked around to the back of the station where there was a car park. Dodge could see that the back door from the car park into the station had an electronic lock linked to an intercom and was covered by a closed-circuit TV camera. He approached the door by following along the station's side wall to stay out of view for as long as possible. Carrying a piece of metal to slip the lock, Dodge placed himself with his back to the camera and his body blocking out his gloved hands. For almost a minute he fiddled with the metal, trying to push it into place and cursing under his breath. Soon he was in and making his way along the corridor. A uniformed constable who looked overweight and unfit passed him and said nothing. Dodge congratulated himself on having perfected the art of looking like you know where you're going. Installing the transmitter posed no problems and within ten minutes Dodge was on his way out.

As he stepped towards the rear door, placing his hand on the electric switch used to open it from the inside, two young constables who had just parked their Astra appeared at the back door. Dodge pressed the buzzer and beckoned them in. One of them noticed Dodge's gloves.

'Ta. Do I know you?' The two policemen were taller than average. Standing close to Dodge the effect was somewhat comical.

'No,' said Dodge warily.

'Who are you then?'

'I'm CID,' Dodge replied, his confidence obviously faltering.

'A five-foot-three copper? I don't think so. Have you got some ID?'

'Yes.' Dodge reached into the black bomber jacket he was wearing and felt the outline of a teargas spray. He brought it swiftly into action, giving both policemen a blast before pushing past and out through the door.

With one of the convulsed policemen shouting, 'Stop, ya bastard!' Dodge fled across the car park and into one of the dark sidestreets.

The next day everybody in the station learned that a suspected robber had been inside the building and were asked to check for anything missing. The Scenes of Crime officer appeared to see whether Dodge might have dropped anything and took the opportunity to give everyone he met a good ribbing about the incident. Nobody suggested that the intruder might have been intent on leaving something behind rather than stealing.

Chapter Eighteen

Lee sat at his desk going through the list of items recovered from the Majestic job to see if it contained any clues about Denton's second package. He was not surprised to find that most of the descriptions were annoyingly imprecise. Deep down he had known it was a bit of a forlorn task, but hoped that doing it might distract him from his domestic crisis. Jane had taken Gemma and headed for the Isle of Wight. She had declined Lee's suggestion that she use the car, saying that they had better get used to living without it. Two hours after Lee headed off to work, giving her a mournful peck on the cheek, she left with one very excited five-year-old to get the tube to Waterloo where they would then catch the train to Portsmouth Harbour for the crossing to the island.

Lee had brushed away her sleepy inquiries about who had phoned in the middle of the night. As much as anything else he didn't want to worry her, so he said it had just been a couple of kids messing around. He decided to try some more rewarding work and started making calls on the Halifax job. Lee recognised that he had been on the verge of giving the whole RACETRACK business up before the phone call. Nothing was worth the grief which he was getting at work and at home, and Jane's crisis at work simply made it vital that he carry on earning as much money as possible. But Lee was bloody-minded and stubborn enough for the threat call to lead him to question whether it was right to drop the whole affair.

The caller's promise to sodomise and murder his wife had

heightened Lee's dilemma. Murdering a woman and a toddler? Lee just didn't believe MI5 would do it. They might threaten it, though.

The call did heighten Johnson's worries about security: of his family and the files. He had kept both sets of papers in the bag taped to the bottom of his workbench. Was the suspected burglar at the police station last night after the files? His things looked undisturbed but that meant nothing. In Northern Ireland they took polaroids of everything before they started a covert search so that everything could be put back in its place. Still, how would MI5 know he had copies? As he mulled over these questions the phone went.

'Johnson.'

'Boss, it's me,' MacFadyen said. 'I've just finished at the dentist; I'm on my way in.'

'How did it go?'

'It was murder. I swear that tooth is connected to my balls.'

'Listen, mate, we had a suspected burglar in here last night.'

MacFadyen giggled: 'Brilliant!'

'I need to give you the second copy of those files. Do you mind? Just to have them somewhere else in case he visits my place.' Johnson looked at his watch: it was already almost noon. 'I tell you what, mate, why don't we meet at my place in forty-five minutes and we can stop by the pub on the way back to the nick.'

'Sure, I'll see you soon.'

As Johnson waited for MacFadyen in the shed he shuffled through the papers. He had noticed a small slip of paper. It was punched with holes down one side, perhaps it had been removed from a record book of some kind. On it was written:

RECORDING RECORD
Tape No: 4786K3/71

SF: CINNAMON, Type 73 mic
Date Rec: 3/6/71

Below these details were a series of withdrawals rather like the Registry records. C. Denton was the last, with a date in 1974.

After MacFadyen arrived the two men went down to the shed together. Lee handed one copy of the papers over.

'Where are we going to take this now if Nicola won't talk?' MacFadyen asked.

'Well, I can try and find her in Brighton. Face to face, there's a chance I might be able to pursuade her to talk.'

'Sorry to be negative, but if she doesn't?'

'I don't know, Badyun. I've got to save my bacon now. Perhaps if I can just toughen up the evidence that Denton was blackmailing somebody, then I could put a copy of the whole lot in the post to the head of CID.'

'If the spooks are involved that might not be good enough,' said MacFadyen. 'Perhaps you should send one copy to him and another to an MP.'

'They'll never forgive me if I get outsiders involved. You know what the Met's like. Still you may be right. I suspect the whole nature of this business is changing.'

'What do you mean?'

'I had a threatening call in the middle of the night. Telling me to drop the whole business or Jane and Gemma would get killed.'

'Jesus Christ! Where are they now?'

'They've gone down to her mum. We had a bit of a tiff about this whole business, but I didn't tell her about the call. I just think that, somehow, I've got to sort all this.'

MacFadyen surveyed his partner and for the first time felt truly worried about the turn events were taking. Johnson was usually a very cool character but he could see that he was beginning to get rattled. Johnson had removed a cigar box from a shelf in the shed and taken a parcel wrapped in an oily rag from inside it. He unwrapped it to reveal a gun.

'It's my nine milli Browning. It's licensed. Personal protection. You know, a hangover from Ireland days, when they reckoned the PIRA might be after me when I joined the Met.' He drew back the well-oiled slide, cocking the pistol's hammer.

MacFadyen nodded silently, tucked the papers into his jacket. How, he wondered, could he help his friend out of this mess?

No more than a minute after they got back to the office, Johnson's phone went.

'Johnson.'

'Lee, it's Elaine Stevens, DS Stevens. I'm in London,' The thick Lancashire accent carried its own reminder.

'How are you?'

'I'm fine. I wanted to take you up on that drink you promised,' she said. 'What are you up to this evening?'

'Well, I thought I might go for a run, but I'll certainly meet you afterwards; where's convenient?'

They arranged to meet in a pub down by the river – one of the ones which Lee went jogging past.

After work, Johnson rang Jane's parents to make sure she had arrived OK and told his wife that he would miss her tonight. The time in which he went running, bathed and got dressed passed quickly.

As he walked down to the pub to meet Elaine Stevens, Lee remembered their previous conversation and how she had flirted with him.

He eyeballed the bar and she was nowhere to be seen, so he sat himself down with a pint of Stella and read the *Standard*. Elaine arrived ten minutes late. As he saw her across the bar and gave her a polite smile, he decided that he would have no difficulty controlling his sexual urges in her presence. Whereas

Jane was dark and petite, Elaine was about five foot eight, had close-cropped blonde hair, piercing blue eyes and a physique rather like that of an olympic swimmer. As she made her way across the bar, Lee studied her shape through the cotton shirt, short skirt and tights she was wearing and decided that Elaine must spend a lot of time pumping iron in the gym.

On first meeting, many of DS Stevens's police colleagues made the mistaken assumption that she was a lesbian. Those who she chose – and she chose them quite freely – learned that this was wrong. Many women who join the police are appalled by the sexism of so many policemen and they react in various ways. At thirty-two, Elaine had no desire for settling down or family. Instead she made sure she was strong enough to cope with those who resisted arrest, shunned the domestic cases which those policewomen who become detectives are so often given and conducted her sex life in defiance of the double standards preached by so many of her male colleagues. The Special Branch had appealed to her largely because she liked the idea of fighting terrorists – it confounded so many senior officers' expectations about what a woman should be doing.

'What can I get you?' Johnson asked.

'I'll have a Bacardi and Coke, thanks,' she replied, sitting down.

Johnson returned with the drink.

'I'm down here because an IRA player has been arrested under the Prevention of Terrorism Act,' she said, matter-of-factly. 'It's somebody I've been pursuing in the northwest. The Met's arrest is taking the piss: they haven't got the evidence to charge him. He'll soon be walking away, back to Londonderry.'

'What's his name?'

'Ryan, Feargal,' she replied without hesitation, showing her trust.

'The Creggan Ryans?' Lee asked.

'Yes,' she said, impressed.

'How old would Feargal be these days, early twenties?'

'Twenty-five, clever clogs. How do you know him?'

'He was just a kid when we put his dad inside. I was with the Londonderry Det – you know, Army undercover surveillance. We had a tip that the Derry Brigade were going to slot this police reservist who worked at one of the dairies as a milkman. We followed Des Ryan and a mate of his to the gates of the dairy where Baz, one of the other Det blokes, rammed their car and I had the pleasure of putting my HK to Ryan's temple and telling him he was fucking nicked.' Johnson could tell she was fascinated, so he concluded the story: 'At that time we would normally have taken out an IRA ASU like that. They would have died in a hail of bullets. But what young Desie didn't realise was that his mate in the seat beside him was our source, so shooting them would have made us rather unpopular with the Branch.'

'You're a dark horse, Lee,' she said and sipped her drink. 'Was that stuff I gave you any good?'

'It was, love. I even went to see Buchanan at his house in Norfolk. He had some interesting things to say. But unfortunately I was enough of a plonker to believe him when he said he wouldn't tell head office about our chat.'

'You're such a daft bugger, Lee,' she said, and then leant forward, putting her hand on his forearm and looking into his eyes. 'I won't give you any more tips unless you promise to use them more responsibly.' And then she winked at him.

Johnson couldn't understand her. He had expected her to be angry, instead of which she was making a joke out of it. He did not understand her fascination with working the system and getting away with it.

'So you're telling me you've put your job on the line?' she asked.

'Well, it's not too good. My head tells me to forget the whole bloody business but there's something in my heart which makes me think I should hand over what I've found out and that might save the situation. After all, something here stinks and it wasn't my decision not to give the files back to the Security Service.'

'I don't know,' she said, looking more serious, 'but if I can help you just ask me. Just don't drop me in it. Don't implicate the Branch, you know.'

'Thank you. You're about the only person willing to help me. Of course I won't drop you in it.'

Elaine seemed to lap this up. Johnson had not told her the whole story but, knowing well how secret documents were meant to be handled, she concluded that his suspicions were in some way justified. 'I think this fella with the deposit box is probably into blackmail. I can't see the Security Service putting their files in safety deposit boxes. They've got so many nasty secrets in their Registry, why treat this one differently?'

'That's what I reckoned. Do you fancy another one?'

'I'd better just have a diet Coke. I've got to watch the drinking, it gets in the way of training.'

'Fair enough,' Johnson replied.

They made small talk for a few moments, staring at their empty glasses.

'I'm hungry, do you fancy a curry?' she asked.

'I wouldn't mind something to eat. But I'm a family man, Elaine. If we go around to the local tandoori I might get a bit of a name for myself!' Johnson replied, trying to make a joke out of it.

'I don't know what you've got on your mind, Lee Johnson!'

They agreed to head for a Nepalese place in Chiswick. As they walked along, Elaine asked: 'Why aren't you with the family tonight then, Lee?'

'Oh, they've gone down to her parents on the Isle of Wight for a few days. To be honest, we'd had a bit of an argument.'

'She's a silly one, honestly. The last time to leave a dishy fella like you on your own is after an argument.'

The food was bog standard: chicken and lamb done without

enthusiasm for a British clientele who didn't know better. The owners played the standard curry-house Muzak. Lee wondered whether Indian and Nepalese music was really indistinguishable.

During the meal, Elaine carried on flirting with brutal directness and Lee began to wonder how he would get himself out of this situation or whether he wanted to any more. He started thinking about what would happen if she came back to the house and he knew he had to prevent that happening.

As they settled the bill – she insisted on paying half – he said, 'I'll be off home then. Where have you got to get back to?' It was about the least complicated signal he could give her. But three pints and Elaine's attentions were gnawing at his certainty.

'I'm staying in a place in Paddington. Shitty it is, full of hookers. I thought I might be saved by a knight in shining armour.'

Johnson did not reply.

They decided to walk together up King Street towards Hammersmith tube station. He looked down at her legs – through the tights he could see her strong thighs; she was quite unlike any woman he had ever slept with. Perhaps it was a measure of his confusion over Jane, his work and everything else that made the prospect of doing so interesting.

As they walked past the Seven-Eleven she stopped, and said, 'Listen, I've got something I want to say to you.' He stopped too and then, in a swift movement she pushed him out of the street lights into a darkened alley which ran beside the shop. With a strength and a confidence which alarmed him, she pressed him against the wall and kissed his mouth. Her tongue went in deep and hard and he felt his jeans tighten with excitement. Feeling him against her, she reached down and began to unbutton his flies.

Johnson had always felt that erections and straight thinking were incompatible, but a little to his surprise and relief his loyalty to Jane and his daughter began to reassert itself.

'Stop it, Elaine, stop it,' he said after prising his mouth away from hers. 'I'm sorry, love, I can't do this.'

She was still obviously aroused. 'You want it, Lee, don't fool yourself.'

'I'm sorry. I can't sell out Jane.'

She was kissing his neck and holding him tightly by the shoulders. 'She's never going to know, Lee.' Elaine dropped one hand into his jeans again and held him. 'I want you inside me, let's go to my hotel.'

'No, I'm sorry, love, you're a smashing girl and if I'm honest, I found myself fancying you a lot tonight, but I can't do this.' He pulled her hand away and began wrestling his erection back into his jeans.

'How do you know she's not getting it on the side?' she asked.

'Who ever knows, Elaine? Maybe Jane and I are not going to stay together in the long term, but I'm not going to do this. I'm not going to be like all those other useless coppers who fuck around and lie to their wives.'

Without intending to, Lee had touched a deep chord in her, defusing the anger which had begun to simmer in her following his rejection.

'You're a good bloke, Lee,' she said, accepting at that moment that she was not going to take him to her bed. 'There's not many like you.'

'I'm not sure I'm good. I've just got to have some respect for Jane and for you; I was never a two-timer.'

They straightened their clothes and began walking again. Lee held her hand and she seemed to appreciate that. A couple of hundred yards up King Street it was time to part.

'Sorry again, Elaine, no hard feelings?'

'No, don't be daft.'

He gave her a safe peck on the cheek and turned away.

'Lee,' she called after him, 'call me any time if you need more help: we've got to keep you in a job!'

'Thanks. You're a star,' he replied and they went their separate ways.

As Lee walked back towards his house, he felt enormous relief. He hadn't been able to put images of his wife and daughter out of his mind when he was kissing Elaine; he shuddered at the thought of how guilty he would have felt if he'd gone all the way.

Sitting on the Metropolitan Line, heading for Paddington, Elaine couldn't stop thinking about Lee. He was the only man who had ever turned her down like that, and she found herself admiring him for it. He was his own person and prized his self-respect. That made them similar. She had only intended to have a quick fling with him, but now she regarded this tall, handsome man quite differently. Elaine began thinking about when they might ever speak again and fantasising about what they would have done if she had pursuaded him to come back to her hotel. As the carriage rocked to and fro on the uneven rails, she found herself becoming quite wet.

Belatedly Lee came to realise what Denton already understood about him if he could only present a dossier of evidence to MI5 next time they came visiting, his chances of beating Rickett, Hacker and the other cringing deadbeats in the CID head shed would be much better. It wasn't about building something which could be used in a prosecution, simply a matter of convincing the big bosses in CID that he had genuine reason to pursue his inquiries in the face of Rickett's refusal to send the papers back to their rightful owners. To this end he decided to do three things: hand back one set of the photocopied papers to the head of CID at the Yard, search for one more piece of evidence that Denton was using information gathered by MI5 to pursue his blackmail scheme and try to get a better fix on where Nicola Dawson was.

Chapter Nineteen

At 7 a.m., Johnson drove his own car to Blackheath. He felt this would be early enough to ensure Denton would still be in. His journey was made less comfortable by the presence of a tape recorder tucked in the back of his boxer shorts and held in place with masking tape. He had run a microphone along his shirt-sleeve, so that its head was held in place by tape close to the cuff. After a series of tests in which he had conversed with the breakfast show on the kitchen radio, he was satisfied that the recorder would give him decent sound.

From his parking place, Johnson could see a light on in Denton's kitchen. He made the lonely walk to the front door. When he had reached a position in which he was satisfied nobody in the flat would be able to see him, he slid his hand behind his back and clicked on the tape recorder.

'Hello?' asked Denton in response to the buzzer.

'Metropolitan Police, Mr Denton. May I have a word?'

'Sergeant Johnson, is it?'

'It is sir, yes.'

Denton was confused, afraid. He looked at his watch. What was the man doing here at this time?

'Mr Denton?'

'Yes, give me a moment, I need to get dressed.' Denton's mind raced: was there anything compromising in the flat? Were there signs of many police outside? He checked his desk, the window. He began to feel a little steadier: it appeared Johnson was up to his old tricks again. He sounded the buzzer and heard the detective sergeant come pounding up the stairs.

'I think you've wasted your journey, sergeant,' he began.

'I hope not, Mr Denton. It's just that I'm about to give a dossier on my investigation to your Service and I wanted to offer you the chance to put me right if I've misunderstood anything.'

'I can't say anything to you about any Security Service matter, you know that. If you have a "dossier",' Denton allowed his contempt to surface as he said the word, 'then you must obviously do what you think is right.'

'I'm going to hand over a photocopy of MI5 files stolen during the Majestic safe deposit box job.'

'Mr Johnson, I don't know what files you mean, but if, hypothetically speaking, you have been copying highly classified material, I suggest you should consider the consequences for yourself.'

Johnson was pleased with that: he hoped the fact that it was clear that Denton knew exactly which files he meant would be evident to anybody who heard the tape. He pressed home his attack. 'I've found Nicola Dawson too, Mr Denton.'

Denton was determined to deny Johnson the satisfaction of any reaction.

'Fairly soon, Mr Denton, I'm confident I'll find the American intelligence officer who I believe you've been blackmailing.'

'I'm sorry?' Denton's voice cracked with stress.

'The American who paid for sex with Nicola Dawson and who you've been blackmailing.' Johnson had chanced his arm on the nationality of the spy, but sensed now that he had been right.

Denton felt himself on the verge of losing control. The girl must have told him it was an American, or was it Mark Buchanan?

Johnson followed up his advantage. 'And I know about the other package you were storing in the deposit box and the dollars.' He savoured his opponent's apparent loss of composure, adding: 'Mr Denton, you've gone very pale. Are you all right?'

'I'm a very sick man, Mr Johnson. I don't expect people to come into my house at this hour accusing me of blackmail, not after a lifetime's service to my country. I think I deserve a bit better than that.' Denton had discovered indignation as his best defence.

'I'm sorry about the time, Mr Denton, but it's pretty clear to me that you've been doing some very bad things.'

'You have no idea what you're talking about. My behaviour was absolutely right. Any contact I may have had with anybody was with the Service's approval.'

'You're saying you've met this American, this very senior, still serving, American spook, with HMG's approval?'

'I'm not saying anything, you've got to refer these questions to my Service; we've got nothing further to talk about.' Denton could feel beads of sweat on his forehead. Johnson now seemed to have an idea who QUASAR was. The sick man felt he was losing control of the situation. 'Just bugger off and leave me alone!' he added, almost shouting.

'You've just been discussing the facts of the case with me, Mr Denton. I've only got one or two more questions—'

'No!'

'Mr Denton, if—'

'I've nothing further to say, sergeant. I will of course be making a report of your allegations to the relevant people in the Service.'

Johnson did not move.

'Go, please. Why are you still here?' Denton asked.

Johnson's mind was still racing – perhaps Elaine would know who had interviewed him and how to get to him.

'Sergeant, please leave now, or I'll call my superiors.'

'Be seeing you, Mr Denton,' Johnson acknowledged him at last. He turned and left without further comment.

* * *

As he drove towards West London, Johnson pulled into a residential road and retrieved the tape recorder. He wound back the tape. There was a recording all right, but its quality caused him despair. Denton's voice was like a faint whisper – he turned up the volume and held it to his ear. He could hear Denton saying 'refer these questions', but his own voice and the rustling of his clothing were deafening by comparison. Johnson had played his last gamble and the results were not what he had wanted. Denton had handled the encounter by the book, except for that one lapse when he had claimed to be under authority. The old spy may have looked very uncomfortable, but that wasn't on tape – and anyway, he was obviously ill. In his disappointment, Johnson allowed himself a moment of grudging admiration for Denton: either he was in the clear or he was a first-rate liar.

As soon as the door closed on Johnson, Denton's composure had gone. He had run towards the toilet, but his guts had emptied themselves before he could get there. He fell on the floor, the smell of his waste tormenting his nostrils and the feel of it on his legs sweeping away the very core of his spirit. Tears began streaming down his face and he sobbed, 'Irene, Irene, Irene.'

At 9.50, a little later than usual, he walked into Gower Street. He had cleaned himself up, thrown on some clean clothes and a composed face. Denton kept telling himself that the next few days would be his last trial. He would retire, and then . . . and then he had his plans. Almost as soon as he had reached the fourth floor and gone into his office, he picked up the phone to Donald Travis.

'Mr Travis, it's Charles Denton in counter-espionage.'

'Yes, what's up?'

'I've had a visit from a policeman, a Detective Sergeant Johnson.'

'I do not believe that man's cheek, he's asking to be kicked out of the force.'

'Do you know him?'

'Oh yes, you're in good company, Charles: he dropped in on Mark Buchanan a few days ago.'

'No?' Denton feigned surprise.

'You'd better come down and see me right away.'

Two hours later, Travis saw the Director General, explaining Johnson's latest attack of chutzpah.

'He accused Denton of blackmail?' she asked.

'Yes. He came back to this theme of the files apparently. It makes no sense to the people in Registry, but who knows? Somebody may have copied them.'

'Is there any chance that Denton did blackmail somebody?'

'DG, we'd have to put a great deal of effort into this for me to give you a decent answer on that.'

'I'm begining to think we should. We've got to find out who's telling the truth, Johnson or Rickett. We've also got to find out what Denton's been up to.'

'He's had a long and honourable career in the Service. He's got a few weeks to go to retirement and he's very sick.'

'Oh, yes, he's got cancer hasn't he?'

'Indeed he has. If we ask him some questions, we'll have to go very gently,' said Travis.

'We can't rule out the possibility that Johnson is barking up the right tree, though.' She opened a notebook and began scribbling, telling Travis the points as she wrote them. 'I think the time's come to get a team working on this. Take two officers – one from counter-espionage and one from vetting: does that suit?'

'Yes, I can think of a couple of possibles.'

'Intercept Rickett and Johnson's phones. Do you think special facilities in the police station would help?'

'It certainly may give us a clue as to who's telling the truth.'

'I'll have a word with the commissioner: I'm sure he won't object. Don't interfere with Denton's phone just yet. I want you to look further into his background, check bank accounts, see if he's been piling up money. We obviously need to find out more about the original operation too.'

'Of course, the possibility could be there of interviewing QUASAR, the American gentleman . . .' Travis ventured.

'Well, that's a big step. If we seek permission from the Director of Central Intelligence in Langley, then it must have the effect of damaging trust – why didn't we tell them about QUASAR's indiscretion for all these years? If we talk to QUASAR unofficially, deniably, then we run even greater risks if DCI finds out. That may be something we have to refer to ministers if and when it becomes necessary. Then, of course, we'll have to tell them about this whole unedifying saga. Frankly I can't think of any conversation I would less like to have.'

'Indeed, we'll just have to hope Johnson turns out to be a loose cannon.'

'He seems to know quite a bit for a loose cannon,' she observed.

'Having met him, I don't think he's completely stable. He's a little shit who's gone into something way over his head.'

'Would he go to the press? Do you want to talk to editors?'

'Not yet. If we get wind that he may be contacting them, then I think we could take that step.'

That afternoon, members of the special Telecom section in Oswestry received the necessary paperwork to intercept four telephone numbers: the office and home lines of Rickett and Johnson. Travis found the officers he was looking for and gave them their instructions. The DG's Legal Adviser had been placed in charge, but he didn't entirely relish the prospect. Treachery and deceit are often difficult to label with certainty in the world of intelligence. Everybody at GWS knew how many thousands of man-hours had been flushed away investigating possible Russian spies within their Service. Even when that inquiry was finished, there were those who didn't believe its findings, including that bloody man who went off to Tasmania and wrote a book. If Denton died soon that might simply feed conspiracy theories rather than finishing off the whole business. Operation RACETRACK was hardly in the same calibre as the great Soviet molehunt, Travis reflected, but it might still soak up a great deal of his time without any conclusive result.

MacFadyen was already at his desk when Johnson arrived in the CID section. Barely looking up from his papers, he said, 'you look like you've been doing something naughty this morning.'

'I went to see Denton. I was carrying a tape recorder.'

'Oh, that's good, I thought it might have been the Queen or the Archbishop of Canterbury, after your recent stunts.' MacFadyen shook his head slowly, but allowed a half-smile to show through.

'I think I almost had him. He was well freaked when I said QUASAR was a Yank, and about his stuff in the other deposit box.'

'Lee, I thought you were kicking all this into touch?'

'I just need a bit more and I think I could nail the American for the girl and Denton for the blackmail.'

'Meanwhile you're oiling up your automatic. It's all getting too heavy. If you think it'll fly as an investigation it's time to bring in some heavies, if you don't it's time to drop it.'

'You're right, mate, but I just need a bit more,' said

Johnson, falling once more into a daydream about how he was going to find Nicola Dawson.

Jim Parker had decided to barbecue steaks that evening. He stood in a Redskins T-shirt one size too small for him and a tall white chef's hat, prodding the huge floppy cuts of beef from time to time. Apart from Vince Dubois, who was single and had come alone, the others were all red-blooded boys from the world of covert operations whose wives sported a variety of gravity-defying hair-dos. There was Alfonso 'Alf' Rodriguez, a Cuban-American who Parker routinely introduced to people as 'our destabilisation specialist'. Alfonso wore $900 snakeskin boots and was gearing up to do his party piece, which involved downing a large mug of beer while humming the national anthem of Batista's Cuba. Deke Clayburn had come too and insisted on keeping his aviator shades on long after the sun had slipped below the Virginia skyline. Deke was the Agency's hot-dog helicopter pilot, a man who flew missions that did not exist in aircraft 'cleansed' of all registration numbers or marks to countries nine out of ten Americans had not heard of. Deke's main claim to fame was having flown three CIA personnel out of the Bekaa valley in Lebanon where they had been searching for the Agency's Beirut station chief after he was kidnapped. Deke brought them out in a Hughes 500, 'flying so low, our exhaust was frying the goats on the hillsides'. As the meat sizzled, Deke stood over Jim, giving encouraging incantations like: 'Let that baby burn'.

After they had devoured the steaks, and 'the girls' were sitting in the yard chatting, Jim, Vince, Alf and Deke who were all well-oiled retired to the den to catch the ballgame on a big-screen television. As they were channel hopping, to everybody's surprise, Hal Canning appeared on a late-night news show.

'Lordy-lord, what have we here?' Parker exclaimed. Canning

was being interviewed as part of an item about 'The CIA and the new world disorder'.

The interviewer started by saying. 'So, Hal, the world didn't turn out to be a safer place after all?'

'Well, as one of my previous bosses in Central Intelligence said, Cary, we may have killed the dragon of Communism, but there are still a lot of snakes out there.'

'What's causing you most concern right now?'

'We're tracking the possible spread of nuclear or chemical weapons around the world; we're tracking growing Islamic terrorism, and of course in the new CIA we're tracking some of the economic threats to our American way of life, like the dumping of goods.'

Parker was livid at the easy questions being lobbed at his rival. 'I can't believe this shit! Nobody told me Mr Blow-dry was doing this.' Parker tugged off the chef's hat as he said it.

'Mercy sakes alive,' Deke added in his best test-pilot's drawl. 'We have a geek at twelve o'clock, treat this geek as hostile, guns are red and clear to fire!'

Vince Dubois was uncomfortable with the speed with which Parker's other guests joined in the condemnation. He had watched Canning enough times in front of committees to know that he was at his best communicating complex ideas in an easily understood way. Canning's silver hair, flawless patter and sharp suit gave the impression of somebody who was more a master of the medium than the person interviewing him.

As Canning conceded: 'Some of us are glad the Nicaraguan chapter is closed,' Alfonso shouted, 'Kiss my ass, cabrón!'

The last question, though, brought the room to silence. The anchor was one of those Americans of Chinese or Vietnamese origin whose voices and lamb-chop suits betray no hint of their origins. The camera remained on Canning's face, primed for any flicker of reaction, as she said, 'Word is in Washington that you are the Agency's choice to replace Director Bateman: is that a challenge you would relish?'

Canning allowed a slight smile, a patronising smile, to cross his lips as he said the Director still had a year to run but that he would 'serve the US intelligence community in any post – high or low – that our President and Congress placed me.'

'Softball question, lady!' Parker bellowed. 'Back to little league, Suzy Binh, Cary fucking Wu, Mary mother-fucking Wong, whatever your goddamn name is!'

There was an embarrassed silence from the other guests as Parker paid off with, 'What's wrong with a proper Chinese name, bitch?'

Deke muttered, 'holy shit!' Parker reflected that Canning and the network both seemed to know something which he, as the CIA's Deputy Director for Operations, did not.

Chapter Twenty

The day after his television performance, Hal Canning's car pulled into the familiar, familial leafy drive. Jean, his wife, was arranging dried flowers in the hallway when he came in.

'Hi hon,' he said.

'Uh huh,' was her only reply.

The Cannings' marriage was loveless, and had been for years. They still had a partnership, though, and she didn't seem to stray in search of romantic adventures. She still looked good: auburn-haired, small, firm legs, a slight belly on her accentuated by her inexplicable desire to wear elasticated tracksuit trousers around the house. Occasionally they still made love, but Hal only got through it by filling his mind with images of younger bodies than hers.

Fantasies had been stirring in Hal's mind for some time and he sensed it might not be much longer before he surrendered to them, as he periodically did, and made his way north to Baltimore where he had a special arrangement.

He spent some time in the bathroom brushing his hair, examining his eyebrows, taking the tweezers to any stray hairs which offended his sense of order. Jean watched him descend in tennis kit, heading for the court at the back of their house.

Hal spent the next few hours hammering a ball against the practice wall on one side of the court. As he went, he mulled over his strokes and how he would play them: how he would mastermind the Agency's new economic offensive; how he would trip Jim Parker up when he next had the chance, and how he would edge his way into the directorship when the new president was elected, as all polls suggested would happen. He decided he would have to contrive meetings with the front-runners for the Democratic nomination. There would obviously be some party hacks to push out of the way but, as Canning volleyed a ball into the green surface ahead of him, he felt he had a good chance of overcoming them. Last night had been good for him in every respect – the congressional staffers would have sat up and taken notice. But whereas Hal should have felt on top of the world, he was troubled by events far away which could ruin everything.

'Hal, phone!' Jean called from the porch, interrupting his thoughts.

'Who is it?'

'Some English guy, didn't say his name.'

Canning went into his den, mopping sweat from his brow with a towel and taking the receiver into his hand. 'Hello.'

'Hello, Pete, it's Charles.'

Canning looked at his watch, it was almost midnight in London, the normal sort of time for Denton to call. Didn't this man have a life, he wondered? 'How's our operation going, Charles?'

'I can't say it's going well. Things have reached a very critical point.'

'You're always bringing me problems, not solutions, buddy!'

'The snooper has discovered quite a bit about you. I don't know how: he confronted me with the knowledge this morning.'

Events in London had, with those few words, taken on an ominous new seriousness. Hal realised for the first time that a noose was being pulled around his neck. 'Oh really!' he replied, hoping to sound as calm as possible. 'What did you say?'

'Nothing, obviously. Well, that's wrong, I did say one thing:

I told him any meeting I might have had would have been done with the relevant authority.'

'You shouldn't have told him anything.'

Denton ventured: 'I had a meeting with our legal boss today; our firm is throwing the book at this snooper.'

'What's your feel for who knows the full facts outside your organisation?'

'Well, just the inconvenient detective really – oh and his partner. His partner has taken a copy of the files.'

'Nobody else?'

'It's difficult to be completely sure, but I don't think so. Not forgetting the girl herself of course.' Denton wondered where this line of questioning was heading.

'Great!' Canning said mockingly. 'I suppose we can be glad it hasn't all appeared on the Internet yet. We might have to go with your idea of removing them.'

'Removing them?' Denton realised that Canning was backing the solution he himself had hinted at during their previous conversation. Denton wondered whether they were in the habit of using this kind of language in Langley.

Canning looked out into the Virginia calm. 'Yes, have your bosses talked about eliminating the problem?'

'It's not our way, as I mentioned before – lots of boring legal problems. I don't think they would order it, even through the people we've contracted to help us,' said Denton, who for the first time had begun to wonder whether there were options worse than the unmasking of himself and his agent.

'I'll talk to our contractors,' said Canning, whose voice had become cold to the point of sounding like synthesized speech. 'Get a grip on this operation, Charles. You're really pushing our relationship.' He rang off.

The following day, Peter Pinchman and Martin Dodge sat in the Croydon offices of Panther Secure Systems Limited. Canning had phoned Pinchman in the middle of the night again and Pinchman was relaying the nocturnal conversation to Dodge.

'Sounds odd to me, boss. This job is becoming really odd, even for this business,' Dodge said.

'You've got no problem with what he's asking?'

'No, of course not. We'll need a bit more muscle on the job, obviously.'

'That goes without saying, Martin. We've obviously screwed a lot more dosh out of them for this. I think we've really arrived in the big time with this operation.'

'It's still odd though, isn't it, boss? Two coppers, what the fuck have they done to these Yanks?'

'Stood on their bollocks for all I know. Ours is not to reason why, Martin. We get the business because people like our American friend and his MI5 oppo know that we're good soldiers. We follow orders and that's the end of it.'

It was 4.15 on a dreary Thursday afternoon. Detective Chief Inspector Rickett had been summoned to Scotland Yard for a meeting with the brass. He didn't have to ask what it was about. Chief Superintendent Hacker was waiting in the Head of CID's outer office when he arrived. Rickett half-expected to be put on indefinite sick leave as soon as he got through the door. Twenty years on the force and he had never tapped the boards in front of the boss before.

'Gents, take a seat,' the Head of CID said, motioning them in. 'Tea?' Both men declined and Rickett began to suspect that he was not here to be disciplined.

'Your man DS Johnson has been upsetting the Box 500 boys again,' the CID boss began. 'He's been to drop in on another one of their officers. He seems to be making a habit of these house calls.'

'Well that's not on, sir, because I had I word with DCI Rickett about the last incident—' said Hacker, turning to his subordinate.

'I told him he was out on his arse if he carried on with this business, sir,' Rickett jumped in.

'Well, I want him suspended PDQ. He's finished. I want him discharged on health grounds. Do it tomorrow morning.'

'Sir,' Hacker asked, 'what about the trial on those safe deposit robbers? It's obviously going to look bad for us if our chief prosecution witness isn't there.'

'I don't give a monkey's. You've got DC MacDonald; you've got the SO19 officers who made the arrests. They're all pleading guilty anyway. No, I want him out fast. There's no room for caped crusaders in my department.'

'Understood, sir,' Hacker replied.

'DCI Rickett, I understand the MI5 legal people are not very happy with your version of events relating to these celebrated sodding happenings. Get it sorted before Travis comes calling again.'

'Yes, sir.'

'You're on very dodgy ground here. Don't mess up, do you understand me?' the Head of CID asked with the menace of a man who had climbed to his job in his early forties and was now in striking distance of a chief constableship.

'Completely, sir.'

'You can go now, DCI Rickett, I need a quick word with your boss.'

Rickett shuffled out.

'Chief Superintendent Hacker, we are going to have a conversation now that never happened.'

'I understand, sir.'

'It's for the sake of all the good graft you've put in over the years.' The CID chief came around his desk and sat in the chair which Rickett had occupied a few moments earlier and leant forward until Hacker could smell his stale breath. 'MI5 don't trust Rickett; they think he's lying to them. I think Rickett's just covering his arse. We're hanging Johnson out to dry but I don't want to do the same to Rickett – he's too close to you, to us. He's not the cleverest of blokes: talk to him, coach him before MI5 come visiting again.'

'I understand, John,' Hacker replied.

'The commissioner tipped me the wink this morning that the spooks are going to bug the CID section in Shepherds Bush. So don't have your chat on the phone or in Rickett's office.'

Johnson spent that afternoon compiling statements on the King Street building society job. He had failed to reach DS Elaine Stevens on the phone. Rickett had also gone out – his secretary said to the Yard. Johnson wanted to have a word with him as soon as he came back, to tell his superior about the copy of the files and his readiness to hand over everything he had discovered. If he were to save anything in the Met, he might as well let Rickett know about the copy, rather than waiting for Travis's next visit.

MacFadyen sat behind his desk typing up notes on another robbery. Every now and then he removed a half-bottle of Scotch from his drawer, put a little in a Styrofoam cup and swilled it around his mouth before swallowing the contents. MacFadyen caught Johnson watching him. 'It's that fucking tooth again: I know it's dying on me; I feel a root canal job coming on.'

'What's that?'

'It's fucking terrible, it's when they use Black and Deckers in your mouth for two hours non-stop. You come out feeling like the bastard's been standing on your lower jaw.'

'I've thought things over and I reckon I've got enough to put a file together for the Head of CID. If that doesn't convince them this thing's worth a proper investigation I don't know what will. So I'm through with it.'

'I've heard this before.' MacFadyen poured his partner a cup half full of Scotch and they began to drink.

'I mean it. My heart's still ready to fight on, but my head's told me I've got to stop. Plus the trouble's given me an ultimatum, she says I've got to pack it in.'

'Have you told her yet?'

'No, I'll call her tonight, she's still at her folks'.'

'Why don't we go out and get pissed then?'

'Yeah, OK.'

Johnson phoned his wife and repeated the same faithful promise. She, like MacFadyen, knew her husband's integrity well enough to believe him. She told him she would be home at the weekend and he wished her and Gemma goodnight. Almost as soon as she had put the phone down, Jane decided she had spent enough time on the island. She looked at her watch: a late crossing, a train, taxi; it might be after midnight before she got home. She decided that didn't matter.

The two detectives went for a curry and then down to the river, to one of the few pubs which Johnson felt really at home in. They had a couple of lagers over dinner and by ten in the pub were, in the Scotsman's words, 'nicely steamin''. At various points in the evening they had resorted to the essentially harmless bachelor practice of discussing the women around them.

'Check her,' MacFadyen said, nodding in the direction of a fair-headed young woman who was looking around the pub for somebody who, fairly obviously, was not there.

'Nice Earthas,' Johnson remarked, studying the curve of her sweatshirt. MacFadyen gave her a genteel wave. 'Over here Duchess! We're waiting.' The girl blushed and about-turned swiftly.

'Don't harrass the locals, Badyun: you'll get me barred.'

MacFadyen's high spirits, far from being diminished, soared as he heard the opening bars of one of his favourite songs on the juke box. The bearded Glaswegian had invented his own words. As the vocals began, he jumped to his feet.

I'm just too good to be true,
Can't take my eyes off myself,
I'm like heaven to touch,
Wanna hold me so much!

As he sang, MacFadyen used exaggerated entertainer's mannerisms, performing to mirrors and touching his body as the song progressed. Fairly soon, even the staid custom at the Ancient Mariner in Hammersmith were clapping along in time.

I love me baby! And if it's quite all right,
I'll make baby gravy in my bath tonight.

The song ended with applause and the customers apparently unoffended by the lyrics which had gone about as far as the Sods' Operas Johnson remembered from his Army days. He couldn't tell whether the punters had understood MacFadyen's slang. The partners walked together into the darkness across Furnivall Fields to the Hammersmith Broadway, the Scotsman draping his thick arm over Johnson's shoulder. At the Broadway, Johnson saw MacFadyen into a taxi. It was one of those exaggerated gestures of friendship which drunkenness can often produce, for in truth Johnson was the worse for wear of the two. With a 'take care, my old mate', Johnson saw him off and returned to his own house.

He was not too drunk to realise that he should take in a good deal of water before going to bed. He knew things weren't too bad when he was able to close his eyes in bed without becoming dizzy. As he began to drift into sleep, he experienced a common sensation: thinking that somebody was standing over him. He opened his eyes and nobody was there. Soon he had drifted off.

Chapter Twenty-One

Charles Denton arrived in his flat just after ten. While Johnson and MacFadyen were carousing in the pub, he made himself a camomile tea and sat down with transcripts of calls from the twenty-four hours up to that evening. Denton's work had never been easy, requiring him to put in as much time as the other MI5 people at Gower Street and then find the hours for his real espionage activities – meetings with Canning included. Now, with his strength and concentration ebbing, he found himself having to take on the burden of running this operation against Johnson.

Denton's CD player was one of the few luxuries he had allowed himself in recent years, and now it consoled him with Chopin. He had been saving for his retirement plans: plans to quit London and return home, but that was all out of the question now. He was wasting away too fast to expect much retirement, and the native land he had left all those years ago no longer existed in the same form. He was very pleased and proud that the country of his birth had evolved in the way it had, but it had nevertheless ceased to be the the place he dreamed about retiring to.

Soothed by tea and piano, he worked his way through the transcripts. As in most recent days, almost all of Johnson's office calls referred to various cases he was working on; only at the bottom did he come across the last one on that day's transcript, the call Johnson had made to his wife.

Denton noticed the number at the top of the call – deciphered simply enough by counting the clicks on the line and usually confirmed by the person answering the phone. Johnson's wife was in the Isle of Wight, and it was clear from the early part of the transcript that her parents lived there.

> **LJ**: I've got stuff together to give the big boss about that case that annoys you so much. I'm not going on with it, it's finished.
> **JJ**: Is it? Are you sure?
> **LJ**: I'm sure.
> **JJ**: Promise?
> **LJ**: Yes, of course, I promise.
> **JJ**: You've done the right thing, darling. I didn't mean to be a bore about it, you know that, but we'd be in so much trouble if you lost your job.
> **LJ**: I know, I know.

Denton realised that he had won in a way. Johnson was giving up. He contemplated what Canning had in store for the detective. Should he ring Canning and tell him Johnson was giving up? Was it time to reverse any orders Canning might have given to Panther Systems? He wondered whether he should head for a call box.

Johnson still planned to hand everything over to the 'big boss', whoever that was. Denton understood that he would be exposed if that happened, but he had become resigned to exposure during the last few weeks. What would be so wrong in him enjoying brief notoriety as a great spy for the last few weeks or months of his life? No, he thought finally, exposure would damage what he was loyal to. There was Canning's last shipment of intelligence to bring in. Johnson and one or two others just might have to die for that. Denton noticed from the transcript that Johnson's wife was not coming home for a couple of days. He realised that, when she did, she would probably be a widow.

It was just after midnight when Johnson was awoken by a sound. He opened his eyes to see three black figures standing over him. In a series of swift movements, one placed a gloved hand over his mouth while the two others took one of his arms each and secured his wrists to the bedstead with plastic ties. He thought of his Browning automatic, still stuck in the bloody garden shed. Johnson struggled briefly but felt the plasticuffs cut into his wrists. The two heavies each sat on one of his legs. The third man, who Johnson had noticed was very short, leant close to his face.

'No noise. OK?' Dodge said, then removed his gloved hand.

'OK,' Johnson replied, his chest heaving with the fear and the adrenalin coursing through him.

'You're a stupid cunt, Johnson. I told you to leave off and you didn't listen. I should have come calling when your wife and kid were here.' Johnson did not reply, but beneath the holes of the man's balaclava, he glimpsed a wispy moustache. He also detected that the man wore overalls which glistened in parts: patches of something wet.

'We want the files you copied. Where are they?'

'Fuck you, titch!' Johnson decided that telling these men what they wanted would probably be a fatal mistake.

Dodge rewarded this insolence with a series of swift punches to the face, his fist bobbing back and forth like a mechanical hammer. Johnson heard his nose crunch and felt blood running into his mouth. Dodge produced a wad of papers from inside his boiler suit and illuminated it with a small torch.

'Your friend wasn't so stupid, Johnson. He gave up the files the first time we asked him. You're not so big now, are you,

Johnson? Surprised your pal shafted you at the first fucking opportunity?'

'Go fuck yourself!' he spat at the man crouched over him, who slapped his face hard.

'Did you open the other package?'

'Which other package?' Johnson thought he knew which one, but wondered what the man was looking for.

'I ask the questions, dickhead.' He slapped Johnson again. 'The one containing the other material: did you open it?'

'No.'

'You feel pretty sorry for yourself now, don't you, you prat!' Dodge was speaking quickly, evidently enjoying his moment. 'Big CID man, aren't you? I could cut your dick off now. Do you realise that?'

Johnson could feel panic rising within him. He couldn't think of a way to get to his gun. He cursed his stupidity for not having it in the room. Every time he struggled to free his hand, the plastic cut deeper into his wrist.

Jane gave up trying to find a taxi on Hammersmith Broadway. She had got the last tube back and she was regretting her heady impetuousness at rushing back with a five-year-old in the middle of the night. Gemma had slept most of the way, but now she was waking, rubbing her eyes and complaining that she wanted to be in bed.

PC Steven Nicholls, who knew Lee well from Shepherds Bush station, was rounding the Broadway in his Rover squad car when he noticed the woman and child. 'That's DS Johnson's missus, isn't it?'

'I don't think I know her,' his colleague replied, bored.

'It is; it is her.' PC Nicholls pulled in at the kerb and wound down the window. 'Mrs Johnson?'

'Yes,' Jane replied, hoping deliverance was at hand.

'Do you need a lift?'

* * *

Dodge disappeared from the Johnsons' bedroom. The other two had said nothing: Johnson decided to talk to them. 'Are you an ex-soldier?' he asked.

One of the men turned around. 'Fucking shut it,' he replied in a distinct Geordie accent.

'I was a soldier. I was a Sapper and I was in 14 Int in Ireland. I've done my bit. Don't let that crazy little bastard do me in.'

'You weren't in 14 Int, you bullshitter,' the Geordie replied.

'I was, Londonderry Det. 1985.'

'Well, you're in deep shit now, pal,' the Geordie replied and both men snickered nervously.

Dodge returned with a jerry can. He told the others to secure Johnson's legs and opened the container.

'I don't think you're warm enough,' Dodge said as he began pouring liquid onto the bedclothes.

Johnson smelt the petrol. 'Fuck you!' he shouted.

Dodge threw the can on the floor and flicked open a Zippo lighter. 'I'm gonna fry you unless you tell me where those papers are.' Johnson did not reply. 'Your little girl's not going to want to see you when I've fucking barbecued you!'

Johnson couldn't stop himself thinking of his daughter. Tears began to run down the sides of his face. He wanted to give in: what was holding him back?

'Cover his mouth. There's a cop car in the street,' the Geordie said from his position peering through the crack in the curtains. Dodge sat on Johnson's chest and clamped his gloved hand into position.

'Oh shit! It's stopped outside!'

Geordie watched a policeman get out and look directly at the house.

'He's gonna come in!'

The other two men moved before Dodge. He struck the Zippo and tossed it towards Johnson before following the other two down the stairs. As Jane's key turned in the lock, they had gone through the kitchen door, past the potting shed at the end of the garden and were vaulting the fence into a neighbour's.

Jane thought she had heard something and could sense there was something wrong as soon as she came into the house. She did not want to take another step. 'Lee!' she called.

'I'm in the bedroom,' Johnson's voice broke with emotion as he realised what had happened.

'What's the matter?' she called as she walked up the stairs.

'I need help, babe. Don't bring Gems in.'

Jane walked into the room and switched on the light. As soon as she saw her husband, bloodied and tied back, her tears began to flow.

'Get the lighter off the floor, quickly!'

Jane picked up the zippo and snapped it shut, stamping out a small patch of smouldering carpet. Dodge had thrown it straight at Johnson, but it had bounced off his forehead, clear of the petrol.

'Get the covers off, babe, the petrol's stinging me!'

She worked quickly, getting nail clippers from the bathroom next door and cutting free the plasticuffs. Johnson took her in his arms and they hugged.

Gemma walked into the room and saw her father's bloody face, heard her mother's sobbing. Very quickly she too was crying. Johnson lifted her with one arm, squeezing her close.

After a few minutes, Johnson stood. He felt unsteady on his feet. He noticed some small patches of blood around the bedroom, evidently not his. He realised they must have come from the three hooded men. Were they hurt? Or was it MacFadyen's blood?

Johnson picked up the phone by the bed and punched his partner's number. He let it ring fifteen or twenty times. 'Babe, I've got to go to Dave MacFadyen's place.'

'I don't want to be alone here – not after these animals have been in our house.'

'Come with me then, let's take the car, but it's got to be quick.' Jane lifted the bag she'd just brought in from the island off the floor and said: 'I'm packed!'

Lee rushed through the kitchen door to the back garden, retrieved the RACETRACK files from under his workbench and pulled the pistol from its covers. Frantically he clicked 9mm rounds into a magazine. Normally he'd want three loaded clips, but he didn't have the time. He snapped the loaded one into the weapon and put the other two into his pocket together with a box of shells. He came bounding out of the front door to find Jane and Gemma already sitting in the car. Moments later they were speeding through Shepherds Bush.

'Where are we going now, Mummy?' Gemma asked from the back of the car as they sped along a darkened Shepherds Bush Road.

'Don't worry my darling, we're off on a journey.' Jane lay her daughter down in the bed she had made up on the back seat.

Lee's Escort slewed around the corner of Parkside as he turned down towards Southfields. 'Let him be out, let him be out!' he implored.

Jane said nothing, sitting grim-faced and occasionally clutching her husband's hand when he was not wrestling the wheel. In her mind a series of emotional bombshells had begun to detonate. She pondered what would have happened if she had given in to her own tiredness or Gemma's and stayed down on the Island for the night. Or if she had arrived without the police car and the men still in the house . . . She couldn't stem these thoughts, and her whole body shuddered with the cold realisation of how the slender thread which held together everything she loved and valued could have been severed only minutes before.

* * *

Johnson parked around the corner from MacFadyen's flat in Southfields. He pulled back the working parts of the Browning, letting them fly foward, putting the first round into the breach. He walked towards the converted Victorian house where his partner lived. 'I'm going in alone baby, OK?'

'Yes, OK. For God's sake be careful!' As he walked away, she couldn't bear the tension and lifted her dozing daughter from the back seat into her arms for comfort.

Johnson had taken the precaution of donning gloves before he pushed open the front door. It had been forced earlier, the area around the lock was splintered. With the 9mm in one hand he surveyed the door frame holding a torch in the other. Johnson had gone only two paces further when he saw MacFadyen's body lying on the carpet. The walls were spattered with blood. His eyes raced up his partner's body once, then twice, before he grasped that his head wasn't there. 'Oh fucking Jesus no!' He didn't pause, he didn't want to look at the body for another second, so he pressed on.

Johnson shone his torch into the sitting room. The intruders had sprayed a message on the wall. 'Four Scousers in jail. Four dead coppers. One down three to go.' He backed through the door, stepping around the pools of blood in the corridor. He could see a heavy trail of crimson droplets, beckoning him into the kitchen. MacFadyen's head had been placed in the sink. It was half-covered with the blood which had seeped out, but Johnson's torchlight caught a lock of ginger hair, an open eye. On the tiled floor lay a Sabatier carving knife with a twelve-inch blade.

He got into the car, said, 'Badyun's dead' and began to drive away. As the vehicle picked up speed, Lee felt waves of hot and cold surge through his body. His head began to spin, his mouth dried up and he began to doubt whether he could keep the car on the road. In a sudden movement that caused the car to screech, he pulled in to the kerb, flung open the door and, as he was trying to open his seatbelt, retched violently into the gutter.

Jane leant across and stroked his head as he vomited until he had speckled the cold black kerb with his green bile. As the convulsions released their grip, Lee turned to face his wife. There were bits of something on his chin; his eyes looked strained and watery. He fixed his wife in his gaze. 'He's dead. He's dead and it's my fault.'

Lee and Jane drove down into Hampshire, to the New Forest. For some time they were speechless.

'Who did this?' Jane asked at last.

'I don't know; I haven't a clue. I reckon those three in our house were ex-Army. I didn't think MI5 would ever pull a stroke like this.'

'Who else could it be?'

'Well Denton obviously wasn't acting alone, that much is clear. He's no small-time blackmailer that man. Maybe it was Five, maybe that's what Buchanan meant when he said that his successor as well as his predecessor had thought the American might be useful as an agent.'

'They would kill people to protect that?' she asked.

'I didn't think so before, but now I suppose it must be true. Maybe the agent is near the top of the CIA, Buchanan hinted as much.'

They parked in a small lane, far from anybody's house. The car sat cooling under a starlit sky.

By three Jane and Lee were trying to sleep in the front seats, but their minds wouldn't let them rest.

'Are you awake my love?' she asked.

'Yes.'

'Hold me,' she whispered.

They began to kiss. Lee felt warm waves of desire surging through him. He kissed the back of her neck and she began to sigh with delight. Unrolling Lee's sleeping bag onto the ground beside the car they lay down, making love under the stars on a balmy late summer's night. Lee lay on his back with her astride him. He held her buttocks tightly, lifting and lowering her as she looked down at him. Every now and then her face lunged down and their tongues entwined in deep powerful kisses. It was a passion as intense as any they had ever enjoyed, fuelled by the desperation of lovers who knew that, but for chance, their life together would have ended that night.

Chapter Twenty-Two

Jane and Lee made their plans. They would go back to the island the next day as foot passengers on the Lymington–Yarmouth ferry. Lee realised there was some risk in going to her parents, but they needed some time to sort things out. His wife could take as much money as possible from their bank accounts while she was there. Lee could then come back, pick up the car and go to ground until he could find out how to guarantee his safety.

With the first glimpse of dawn, after no more than a couple of hours asleep, Lee tapped Jane's shoulder and led her from the car once more. They walked away, so that Gemma could not hear.

'How are we going to get out of this?' Jane asked.

'I don't know who we can trust now. It's all such a mess. I know one thing though. It came back to me while I was sleeping in the car. The guy who was at the house wanted to know whether I'd seen the material in the other package before he killed me. You see, Badyun and I had already discovered from the safe deposit man that there'd been another that we'd never noticed and it had been recovered by the same bloke who had the files.'

'*Seen* the material? Photos maybe?'

'Come to think of it I'm not sure he did ask whether I'd seen it, just said that it contained "other material" or something like that. Denton had looked dead scared when I mentioned the other package to him. I suppose it could be photos, but we know it was quite a small package. It could be another transcript, but I suppose that would have been in with the other one.'

'Maybe it was a tape,' Jane prompted.

'Yeah, maybe you're right. Anyway, I think it could be the key to the whole thing. If it's photos or a tape of what went on at the brothel then the stuff in the documents can't be wished away, can it?'

'You want to go after it, don't you?'

'I think it's our best chance. I've got to watch Denton, see where he goes, who he meets. Then I've got to confront him and get whatever was in that package.'

'All right so far,' said Jane, setting herself down gingerly on a tree stump, 'but what do we do with the stuff when we've got it? Who do we trust?'

'Maybe the Head of CID, maybe the commissioner, I don't know. Let's cross that bridge when we come to it.'

'Lee, you know what I think we should do?' She beckoned him towards her and held his hand. 'I think we should get the passenger ferry from Lymington over to the island, clear as much money as we can out of the bank and then I think you should go back over to the mainland and hunt this Denton bloke on your own.'

'I'm not leaving you and Gemma, not when those bastards could get you. No way.' Lee sounded adamant.

'Think it through, my love. You can follow him. You can get into his flat. You can take care of yourself. You've been trained to do all that. Gemma and I will be like a millstone around your neck. You can hide out, sleep rough: where would we go?'

'I promised myself after what happened to Gemma that I would never let her down again.'

As Lee became more distressed, Jane's tone hardened. 'You'll be letting us down if you don't take the one chance to end this mess. I can work on the American end of it, perhaps try to work out who this bloke might be. You go for Denton.'

Lee couldn't help but smile. So often he thought of himself as fighting her emotion with his own hard-headed logic. Now he knew she was right. He stood a much better chance of getting to Denton undetected if he went alone. 'Do one thing for me, Jane –' he took the Browning out of his waistband – 'take the nine milli and kill that little bastard if he ever comes near our Gemma.'

'The gun? No way!' As she looked at the black form in her husband's hand, her distaste could not have been more obvious if it was a turd.

'Take the weapon. I'll look after myself. If I'm away from you, they probably won't touch you. If they do want to have a pop and you've got the tool, then you can protect yourself and Gems.'

'I've got no idea what to do with that thing; I'd be a danger to everybody.'

'I want you to be a danger to everybody except Gemma. Take it!' He thrust his hand forward, aggressively.

'OK,' she said finally, and was immediately struck by the weight of the thing.

Lee strolled back to the car, took a newspaper from the boot and pinned it to a tree. Without words, he put his arm around her and walked her about fifteen feet from the makeshift target.

He began to instruct her with the fluency and calm of a man who had spent so many hours on the range in Ireland that he could use his weapon to hit targets without the conscious process of aiming it. He pushed and guided her body into what they called the 'CQB', the Close Quarter Battle posture – a crouch holding the weapon forward with crooked arms.

'If you shoot in a CQB it'll give you steady aim, and if he does manage to plant a round on you, standing like that will give you your best chance of remaining upright.'

Jane felt self-conscious as he made her repeat phrases aloud about the procedure for drawing the weapon.

'Once you draw the weapon, you use the weapon: it's not for waving around at people. Aim for the centre of the trunk. Repeat.'

'Aim for the centre of the trunk.'

'As you fire you'll feel the muzzle of the gun climb with the recoil.' He imitated the front of the gun flipping up. 'Aim again. Fire again at the same aiming point. That's what the boys call a double tap. Never give less than two rounds. I'd give someone three or four minimum myself, but you make sure you give them at least two, OK?'

She nodded.

'Once the immediate threat is down, look around, is there anyone else in a position to get you? That should only take a second, then check the first target again. If the target's gun is well away from the body – and I mean more than six feet, then fine. If the target has the gun and is unconscious, approach while maintaining your aim and kick the gun to a safe distance. If they're still conscious, get good and close, say five feet, and give them a touble tap in the head.' He played out the action pointing down at the imaginary target.

'The head?'

'It's you or him, Jane. Leave somebody with a gun wide awake and they'll shoot you in the back as you're walking away feeling like John Wayne. Give him a double tap to the head and there'll be no misunderstandings. We used to call it the 9mm pension plan.'

Jane did not even notice his Army gallows humour. She saw something else emerge in her man as he explained the business of shooting somebody with cold precision. She realised that he had buried away within him during their years together the attributes of a machine-like killer. She found that disturbing at first, but then her inner confusion simply compounded as she began to feel secure that he had the qualities not to end up like his partner, the qualities which she knew she did not have.

As her thoughts returned to the pistol, she noticed Lee loading the clip into it.

'OK, now we're going to use the weapon against the target. That paper square is the same size as the chest of a man. When I say "go" I want you to draw the weapon and put three rounds into it.'

Jane nodded.

She couldn't believe the noise it made and the number of birds that swept up into the sky from the surrounding trees. As the beating of hundreds of wings subsided they could hear Gemma wailing in the car. Through her ringing ears she heard Lee saying, 'Jane, what about the other two rounds? Two more rounds down on the target in the next five seconds please!'

Johnson did not linger on the Island. He took a bus from Lake to Ryde and then one to Yarmouth as soon as Jane was able to give him £200. Her parents had realised that something was wrong, of course, but he did not want to find out how much they had already learned of their son-in-law's difficulties during Jane's recent visit.

Although he was a Londoner, Johnson always found the ferry trip back from the Island touched emotions in him. It was leaving a self-contained, vaguely innocent world, steeped in the old-fashioned values of its ageing population and heading back to the unpleasantness of 1990s England. Now his melancholy was accentuated by guilt at having left his wife and child behind. They had a plan, but that didn't stop him feeling he should be protecting them. But now he had to disappear and so did Jane and Gemma. Jane had her own hunches about what could be done to guarantee their safety and she intended to play those in her own way.

Johnson knew that the Security Service had very considerable powers to track them. He had spent much of the time before leaving the Island making out two copies of a code which he and Jane would use over the phone. It was a simple equivalent of the one-time pad used by espionage agents for decades, a series of tables in which letters could be converted into other letters or numbers. When they spoke on the phone, they could arrange meetings in code – one which would be virtually impossible for the spooks to break quickly. He had already come to the conclusion that the phone conversation with MacFadyen after his visit to the dentist had resulted in Dave's murder and very nearly his own. Every few minutes Johnson found himself coming back to the guilt at his carelessness which alternated with his terror about what would have happened but for his wife's early return.

It took him more than an hour by public transport to get from Lymington to where he had left his Escort. He smiled when he noticed the flattened grass beside the driver's door.

An hour later, the Escort was heading up the M3, when he turned off at the Fleet Services area. Johnson put a tenner's petrol into the car. Money would be his Achilles' heel. He and Jane didn't have enough for him to stay underground for long.

He went to one of the phone booths and dialled the familiar number.

'DCI Rickett please. It's DS Johnson.'

'Johnson?' Rickett came on the line.

'Do you know about MacFadyen?'

'Yes, where are you?'

'I can't say.'

'Don't be stupid, you've got to come in and give a statement. Or would you rather be the prime suspect?'

'Even you're not that bad a detective.'

'His blood is all over your house. It doesn't look very good fleeing the scene of a murder, Johnson.'

Lee understood that his own house was probably being taken apart at that very moment by Forensic. 'Don't talk crap. The two officers who dropped my wife off will tell you what time they were there. She's my alibi. They tried to kill me too, or haven't the SOCOs told you my bedroom was doused in petrol and a fair amount of my blood too?'

'I don't think you did it, Johnson, but if you go on the run who's going to believe you?'

'I've got to keep my head down. I don't want to give MI5 another chance to kill me.'

'MI5? You don't believe that, do you?'

'I've not got any other explanation.'

'It was mates of Doherty, those Scouse nutters,' Rickett said, a little uncertainly.

'No, they wanted copies of the files. They got MacFadyen's and killed him and they wanted my set.'

'You copied them?'

'Yes.'

'And you made a fanny of me in front of Travis without telling him that you had copied them?'

'You made a fanny of yourself, boss,' Johnson said, jotting down the MI5 man's name.

'You're a lousy piece of shit, Johnson. You were suspended as of this morning. That's where your visit to Charles Denton got you, dickhead. The Head of CID says we should get rid of you ASAP. What have you done with that 9mm personal protection weapon you've got? We didn't find it at your house.'

'I've mislaid it; you can have it back as soon as I find it.'

'Don't be an arsehole, Johnson—'

He put the receiver down and walked across the car park towards the Escort. Any hope Johnson had entertained that he might get a fair hearing from the Head of CID or even the commissioner had evaporated. He tried to put this out of his mind and worry instead about the practicalities of making himself invisible. As he was strolling back, Johnson noticed another dark blue '87 Escort 1.6 GL. He walked around the car and studied it closely. He took a note of the registration number and when the tax disc expired. The upholstery was the wrong colour: other than that it wasn't a bad Ringer – that's what the IRA called the cars which it used to beat the vehicle registration computers in Northern Ireland.

I-95 from Baltimore to Washington is much like any other freeway, a river of dull concrete meandering through the boredom of the American automotive landscape. Anybody who knew Hal Canning would not have found it easy to understand what he was doing driving a '78 Ford pickup past those exit signs, fast food outlets and gas pumps. Canning wore a greasy baseball cap, lumber shirt and jeans. As far as the Agency was concerned, Canning's use of the vehicle and his occasional absences from Langley were needed to meet 'confidential informants'. It was not unusual even for very senior CIA officers to maintain a handful of sources which they might rendezvous with occasionally.

In fact, the lengths to which Canning went to disguise himself on these visits owed nothing to the tradecraft of meeting agents and everything to his desire never to be placed in the same position which he had put himself into as a young man in London all those years ago. Canning's visits to Baltimore did not involve going to the 'combat zone' of sleazy cinemas and adult bookstores but to a lower-middle-class suburb where he would have sex with a young girl he knew only as Maria. He had found Maria through a contact magazine. The ad had promised 'broadminded adults ready to share family experiences'.

Canning had the radio tuned to a country station – something he would never normally do but which seemed to fit with the part. He called himself 'Chuck' on these trips and found himself using redneck words to people in Taco Bell or the gas station. He knew he was doing it but found the role-playing quite thrilling. When he went to Baltimore he was usually in a state of nervous anticipation. He didn't do it often, only when the pictures he held in his mind when he made love to his wife began to fade and needed to be replaced. Coming back from Baltimore he experienced a mixture of satisfaction and guilt. He would hum along to the radio, even though he didn't really know the songs, making mistakes like a self-conscious child trying to sing a song he has never been taught. But it was the knowledge that he had penetrated a child only hours before which made Hal mess up the songs.

For some years after his conversation with the two MI5 men in London, Canning had kept his desires in check. He had become frustrated, morose and, he would often remind himself, experienced the only really difficult patch in his marriage. Things had unravelled again on an Agency trip to Thailand in 1977. It had just been too easy there and all for five bucks. There had actually been a succession of Marias during the last few years, all provided by the same couple in Baltimore. Canning did not understand how they persuaded people to lend their daughters for sex, but the sums of money involved were not enormous. He speculated that the fathers or mothers of these children were beholden to the Schmidts themselves for various sexual favours.

The current Maria was close to losing the bloom of childhood which Canning searched for. He had been with her a couple of times during the last few years. In truth, 'Maria' was a small, poorly-developed Hispanic girl of thirteen. The Schmidts had convinced Canning that she was nine: they had learned early in their trade that their clients would believe virtually anything they wanted to about the sexual partners they craved.

Washington, so the joke at Central Intelligence goes, is a place surrounded on all sides by reality. Canning called the Beltway which encircled the capital the Reality Expressway. Now he steered the pickup onto it, towards the Agency garage in Crystal City where he would shake off the trappings of

Chuck, his paedophile *alter ego*, and don the charcoal grey suit and Brooks Brothers tie of the CIA's Deputy Director for Intelligence.

Johnson found a good camping store in Kingston Upon Thames. He had removed a sleeping bag and his Goretex anorak from his house the night before, but there were quite a few other things he needed. Johnson bought a small camping gas stove, a foam sleeping-bag mat, a dark green groundsheet, small shovel, torch and, most importantly, a waterproof bivvy bag – a man-sized tent which would allow him to stop his sleeping bag getting wet in all but the worst weather. After buying these goods, Johnson had only £17. He decided to go to Safeways. Johnson bought food there and one or two other items, including toilet rolls. He left with £52, having used his Switch card to draw cash.

It was on his way back from the supermarket to the car that Johnson had his greatest stroke of luck of the day. Prior to going to the supermarket he had spent two hours cruising around suburban streets trying to find a good match for his car. It was typical that you couldn't find one when you were looking for it. But as he carried his shopping he noticed, parked near the public library, a dark blue '87 Ford Escort 1.6GL with the right colour seats and a tax disc which expired in the same month as his. Even better, Johnson realised the owner of the car was probably a young man, as its back seat was strewn with dirty football kit, cassettes and several letters. These all had the same name and address and had been opened. Johnson now had not only the registration number of a car that looked exactly like his, but he also had something the IRA considered vital for a really good Ringer – he could give the police an alias with address to match if he was ever stopped.

That afternoon he travelled to a garage in Roehampton

where he had known criminals obtain numberplates before on a no-questions-asked basis. They cost him £40, but he considered it a good investment. With a vehicle now registered to Mr Paul Rampton of 16 Nelson Crescent, Sutton, Surrey, Johnson believed his chances of evading any dragnet which the police or MI5 might put into operation had been considerably improved. During the training course on which he had met Elaine Stevens in Manchester, Johnson had heard of a plan to introduce a numberplate-recognition computer able to scan the output from the traffic monitoring cameras all over London. He did not think the system had yet come into service, but it comforted him to know that his counter-measures would now defeat it.

As he drove up the hill towards Wimbledon Common, he felt satisfaction that something was going his way at last. He couldn't help a boyish excitement at the thought of sleeping out and cooking up some of the food with his newly-acquired stove.

After parking the car in a residential street, he walked towards the Common carrying the things he would need for the night. It was still not dark as he struck across the open grass in search of a place sufficiently deep in undergrowth to hide him.

Quite quickly, Johnson realised that things would be very difficult on the Common. Even at nine and ten there were joggers in the most surprising places. He noted one or two gay-looking men, presumably in search of trade, and straight lovers too, teenagers giggling and stomping around in the undergrowth. Johnson felt that using the stove was impractical under these circumstances and ate his baked beans cold with tinned ham. He had used his groundsheet and bivvy bag to create what soldiers called a 'basha', a sheltered, hidden sleeping place.

He wriggled into the bag, having repeated his old routine of placing his boots with their necks under his head as a pillow and the soles facing outwards. The stale smell of down inside his sleeping bag kept too long folded and unaired in his attic pricked his nostrils. It took him a long time to get off to sleep. He thought about finding a better place and about how he would guarantee his safety and the safety of his family, but the thought that he could not expunge as he lay, wriggling in the search for sleep, was of what would have happened if the lighter thrown at him the night before had found the petrol soaking his body.

Chapter Twenty-Three

The radio on the kitchen sideboard pumped out the *Today* programme. Speculation was rife in the City of an interest-rate cut to defend Sterling. Jane Johnson was no expert on financial news but she interpreted the news to mean that Britain was continuing its steady slide into economic torpor. She had decided to leave that morning – she had already been on the Island more than twenty-four hours and, as Lee had pointed out, she had to move frequently. She and Lee had arranged a schedule of calling times and meetings which she was terrified she would forget. Against his advice, she had made a note of them on the back of an Access slip and put it into her purse. As she and Gemma tucked into their cornflakes at the kitchen table, Jane felt the rising tension of knowing that she must leave and that she would have to explain certain things to her parents in order to have their help.

Jane's mother, Pat, shuffled into the kitchen in her slippers and an unseasonally thick dressing gown.

'Mum, I'm going to have to go back to the mainland for a couple of days.'

'All right,' Pat said.

'Can you look after Gems while I'm gone?'

'Of course, we'd love to.' But Pat could read the concern in the five-year-old's face. 'Gemma, run and see if you can find grandpa upstairs and tell him his tea's nearly ready.'

She scurried off, clutching a piece of toast, a transgression overlooked by her elders.

'What exactly is going on?' Pat asked.

'Lee's in big trouble with somebody, we don't know who: we think it's the Secret Service. We've got to straighten things out.'

'You know you're welcome here for as long as you like, but wouldn't it be better for the little one if you went home and worked things out there?'

'We can't go back. I don't want to go back. I wouldn't want to be at home now.'

'What on earth has happened?' Pat's eyes began to cloud and she sat down beside her daughter.

'Our phones have been tapped; somebody came in and tried to kill Lee.' Jane too was close to tears now. 'I don't want to go back, I don't know if I'll ever be happy living there again, and I feel partly to blame.' Jane told the story of Dodge's visit in the guise of a phone engineer.

The tears had begun to trace across Pat's wrinkled cheek.

'I can't stand the thought that I allowed our home to be violated like that,' Jane said.

'Don't be so harsh on yourself, how were you to know what was going on?'

'I know, I know. But I've got to do what I can to get us out of this mess. Lee's got to disappear now; he can't show his face. There's lots of things I've got to do for both of us. You'll look after my baby, won't you?'

'I'm so sorry my love. You know your Dad and I will do anything we can to help.'

'I know Mum.' Jane put her arms around Pat's shoulders and kissed her. 'Gemma may be in danger when I'm not here: never let her out of your sight. Try to stop her playing at the front of the house, where people might see her.'

'I'll try, but you know what a handful she can be. I shan't sleep a wink with the worrying.'

Jane readied herself for the journey. There were a number of people she intended to see in London: she would stay with friends. She walked down to Sandown station to catch the clattering old London tube train which had been palmed off on the Island some years ago. She wedged herself into one of the seats and tried to read her *Mail on Sunday*. She couldn't help but remember lying on the sleeping bag in the New Forest with Lee after they'd made love the other night. The next morning, after her lesson with the gun, they had sat in the car together. He had held her hand so tight it had hurt and whispered so that their daughter would not hear. 'He's killed before; he'll kill you if he gets the chance. If you see that little bastard again, don't take the slightest chance, drop him.' That's what Lee had told her. It was the Army training talking, she knew. 'The meanest person walks away alive, hesitation means you'll be the dead one,' he had said. She had been shocked by the incongruity of it, these obscene words about killing and 'double taps to the head', the morning after making love under that canopy of stars. There was no point being naive about her husband, she thought, as the old veteran of the Northern Line pushed and pulled at her, swaying on the uneven tracks. When they taught him to survive in Ulster, they had stirred the animal in him.

The train stopped; other passengers entered the carriage, eyeing up the free seats. Jane picked up her battered Mulberry bag from the space next to her, feeling the weight of the 9mm pistol as she rested it on her lap.

Lee had gathered his gear and moved off from the Common early, about six. He had slept little; today he would try his ideas about better hiding places. Lee understood he'd have to go further out of the centre, but didn't want to hide out in the countryside: it was too far from what he'd come to do. He had driven down from the Common to Raynes Park, an ugly dormitory on the main line to Waterloo. In the station toilets, he shaved and decided he would treat himself to some breakfast. He found a greasy around the corner and settled in with a cup of tea, and a full fry for £2, which seemed reasonable to him. It was then that he noticed the *News of the World* sitting on the counter. 'Can I have a look at your paper, mate?' he asked the fat, stubbly Cypriot who had taken his order. The man grunted and tossed the newspaper over. Well, they had made the front page. The headline, 'Hero Cop's Gruesome Murder', stood out over a dated photo of MacFadyen. Below it, Johnson read the breathless text:

Police are hunting the perverted killers of a hero detective who foiled an armed robbery two months ago. The sick criminals hacked off David MacFadyen's head with a kitchen knife at his London flat on Friday night. A source close to the hunt for the cop-killers described the assailants as 'no better than animals'. MacFadyen earned a bravery award when he disarmed four armed robbers in London. One of his colleagues last night told the *News of the World* that the ace detective's murderers were out for revenge. The police source said prime suspects for the murders were friends of four Liverpool robbers arrested by MacFadyen. The four are awaiting trial and cannot be named for legal reasons. The 35-year-old detective was found murdered at his London flat. Police colleagues said MacFadyen, who was single, was married to the force.

Johnson wondered whether Rickett had talked to the reporter. The journalist had certainly spoken to somebody: he knew about the kitchen knife. There was no mention of his own disappearance in the article. It was a catalogue of exaggerations and distortions and it was putting on record the idea that his partner had been killed by Sancho Doherty's mates. Ireland had nurtured a dislike of the media in Johnson. Reading the

News of the World, he decided that taking his story to the press could only be a last resort.

He drove to Blackheath after breakfast. He parked a good distance away from Denton's flat, but he had come to eyeball it. Johnson had toyed with several ideas about contacting Denton. He found himself fantasising about cornering Denton at night, in his bedroom when his mind was nagging him with thoughts of death. How well would Denton speak with the barrel of a nine milli in his mouth. How would that little shit like it if the tables were turned? First question: did those three bastards who visited me at midnight belong to your firm or have you been running a little freelance operation? Second question: if they did belong to MI5 and I let you live, will you give me the evidence I need to get these people off my back? Alternatively, if you were freelancing, give me one good reason not to blow your head off?

As he walked past two laughing children with a sorry-looking homemade kite, he got his mind back on track and told himself these were stupid thoughts. He wasn't going to kill Denton. Apart from anything else, he'd given Jane the gun. There were various places he could have picked up an illegal shooter – but that would cost him £300 or £400 and he didn't have that kind of cash.

On the open heath, there were no good places to hide himself with a view of Denton's flat. Johnson kept moving, in case he was being observed. Occasionally he sat on a bench, looking paternally over towards kids rushing around the grass. He had considered staking out the flat, seeing whether anybody interesting turned up, logging Denton's movements. It was the kind of work he had done in Ireland; he was good at it; but he couldn't see how it was going to help him put his life and the lives of his wife and daughter back together. Maybe he should do it anyway. 'Don't confuse activity with achievement,' he had sometimes told green new subalterns in the Sappers. But Johnson knew that this dictum was ignored every day in garrisons of the British Army: much of life in the peacetime forces was activity for the sole purpose of preventing everybody asking too many questions about why they were there. Anyway, once he'd established Denton's movements and who he was meeting, he'd need to find out what was in the second package. In the meantime, keeping Denton under observation might stop him surrendering to despair, falling victim to the longing which was already stirring in him, to be beside his wife and child again. As he turned to watch Denton's flat for the last time, he could see the outline of a man at the window.

Denton had not spotted Johnson as he sat down with a cup of herbal tea. He wanted to get down to work, but he couldn't help surveying the clutter of his flat. The photographs of his school, of Irene and him by their Austin Seven on a weekend outing to the Essex coast in 1963, the rows of literary classics which he had always promised himself he would read. Soon he would be packing everything up, heading off for retirement, what little of it he would have. Arrangements for his departure from Blackheath weighed on his mind more and more these days. His last day at GWS would be very soon – Personnel had told him they were recalculating the amount of leave the Service owed him. Retirement day was rushing forward.

The goons at Panther had intimated at first that both MacFadyen and Johnson had been 'taken care of', but the press had only mentioned the Scotsman. He took some satisfaction that the police and press had picked up the idea that the killing was related to the Doherty arrests: it had been his own inspiration.

The intercepts on Johnson's home and office phones had yielded nothing since that fateful night. Denton had overheard somebody in the restaurant at Gower Street mentioning that the Legal Adviser had put together a team to examine the whole saga. Denton had hoped to find out more about

Johnson's fate by using his knowledge of the directorate's operational database on the computer, but Travis was outside the counter-espionage area and used a different compartment of the Service's electronic mind.

Denton had spent the weekend putting together a package for his masters. It was not his last: that would have to await Canning's final delivery. His work had always divided between what he had done in the office and his out-of-hours efforts. Over the years the pace had varied very considerably. He had spent nearly ten years as a training officer. There was very little he could offer then, just the tittle-tattle of who was in and who was out in the Service. Canning's career, by contrast, had rarely troughed, although some years had been spent in postings which were not of such overriding interest. As long as Denton had Canning, his out-of-hours importance had always been maintained. Denton did not regard his record in the Service as a poor one. After all, it was remarkable enough that he had made it in at all considering where he had come from. He accepted that chance had played a part – it certainly had in allowing him to carry on for the last few years, when such change had swept through the world. Ultimately he had to concede that it was Canning who had really kept him in the first division. He thought about the successor who was being trained to run Canning and he could not help but feel jealous that the orchestra of his particular theatre of espionage would play on under a different conductor.

Chapter Twenty-Four

Nicola Dawson had received a summons to appear in court in London. Ensconced in her Brighton bedsit, surrounded by cigarette smoke and empty Special Brew cans, she did not take this news well. She had put Johnson out of her mind; she hadn't trusted him – but now she wondered whether she had anything to lose by talking to him. She rummaged through the tissues, tampons and cigarette packets in her huge handbag and plucked out a bus ticket with 'Lee Johnson' and the detective's phone number written on it. After pulling on her Doc Martens and straightening her hair, Nicola went to her usual phone box and rang the number. It rang for a long time; in fact until somebody from the neighbouring office had come through.

'CID, DC Merton,' a voice replied.

'Lee Johnson, please.'

'He's not here, love. Who's calling?' She was silent, unsure of what to say. 'Hello, who is it?' he asked.

'Can you just tell him Nicola called –' she looked at her watch – 'and that I'll ring back at four o'clock tomorrow afternoon.'

'You can try, missus, but we haven't seen him for days.'

'I'll try anyway. Thanks.'

Travis's office had filled with an assortment of people brought in from specialised departments of the Service to discuss their new mission. That day, Travis had chosen BASTION from the weekly list of codenames generated by the JIC Secretariat. Without the JIC's randomly-generated list, MI5 and MI6 officers would constantly be displaying their lack of imagination by chosing similar codenames, usually plucked from sport or ancient history. A team of three other officers, each backed by an assistant, had crowded into his panelled office and were sharing out cups of coffee. Some had already been working on the project before the weekend.

'Having reviewed the papers, it's clear that Johnson could have learnt everything he said to you and the former DG from a couple of the files,' his principal investigator, Monica Davies, said. She was thirty-eight years old, a fast-stream entrant who had just finished two years in Northern Ireland running sources and was about to take up a section head's post in counter-espionage. The DG described Davies as 'brilliant'; Travis couldn't help but wonder whether the DG's own pedigree wasn't too close to Davies's to dent her objectivity. He had quickly noticed that Davies had a slight lisp and a fearsome nervous twitch. He wondered whether it was her nature, or too long in Ireland. 'Obviously the records for the files indicate they haven't left the Service, so it's fairly clear we must be dealing with copies,' she concluded.

'Monica, as you'll have seen in the press, things have changed quite a bit since we were given this task last week. MacFadyen is dead and Johnson has disappeared. Johnson has gone walkabout with a 9mm pistol. DG informed me this morning that we should consider Operation BASTION to extend beyond its original remit as a leak inquiry. In order to find out what's been happening we will have to find Johnson.'

'Knowing the unit he served with in Ulster, I can't think of anybody harder to track down.'

'Where are his wife and kid?' Sam Boswell asked. A couple of grades lower than Davies and in his forties, Boswell had been brought in as a specialist in vetting.

'We don't know, they've gone too. But you could start by checking her parents and friends, intercepting phones where you feel necessary. Move quickly, don't worry about paperwork. It's all covered under the original warrant for Johnson,' Travis replied.

'What about a NEWMARKET trace?' Monica Davies asked.

'We had a memo from Special Support telling us to confine NEWMARKET requests to terrorists because of overload on some datalink or other,' said Tim Ashman. An impressively fit figure despite his balding pate and the fact that he was well into his fifties, Ashman was attached as the team's technical officer. He had spent eighteen years in the Royal Signal Regiment, before reaching sergeant major and switching into MI5.

'Pardon my ignorance, but what is a NEWMARKET?' Boswell asked.

'It's our interception of the cash card and credit card warning systems operated by the banks,' Ashman explained. 'Once you've got the suspect's account number it's very straightforward. It's how we knew that we would find those Paddies we lifted in Nottingham last year living close to a particular branch of the Midland—'

'Use it,' Travis said, reasserting control over the meeting. 'Tell Special Support to ring me if they have a problem. Sam, have you checked up on Denton at all?'

'Well, I've been through his bank account records for the past fifteen years. Nothing untoward. He's accumulated £22,000 in his deposit account over the last few years, but that's hardly surprising as he's a widower. He looks pretty clean in that respect.'

'Vetting?' Travis asked.

'That's a bit tricky: his two PV interviews were done by some SB sergeant in Salisbury, who I would wager will now be either dead or impossible to find.'

'It can't be that difficult? Surely we can stretch to a return ticket to Wiltshire?' Monica Davies inquired.

'Salisbury, Rhodesia, Monica,' Boswell replied deadpan, savouring a rare victory over the GI fast stream.

'Is there anything suspicious about the interviews themselves?' Travis probed.

'We don't have them.'

'Sorry?'

'We just have a short note from the Branch in Salisbury giving the names and addresses of the people interviewed and basically saying that Denton is a good egg.'

'Oh that's really good, that is!' Travis rolled his eyes in exaggerated incredulity.

'It's not that uncommon for somebody who came into the Service from a Commonwealth country that long ago,' said Boswell.

'Why should we suspect Denton at all?' Monica Davies asked.

'There's no firm reason,' Travis began. 'The DG believes we should look at him as virtually the only person left who was party to the original operation and of course, Denton told us when he reported Johnson that Johnson had accused him of blackmail.'

'Do we suspect Denton of blackmail?' she asked.

'We do have to ask why Johnson would drop in on him in the first place, whether we believe Denton's version or not. We have to establish exactly what excited Johnson's suspicions.'

'A connection between Denton and the files which Johnson says were recovered after the deposit box robbery,' she said.

'Monica, I think you and I need to give Denton a proper interview.'

'There is another direction we could proceed,' Davies said, shifting forward in her seat. 'It's fairly clear that whether our security was breached verbally or whether, as I think we all now believe, copies of documents went missing, the breach appears to refer exclusively to Operation RACETRACK. There's only one really unusual thing about that operation, and that was the gentleman of unsavoury lust who accidentally became one of the *dramatis personae*.'

'And . . . ?' Boswell prompted, while wondering when she would finish showing off and get to the point.

'And therefore we probably need to find out a bit more about that gentleman. It might allow us to establish exactly how the papers went adrift and whether somebody in this Service was responsible, either for personal gain or for the benefit of another state.'

'I'm sure it won't surprise you to learn that QUASAR's identity is a matter of great sensitivity even within these walls, even today,' said Travis.

'Well, it's pretty clear he's American,' she replied.

'I can't go any further than that I'm afraid, Monica. DG regards his identity to be a matter of exceptional sensitivity.'

Boswell bridled at this. 'That seems a little odd, if you don't mind me saying, Donald. After all, we're all cleared to buggery, pardon my French. There aren't really meant to be any secrets in this Service that can be concealed from a tight operational group like this one.'

'It's not a matter of concealment,' Travis began, understanding the indefensibility of this position. 'I know, I'm batting on a sticky wicket. You're all smart enough to realise that QUASAR still occupies a very senior position in the United States. As it stands, DG has specifically told me to restrict his identity.'

'Given his current status, it's fairly obvious that QUASAR would be an eminently suitable target for blackmail,' said Monica Davies.

Travis agreed to ask the Director General to rethink her decision in the light of the fact that the team felt they had a need to know.

* * *

On the floor above, Denton was scrolling through the menus on his computer, killing time. He was scanning the counter-espionage department staff list when he noticed:

Davies, M. V. detached Op BASTION

He saw that the file had been altered that very morning. Denton went to the counter-espionage branch list of current operations and typed the command 'fi bastion'. After a few seconds the computer returned the message 'can't find'. Seeing that this officer was serving on an operation outside the Branch, Denton's curiosity was aroused. He had suspected for some time that the Service would be responding to Johnson's allegations: perhaps this was proof. Under the system of restricted access passwords, Denton was not meant to be able to check the operational files of other branches. But he had already found a number of loopholes in this security system. He went to the list of current communications interception warrants and typed 'fi bastion' once more. The header for an OP BASTION communications interception warrant appeared. He could see only that it had been created the previous week and that further enquiries were referred to 'LA to DG'. Denton could not get into the file without a further password, but he had already discovered enough to become convinced that Operation BASTION and Monica Davies merited further attention.

Johnson had spent all day looking forward to his journey to the phone box. He had found a much better hiding place and the old-fashioned red box stood fifteen minutes walk away. He had arranged to ring Jane that evening at her friend Tania's, at seven o'clock. He dialled the number to find it engaged. He repeated the action: once, twice – busy again. He glanced at his watch: 7.07. So it went on until he looked at his watch again: 7.16. Johnson was becoming increasingly annoyed with Jane. Hadn't she told Tania that she was expecting a call?

A few minutes later he got a ringing tone.

'Jane?'

'Yes.'

'It's me. Why was the phone engaged?'

'Tania, talking to her new fella. Sorry.'

'She certainly gives it GBH of the ear'ole, your friend Tania.' He said nothing for a few moments, regretting that he had allowed his anxiety to spoil this moment.

'Are you all right Lee, is everything OK?'

'Yeah, I've had trouble finding a nice place to live but I've got somewhere that'll be good for a while. How are you, my darling?'

'Missing you.'

'Me too.'

'Wishing we could be flattening grass in the New Forest.'

'Christ, me too. It's proving more difficult than I thought. I thought it would be like being back in the Sappers, but it's . . . it's just miserable.' As he made this confession, Lee understood how depressing the last few days had really been. Lee thought he could hear her sniff. 'Are you all right?'

'Yeah, I'll live.'

'How's the little one?'

'Mum says she's a bit miz without us.'

'I was desperate to phone there tonight, but I reckon I can't risk it. They would trace the call back too fast. You've not rung her from anywhere near where you're staying?'

'No, I've been following orders,' said Jane.

'Have you found anything out yet?'

'No, I'm going to get started tomorrow.'

'Listen, we're going to have to rethink who we give our stuff to. I spoke to my boss and he told me the big boss had fired me. So I think we're going to have to go outside my firm.'

'Yes, I've been having some thoughts on that too,' she said. 'I think the higher up they are the better.'

'Shall we meet up tomorrow evening?'

'Yes please. Where?'

'Are you standing by?'

'Yes, fire away.'

'We'll meet at NBVXPZDFGRS at FTRSUY o'clock.'

Jane went to the first sheet of code which Lee had made out for her on the Island and began transcribing the letters.

'Fine, understood,' she said, feeling triumphant.

'I've still got another fifty-two pence. I've had a couple of ideas.'

They carried on talking until the money had run out. Lee walked up from the main road, past the sign reading 'Kingston Down Golf Club' and up a lane leading past its clubhouse. He skipped over a fence and disappeared into the trees, making his way to a point deep in the undergrowth which he reckoned to be the furthest from any of the fairways. Johnson had discovered that an exclusive golf course was a good deal quieter than Wimbledon Common, except perhaps at weekends. But he didn't intend to be there by then.

After returning to his basha, Johnson lit up the camping gas stove, opened a can of beer and prepared his first cooked supper for days.

Chapter Twenty-Five

It was a little after four on a rainy Brighton afternoon as Nicola Dawson stood in her usual phone box listening to the unanswered rings of a phone in Shepherds Bush police station. She had decided to let it sound a few more times.

Then at last. 'CID, DC Merton.'

'Hello, is Lee Johnson there please?'

'Are you the woman I spoke to the other day? Nicola was it?'

'Yes.'

'He's not turned up I'm afraid, love.'

'Oh. Did you tell him I rang?'

'I haven't seen him and I'm not sure I will.'

'What do you mean?'

The detective chose his words carefully: 'He's just not likely to be around for a while.'

'Look I'm desperate to talk to him. I need to speak to him quickly.'

'It's police business right?'

'Yes and it's urgent.'

'Well I don't know anything about his cases and if I'm being honest – I mean between you, me and the lamp-post – he's disappeared; we don't know where he is.'

'He's disappeared?' Her spirits sank.

'Can anybody else help?'

'No, I was just hoping he might turn out to be a friend. Bye.' She rang off.

Nicola walked out of the box, banging its door furiously. She passed the parked red Sierra which Dodge and Phil, his Geordie mate, had taken down to Brighton. Dodge was on a carphone to Pinchman, who sat in the flat in Hammersmith where their bug on Johnson's phone was monitored.

'It was her all right,' said Pinchman.

'Understood,' Dodge replied and cut the line, throwing the phone aside and starting the car. They cruised along a short way behind her, like punters searching for tarts.

'Not a bad arse. Shall we screw her first?' Phil asked.

'Don't be a cunt. We're supposed to be fucking professionals.' Dodge had flushed with anger. He was already psyching himself up.

Dodge rang the bell on the flat. She opened it on the chain, but with one smart push Dodge broke it, sending her flying back into the room. Quickly Dodge was on top of her, taping up her mouth and holding her limbs. Nicola hardly struggled at all. Dodge told Phil: 'Run the bath.'

There were a few moments of thrashing about after they dropped her in, but soon her struggle had been followed by a stream of bubbles from her nostrils and mouth. Nicola had only emerged from the cold embrace of her fear a few moments before her death, realising belatedly that these men were not after loot or rape but intended to kill her. Dodge had bruised her neck slightly, holding her under, but Nicola's body would not be found for six days, and after that period the marks were academic. In her death throes, Nicola Dawson had scratched Dodge's cheek, but that wound had largely healed by the time policemen, gagging at the stench, zipped into a body bag the little girl who Hal Canning had used for sex all those years ago. Phil had looked on through the bathroom door while Dodge did it, his face flushed, a turmoil of mixed emotions, a nervous apprentice who dreaded the moment when he might be called upon to commit a similar act but sensed that he would not be accepted into Dodge's strange brotherhood until he did.

Tim Ashman, the Op BASTION technical officer, had gone down to Shepherds Bush with Ted, his assistant, a man of similar, middle age but larger waistline. The Met had been asked to clear their visit. Curious detectives had to be shooed away as the two specialists began combing the CID section for bugging devices. Ted lifted the receiver of Johnson's phone and dialled the speaking clock. Ashman then used a portable scanner which raced through the frequencies used by commercially available bugging devices until it found one giving out a particularly strong signal. The display on the machine put up the word 'locked' alongside the frequency and a measure of signal strength. Ashman carried the scanner into the corridor and plugged a headset into it.

'At the third stroke it will be ten forty-nine precisely.'

'It's wired all right, you'd better start at the receiver end,' Ashman said.

It didn't take Ted long to unscrew the small junction box on the floor and find the device.

'Dear oh dear, look at this, boss.'

Ashman peered over. 'A V-50? Don't like the look of that connection.'

'Whoever did this rode in on horseback,' said Ted with disgust. 'Look at this bodged hookup!'

'Done in a hurry, that's for sure.'

Neither of the men made any attempt to remove the device. Instead they carried on scanning different frequencies. Then Ted had an idea.

'Shall we get a call in from outside in case there's another one outside the PBX system?' Which led them twenty minutes later to the device in the junction box on the street outside.

They carried on working throughout the morning before moving to Johnson's house to begin a sweep there.

At four o'clock Ashman arrived back at Gower Street and went to Monica Davies's office.

'I'm glad we decided to check Johnson's phones,' he began.

'Find something?' She looked up from her transcripted intercepts.

'I'll say: more wiring than the Blackpool illuminations. We've found three devices so far.'

'Who's doing it?'

'Your guess is as good as mine. It's commercial gear, nothing too flash, but then past experience teaches us that foreign governments often use off-the-shelf stuff too. Put in by an amateur, mind you.'

'Can we find the place where the intercepts were being recorded?' she asked.

'Very tricky. The receiver will give off a small signal that we can detect but we would need to get the bugs transmitting in order to stand a chance of homing in on it. If Ted rings the speaking clock every hour for the next few weeks then even if the person monitoring the devices is as big a moron as the one who put them in, it's not going to take them long to suss out that somebody's homing in on them.'

'We'll have to be imaginative, Tim. Let's say that Ted is a member of the local CID who keeps nipping out of his own office to use Johnson's phone to call my secretary who happens to be his lover. Well of course, being lovers, and married ones at that,' she smiled knowingly at Ashman, 'they might go on and on talking for thirty, forty minutes at a time. Would that be what you needed to home in?'

'Well, we'd certainly be in with a chance: the devices we found have a pretty short range and if we assume that the reception point is somewhere within that distance of both

Johnson's home and office, then that narrows the options considerably. We'll get Fred onto it.' 'Fred' was a specially modified Bedford van, designed for the specific purpose of finding radio receivers, employing glorified TV detector van technology.

'Good. We'll have to think of some excuses for other people to use the phone too, perhaps calling out for a pizza, invent a new detective who's been given Johnson's desk?'

'Yes, OK.' Ashman was now convinced that they might find the receiver station.

'Anything else?' Monica Davies asked.

'Nothing really, we'll get onto it.' Ashman turned to leave, but then remembered something. 'Oh, by the way, we thought that while we had access to the CID offices we might as well take the opportunity to install the special facilities which Mr Travis wanted for monitoring Detective Chief Inspector Rickett's office and phone.'

'Well done, you've saved some mileage on Service vehicles!'

'We aim to please,' he said, making his way through the door. 'Ted did a lovely job on them.'

By 6.15 p.m., Johnson was conducting his counter-surveillance drills outside Southfields tube station. He had not thought, when he arranged to meet his wife there, that virtually the first person he would run into as he came out of the station was the flower seller he had bought lilies from with David MacFadyen. For a moment he felt quite ill, recalling again the events of a few nights before. But then he savoured the memory of MacFadyen's thoughtfulness and his knowledge of the most unexpected things. The flower seller did not appear to recognise Lee, but then that wasn't surprising given the number of customers he must have. While he lost himself in this reverie, Lee was not paying attention to the area around the station and whether it was safe.

The main entrance looked onto a busy crossroads; it was difficult to monitor – just too many passing vehicles, too many faces to try and memorise. Johnson had seen MI5's A4 Units, more popularly known as 'Watchers' in action – they had helped train his lot for Ulster and they were very good. Unlike the special Army unit he had served in, A4 surveillance teams contained a good balance of people of both sexes and a variety of ages. With 14 Intelligence Company, spotting covert surveillance was often as easy as finding two fit-looking men in their late twenties or early thirties cruising by in a newish British-made saloon. Johnson watched a fruit and veg seller across the road, a waiting cabbie: he became uncertain, nervous. They didn't seem to be watching him, but then keeping tabs on somebody by means of the most occasional, and apparently casual, glance is a basic skill of a good surveillance operator. As he weighed up who might not be what they seemed, he noticed that the flower seller was looking at him. Had he recognised his client belatedly? Or was the stallholder simply suspicious of him for hanging about in this manner? He considered a last-minute dash to the next station up the line, to return to Southfields by tube in time to stop his wife on the platform and take her elsewhere. He rejected the idea – why should he believe that the spooks had even heard their conversation, let alone deciphered the code they had used to denote the time and place of their meeting? Lee realised that it would be tricky to remain vigilant without becoming paranoid.

His thoughts were broken as he sighted her coming up the station stairs. Jane was wearing sunglasses and a raincoat which he did not recognise. Her own attempt at disguise?

'Hello, my love.' She kissed him on the cheek.

'Hi, babe, it's been too long.'

They walked together, sometimes holding hands, the few hundred yards to the place on the steep hill overlooking the station where Lee had parked his Escort. She did not appear to notice the different number plates.

'Where are we going?' she asked.

'Somewhere quiet enough to make love.'

She smiled and winked at him. As he drove, they spoke about their strange rituals, the changes in their lives apart, undercover.

'I've decided that Gems can come and stay up here,' she began. 'Tania doesn't mind having her around for a bit.'

'Don't stay there too long; is there anybody else who'll put you up?'

'I can go to Sarah's for a bit.'

'Your sister? That's a bit too obvious isn't it?'

'Well my parents' place is pretty obvious if you think about it – remember the phone calls before MacFadyen was killed – and anyway, if I bring her up here, you can see her too.'

'I'm all for that. It's like a physical pain being cut off from her.'

She stroked his hand. 'You're too good a family man to have stayed in the Army, Lee. It's one of your sweetest qualities.'

'And I'm no good at kipping in a sleeping bag any more.'

Four hours later, Lee was driving Jane towards Richmond station. They had talked and caressed for most of that time, holding one another on Lee's sleeping bag, opened out under the trees on the golf course. They had drunk a couple of beers: for a while it had all seemed like some romantic adventure.

'How much longer do we have to take this?' she asked.

'Long enough for me to stitch up Denton and for you to work on the other end.'

'Could it be months? Why don't we just take our chances and hand over what we have now?'

'We need more to nail them. We don't want all this to have happened just to see those bastards wriggle off the hook.'

'Will we ever nail them? Aren't they above the law?' Jane looked across in despair.

'Bumping people off is out of order; I don't think they'll get away with that.'

'Listen, I've been thinking we should give the stuff to an MP,' she said. 'Someone independent-minded who can act as a middleman with the CID and spooks.'

'Makes sense,' Lee replied.

The car pulled up outside the station. She moved to get out, but stopped, looking back across towards him. 'When?'

'I'll give you a ring in a day or two: there are some places I've got to check out.'

'I know your hiding place now: you may slink back one night to find me in your sleeping bag.'

'Don't be naughty!'

They kissed and she disappeared into the yawning entrance of the building. As Lee put the car into first and pulled away, he felt a deep well of despair opening up within him and wondered whether he had the will to see things through.

Chapter Twenty-Six

Jane did not feel at home at the offices of Middlebrook, Bloomfeld and Singh. Ever since John Middlebrook had told her that her hours were being cut she had begun to disengage herself from the place. She now regarded it as a rather sad solicitors' office in a part of West London too poor for it ever to be anything better. There were stacks of legal papers tied with red ribbons, discarded tomes whose covers bore the stains of coffee cups: the firm was descending into Dickensian seediness. John Middlebrook didn't care about the trappings of his job. As a radical lawyer who had qualified in the sixties he had never wanted wealth, which was just as well, as his practice of letting many poorer clients off their bills was at least in part a cause of the firm's difficulties. Middlebrook's response to Jane's late-night phone calls in which she had hinted at her and Lee's predicament had been heartening. As a veteran of the Grosvenor Square demo of '68, he fancied himself as something of a spook-spotter. In the first place that support consisted of allowing Jane to make use of the photocopier; he did not enquire why she needed it. When she finished, he summoned her into his office.

'Everything OK?' he asked.

'Fine, thank you. You've been very kind, what with me bunking off work and everything.'

'It's nothing, I owe you one. Listen, Jane, I looked these out at home, they may be of some interest – know your enemy!' He handed her a plastic bag full of books.

Jane delved into it, noticing *Spycatcher* and some more obscure titles presumably picked up during Middlebrook's earlier life: *Dirty Work*, an anthology about the CIA; *British Intelligence and Covert Action*, self-explanatory.

'You're very sweet John, I just hope I've got time to read them, I didn't expect a reading list.' She smiled weakly, wondering how she was supposed to lug useless books around.

'There's a lot in there: it might help you figure out what's happening to you and Lee.'

'Thanks again.'

'Listen, there's something else, Jane. You haven't told me exactly what's been going on – I don't expect you to. But you know me, I've been round the block a few times: it's obvious that the murder of Lee's partner is connected with all this—'

'They tried to kill Lee too.'

'What? Oh Jesus!'

'That's why we've got to hide, until we can find out how to straighten things out.'

'That's what I wanted to mention, Jane. Sooner or later it's all going to have to be settled. If the Security Service have killed a policeman or are connected with it in any way, then there are really major issues here.'

'Surviving is our only issue now, John.' She spoke quickly, passionately. 'We don't want to live like animals, like fucking Bonnie and Clyde—'

'I know, I understand – well I *think* I can understand; what I'm trying to say is this. I'm friendly with a couple of reporters, one on the *Independent*—'

'Lee doesn't want to go to the press.'

'All right, what's your idea then? Because surely it's all going to get out sooner or later.' Middlebrook was losing his temper.

'We don't want to get the press involved. Lee thinks his bosses will never let him square things up if he goes public: we need somebody who we can use as a confidential middleman with the CID and MI5, and who knows who else. We were thinking of an MP.'

'I don't know what's going on with you and Lee. It's true an MP could table some cleverly phrased questions in Parliament. I've got some contacts there too – Labour of course. You must tell us what to fish for.'

'OK, I see what you're saying. It's a kind offer. Don't you think they'd have to take it more seriously if we gave our stuff to a Tory?'

'A Tory? Who are you going to trust among that lot? It'll be thank you very much Mr and Mrs Johnson and then he'll get nobbled over dinner in his London club and you'll never hear another word about it.'

'That's the value of photocopiers, John: they insure us against that. The left is simpler for the spooks to ignore – easier for the Tory press to dismiss if it comes to that. A Tory might be better – some minister sacked by Mrs T for having a conscience or somebody who's stayed on the back benches because he was too much of an individual – I'm just thinking aloud, John.'

Middlebrook was silenced. He was surprised by her political sophistication and felt vaguely ashamed of himself for under-estimating her.

Jane said her goodbyes, told him she would keep in touch and headed off with her books and photocopies. Funny, she reflected as she walked to the tube, how some people want to involve themselves in the misfortune of others. As she passed a dustbin she considered hefting the bag of books into it. But she realised Middlebrook would expect them back at some point.

Denton did not envisage making many more runs to deposit material for his bosses. He had this one, then the last special delivery from Canning, then it would be finished. The old man put the photocopied papers into a Sainsbury's carrier bag and donned his mac, ready to leave Blackheath. He wore gloves, despite the fact that it wasn't particularly cold – that was a new precaution to keep his prints off the bag. Before setting off down the stairs to the front door, he had spent some time observing the scene outside the flat, his usual counter-surveillance drill. Now, though, he was not just fighting the complacency that comes from following procedures for thirty years. Increasingly, pain, and the effects of the drugs he took to try to keep it under control, were blunting his senses.

He had visited the doctor who had given him a little battery-powered unit which was hooked into him through a small pipe tapped into one of his veins. Every few minutes it made a bleep to indicate that it was working and pumped a little diamorphin into him. These were very small doses, but Denton knew enough about medicine to know that this little machine and its supply of opiates hooked him into what they called 'palliative care' or, less ambiguously, 'terminal care', at the hospital. He who goes on diamorphin, Denton reflected, is on the last lap of the cancer marathon. The doctors were impressed by the way Denton still moved around as much as he did, and they were surprised too that he had held up so well psychologically. As he moved out of the front door, he heard a bleep from under his coat and allowed himself a smile. Was this any way for a secret agent to be carrying on? If there was one thing he had always known, it was that there would never be laurels and public plaudits for somebody who had spent his life in the shadows – but at that moment he longed for somebody to give him a little recognition for carrying on to deliver the goods even while a machine pumped morphine to dull his pain.

On the bus, his mind drifted to the way his tasks had changed over the years. Early on, everything was based on spying, MI5's order of battle, the CIA's operations in Britain or eastern Europe. For the last couple of years, since his 'rebirth', there had been different priorities. He knew that the paper headed 'French Interest Exchange Rate Strategy', written by a member of the Joint Intelligence Committee Economic Assessment Section, would probably be of most interest to his masters. The new obsession with matters economic was difficult to detect in the Registry, where the reams of paper produced weekly by the JIC staff generally rested unread. These reports were done at the behest of the Bank of England and the DTI, and the officers who compiled them did not regard their work with much enthusiasm. The economic tasks of today reminded Denton of the counter-subversion work of F Branch during the sixties and seventies. Officers were usually lukewarm about serving with F Branch because in their heart of hearts they knew that the National Council for Civil Liberties or Scottish TUC represented no real threat to parliamentary democracy. Reading the mail of some union leader, or writing copious reports about his holiday in Bulgaria, were instead simply symptoms of the ideological conflict of the time, one which had now given way to economic rivalry.

As he strolled, apparently nonchalantly, onto the trading estate in south Wimbledon, he noted that a small circular yellow sticker had been left on the lamp-post just before he turned off the main road. This was the signal that it was safe to proceed, the area around the drop had been checked for surveillance. Heavy lorries carrying bottled oxygen thundered past Denton as he made his way towards a small office building with a sign over the entrance saying 'BBG Plastics'. Whoever ran the oxygen company on the next lot was clearly doing well, but it was difficult to tell whether BBG Plastics was alive or dead: there was no sign of staff; its empty offices could be glimpsed through filthy windows. Outside there was a skip containing bits of plaster, a selection of 1988 phone books and discarded office furniture. As Denton went past, he casually lobbed the Sainsbury's bag into the skip.

After making the drop, Denton walked smartly into south Wimbledon tube station, stopping to buy the *Standard* – a convenient opportunity to have a good look around. As he grappled with the paper, Denton realised he could remove the gloves from his sweating hands. He did not notice the passing dark blue Ford Escort. Even if he had, its driver had disguised himself cleverly, and its numberplates identified the car as belonging to one Paul Rampton of 16 Nelson Crescent, Sutton, Surrey.

For several days Martin Dodge and his hapless Geordie sidekick Phil had spent their time observing places where they thought there was some chance of Lee Johnson materialising. It was boring work, made all the more so by the fact that they knew their chances of running into him were minimal. Dodge had decided that enough was enough and returned to the offices of Panther Secure Systems in Croydon. He found Pinchman engaged in a conversation with some local businessmen – they were talking about a contract for an undercover operative to break a ring of criminals operating in a local DIY superstore. Dodge spent a few minutes flicking through *Handguns* and *Majesty* as he waited for Pinchman to see off the unfortunate timber merchants.

'Martin, what's new?' his boss asked, turning away from the front door. His tall frame looked faintly ridiculous beside Dodge. The smaller man waited until they were sitting down and more equal before beginning.

'We're not getting anywhere with Johnson. He's too smart, we're never going to dig him out at the current rate.'

'So what do you suggest?' Pinchman replied.

'Well, if the Box 500 people are trying to find him, and

possibly the Yanks as well, surely they can give us some better info?'

'My understanding from Mr Ryan is that they don't know where he is themselves: remember Johnson led an interesting life in the Army; he's as difficult a bloke to track down as any.'

'Well, I'm fucking pissed off with it.'

'Don't give me that, Martin, you did a great job tracking down the girl. You've cracked it once, you can crack it again.'

'I've been thinking about it . . .' Dodge paused for effect. 'The wife and kid are a millstone for him; they must be much easier to find. If we have them, we've got Johnson by the balls.'

Pinchman looked around the office conspiratorially, unnecessarily given that as they were the only ones still there. 'What are we going to do with them when we've got them?'

'Well, she must know a fair bit, the missus. For all we know, she might be the one with the documents now, not him. We've obviously got to use them to smoke him out –' Dodge looked down at his feet – 'but we've . . . obviously got to top them too.'

'This is getting too fucking heavy for me, Martin, I'll tell you.'

'She's seen me, remember! When I went into their house. I don't like the thought of her being around.'

'We can't top a five-year-old girl, mate. No way. That's really overcooking it.' Pinchman was shaking his head slowly.

'Why don't you ask the Yank?'

'This has all gone too far. The spooks have kept their distance from us, Martin, remember that. If we're caught – if you're caught – we're up the swanny, they don't know us, we'll be as exposed as a turd on a fucking billiard table.'

'What choice do we have? If we back off now, sooner or

later Johnson's going to reappear and it's going to be all over the *Sun*. If we're caught do you really think we're fucked? I don't: all previous experience with the spooks tells me we'll be out of whatever cop shop we've been taken to in five minutes. If we go down, they go down too.'

'Our necks are wound out too far, Martin. I don't know where to get hold of this Ryan; that's probably not even his real name. We did it on behalf of MI5, but I can't tell you who or where to find him! Very convincing! We've been played along like a fucking violin!'

Dodge leant forward, fixing Pinchman in his dull eyes: 'Look, there's no going back now, we're in too far. We've got to finish the job and the best way to do it is to lift Johnson's wife or kid, preferably both, then he'll come running soon enough. We've got to lean on the spooks to find them for us. Get more money out of the Yank.'

'He's already in for 900k,' said Pinchman, apparently reviving with the talk of money.

'So make it one and a half mill. Think what this job will have done for Panther. New offices, a new place for you!'

'Yeah, maybe.' Pinchman's tone was resigned rather than enthusiastic. He reached into the cupboard underneath his desk and plucked out a bottle of Scotch and two glasses, pouring generous helpings. 'You might as well try going down to the Isle of Wight, to her parents' place.'

Dodge smiled and raised his glass. 'Cheers!'

Chapter Twenty-Seven

Elaine Stevens walked the short distance in the half-light from her car to the sixties-built semi in Wythenshaw that was her home. She carried a briefcase, which held her things from work, and a holdall with her gym kit. Elaine had spent an hour and a half at the gym on the way back from work. Her body felt stretched, tired but good. Her powers of observation were sufficiently good to detect the parked Ford Escort with a man behind the wheel, apparently reading a newspaper, a little way up the road from her house. She was determined never to allow the fear which grips so many women in British cities to rule her life. She was good enough at Karate and had hit enough blokes in earnest during her years on the beat in the GMP to know her chances were good against most men. Then the newspaper dropped and she recognised the figure behind the wheel as the door clicked open.

'Looking for me?' she asked.

'Might be, might be. How are you?' Lee said, walking swiftly towards her.

'Things are looking up by the minute.' She cracked a grin and fixed him in her clear blue eyes as he leant forward and kissed her cheek. She moved her head back, not expecting him to repeat the gesture on the other cheek.

'We'll do things the continental way,' he said.

She showed him into her house. Lee felt a little unnerved by it: there were few signs of her or easily detectable traces of femininity in the place. There were a good number of books on the shelves which stretched away on each side of the TV and hi-fi, although a fair number were of the horrifically boring variety read for police promotion exams. He noticed one large photograph of Elaine with an old man, presumably her father, but little other evidence of family.

'Tea or something stronger?' she asked, hurling her gym bag onto the bottom of the stairs.

'Tea will do me.' He carried on looking along the bookshelf until he noticed a number of paperbacks whose spines bore florid titles like *Knight's Conquest*, *Realm of Fire* and *The True Champion*. He pulled one off the shelf and studied the illustration on the front. All of the artworks were similar, featuring trembling maidens in shimmering gowns either being embraced by or carried off by hulking knights with eyes like lasers and a musculature which would shame Schwarzenegger. Lee felt a little uncomfortable, shouting to her in the kitchen: 'I don't mean to impose, but if you've got a spare room I wouldn't mind staying over tonight.'

'Yeah, no probs,' she called back from the kitchen, and then teased: 'although it might get a bit chilly in that spare room.'

Lee wasn't sure what to make of that: he had not come with the intention of inciting further advances. The idea of getting through the night began to make him nervous. For a moment he saw himself in the shimmering gown trying to resist an armour-clad Elaine, and smiled at the absurdity of it.

Later, Lee and Elaine got a Chinese take-away and sat eating with the TV on, occasionally glancing at it as a means of soothing their mutual embarrassment, filling the conversational pauses. He learned a lot during that conversation, about her childhood with her uncle – man in picture: her father had run off and her mother hit the bottle. The police had been Elaine's salvation, harnessing a strong and wayward spirit which might otherwise have gone astray. Elaine intended to study for a law degree; it was her greatest regret that she had left school before her A levels. She had hopes to go to the top of the police.

'Don't ruin your career chances by doing me favours, then.'

'I'll always be careful about what I do for you – leave that to me. It's not something for you to worry about. Anyway, you're here for a reason. I don't suppose you're really that interested in my childhood.'

'I am, but well, you're right. I need more info from the Security Service databases.'

'OK,' she said, and then looked up to savour his reaction: 'in return for sex.'

Lee was silenced.

'Don't look so serious, chuck! I'm only teasing you.' Both of them blushed.

'Listen, I'm in big trouble, Elaine.'

'I guessed that when I saw your mate had been murdered.'

'You saw that, then.'

'I wanted to ring you up, talk to you about it, but something told me to go carefully. I suppose I already knew about the security angle from what you'd told me. For my own protection, you might say, I decided to check the list of current warrants before ringing your office.'

'Oh yeah?' Lee was impressed by her instincts of self-preservation.

'The Box 500 boys had a warrant for both your house and office. BASTION is the codename for the operation.'

For Lee the news produced satisfaction and despair simultaneously. His pride was helped by knowing that the attacks on Badyun and him really had been nothing to do with the Scouse mafia, but within an instant he knew that that should have been obvious and that the news of the warrants was ominous because it meant they were up against the first division, not a bunch of amateurs. 'Have they got the watchers onto me too?' he asked.

'I don't think so: they've got a big op running in Preston at the moment with some IRA suspects. Most of them are tied down there.'

'Who's running the op against me? Is it Denton?'

'There's a lot of things I can't get easily out of the databases, Lee. I only found out about the intercepts by going through the motions of putting in for my own intercept on your numbers – so the computer told me somebody else was already doing it.'

'Did they kill MacFadyen?'

'Come off it, you don't believe that do you?'

'It's not such a stupid idea. Whoever killed MacFadyen did it because of a conversation I'd had with him on the phone.'

'Murdering coppers? Come on, Lee! I just don't think they'd do it.'

'You don't believe that crap about the Scousers killing him then?'

'I don't know. You've probably got the best idea of who's doing it.'

'MacFadyen died because they knew – somebody knew – that he had a copy of the files on Operation RACETRACK. They came to get my copies too, and they would have killed me but for a stroke of luck.'

'Shit! I didn't realise.' She wanted to reach across and hold his hand but thought better of it. 'What sort of blokes were they?'

'They were ex-Army, I think. One titchy little bloke, two bigger ones. I don't know, they could have been Five; they could have been freelancers working for Five; they could have been working for somebody else – who fucking knows? If I could figure it out, I'd know what to do next.'

'Has it occurred to you that MI5 might be interested in you because they're as puzzled as anybody else as to what's going on?'

'Yes, I've thought of that,' he replied with an unconvincing hesitancy. It was not a hypothesis to which he had really given much weight.

Lee asked Elaine for a couple of favours, things she could try and dig around for in the computers. They finished their meal and she showed him to the spare room – equipped with a tiny single bed. They said goodnight and Lee took the opportunity to have a long, hot bath and slid into bed just after midnight.

It was difficult getting to sleep. Lee's mind would not stop racing back and forth – evidence that the Security Service was bugging his phone – what was Denton's game? Who was pulling the strings? The creak of an opening door made him stop.

Elaine tiptoed into the room, a silk kimono tied at the waist. 'Honestly, a girl could wait all night for you, Lee Johnson!'

'Come on, love—'

'Shh!' She put her finger to her mouth and slipped the bow on the kimono. 'I've been lying there for an hour, unable to sleep. My body's burning, Lee, I want you to touch me.'

He surveyed her silhouette against the door, the shock of hair, her strong shoulders and thick things. 'Look, I'm really sorry, Elaine. I just can't, me and Jane, you know we don't fool around.'

Elaine ran her hand between her legs as she knelt beside the bed. 'Come on, Lee, touch me: You're too sexy for your own good. Just for tonight, who's it going to harm if it's our secret?'

'I can't, I'm really sorry. It wouldn't be fair on Jane and it wouldn't be fair on you: you deserve better than somebody who's going to disappear tomorrow back to the wife and kid.'

'Just tonight, just hold me, that's all I need.' As her confidence faltered, her voice became more like a little girl's: 'I'm so lonely.'

★   ★   ★

They spoke for another ten or fifteen minutes. In the end, Lee agreed to go to her bed if it was just for company. As he slid beneath the covers, he doubted the wisdom of this 'deal', but Elaine was good as her word and he woke up in her arms.

Hal Canning got off a night flight from New York and shuffled his way into the harsh light of Terminal Three. He did not look his usual immaculate self: the jeans and Reeboks were used intentionally as disguise, but the hollow eyes and messy hair were evidence of the deeper change in psyche which had come over him in recent weeks. The crowd behind the thick glass in the departure lounge wore brightly coloured shorts, shellsuits. He watched fat women guffawing, men working on their beer bellies – it was 7 a.m., dammit! Canning thought back to his days in London in the early seventies: surely things had been better then. This gang of holidaymakers symbolised well the human dimension of a nation with broken confidence and sliding expectations. Canning passed through the passport control on a Canadian document which he had used before for sensitive journeys in the Middle East.

Pinchman did not regard it as odd that Canning appeared at his front door at eight in the morning on a Saturday. He mumbled to his wife to stay in bed, donned a red-trimmed black silk dressing gown and went downstairs to answer the door.

'Mr Canning, I presume. How are you?'

'Good, and you?'

'I can't complain.' Pinchman noticed the curious limpness of Canning's handshake; it was almost feminine.

'Forgive the earliness of my call, but I'm here for a very short period and I think there're matters which need our urgent attention.' Pinchman picked the *Express* off the doormat and led his guest through into the kitchen. 'Coffee?'

'Please.' Canning placed his overnight bag on the floor and made a play of studying the paper as Pinchman busied himself. 'You earned your dollars taking care of the girl. Outstanding!'

'Martin did very well with that one. I must admit I was pessimistic about finding her. He's a good operator, Martin, although –' the toaster popped and Pinchman pulled out the slices '– he frightens even me sometimes.'

'I'm very concerned, we're all very concerned at Langley, with your failure to take out Johnson.'

'Marmalade?'

'No thank you. Are you any closer to finding him?'

'It's been very tough for us, Hal.'

'For the money you've been taking, we expected better. People at Langley are telling me Panther is a one-horse outfit. I'd like to tell them they're wrong.'

Pinchman ran a hand across his forehead. 'Johnson is a needle in a haystack, I don't believe anybody could have done much better. We've cracked some of the problem, it's just the longer things go on, the bigger the problem gets.'

'That's why the thing has to be taken care of now. What are you going to do about it?' Canning wound up the pressure.

'We have an idea . . . We think his daughter may be with the wife's parents. Perhaps we could lift them – the kid and the wife, I mean.'

'That would certainly get his attention,' said Canning, drawing on his coffee. Pinchman's expression was pained; he was having trouble forming his next sentence. Canning prompted. 'Do you have a problem with something?'

'I'm worried about the length of time that all this has gone on. I'm worried that Johnson or his wife will have told somebody everything they know by now. It's getting harder and harder to put the genie back in the bottle.'

'They're scared; they don't know who they can trust. The important thing is to eliminate Johnson as a possible witness.

All sorts of things might or might not be drawn from the papers, but the main thing is to take care of key witnesses – you've done it with the girl and it has to be done with Johnson.'

'Martin feels that the wife is also probably a threat by now; he must have told her a lot. Also, she was in the house when Martin visited Mr Johnson.'

'Go with Martin's instinct: she's a loose end. Don't worry, we'll take care of the expense.' Canning studied Pinchman. He did not have the look or values of those guys in Miami or LA who could be bought by the Agency for so little and who never showed any sign of mercy or doubt. Pinchman looked about as comfortable as somebody in a dentist's waiting room. 'You're in the major league now, no going back.'

'I know, I know.'

Canning drew an envelope from his leather jacket. 'There's another cheque here. It should cover everything. You guys must be making a lot of money on this deal!' He slapped Pinchman's back. 'Only kidding!'

They finished breakfast and Pinchman called a mini-cab for his guest. As the two men walked towards the door, Canning turned to his host.

'What did you do with the papers that you recovered from the other guy, MacFadyen was it?'

'We returned them to Mr Ryan. Is that OK?'

'Sure. Was it just papers?'

'Yes, just some photocopies. We didn't take too close an interest. Why, is there a problem?'

'No problem, no problem. Give me results, Pinchman: we need them fast.'

Chapter Twenty-Eight

Martin had given Phil the evening off – it was Saturday after all. The plan was that they would head down south on Monday, Phil hadn't been told exactly where, to stake out the target's missus. Phil did not know whether Dodge had the same treatment in mind for her that the girl in Brighton had got, but he would draw the line at doing the kid too. He decided there was not enough time to head home, up north, to see his mates and instead retired to the Lancaster, one of those pubs near Leicester Square which are usually populated entirely with foreigners. Martin had given him £500 in fifties and he decided that a dump like the Lancaster would be the best place to pick up some tourist.

It was not Phil's first experience of working for the spooks. After he had left the RAF Police, Phil had been hired by a bunch of 'Foreign Office' berks to work in Namibia and Angola on six-month contracts. They had given him an AK-47 and told him to mind this bloke from the embassy on his trips up-country for meetings with UNITA guerrillas. There had been a couple of other lads on the same work and it had been a good crack. He had gone home to Gateshead with £12,000 at the end of each contract, which was good money in anybody's book. Francis, the embassy bloke, had given Phil a slip of paper showing the money had been won in a betting shop in Northampton or somewhere. Each trip he did, the cheque was drawn on these bookies and Francis said to keep them handy in case the taxman asked too many questions.

The work in Africa had been good, and Phil missed having a beer with the other lads in Windhoek, but the contracts had dried up after Namibian independence. Phil thought Francis was all right – for a southern bastard. Francis had never let on much about why they were there – although it seemed obvious to Phil he was getting weapons through to the guerrillas – but he was a fair bloke who took care of them in his own way.

For about an hour, Phil played pool against himself, sinking a couple of pints of Lowenbrau and giving the eye to every likely-looking bird who came in. He then found a couple of Danish blokes willing to give him some games, and they packed in as many drinks as anybody could manage. They had started betting a tenner a game, and by 10 p.m., they had taken more than £100 off him. Phil couldn't keep track of the number of beers he had had by then, but it could easily have been ten pints. He was on his way back from the toilet when he noticed one of the Danes altering the position of balls. Something broke inside him, and without a word, Phil ran forwards and swung his pool cue, beating the Dane around the head several times. As the man went down, Phil kicked his face, breaking the front teeth as the other Dane came at him in a hail of fists.

Sunday morning found Phil in a cell at West End Central police station. He was due to be put in front of a magistrate the following morning on a charge of Grievous Bodily Harm. As the light streamed through the bars of his cell, Phil propped himself up. The stench of the cells pricked his nostrils: he retched but nothing came. There was plenty of vomit on the floor, and he remembered how he had spent much of the night. The Dane had landed a few good punches and Phil could feel a couple of cuts inside his cheek and a painful bruise above one eye.

The key turned in the lock. 'Breakfast, you dirty bastard!' The copper slid a tray onto the floor.

'Ta. I'm sorry about the mess, give us a mop and I'll take care of it.'

'I'll get one in a minute. Is there anybody you want to phone. I tried asking you last night but you were too far out of it.'

'Yeah, there is a number.' Phil groped in his wallet for a business card which Francis had given him in Pretoria two years before. There was a handwritten phone number, but no name on it. 'Call this and they'll vouch for me.'

'Are you in the forces or something?'

'Sort of. Call the number, mate, they'll get me off your hands.'

Denton and Canning had agreed to meet in Hyde Park. They strolled among the Sunday afternoon revellers, but not very far before Denton's ebbing strength forced him to rest on a bench. It was their last meeting. Canning had contacted him at short notice and told him he was coming to London and needed to see him. Denton's successor as Canning's handler would not be able to get there in time: they had planned the handover for a couple of weeks' time. Canning did not know about these arrangements, although one look at Denton's sallow face told him there would not be many more meetings.

'Hal, Pete, whatever I should call you. I'm sorry to say this is our last time.'

'Oh. Well, I've brought you the papers you wanted.'

Denton peered into the carrier bag which Canning had shifted over towards him.

'You've got a lot of goodies there, my friend. All our sources in Iran, Israel, France, the Balkans. Use it wisely, there's a lot of butts at stake. That's twenty years of casework in some cases.'

'Excellent, really excellent and, er . . . any luck with Germany?'

'Yeah, it's all in there. You getting greedy?'

'That's really most excellent. It was very important to me that our last joint effort be the most impressive. Thank you.' Denton surveyed a passing couple before resuming. 'I was meant to introduce your new . . . friend, but I'm afraid there wasn't the time to get her here today.'

'I won't be meeting her, Charles.'

Denton's alarm bells sounded. 'Why?'

'I'm not going on with this. I'm sure you guys would like nothing more than to have somebody at the top of the Agency, but I'm finished with helping you.'

'Come now,' said Denton, although he found himself feeling satisfaction at the idea of this super-agent going dormant because he would deal with nobody else, 'I'm sure my successor—'

'It's nothing to do with who . . . I'm sorry, Charles, I mean nobody would match your way of doing things. You're one of the old school, Brits aren't made the same way any more. No, that's not my reason.'

Denton was disappointed not to have his ego stroked. 'What is?'

'I can't carry on. We were told enough times at the farm and you must have heard it too – blackmail is a lousy basis for recruitment of agents.'

'Hal, you're not an agent, you're—'

'Cut the bullshit, Charles; that's exactly what you've had me be these last twenty years. You've always given me this line about "a little help to the old country", but you and I know exactly what I've been all these years. I've deluded myself in the past, taken in all this friendship stuff, convinced myself this was all some dumb game and I wasn't really harming the US. Well, blackmail has its limits and I've reached mine. This crap with the files and this tearaway cop. I just want it finished. Tell your bosses I'm through: there'll be no more.'

'All you've done, Hal,' Denton was choosing his words carefully, 'is provide a back-channel, something extra for two very closely allied intelligence services. You've just been a very good friend.'

'Cut this friendship business, you sound like the KGB! I could justify what I did because it was giving a little extra help to Britain: if it had been anybody else I would just have had to accept that my career was over in 1971. But over the years, you guys have been so cheap. I would have expected some recognition from the heads of your service or something. At times I've wondered whether I really was working for the Brits.'

'Don't be so ridiculous!' Denton countered.

'It don't look like it to me sometimes. This business with Johnson: do you know how much it's cost me? You guys can't protect what must be one of the best intelligence relationships you've ever had – you couldn't even wipe your own butts without dollar bills for paper!'

Denton sat silently, hoping the storm was blowing itself out. He wondered where to start. 'You know I'm dying, don't you, Hal?'

'I'm not trying to bawl you out, for chrissakes: it's your organisation that sucks.'

'You're right. What can I say? I don't think you know how much this friendship – and that's what it is for me – has meant to me. I can honestly say it's given meaning to my life, especially since Irene died.'

Canning was beginning to squirm on the bench: he had honestly not meant to hurt Denton's feelings. 'You know the strangest thing, Charles? Sometimes I've thought about our . . . relationship . . . over the years: what you've been interested in, all that kind of stuff, and I've wondered whether you're really playing me for the Brits, or whether something else was going on.'

'Don't be ridiculous,' Denton spluttered, a cool shiver running through his emaciated body.

'I'd kill you if it were somebody else,' Canning said slowly and purposefully.

Denton struggled to read whether the threat resulted from a deep-seated suspicion or was a device Canning was using to end the relationship. He decided to keep going for the sympathy factor. 'I'm dead already, dear boy. I'm just a bag of bones. I can't make it down the stairs without my little pain-killing machine.'

Canning realised the emptiness and cruelty of his taunt. 'I'm sorry, Charles. I'm not talking like myself: this business is finishing me.'

They spoke for a few more minutes. Canning composed himself, trying in a back-handed way to compliment Denton on the way he had handled things over the years.

'Be a good chap, don't break things off at this stage,' said Denton, finally.

'No, I'm through. I might have told you this five years ago, but I didn't. I'll try and tie the loose ends with Johnson and his wife—'

'His wife?'

'She's got to go too. I've discussed it with Pinchman, made more funds available. Then that's the end of it. I want no more to do with your people. I'll just smile at them at conferences and it'll be our little secret.'

They walked together as far as the tube, and Denton said goodbye for the last time.

As Denton was turning to leave, Canning asked: 'What did you do with the papers that were taken back from the dead guy? I'd like to see them.'

'I destroyed them, Hal. You wouldn't want anybody else to learn our secret would you?'

Canning felt a moment's fondness for Denton and his sharpness. He had wanted desperately to read them, if only to try and make sense of everything that had happened since 1971. With time, Denton's answer would feed his suspicion that their relationship was never what it had seemed, but for the moment he simply admired the dying man's presence of mind in being forearmed with this answer.

As he clattered along in the train, Denton felt satisfaction that the relationship with Canning was unlikely to outlive him. He had always believed that a special chemistry between the two of them had made the whole thing possible, and now that was finished. In a way, Canning's refusal to continue would be his best epitaph. He had, after all, done his best to persuade his agent to carry on. Until the end, he concluded in his haze of diamorphin, he had been the professional – too bad for his bosses if this most prized of sources would work for nobody else.

The drug meant that Denton only had a few hours in the middle of the day in which his mind worked acutely any more. As he began to sink deeper into drug-induced numbness, he experienced vivid daydreams. He saw himself in a great hall walking foward to receive medals and tributes. The bosses giving him eloquent panegyrics, the adulation of his peers. A few understated words of his own, an exit to thunderous applause. A few more months of life in the warm glow of public recognition, perhaps some newspaper articles about the spy of the century.

Denton realised he had missed his tube stop. He got out of the train and switched platforms to go back. It was good counter-surveillance anyway. His mind came back to the present. Denton felt relieved that he was about to begin his last week at the Security Service, and then he would be away to enjoy what little remained of his life. Some thoughts still nagged at him: had he bungled the Johnson business? How long before Canning gave further thought to the idea that he had not been run by the Brits?

A youngish man, perhaps twenty-nine or thirty, in blue cords and a Guernsey sweater, had arrived at the police station a couple of hours after the desk sergeant called the number on

Phil's card. He was let into the cell by a copper who then withdrew with the discretion of a madam. Phil was sitting on the bed, looking up at him. The Geordie had been softened up by a few hours in the cell – he had put plenty of people inside them in the RAF Police, but his own sheet had always been spotless.

'It's a pain in the arse being called in on a Sunday, Mr Rogers. You had better have a good explanation for your actions. Your Danish friend is critical by the way. Massive concussion, he's in a coma. No coincidence I suppose if you hit somebody round the head seven or eight times with a pool cue.'

'I was expecting Francis,' Phil mumbled, a little like a child in the headmaster's study.

'He's abroad. He won't be pleased that you used the number. It's only for use if you're arrested doing something operational for us. What was your operational reason for beating people up in the Lancaster pub? I don't believe you're on contract to us at the moment.'

'Well, I'm on contract to somebody – our blokes and the Americans as far as I can make out.'

The 'Foreign Office' man ran a hand through his thick blond hair. Phil thought him a little like a younger Heseltine. 'If you're working for the Security Service then that's their problem. You understand the difference?'

'I think so. The Africa job was MI6?'

'Precisely. If the proles in Five can't give you an emergency number it's not our problem. Frankly, even if you had been doing another job for us we probably couldn't help you on something like this. The plods aren't that easily pursuaded any more.'

'You can't help me then?'

'Nope.' He turned to leave. 'You'd better get yourself a schnorkel, Phil Rogers, because you're deep in the shit. You could be looking at murder or attempted murder, my friend.

Sweet dreams.' The MI6 man turned and the door banged behind him.

Phil jumped to his feet and almost shouted: 'Help me! Jesus Christ, help me!'

There was no response, but Phil could still hear him at the end of the corridor making small talk with the desk sergeant. 'We've been killing people!'

Another prisoner shouted. 'The Geordie Ripper wants his mummy!'

The MI6 man walked back to the cell door and whispered through it: 'Who has?'

'The team I'm working with. Please help me!'

The key turned in the door and the young intelligence officer went back into the cell. 'So, Mr Rogers, are you making this up?'

'People at Panther have been bumping people off for our government and the Yanks.'

'Bollocks!'

'It's true.' Phil was sniffing back tears.

'I'll give you five minutes to convince me.' The MI6 man turned, closed the door and sat down on a chair, beckoning Phil to be seated.

'I don't want to incriminate myself.'

'Tell me what you know.' The spook's voice had softened dramatically. He sounded less the public schoolboy and more like the host of a late night radio phone-in programme.

'Get me out of here and promise you won't do me for any of this.'

'I can't make promises here and now, Phil. I can make some phone calls in a couple of minutes. You tell me what you know and if things don't work out for either of us, the conversation never happened. Fair?'

'OK.'

'Who's been killed?'

'A CID man, a couple of weeks back. MacFadden or

MacFadyen, I think it was in the papers. And a girl, I don't know her name. She was done in Brighton.'

'Who's paying Panther for this job?'

'I don't know. All I know is that they talk about an American and a Brit. We went after the CID bloke – and another CID man called Johnson – because they had some papers, very sensitive stuff.'

'Did you read them?'

'No. Martin took them—'

'Martin who?'

'No, I'm not grassing him up. He's fucking mental, I'm not crossing him.'

The MI6 man pondered what he had been told and then looked up at Phil. 'So what makes you think you were in the pay of somebody in government? There could have been anything in those papers.'

'I was going to tell you. I did catch a glimpse of the papers: photocopies. I saw it said "Top Secret, DG's Eyes Only" on the photocopy; I remembered that bit about "DG's Eyes".'

The MI6 man made a mental note. Their boss was known to all in Whitehall as the Chief; 'DG' meant Security Service.

'And Martin said,' Phil continued, 'he said several times that what we were doing, we were doing it for government people but that it was all too sensitive for them to own up to if something went wrong.'

'Well, you've buggered them up good and proper, haven't you?' The MI6 man left Phil to ponder this thought and disappeared into the hallway. Phil heard him murmur something to the policeman and then the cell door banged shut and a key turned in the lock.

Chapter Twenty-Nine

That Monday morning, Denton was slightly late for work, although that was not so unusual, his appearances at Gower Street had become erratic during the last few weeks. It was a fine day, bright sunshine, the begining of his last week in the Service. He made his way in through the entranceway. Before Denton could get to the security doors inside, two solidly built A Branch types walked towards him.

'Mr Denton?' the first enquired.

'Yes.'

'Could you come with me, please.'

'Where are we going?'

'We're going somewhere quieter. There's an investigation going on and they'd like your help with their inquiries. Your section head has been told that you'll be absent today.'

'I see,' Denton said, as the two men gently turned him around and swept him back through the front door. 'So this is it,' he thought, the moment he had lived in fear of for twenty-five years. As they stepped onto the pavement of Gower Street, a Rover pulled up in front of them, the doors clicked open and the minders slid him into the car. Denton assumed others would be taking his flat apart. That was all right, they wouldn't find anything. Canning's last package of documents was already on its way to his masters. He felt intensely relieved that he had already dropped off his last package of material in the skip at BBG Plastics: it would have finished him.

'Don't take the South Circular,' one of the minders said to the driver.

Denton watched the shops flashing by, the bustle of ordinary life in its monotonous regularity. It would be OK, he convinced himself: after all he had had an entire professional life anticipating this moment.

The car had drawn up at some traffic lights. They were in Kent somewhere.

'Alan!' one of the minders said to the other with urgency, 'you see that place on the left?'

'Oh yeah?'

'They've got those aluminium frame windows that we're putting in at the moment.'

'Very nice. Double glazing?'

'It's got to be hasn't it, really, where we live.'

That was the only conversation of the trip. Eventually the Rover pulled into the drive of a large detached house near Sittingbourne. It was one of several owned by the Service and used for putting up nervous touts from Ireland and visiting bigwigs, or for staging special conferences. It was a large, late-Victorian, brickbuilt house that might once have been home to a family with six or seven children. Denton was shown through the hall into what he presumed had been the sitting room. There were two men and a woman there: he recognised two of them vaguely from GWS.

'Mr Denton, it's very kind of you to join us,' said the woman, lisping slightly. 'I'm Monica Davies, I'm a Head of Section running a special investigation.' She turned towards the others: 'This is Sam Boswell, he's my number two.' They did not shake hands. 'I thought you should meet Doctor Smedley. He won't be here throughout our conversation, but he'll always be on hand in case you feel poorly or need medication.'

'That's very thoughtful, thank you,' said Denton.

A reel-to-reel tape recorder sat, primed, on the table. Virgin notepads and biros had been placed beside it. Denton was offered a chair on the other side of the table.

'Charles,' she began, 'you very properly came forward following the approaches made to you by Detective Sergeant Johnson. The matters which he raised with you have caused us to go back and look very closely at material relating to Operation RACETRACK and to your own career in the Service.'

Denton struggled to maintain his concentration. It was vital that he consider every word she said for signs of what they did and didn't know. Try as he would, he found the pain killer blunting his concentration. Shortly after sitting, he made the decision that he must switch the little machine on his belt off if he was to regain his full concentration for the next few hours. Within an hour or two he would be at his most attentive, then after that the pain would begin to gnaw away at him. The interrogation would test him doubly: whether he could recite flawlessy the story he had thought out for twenty-five years and whether he could get through it without having to switch on the pain killer again.

'Mr Denton –' Boswell was leaning forward – 'we'd like to run through your career in the Service.'

'Certainly.'

'When your Positive Vetting was done in Rhodesia, do you know why the investigating officer did not file details to us?'

'I'm afraid I was never aware that he hadn't.'

'Why did you join the Service?'

'Well, I was fascinated by the idea of intelligence work. I'd read a certain number of things dating back to the War. One of the masters at the Bishop Livesay school suggested that London might be a better place to do such work.'

'Who was the master?'

'Mister Kemp, we called him, of course. I think it was Nigel

Kemp. I had the impression he had done something in the Secret Service during the war.'

'Are you still in touch with anybody from your school? Is there anybody we could speak to?'

'Well, I think an awful lot of those I did remain friendly with have passed on. Irene and I didn't really keep up with them. After a few years here, they sort of fell by the wayside.'

And so it went on until lunchtime, a minute examination of his career which did not progress past 1970. At 12.30, Monica Davies and Boswell withdrew, Dr Smedley reappeared and a tray with easily digestible food was brought for Denton. He didn't feel like eating anything. There was pain, he had expected that, but other things were happening to him too. He was feeling waves of nausea and breaking into sweats; his hands were shaking. His mind was clearer, but he was desperate to switch the diamorphin back on to stop himself showing these signs which could be interpreted as stress by the interrogators. Denton forced some of the food down.

The two interrogating officers ate in a small dining room at the back of the house. A lady retained by the Service as caretaker and factotum placed plates bearing unappetising meat and two veg in front of them.

'Were you happy with this morning?' she asked Boswell.

'I find it fascinating. His recollection seems pretty good considering the time passed and the state of his health. Yet there's nothing very concrete there. Nobody who grew up with him who he's still in touch with. His best man's dead, all his friend's seem to be dead.'

'What are we driving at here exactly, Sam?'

'Well, we've got no evidence to prove he isn't a fake.'

'What on earth do you mean?'

'There could be something in his past which placed him open to blackmail, or indicated that he might have a propensity for it himself. That's all I'm driving at.'

'Have you got any corroboration?'

'I haven't found anybody yet from his college. The SB sergeant who did the vetting died in 1965. Both of the references are dead. The only lead I've managed to turn up is one Gerald Porton who was head boy of that school in Bulawayo during Denton's last year there. I've got an address and number for him – he lives in Cambridge – but he's unreachable on some holiday at the moment, which pisses me off.'

'You did well to find him, Sam,' she said in a mildly patronising tone. 'The problem is that we haven't got time to develop very good hunches like yours. We're under too much pressure on this inquiry. I think we've got to get him onto the whole business of Operation RACETRACK as soon as possible. I'd like to have a couple of hours with him on that before Donald arrives.'

Denton was allowed an hour's rest, lying on a chintz-covered sofa, before questioning resumed. Then began a detailed discussion about Operation RACETRACK: who had dreamed it up, how it was executed.

'When did you become aware that our friend QUASAR had fallen into the trap?' Monica Davies asked.

'Well, I can't really remember. I think there was a certain amount of ribald humour among the watchers. It was actually one of the other officers in K3 who recognised him.'

'Were you told his name?'

'Oh yes, several of us on the operation knew who he was. It was the talk of the Section. "You'll never guess who we photographed . . ." That kind of thing.'

'The papers suggest that the DG at the time believed we should keep open the option of recruiting QUASAR, a decision subsequently rejected by his successor. Do you know what DG had in mind?' she enquired, scribbling as she spoke.

'Well, of course I was just one of the poor bloody infantry.

DG didn't really know I existed,' said Denton. 'I got the impression from Michael Martin, my Head of Section, that we did not want to throw away such a valuable potential agent, even if the Service judged it far too risky to try to exploit that potential at the time.' Denton had them on ground he relished. Nobody who was party to the key decisions was in a position to contradict him. His interpretation of these facts would allow him, if things went badly in this interrogation, to protect himself.

Monica Davies resumed the attack. 'When you saw QUA-SAR with Michael Martin, what exactly was said?'

'I can't remember that much. Naturally I was just there as a bag carrier really. Michael did almost all of the talking. He made it clear that he had been a naughty boy, that we had caught him and that we did not intend to drop him in it with his own side. He was told that he was only getting the kid-glove treatment because of the special relationship.' A mischievous half-smile played across Denton's wrinkled face. 'You understand of course that our friend was an American?'

'We understand,' Davies said so curtly that it carried an implicit admonition for Denton's indiscretion.

'Then Michael said something to him like: "You must understand the special relationship cuts both ways, old boy. There may come a time when we need some help and we expect you to return the favour." That was the gist of it, anyway.'

Davies and Boswell shifted uncomfortably. The notes on Denton and Martin's meeting with QUASAR had made a suggestion that an implicit threat had been left hanging over QUASAR, but had not expressed it in such stark terms.

'Michael told him that the whole business would be held under the tightest possible distribution within the Service. QUASAR seemed nervous that SIS would be alerted. We assured him that it wouldn't. He indicated that he appreciated our discretion and that he understood the bargain that existed between us. Michael made it clear that, if we ever needed his help, somebody would contact him, probably one of the two of us, with a password.'

'Which was?' Boswell asked.

'Well, it would be a sentence containing the phrase "sleeping dogs". Michael thought that terribly witty. I considered it rather unsubtle myself.' Denton faltered. 'I'm afraid I'm feeling terribly weak. Will we go on much longer?'

Both officers had noticed the marked deterioration in their interviewee's appearance as the day had gone on. Denton's face was completely washed out; an area around the collar of his shirt had become moist with sweat; occasionally he seemed to be gritting his teeth in pain. 'Not much longer, although we may all reassemble tomorrow. Do you want Dr Smedley?' Boswell said.

'I can manage for a little longer.'

Boswell resumed. 'None of this is in the minutes of your meeting – about sleeping dogs I mean.'

'Would you expect it to be?'

'I would if anybody else was expected to activate QUASAR. How else would they know?'

'There seems to be some uncertainty surrounding the destruction of the tapes made from the Kandahar Road special facilities.' Monica changed tack. 'Mr Buchanan ordered them destroyed, but our own enquiries suggest they remained in existence for a year or two as a result of some administrative delay. Did you ever withdraw the tapes?'

'No, I didn't.' Denton knew they were moving onto more dangerous ground.

Tea was brought in during the mid-afternoon, with stale digestives and longlife milk. Davies was moving the interrogation to its decisive phase.

'Charles. Did you ever contact QUASAR and activate him as an agent?'

'No, I did not.'

'Did you ever contact him for any other purpose?'

'No.'

'Have you ever seen him since that day?' she probed.

Denton's anxiety rose. Had they been under surveillance yesterday in Hyde Park? He did not believe he had – he had been hacking into the operational databases regularly to check that no suspicious surveillance operations were underway. He felt reasonably confident and replied: 'I once saw him in the corridor at GWS, early eighties sometime. I think he was over on counter-terrorist business. Naturally I cut him.'

'Charles. Some people would say that your meeting with QUASAR in 1971 put you in a perfect position to blackmail him.' She groped for the words. 'Did you ever exploit that . . . advantage . . . for financial or other gain?'

'No, of course not.'

'You've taken an accusation of blackmail very calmly,' Boswell interjected, 'but I suppose if you had blackmailed him, you'd have had many years to prepare yourself for this interview. Do you think it's fair of us to ask you these questions so near to your retirement?'

'Whether it's fair or not doesn't come into it. You must remember, I served with K Branch during the height of our paranoia – our *concern* would be a better word – about Soviet penetration. It occurred to me then, "how would I feel if I were being asked all these questions after a lifetime of service to the state?" So I've been here before on the other side of the table.'

'I think you're really saying to me that I don't stand a chance of tripping you up.' Boswell's voice carried a more aggressive tone.

'Not at all. Perhaps you're not as good a psychologist as you think you are.'

'Why did you take Operation RACETRACK files out of Registry and put them in a safe deposit box?'

Denton thought: 'Now the fun begins,' but naturally he kept a poker expression and replied: 'I didn't.'

'I think you did. You realise, if we catch you lying on this, that nothing you have said to us will still be credible?' This statement was an invitation for him to put his head on the block. Had they conducted special tests on the Registry records for the files? Had he been under surveillance since the day he went back to the Majestic company to recover them? What harm was there in admitting to having squirrelled away the papers? 'I did not put any documents of the kind you described into any safe deposit box.'

Their thoughts were broken by the crunch of a Service Daimler gliding across the gravel drive.

The door opened and Donald Travis appeared, closely followed by another man, clad in a similar dark blue suit and polka-dot tie. Denton's spirits sank. The two men sat down, joining Davies and Boswell, fanned out in front of Denton. Travis and the other Security Service officers exchanged a few terse greetings.

'For the record,' Travis nodded at the turning reels of tape, 'I am Donald Travis, Legal Adviser to the Director General, the person to be questioned next is Oswald Pew, managing director of the Majestic safety deposit company.' Monica Davies and Sam Boswell remained hushed as Travis began. 'Mr Pew, do you recognise this man?'

'Yes, I do.'

'By what name do you know him?' Travis inquired, his eyes fixed on Denton, looking for any sign of reaction.

'Paul Ryan,' Pew responded.

'How many times did you meet Mr "Ryan"?'

'Only on one occasion, when he recovered some papers and a package stolen during the robbery of our premises. I also spoke to him on the telephone a couple of times.'

Denton did not want to give Travis the satisfaction of eye contact. He looked down at his fingers instead.

'Mr Pew, how long had Mr "Ryan" hired the two boxes held at your company?'

'They had been held under his name since 1973, five years before I arrived at the firm.'

'I understand that something was not claimed by anybody following the raid. What was it?'

'It was a bag containing a large sum of money, American money. My recollection is that it was about a quarter of a million dollars. Nobody came forward and, of course, Mr Ryan had held two boxes.'

'You were suspicious?'

'Of course.'

'Thank you, Mr Pew, I have no further questions.'

Boswell leaned forward and clicked the tape recorder off. Travis nodded and Pew stood up.

Denton's eyes flicked up. 'May I ask one question?'

Pew looked at Travis and the other officers, uncertain of what to do. Denton's interjection was not part of this scene as they had imagined it.

'I suppose so,' said Travis slowly, dragging out the word 'suppose'.

'Mr Pew,' Denton's voice croaked slightly, 'I'm sure that you took your duties of confidentiality towards your clients very seriously,' he said with just a trace of irony. 'Did you ever examine the contents of the envelope which I recovered from you?'

For what seemed like a minute, Pew said nothing, glancing first at Travis, then at the floor. 'No, I did not,' he said at last.

Pew was shown out of the room and into the corridor by Travis, whose bearing and tone betrayed the significance of the last exchange.

'Thank you so much for coming, Mr Pew, most useful. My car will return you to your office.'

'Glad to be of service,' said Pew, extending his hand.

'No really, we rely on people's willingness to help.'

'Glad I could be of some service,' Pew repeated before leaving quite happily. For him the encounter testified both to his willingness to help in Defence of the Realm and a reaffirmation of what he liked to call the sacred trust of his clients.

Travis returned and the tape recorder again stirred into action. Boswell resumed the attack. 'Denton, you've not told the truth about your safety deposit box. You've used a pseudonym to hire a box in which you stored documents relating to Operation RACETRACK. You have carried out blackmail and made at least a quarter of a million dollars from these activities.'

'Young man,' Denton replied, hoping the form of address would antagonise his blustering accuser further, 'you do not have an ounce of proof for your allegations. I hired a box to store personal papers, precious things relating to my life with my late wife. I know nothing about the money; your allegation of blackmail is offensive and unwarranted.'

'Your demeanour is very shifty, it suggests you are guilty.'

'It suggests only that I am wasted with cancer,' Denton replied through teeth gritted in anger and pain, 'and that I stopped taking my pain killer some hours ago in order to be able to give you the fullest possible answers to your questions!'

His outburst had the desired effect. There was a good, long, awkward silence. Boswell knew he had been out of court and the effect of the exchange was to make him feel so guilty about pushing this sick wizened man in this way, that he could not bring himself again to play an incisive role in the interrogation.

Travis leaned forward. 'If what you say is true, Charles, why did you hire two boxes and why didn't you hire them under your own name?'

'The second box contained Irene's jewels, a necklace, two diamond rings. I had taped them up inside a padded envelope, that's the one Mr Pew mentioned returning to me. I decided not to put the boxes under my own name because of an old standing Service convention to avoid actions which attract the interest of the tax authorities. I understand that they regard deposit box owners with particular suspicion.'

'That seems implausible to me.' Monica Davies spoke for the first time in an hour.

'Well, I agree it seems a little foolish now, but back then the atmosphere was different.'

The questions petered out about twenty-five minutes later. Monica Davies and Sam Boswell regarded the whole episode as unsatis-factory. She had always argued for more time to gather evidence, but Denton's imminent retirement had pressed them into precipitate action. Travis asked Denton to stay away from GWS until Friday when he could clear his desk and attend the modest retirement reception being planned in his honour.

By 7 p.m., the Rover was whisking Denton back towards Blackheath. As they drove along, Denton started his diamorphin again. Immediately he felt markedly better. He was triumphant at defeating the interrogation and keeping the pain killer switched off for so many hours. But as the opiate coursed around his veins again, one nagging thought went through his mind before it was swept away by the chemical euphoria. Charles Denton realised that on top of everything else this fucking cancer had done to him, it had turned him into a junkie.

He closed his eyes and seemed to be sleeping. He re-entered his favourite daydream. The great hall, the applause of his peers, medals pinned to his chest.

The driver looked in his rearview mirror and observed the look of contentment on his passenger's face.

Chapter Thirty

Jane turned into the road which led to her parents' home in Lake. She had decided to take her daughter away, back to the mainland. Gemma had been there seven days and that was enough. As she had walked up the broad street to their bungalow she had scanned neighbours and passers-by, looking for the tell-tale signs of surveillance drummed into her by Lee. For the last two hundred yards, her right hand had rested on the automatic pistol in her shoulder bag.

The joy of seeing Gemma again had left them both drained. They had hugged and kissed for what seemed like several minutes, although it had only been a week. She had said little to her mum and dad – a few cryptic phrases describing their existence over the water. After dinner, Jane put her daughter to bed and retired to the sparsely furnished spare room. She had pulled out papers and the books given to her by John Middlebrook. She sat on the bed at the centre of a white fan of paper. Two items captured Jane's interest: one of the books lent by John Middlebrook, and a stapled photocopy of an official document. It was headed:

TOP SECRET: DG/DDG's EYES ONLY
Report on Meeting of K Branch Officers and QUASAR,
6th July 1971.

Jane was in no doubt that it was among the most significant

documents of all of those hidden in the safety deposit box. Turning the page, she saw that it was a report to the Director General about a meeting between Michael Martin, Charles Denton and the man whose identity she was making it her business to discover.

1. On 6th July 1971, at approximately 3 p.m., QUASAR arrived at Bow Street police station, following a letter inviting him there to discuss a summons over an alleged parking offence. SLO to the MP had arranged for the two K Branch officers to use an interview room at the station.

2. Following QUASAR's arrival, Michael Martin introduced himself as a senior officer of the Security Service and Charles Denton as one of his section officers. Surveillance material from Operation RACE-TRACK was produced. On recognising himself in the photographs and reading the transcribed CIN-NAMON material, QUASAR broke down and the interview was suspended for twelve minutes.

Jane could imagine certain elements of the scene: the grey-faced men of MI5 doling out their sordid revelation; the nicotine-stained walls of the interview room. However, she could not yet put a face to the sobbing man holding centre stage.

3. When QUASAR regained his composure, he said that he was covered by diplomatic immunity and that he did not intend to answer further questions.

Jane's right hand snapped into action with a yellow marker pen, illuminating the words 'diplomatic immunity'.

Michael Martin locked the door and told QUASAR

that prosecution was out of the question and that he should hear them out before leaving.

4. Mr Martin told QUASAR that the Service had no intention of informing either the police or his own authorities about the incident and that the whole thing should be looked upon as an unfortunate accident. QUASAR sought and received assurances that SIS would not be informed either and would be excluded from the distribution of any RACETRACK material.

5. After hearing these assurances, QUASAR regained his composure and suggested that he would not forget our sensitivity in the matter. At this point Mr Martin stated that QUASAR's gratitude would be borne in mind by HMG.

6. Mr Martin suggested that if the matter were ever to be discussed again it would most likely be himself or Mr Denton who would make contact, as the nature of the Operation RACETRACK material was so sensitive that few other officers were ever likely to be indoctrinated into it. It was made clear, and QUASAR agreed, that no attempt had been made to recruit him as a source.

The final paragraph perplexed Jane as she underlined 'himself or Mr Denton who would make contact' and the last sentence. What kind of strange bureaucratic self-delusion had gone on in Bow Street police station all those years ago? They let the pervert off the hook, but made it clear that they regarded it as a favour. She remembered the DG's annotation about the sensitivity of recruitment being too great. QUASAR's abortive invocation of diplomatic immunity had turned a wheel in her mind. She had lugged the books lent to her by Middlebrook to the Island with a certain resentment. On first examining *Dirty Work* she had dismissed it as a boring collection of essays by seventies CIA-hating lefties. One chapter, however, merited re-examination.

'How to Spot a Spook' by John Marks.

Lee had already confided his feeling that they were looking for an American and in this chapter, Mr Marks showed how skilful use of the US State Department's Foreign Service List and Biographic Register could reveal the identities of CIA personnel in embassies around the world. With samples from the biographies of various hapless individuals, the author had shown the tell-tale signs of spookdom: a 'Reserve' Foreign Service officer status, unexplained gaps in biographical references and mentions of time spent as an 'analyst' in the military.

Jane realised that once she had compiled her list of possible CIA employees in London in 1971, it would still be very difficult to work out which ones were still working for the organisation, but she also remembered Lee confiding his suspicion that the man they were looking for still held a senior position. She looked at her alarm clock: 11.23 p.m. Where was she going to find these US Foreign Service reference books dating from 1971?

Jim Parker's visit to London was scheduled to last a swift thirty-six hours. Its main purpose was to talk to members of his branch of the Company, the agent-running and covert action branch, in the London Station. Only three of the twelve London-based CIA officers worked for him in the Directorate of Operations. The rest filled liaison and political reporting jobs for Hal Canning, the Deputy Director for Intelligence. Several presidential findings limited DDO's ability to run agents in this friendliest of countries. Nevertheless there were some, including several MPs, journalists and other high-ups. These relationships were handled with great tact by the

Company: no dead letter drops, rarely any payment or many meetings in public places. Instead the source was cultivated over many years, often invited to embassy receptions and rewarded with sumptuous lunches at Le Caprice or Langan's. On this visit, Parker was to discuss the recuitment of new sources as part of the Agency's plans to step up offensive economic intelligence gathering.

The DDO was sitting in one of the secure fifth-floor meeting rooms at Grosvenor Square discussing career development with his London number two, when one of the secretaries put her head around the door. 'VIP call for you, Mr Parker.'

Parker loosened his thickly knotted tie and pushed the sleeves up his chunky forearms a little as the series of clicks on the receiver heralded his caller's voice.

'Jim? It's Peter, how are you?' the caller announced with the effortless informality of the well-bred Englishman.

'Sir Peter, good morning. I'm good. To what do I owe this pleasure?'

'I'd like a quick chat with you while you're here. I realise you're busy, but could you make it over for tea?'

Of course Parker had other plans, but he rescheduled quickly in his mind. Protocol demanded a favourable response to an invitation from the Chief of the Secret Intelligence Service.

At 3.55 p.m., Parker was dropped by an embassy car at the entrance to Century House, SIS's brooding concrete tower south of the River. The Chief's assistant, a middle-ranking SIS officer, was there to meet him in the doorway. A pass had already been made out and soon the two men were travelling upwards in a lift. The Chief's assistant had done his homework and engaged Parker in conversation about his Marine Corps background. The two men swept past Lucy, the Chief's PA, and into the incongruously panelled office overlooking Parliament where 'C' did his business.

Sir Peter was about six foot two, silver haired, the average person's idea of a Whitehall mandarin. He came round his desk swiftly to meet his guest, shaking his hand firmly and cracking a reserved sort of smile. 'Take a seat. So nice to see you, Jim.' The two men moved to armchairs as Lucy brought in a tray bearing a distinguished-looking Wedgewood tea-set which was also thoroughly inappropriate to the sixties environment of Century House.

After a few diplomatic exchanges, the Chief's assistant withdrew and Sir Peter's eyes seemed to signal a change in mood from the cordial to the grimly businesslike. 'Jim, you know that we in this Service have always felt that we live and die by the special relationship.'

'Of course, Sir Peter, it's appreciated in Langley.' Parker shifted around in his chair, seemingly uncomfortable, his big, squat frame restricted by a normally discarded jacket and tie.

'The convention that we only operate in one another's countries with the agreement of hosts must be maintained, I'm sure you agree?'

Parker's thoughts were beginning to race desperately. He had clearly been called here for some kind of dressing down, but he couldn't work out why. He replied, 'Of course.'

'Without that convention, our relationship would deteriorate. There will be suspicion, everything that we had worked for would slip away, the fight against our common foes would inevitably suffer.'

'What's on your mind, Sir Peter?' said Parker, trying to short-circuit his host's discourse.

'It has come to our attention that the CIA is financing an operation in this country by a rather second-rate company –' the Chief's face wrinkled slightly, like somebody tasting something sour – 'called Panther Secure Systems Limited. Does that ring any bells?'

'No, I can't say it does.'

'Well, Jim, we have some information which suggests that Panther has killed at least two people in Britain during the last couple of months as part of its contract with your organisation. They've killed at least two British citizens, one of them a policeman.' Parker's confusion about the allegations gave way to simmering anger.

'I have a two-word response to that and the first one is "bull"!'

'You don't think I would be having this conversation unless I had some reason to believe this information, do you?'

Parker said nothing, instead shaking his head in a vigorous way.

'Jim, we have established that there have been at least three transfers between a company called Mountain Resources Incorporated and Panther.' The Chief produced a slip of paper and pushed it across the coffee table. 'I've taken the liberty of noting the dates and amounts. It's been possible for us to establish that Mountain Resources has been using CIA funds.'

Parker studied the figures quickly, his anxiety settling a little as he composed his reply. 'All I can say is that Clandestine Service knows nothing about any such operation. It may be that some crazies in Army Intel are goofing around here, in which case I apologise. I'm going to look into it when I get back to Washington and get back to you with an answer within twenty-four hours.'

'Jim, you must understand one thing. We are almost as certain as we can be that Mountain Resources is transferring these funds on behalf of CIA, not any other organisation. We've kept all this on a very tight net. We haven't told our fellow intelligence organisations in this country and, of course, we haven't told ministers yet. But without a satisfactory answer, ministers will have to be told – and once the politicians get involved, who knows what damage might be done?'

Parker's certainty about his own department's lack of

involvement fortified his response. 'I can only repeat what I know, which is that we have no involvement with this Panther outfit. It's out of the question that we would authorise the killing of British citizens. I'm sure there's been some misunderstanding here and I wish you'd come to us before –' Parker went carefully towards his counter-attack '– before obtaining this kind of information from what may be an asset of US intelligence.'

The Chief ignored this admonition, replying instead: 'I would have thought that we'd done enough over the years to avoid this kind of attention from your people. If you'll excuse me?' He stood, indicating that the meeting was over. Parker left swiftly. Neither cup of tea had been touched.

Less than an hour after Parker's frosty meeting at Century House, a black Security Service Daimler pulled up outside a bungalow at Lake in the Isle of Wight. A tall, slightly portly figure, smartly dressed, made his way up the drive. Apart from his driver, he was quite alone. Jane Johnson heard the footsteps as she sat in the kitchen. Swiftly, she called her daughter's name and moved into the spare room. As the doorbell sounded, she was taking the automatic from her handbag and beckoning her daughter into the room. Her father was out, but she heard her mother going to the door.

'Can I help you?'

'Yes, I hope so.' The voice seemed rich, almost jovial. 'Is Jane Johnson here?'

'What do you want with her?' Jane's mother replied, her voice showing signs of strain.

'Just a quick chat if that's all right.'

Jane was scanning the street from the window of the spare room. She could see the man's back and his car but apparently nobody else.

'My daughter lives in London,' her mother said.

'I've reason to believe she's here at the moment,' he replied.

Jane cursed herself for making a phone call earlier that afternoon to the British Library, but not travelling to a box to do it. She felt despair at being found, but at the same time some glimmer of hope at this opportunity.

'Who exactly are you?' Jane's mother asked.

'It's OK, mum, I'll talk to him.' Jane had entered the corridor behind her. She had placed the pistol in the deep pocket of her cardigan and kept her right hand thrust into the opening, her index finger curled around the trigger.

'I'm Donald Travis.' He proffered his hand, Jane's remained firmly around the weapon. Her mother stood aside.

'Come in, Mr Travis, perhaps we can talk peace.'

'Indeed!' he replied, with a gusto that confused her slightly. The two of them moved into the sitting room.

Travis sat on the red Victorian sofa and Jane perched on the arm of a large chair opposite. He seemed to be eyeing her right hand. Jane took the cue.

'Before we start, Mr Travis, you should understand that if you make any move to harm me or anybody else in this house, I'll kill you.' She delivered the words slowly and drew the weapon out of the pocket for effect. Travis's earlier *bonhomie* evaporated.

'I'm not here to harm you, Mrs Johnson. I'm here because we want to find your husband.'

'Who's we?'

'The Security Service.'

'Why did you try to kill him?' Her voice was cold.

'We didn't—'

'Who did?'

'I honestly don't know. We want to get to the bottom of this riddle as much as you and Lee do—'

'Nobody's hunting you like a dog,' she cut in again. 'Why should I trust you? You've already messed up Lee's life. There's no going back for us.'

'That's one of the reasons I've come here, Mrs Johnson.

I want you to assure your husband on our behalf that he can return to the CID if he wants. We have evaluated his allegations and we believe him. There will be no repercussions for him.'

'And then one day, in a couple of years' time when it's all died down, the brakes on our car fail and we all die. Is that the plan?'

'I must assure you that we have no intention of harming you, absolutely none whatsoever.'

She digested his claim.

'In fact,' Travis continued, 'we are grateful to him for alerting us to a serious breach of security—'

'We'd want your guarantee about the job in writing. We'd want our safety guaranteed too by somebody we could trust.'

'We're both lawyers, Mrs Johnson. I think you must realise it would be very difficult for us to give such guarantees.'

'Really? It might be difficult for us not to distribute copies of the Operation RACETRACK files to all members of the Home Affairs Select Committee.'

Travis blanched at this.

'You and I must sit in a room with somebody we can trust – a judge or an MP – and you must give us guarantees about our safety, so that if we go the same way as MacFadyen, people will know why.'

'We didn't touch MacFadyen,' he countered swiftly, then slowing to a more considered pace: 'It may be possible for us to give certain assurances. The Met will put it in writing as far as Lee's job is concerned. As for us, that will be more difficult. I'll need to talk to the Director General. Where can I reach you?'

'You didn't do a bad job finding me here, did you?' Her mood had lightened slightly and she said it almost mockingly. 'I'll call you in a couple of days, give me a number.'

Travis plucked out a business card which said simply:

Donald Travis,
Legal Adviser.

There was no address or phone number. He wrote the latter on. 'This is my direct line, you can reach me there.'

'We'll consider your offer. Tell me who tried to kill Lee?'

'I can't offer any really convincing theory. We're devoting quite a lot of man-hours to this subject ourselves.'

'You must have some idea?'

He shook his head, determined to deny her the benefit of his Operation BASTION inquiry.

'That's very convenient for you. So the same anonymous force could still kill us despite any guarantee you give us?'

'*Nemo dat quod non habet.* I cannot give you what is not mine to give. There may still be somebody out there who wishes to harm you, but I can assure you that it is not an arm of our government.'

Jane watched Travis's Daimler pull away into the street. The whole encounter had surprised her and she set about trying to scribble a record of the conversation from memory. For the first time in weeks she felt herself warmed by a ray of optimism.

Chapter Thirty-One

Jane had been expecting the papers to catch on to Lee's disappearance eventually, and that Wednesday morning, as she sat scanning the *Mail* over breakfast, she saw the first evidence that they had. It was a small piece on an inside page of the paper:

Fears For Missing Detective Grow
By Our Crime Staff
London police last night confirmed that the partner of a detective murdered four weeks ago has not been seen since the night of the attack. The missing man, Detective Sergeant Lee Johnson, is not a suspect in the brutal killing of Detective Constable David MacFadyen.

Colleagues fear D.Sgt Johnson may have suffered some form of breakdown as a result of the incident. One source in the CID who worked with the detective said he had been under 'a lot of strain' in the weeks leading up to his partner's murder. The two detectives were commended for bravery after foiling a raid on a Kensington safe deposit box company earlier this year.

There was little else of consequence in the story. She didn't like what she had seen at all. The implication of nervous collapse would undermine Lee's credibility in the eyes of anybody they contacted in the search for help. Was the article the work of the man she had met the previous day? She had her suspicions. Still, he had been prepared to discuss doing some deal with them and that still gave her hope. In a curious way Travis's apparently honest inability to explain who was after them boosted his credibility in her eyes.

As Jane and Gemma were finishing their breakfast, she heard the sound of breaking glass.

'Stay here, darling!'

Jane moved swiftly through the bungalow to the spare room and took the gun out of her handbag. The cool rush of adrenalin was beginning to surge through her. She walked into the living room to see a hand coming through the broken pane to open the window. As she came through the door, the man looked up and his eyes met hers. The small, pinched face and wispy moustache were instantly recognisable to her as those of the man who she had found on her doorstep in Hammersmith weeks before in the uniform of a Telecom engineer.

'*If you see him again, don't hesitate. Kill him.*' Lee's words went through her head. She levelled the gun.

Dodge did not seem to think she would fire: to her disbelief he carried on with what he was doing, opening the window and stretching his leg up onto the sill, climbing into the frame.

'Stop!' she shouted. He seemed to move all the faster.

'Mummy, what's happening?' Gemma was suddenly behind her.

'Get back into the kitchen now!' It was a scream. Jane could hear her daughter scurry away snivelling. Why wasn't she firing?

Dodge was through the window now. He had jumped down from the still and was walking across the living room towards her. He drew a commando knife from inside his flight jacket. He was only a leap away from her now.

'The one who kills first survives!' Lee had said. It wasn't so easy for her. Kill a man in her own mother's living room?

Jane squeezed the trigger, but closed her eyes as she did.

The Browning made a terrifyingly loud bang and jumped in her hand. Dodge was down on the floor. She backed through the living-room door, banged it shut behind her and locked it.

Dodge had heard the crack of the bullet winging over his shoulder and took it as his cue to leave. She was ready to use the weapon. In this particular contest of nerve, he had lost. He ran down the path to a van where two other men were waiting. Phil had gone missing and was not among them.

As they sped off, Dodge said: 'We're going to go back in there tooled up; I'm going to have that bitch.' But he knew that guns would take a while to organise and his intended victim would probably soon flee. As soon as he had begun planning this operation, he had become concerned about how they would get off the Island if they did snatch the woman and girl. If the police were alerted, it would be very simple for them to block the couple of ferry routes to the mainland. To this end, Pinchman had arranged for a motor yacht to pick them up at a small inlet near Freshwater.

Dodge and the others abandoned the van, setting fire to it before they walked down the steep slope where the Zodiac was waiting to take them out to the larger boat. Dodge said little to the others, his frustration turning inwards as he regretted not moving faster to disarm the woman. He found himself wanting another chance to take care of her, to restore his pride in front of his silent companions.

Jane had talked to her daughter in a strange calming monotone, almost without drawing breath, for a long time after the screech of tyres outside. 'Everything's going to be fine . . . we're all safe . . . we'll see Daddy soon.' She felt guilt at not leaving the Island as soon as Travis had departed the previous afternoon. She was afraid that Lee would reprimand her for that, and for not shooting that little shit dead on the spot. At the moment of truth, everything Lee had told her about adopting the CQB stance and firing two or three shots had gone out of the window. If MI5 knew where to find her, that was a very bad sign. How plausible was Travis's denial of their connection with the people who kept trying to get them?

By seven that evening Jane and Gemma were ensconced once more in Tania's flat in London.

'Will you be staying long?' Tania asked as they sat in the kitchen drinking tea.

'No, a couple of days. Is it a problem?'

'No, not really.'

'Not really?' Jane asked, wondering whether it was time to take up Lee's suggestion of going to stay with his uncle in Cheltenham. Jane had no way of knowing that Travis had rung her parents' home on the Island a few hours after her flight to discuss peace terms further.

'No it's fine, really,' said Tania, closing the conversation.

It was some time after Jane had put Gemma to bed, when she and Tania were sitting in front of the television watching the news, that the phone went. Tania answered and almost immediately passed the receiver across. 'It's for you.'

'Hello,' Jane said nervously.

'Babe, it's me. I'd been hoping you would be in.'

'Darling, it's so good to hear your voice.'

'I've been so miserable. I want to see you soon,' said Lee.

'Me too. I've got the little one with me, I expect she'd rather fancy seeing you too.'

Jane decided not to tell Lee about the attack. She couldn't face going through it with Tania sitting there, picking her nose, staring at Martyn Lewis.

'OK, I'm not in London at the moment: what about Sunday, three days' time?'

'Of course, of course,' she replied.

'Have you got your pen and paper handy?'

'Hang on.' She fumbled in her purse and from behind the crisp banknotes she had got out of the machine on the way to Tania's, pulled out the slip of paper bearing codes which Lee had written out for her on the Island a couple of weeks before.

'Let's make it at BNND o'clock at HTERDXCLJBR. All right? Do you want to read them back to me?'

Jane did, and added: 'Honestly, Lee, I have got the hang of this, you know.'

'Has everything been OK with you two?' he asked.

'Not exactly, but we're all right now.'

'What happened?' Lee was becoming nervous.

'It's too difficult to go into now.' She eyed Tania with a certain resentment.

'Tell me!'

She said nothing for a few moments, searching for the words. 'I saw that man again . . . the phone engineer.'

'Jesus! What happened?'

Jane had heard the crash of Lee kicking the side of the phone box and answered quickly. 'We're safe, that's all that counts.'

'Did you . . . use my present on him?'

'Yes,' she said with some small pride, 'but he'll live to fight another day. I only got one round off. I'm sorry.'

'Good! Well done!'

She felt a strange relief that Lee was not telling her off for not killing the man.

It was about an hour later that Sam Boswell walked up Clissold Street in Balham, a couple of roads away from Tania's flat, and tapped on the back window of the Renault van parked there which he recognised as one of the Service's current surveillance vehicles. As the door creaked open he noticed Tim Ashman in the back with another person he vaguely recognised as an A1 type – people who specialised in covert entry. Boswell looked around self-consciously before climbing in. He wondered how often men in suits walking along suburban streets climbed into the back of parked vans at ten o'clock at night.

'What's up then, Tim?'

'I think we've had a bit of a result here,' Ashman began. 'I already knew about two withdrawals by Jane Johnson from the Midland cashpoint machine in the High Street through the NEWMARKET trace. I checked that and noted the proximity of the bank to the flat of one Miss T. Easton whose number was on the list we had from Telecom for numbers dialled from the Johnson's house in the last month before the detective sergeant did his bunk.'

Boswell had begun to take notes in a small police-style pad drawn from the inside pocket of his suit. 'Very smart, Tim, very smart,' he said encouragingly.

'Well, not a couple of hours after Mr Travis tells me she's gone Awol from the Isle of Wight, the NEWMARKET bells sound and she's made another withdrawal from the Midland on the High Street. I took the precaution of having an intercept put on Miss Easton's line, PDQ.'

Boswell had already noticed the reel-to-reel with tape cued up on a rack on the opposite side of the van. Ashman leant forward and switched on the machine. The three men listened to Lee's conversation with his wife.

'Do you think they're using some kind of one-time pad?' Boswell asked, as he pondered the series of letters he had written down in the notebook.

'Well, I've tried various simple codes –' Ashman glanced down at a notepad covered with attempts to crack Lee Johnson's secret message – 'and I rather came to the same conclusion.'

'And you think she's got some kind of decoder with her there at the moment?'

'Well, she's obviously got to be carrying it with her. If we can get it, we can be there for their next meeting and Mr Travis can talk to the organ grinder himself.'

'What if she's burnt her pad after decoding the message?' Boswell asked.

'Well, it's obviously possible. They're a bit Colmans, these two, but she has been making mistakes. She hasn't exactly got the world's best tradecraft, has she? After all she went to that same branch of the Midland three times. She's been back to her parents' house twice. It's got to be worth a look, hasn't it?'

'Enter the flat?' Boswell asked, somewhat unnecessarily.

'Yes, if we find it and Johnson turns up for the meet, then we've cracked it, haven't we?'

Boswell was the ranking officer on the operation. Travis and Davies had both been unavailable for some reason. He used the cellular phone to try Monica Davies's number again. Ashman and the other man looked around as Boswell sat with the ringing in his ear. She was evidently out late. It was up to him, the first time in all his years in the Service that he had been asked to make this kind of operational decision.

'And . . . ?' Boswell nodded at the third man.

'Bill,' the man replied, speaking for the first time.

'Yes, Bill is the expert,' Ashman said, cracking a sly smile.

'OK,' said Boswell after a little more reflection, 'we'll go in there at 3 a.m., and see what we can find.'

Bill immediately began rooting around in the grip which he had at his feet. Inside, Boswell could glimpse some of the tools of Bill's trade: a huge ring of keys; a polaroid camera to record the position of objects before beginning the search; a packet of surgeon's rubber gloves.

A few hours later surgery began in the ground floor of the flat as Jane, Tania and Gemma slept upstairs.

Chapter Thirty-Two

Jane noticed nothing unusual as she tucked her purse into her bag and got her things ready for the journey into the West End. She was taking Gemma with her – there wasn't much else she could do with her. Tania had gone out to work earlier. She had a job as PA to some banker in the City.

After washing up the breakfast things, Jane and her daughter left the house in Balham and took the tube to Marble Arch. They walked together into Grosvenor Square and passed by a small gaggle of Palestinians who stood behind barriers outside the US embassy. Every now and then, one of the men would start a chant with a loudhailer and the others would join in. It was a forlorn sort of protest – several of the men had covered their faces with their checked headdresses. Seeing the lack of interest from the five policemen in front of them and those entering the embassy, she was not sure why they had bothered to disguise themselves.

A couple of phone calls had established that the United States Information Service library on the far side of the square could obtain Foreign Service handbooks from 1970–1972 for her to look at. They seemed very friendly over the phone and did not seem at all curious about why she wanted to look at them. They were expecting her and the books were ready. They also obliged Gemma with a Dr Seuss book, which Jane hoped would distract her for long enough.

She had memorised the spook-spotting criteria from *Dirty Work* and soon began working her way through the embassy list for 1970. Every now and then she stopped and jotted down a name in her notebook. Within about thirty minutes she had gone through the three books, cross-checking the names with the State Department's biographical register. Her list of suspect CIA officers contained sixteen names. Although she felt a glow of triumph at having done this, it was an insipid one, because the really difficult task of working out which of the sixteen might still be serving remained to be solved. She found a 1992 biographical register and checked the index. Only four were still in there. She placed ticks beside the relevant names: Brook, Cisjevic, Pollock and Turnley.

'Mummy, I'm bored; can we go now?'

Jane found another book. 'Look at this, darling, it's lovely.'

'I don't want to look at it. Can't we go?'

'Just let Mummy finish what she's doing. Five more minutes.'

As Jane was running through her options about how to find these people, a fat red book on a shelf of reference works caught her eye: *Federal Staff Directory, 1991/2*. She walked over and pulled the book down. To her surprise, she found an entry for the CIA; however, there were only six names listed. One immediately caught her attention:

Deputy Director, Intelligence . . . Canning, H.N.

The entry even had his phone number, but unfortunately, unlike several of the other senior CIA officers, there was no biographical note. Despite that she felt her senses tingle: his name was on her original list and she felt certain that H.N. Canning was her man. She was not bothered that his was not one of the four names still listed in the Biographical Register – this simply meant that they were still serving abroad under diplomatic cover. Canning had become too big a fish to carry on with that particular charade.

'Mummy!'
'Yes, all right, we're going now.'

Tim Ashman was in an infuriatingly good mood that morning, strolling down the corridors of Gower Street whistling away, occasionally filling in a few lyrics like 'When I fall in love' or 'You don't have to say you love me'. His chirpings and singing were delivered in the warbling tones often used by the self-appointed men of music who perform in pubs. He entered Monica Davies's office and deposited a neatly-typed transcript of the phone conversation between Lee and Jane on her desk: he was beside himself with delight. In place of the gobbledy-gook code which Lee had used to disguise his plans for the assignation, the words 'FOUR o'clock at TURNHAM GREEN' had been inserted. He turned to see her standing behind him.

'Good morning, Sam.'

'Morning. These are the transcripts. We've intercepted a conversation between Johnson and his wife. We tracked her down to a friend's flat in Balham and we cracked a code they were using.'

'How did you achieve that?' she asked suspiciously.

'We conducted a covert search of the flat during the early hours and found a one-time pad in her purse. Bill used his hand-held wotsit – you know, his photocopier – and we replaced it and let ourselves out.'

'I understood an operation had happened last night from Sam Boswell's messages on my answerphone at home. I must say I was slightly surprised he didn't wait for higher authorisation before going in.' She could not contain her annoyance at being unable to take a key operational decision.

Ashman was mildly irritated. 'Well, we were trying your number for a couple of hours. Anyway, all's well that ends well. We only had one difficult moment when we heard one of the ladies upstairs walk across the landing to the loo. We had to stand still for about forty minutes after that.'

At 11 a.m., a meeting was called in Travis's office to discuss how the intelligence obtained the previous night might be exploited. Travis summoned Monica Davies five minutes before the others.

'I understand you weren't able to authorise Boswell's nocturnal ramblings, Monica?' he said in the distracted manner of an MI5 mandarin administering a gentle bollocking.

'No, Jeremy and I had tickets for *Don Giovanni* at the ENO and the car broke down on the way home. All a bit of a disaster . . .' She was unable to suppress a nervous twitch – more of a shudder through her whole body.

'Well, of course Boswell is entitled to make that kind of call in an emergency. He's not the best and brightest in the Service, but of course, he's a perfectly skilled officer.'

'Our answerphone wasn't working properly I'm afraid, Donald . . .' She was becoming mildly irritated at being put through the mangle by Travis in this way. Nothing had gone wrong, after all. The Legal Adviser was unaccustomed to the role of operational commander and she felt he was playing it with too much melodrama.

'It's just the combination of Boswell and Ashman – very different chaps of course, but you know how these ex-Army boys egg one another on. Anyway –' he let the word hang, signalling that he had the good grace to change the subject – 'they did bring back some very tasty morsels. In particular, Ashman was very smart in putting a NEWMARKET trace on that bank in Balham.'

'Indeed he was. I think the question now – the question which I expect you were about to ask me – is how best to exploit the intelligence. If we turn up to greet them, will Detective Sergeant Johnson run like hell?'

'Well, at least we know he isn't armed. She has the gun.

Boswell noticed it had been fired, which chimes in with the police on the Island logging a report of a suspected gunshot the other day and with the intercepted phone conversation with Johnson.'

There was a knock on the door as Boswell and Ashman arrived. Travis waved them in and mouthed the word 'coffee' at his PA, who repeated the same word audibly to each of the guests. The conversation swiftly moved beyond some gentle congratulation for the previous night's efforts towards the formulation of a plan of action for Turnham Green.

'The desirable outcome from my point of view is for somebody to take Johnson gently by the arm and lead him to me so that we can have a quiet chat,' Travis began, adding: 'I don't think I should confront him personally on a busy street, it might alarm him.'

'I don't know,' Ashman countered. 'Here's a bloke who probably thinks we want to top him. The busier the place, the more likely he'll believe that we're not about to. Plus, you're the one person he knows really does work for the Security Service.'

'Point taken, Tim. I still believe it's better for a couple of people to approach him, lead him to me. I gain his agreement to take him and his family to Sittingbourne where we debrief him at length and get to the bottom of this whole business.'

'Bill and I can waylay him, Mr Travis.' Ashman's success the night before was making him more adventurous than usual. 'It's probably best for any A4 people on the scene not to compromise themselves.'

'Hold on there, Tim; we haven't decided whether we need to have Watchers there,' said Monica, trying to reassert her leadership.

'We have to, don't we?' Travis countered, leaving her becalmed.

'Well, I think we do; good surveillance operators on the

ground are essential for this sort of op,' Ashman confirmed authoritatively.

'We'll only get one crack at this.' Boswell was talking now. 'If Johnson takes fright and does a flit, the mobiles from A4 won't stand a chance going after him. Anybody can spot a tail if they're driving at 90 m.p.h. through Turnham Green. But we'll need plenty of A4 bods to secure the area for the meet itself.'

Each had their own say: in Lee's mob in Ireland this kind of free-for-all had been known as a 'Chinese Parliament'. At Gower Street it was not the usual way of doing business. A plan was formulated and Travis handed out a list of actions for each of those present. Monica Davies was told to 'cost and task A4 operation', which struck her as something of an insult. As Travis concluded, Ashman caught his attention one more time.

'I know we don't want to chance our arms again at the house in Balham without good reason,' the ascetic-looking technical officer began, 'but I think I and all the other bods on the ground would feel much better if we knew that old Calamity Jane's nine mill had been spiked. I've got the necessary experience from NI to file down the firing pin. If, in the confusion of the moment, she decides to let rip with the Smith and Wesson, I think all of us on the ground would feel better knowing it wouldn't go off.'

Travis pondered Ashman's request. It was always pushing one's luck to attempt a covert entry in an occupied house two nights running, but he also had to consider the risk of letting Jane Johnson endanger everybody at a very tricky meeting. 'Let me think about it, Tim. I'll call you later.'

Ashman nodded silently and extended his long-limbed body as they all rose to leave Travis's office.

Lee had spent a busy but fruitless few days playing hunches, trying and failing to pick up Denton's trail again. Nothing had borne fruit since his coup following him to the drop-off in Wimbledon. He found himself at a filling station in Deptford putting his last cash into petrol. There were a few cans of food in the boot, but no more notes or coins in his pocket. Several times, he had played his supermarket trick for drawing money, but he knew his account was in the red. The previous day this had been confirmed when a checkout girl had summoned her manager at Asda and he had insisted on keeping Lee's cashcard. There was nothing else left and he hoped that Jane would have some money when they met. He had spent many hours wondering what had happened to his wife and daughter when the killer had appeared, and feeling guilt at not being there. She had used the gun – that much was clear from her conversation.

Lee shook every drop from the nozzle of the petrol pump as he finished and surveyed the surrounding street as he strolled across the forecourt. Nothing rang alarm bells – a couple of neighbourhood boys wobbling around, the two of them on one bike. An elderly lady pushing along a wheeled whicker basket with two bottles of sherry in it. All three were black and while Lee reckoned there were some non-whites in the Watchers, he didn't think they could field the cast he saw on this impoverished street.

Lee saw that the cashier was watching the news intently.

'It was the Franc's turn to feel the heat of the Deutschmark today,' the TV presenter said. 'Bankers in Paris spent an estimated £2 billion trying to defend their currency.' The commentary continued. 'In a repeat of Sterling's disaster on Black Wednesday, those deserting the Franc for the Mark never seemed to believe the French government would go any further to defend its position.'

Lee paid up and returned to the car. The Escort pulled away and headed east. Lee had memorised the address of his destination, an Army quarter in Chatham, but that would wait until Saturday. He wanted one more day observing Denton's flat. He calculated that he would have enough petrol to get him to Chatham and back to Turnham Green in time to meet Jane on Sunday.

Chapter Thirty-Three

Friday morning had come as sweet deliverance to Charles Denton. Since the unpleasantness of his little trip to Sittingbourne earlier in the week, he had busied himself boxing up his things at home and preparing for his last day at work. Colleagues had told him there would be a small retirement party – Denton had insisted that it wasn't necessary but they would not hear of it. He would go in a couple of hours before and clear his few possessions from the office on the fourth floor. Was he leaving under a cloud? He didn't much care any more. Monday's 'interrogation' had been inept. Denton felt a vague sense of anti-climax, having spent his professional life preparing for that moment only to get off with a single day's not-very-clever questioning. Nobody in counter-espionage was supposed to know why he had taken the week off. Travis said Denton should simply tell the curious that he had been too sick to come in.

Denton had spent much of the morning wandering around the West End and Bloomsbury rather like a tourist. His days in Britain were numbered now – his days alive were numbered too. He thought he would pass the time wandering through the streets, gazing at the solid architecture which was one of the few things he really admired about this country. Every so often he had to rest on a bench or a wall. While sitting in Tavistock Square he looked down at his bony, wasted hands. He was taking on a jaundiced hue. The yellow had been visible in his eyes for a couple of weeks; now it was seeping into his skin.

The doctor told him these were the signs that the cancer was eating his liver. Going to the toilet had filled him with despair since the vile illness had taken his bowel in its deadly embrace. Now that his liver was going too, his piss was changing colour, becoming almost orange. That saddened him so deeply that he would have tears in his eyes as he stood at the urinal. He preferred to look away.

The walk from Tavistock Square to Gower Street took only a few minutes. Nobody seemed interested as he came in and took the lift to the fourth floor.

The few pencils, framed picture of Irene and other bric-a-brac took only a few minutes to tidy away. Denton waited until 5 p.m., when people started thinning out, to log on to his computer. He had been gripped by the impulsive desire to have one more go at teasing out details of Operation BASTION. He went to the files he had seen before in the Admin and Legal Adviser's areas of the computer – they all remained locked. As he was about to log off, he had the idea of going to Monica Davies's section of the counter-espionage database. He found a file headed 'A4 Req' with the following day's date. He tried to read it, but the computer prompted 'key'. He held his breath and typed 'B-A-S-T-I-O-N'. The screen changed, he was in. He read on.

It is expected that Jane Johnson will arrive in the area with her five-year-old daughter. It is unclear where in the Turnham Green area she will meet her husband, but we believe at least four mobiles will be needed to take up initial positions at the tube station, and the bus stops on King Street and Goldhawk Road (marked below). Statics should concentrate around the tube station and in Ravenscourt Park.

There were some other details – most importantly that the meeting was due to take place at 4 p.m. The plan also contained details about moving the Johnsons down to the house in Sittingbourne where he had been questioned earlier in the week. Monica Davies had noted:

> All operators should know that Lee and Jane consider their lives in danger and may act irrationally. Lee Johnson may be particularly skilled at detecting surveillance, and this should be borne in mind. If confronted, operators must respond with great tact and calm.

Denton memorised as much as he could and stored the file. It was already 5.30 p.m., and time for him to take the lift down to the Patio Restaurant.

Jim Parker had spent the morning at Langley holding interview boards for those seeking the job of Head of Far East Division of the Directorate of Operations. Parker's interviewing technique was usually brutal. That morning he had asked a middle-ranking black CIA officer who had ambitions for the job: 'Don't you think a negro might be a little conspicuous meeting sensitive sources in Singapore or Hong Kong?' The representative from 'Human Resources' on the board had sighed audibly after that one. Parker maintained that there were certain aspects of race and gender which simply could not be ignored and resented any implication of prejudice. On leaving Parker's room, the crestfallen black officer asked Vince Dubois, Parker's chief of staff who was waiting in the outer office: 'Who put a fly up his ass?' It wasn't the kind of question that required an answer, but Dubois knew that, if he had to give one, he would say that the culprit was the Chief of MI6 in London. Parker's principal worry had been that some of his own people might have gone out on a limb without his knowledge – in which case he would kick their butts all the way to Bangor, Maine, and back. Today, as he nudged past the other members of the interview board filing out of Parker's office, Dubois had gathered enough information to answer his boss's questions.

'What gives?' he asked Dubois as he saw him coming in.

'I've been looking into the London business for you.'

'What have you got?' Parker's brow dropped in anticipation.

'Well, where do you want me to start?'

Parker sensed that Dubois was afraid of what he had to say. He wanted to reply, 'Get on with it!' but bit his tongue and said instead: 'Well, what can you tell me about Mountain Resources Incorporated?'

'It's an Agency front all right.' Dubois studied his boss carefully, fearing the coming explosion. 'It was set up in the early 1980s as part of an operation in support of the Afghan resistance. During the last few months there have been transfers of about $2m into it from one of our operating accounts. Mountain Resources has been paying the money to Panther Secure Systems Limited, operating out of Croydon, England. The amounts tie up pretty much exactly with the figures Sir Peter gave you in London.'

As Dubois's narrative unfolded, Parker stood up, pulled down the knot of his tie, flicked open his collar button and began to pace the office. He glanced at his watch, stopped by the desk and pressed a key on his intercom. 'Melissa, could you ring Senator Rigby and tell him I may be fifteen minutes late for lunch.'

'Uh-huh,' Melissa replied from next door.

'We've been paying for Brits to get whacked?' Parker's voice, normally ebullient, was almost a whisper.

Dubois had noticed beads of sweat on Parker's forehead, something he hadn't seen in years. 'Well, of course we haven't been able to discover much about what exactly Panther has supplied the Agency in return for these two million bucks, but it's certainly true that we've been paying them to do whatever they've been doing.'

'Who authorised the payments into Mountain Resources?'

'That's not proving easy to discover. But there's something you should know about Mountain Resources, Jim. It wasn't a Clandestine Service front. When it was used before, it was used by the Directorate of Intelligence people to fund covert forays into Afghanistan by people gathering stuff for their analytical guys.'

'So you're telling me that fuck Canning is running his own operations in Britain?'

'Well, face it – we know it's not our directorate. The evidence points towards DDI, Jim,' Dubois frowned, suppressing a nervous smile.

'When Congress gets this they're going to tear his head off and shit down his neck!'

'I thought there might be a silver lining to this one.' Dubois allowed the smile to escape.

'There's no silver lining, Vince. If we've been whacking UK nationals there's going to be hell to pay and the whole Agency's going down with Canning. It'll make the Tower Commission look like a Fourth of July picnic. We'll all be tainted, Vince.'

'What if there's some presidential finding authorising Canning's operation? He could be watertight.'

'Vince, we've had some stupid presidents, God knows, but none is going to be stupid enough to sign a finding authorising the DDI to go around terminating Brits with extreme prejudice. It really is Canning or me now and either way I don't see it being resolved without enormous damage to CIA.'

'Why you or him?'

'If the Agency's chief analyst was authorised by the Director or President to carry out some operation, and I never knew about it, then that makes me about as useful as a tub of chicken shit at a ladies' bridge night. If Canning's out there on his own, doing fuck knows what, then I'm probably

OK. Either way, if the Hill gets to hear, we'll all be sellin
insurance.'

Denton shuffled into the near-empty Gower Street cantee
in an embarrassed sort of way, but then who arrives at thei
own retirement party full of self-confidence? As he rounde
the corner into the room he overheard Shirley, his secretar
saying the words 'terribly sad' – that was him, he presumed
She was standing with a couple of other stalwarts from hi
branch, all middle-aged ladies who did clerical work of on
sort or another. In all there were seven people – about on
for every six glasses laid out on one of the tables with
few bottles of wine. Somebody had put out three bow
of peanuts which people nibbled at in an awkward sor
of way.

'Charles, have a drink!' said Peter Johns, one of the fev
others in his branch with service going back almost as long
as his own.

'I'll have a white wine, please, Peter,' Denton croaked.

They stood around Denton in a huddle. Inevitably the firs
question was: 'What are your plans now?'

Denton talked plausibly about his little flat near Malag
where he hoped to spend whatever time he had left, in th
sun, reading those great works of literature which he ha
missed out on during his life. As he repeated these word
to each person who asked, he fantasised again about th
cheering, the medals and the adulatory newspaper articles
These people would soon know his true greatness.

'Ooh, how lovely,' said Elsie, one of the Registry women
'I might come and visit, if that's all right!'

'Please do,' said Denton, knowing the seriousness with
which she had made the remark.

After about half an hour, the Director of Counter-Espionag
arrived with his assistant and everybody stiffened their back
a little. When it was clear that the group of ten standing in

corner was not going to get any bigger, the Director tapped a table with a spoon to bring the group to order.

'We're here today to say goodbye to Charles Denton – one of the old school. Without any disrespect to the younger people present here, I can really say that Charles is a man of a kind we just don't get in the Service any more.'

Denton looked down into his glass, surveying the untouched Bulgarian Riesling.

'Having come here from Rhodesia, Charles entered the Service with the kind of commitment and willingness to serve which was not uncommon among Commonwealth recruits, but which has ebbed away as one by one, the countries shaded pink on the old maps gained their independence.'

Denton was emerging from a diamorphin daydream, a jumble of images and impressions of those early years in England. His spirits started to lift a little: he was about to cross the finishing line in a race he had never expected to complete. Thirty years living with the fear of exposure were about to end. He was going home – even if it was only for a few months. That made him happier than any of these people could ever understand. Denton began to sip his wine.

'It's not the custom at these occasions to delve too deeply into the details of somebody's service, but many of you will know that Charles served in K Branch for much of the 1970s before taking on a training assignment for several years and then coming back to counter-espionage in 1989. Within the last few months, despite the pain and discomfort of his illness, his diligent work allowed us to mount a major operation against the Iraqis.'

The boss wound up his speech with a toast to Denton's happy retirement and the presentation of a small stereo. There had been a whip-round among the staff which had yielded £17; the remainder had come from B Branch welfare and Shirley had bought the gift on the Tottenham Court Road. The assembled company called on Denton to say a few words.

He tried to refuse at first – even the few sips of wine had made him quite lightheaded – but eventually he allowed himself to be persuaded.

'All I would say is that the secret world is often a lonely one.' Some of the audience began to fear it might be one of those embittered retirement speeches which leaves everybody with a sour taste. 'I have served my country to the best of my ability and that has compensated me for the disadvantages of this secret existence. I'm not going to go into what I regard as my own highpoints – my own triumphs of working here, but I might say there have been some. I'll be going home with the knowledge that I made a difference and that's all that counts.'

Denton raised his own glass and the others followed. He added: 'Thank you all for coming' and there was polite applause.

The Director of Counter-Espionage took Denton into a corner and put his arm around his bony shoulder.

'I'm sorry about that business on Monday, Charles. When I found out what had happened, I gave Travis a rocket. They had absolutely no right to talk to somebody with your record of service like that.'

'It's nothing,' Denton replied. 'I'd almost have felt let down if my years here ended without me coming under suspicion of something!'

The Director smiled politely, murmured, 'good luck' and left. The others were soon filing out of the door. A couple of the secretaries put corks back into undrunk bottles of wine and tucked them into their bags.

Shirley turned to one of them and whispered: 'It's so sad. I think he's a bit overwhelmed and confused, poor love. He's not going home, he's going to Spain.'

Chapter Thirty-Four

Having been banned from the office, Denton was able to complete most of his packing and tidying. The flat was on the market, but so far there had been no takers. Its sale would be handled by an agent and the money forwarded to him, if he was still alive. Instead of packing, Denton spent the day getting increasingly anxious as he sat around the flat; anxious about his last day in a false existence which had spanned his entire working life. Just after 2 p.m., some international removals men came and took away his things. He watched the photographs and CDs disappearing into packing boxes and looked forward to being reunited with them in the home he had been told awaited him. He was surprised by the kindness and consideration of the packers, but he forgot that they could read his fate in those hollow eyes and waxy, yellow complexion. If his former workmates had been watching him all these weeks, would this be the time that they would swoop? Or would they do it at the airport?

Denton's nervous excitement about his last journey turned suddenly to panic. He had forgotten the details of how to get to the place where he would spend his last days. They had told him a couple of days ago. A man had met him outside the plastics factory in south Wimbledon and told him: 'Your work is at an end.' Of course, Denton had not made any note of the instructions this man then delivered, committing them instead to memory. Now he was sweating though, because try as he could, those fucking details had slipped into some chasm of his mind. For a few moments, he surrendered to blind panic, running his hand over his pate, across his chin, shaking his head and sighing audibly. He tried to reassert control of himself by marshalling up thoughts like: 'Get back to basic training' and 'It's the final furlong, don't let it slip'.

Before he and Irene had taken their roundabout journey to Rhodesia, they had been taught various ways to memorise things. One involved a room: each object in the room was attached to some aspect of what you wanted to remember – they would connect wherever possible: the clock in the room would bear the time of a meeting, a picture on the wall would be a description of the place where the meeting was happening, and so on. But the room in his mind now seemed as empty as the one he was standing in.

In despair, Denton set out for a phone box in order to check in with his controllers. The call was scheduled but he did not relish having to admit to them that he had forgotten some of the detail of his exfiltration plan. He decided to use an unfamiliar box just in case. He called the number which he had memorised but never used before.

'Hello,' a voice answered. It was electronically disguised; it sounded almost like a computer talking to him.

'It's Alfred checking in.' Denton's confidence had sagged so much because of his memory problems that he wondered for a moment if he had given the right pseudonym.

'You are late.' The computer voice was unforgiving.

'Listen, I have a problem with the plan—'

'It is not important, the plan is changed. You are to be ready to leave at 08.00 tomorrow. You are to walk to the south side of Tower Bridge. You will be picked up there.'

'What about the airport?'

'You will be picked up there.'

Ordinarily Denton would never have questioned an order, but he was shocked by this last-minute change. It seemed irregular, even dangerous. 'What is the procedure if I am not met?' he asked.

'Call this number at 11.00 if you are not met: a new rendezvous will be arranged.'

'Is everything OK? May I ask why the plan has been changed?' Denton didn't care any more about the rights and wrongs of tradecraft: why was something that had been done in the proper way, face to face, just a few days before, being altered?

'We share your concerns about the possible attentions of your company. The airport is not considered secure. You will be taken to a place of great safety.'

'Fine,' was all Denton could say. He replaced the receiver and immediately wondered about the last phrase. Did they suspect him of something? His favourite daydream about going home and receiving the acclamation of his chiefs suddenly seemed fragile. The mood of near-panic which preceded the call had worsened. Denton had only walked a few steps when something wracked his body. It was pain like none he had felt before and it seared through the feelgood haze of the diamorphin.

Lee was careful about timing his arrival at Bill Jessop's quarter. He knew Bill and his wife would be out socialising if he left it too late. So, even before the sun had slipped down, he rang the doorbell of the quarter where he expected to find his old friend.

'Fuck I! What brings you to these parts?' Jessop's accent, a hard Mancunian, was as thick as ever Lee remembered from the nights when the two of them were sergeants pissing it up in Munsterlager.

'Well, I thought I might drink all your beer, take your money, throw up all over your spare room and then leave you to clear up,' Lee replied, noticing that Bill already seemed to have taken a couple of drinks.

Walking into the living room, Lee immediately noticed a chaos which would never have been tolerated in their quarter in Germany.

'Where's Dee?' he asked.

'Well, things have been pretty rough, Lee. She's not been here the last few weeks.' Jessop's drooping black moustache seemed to accentuate his mournful demeanour.

Bill's story unfolded. His wife had been increasingly unhappy since the posting back from Germany. As a sergeant major at the training regiment up the road, Bill was entitled to a fancy quarter but that had not been enough to stem Dee's unhappiness. Bill described her descent into 'mid-fucking-life crisis'. He had suspected for weeks that she had started having an affair with some estate agent in the town and now apparently she had moved in. As Jessop told this tale, he pulled two cans of Carlsberg from the fridge, where another fourteen waited on ice, handed one to Lee and the two of them had sat down together. Bill sat there on his unevenly stuffed Army sofa staring into his can of lager and muttered: 'I've been thinking about driving down there one evening and slotting the pair of them.'

'Don't be daft; don't piss your whole life away.' Lee tried his best to comfort his friend. He found himself feeling vaguely annoyed at having to deal with this crisis rather than his own drama. Lee decided he would leave that until later and get Bill onto a different subject.

'So you never really told me about the Gulf, what did you get up to out there?'

'That was an anti-fucking-climax, the whole thing, Lee.'

'It looked pretty exciting from my living room in Hammersmith, I can tell you – people ducking Scuds, burning oil wells.'

'Well, we did a month of work up in the desert, then we had a war that lasted a hundred hours. Eighteen years in the Sappers for a hundred hours of fucking warfare: it was bollocks.' Bill cracked another can. 'At the end of it all we get volunteered to go and clean up the road north of Kuwait City – well you might have seen that on your telly, the Mutla-fucking-Ridge.'

'Oh, yeah, I think I know the place – the Shermans turned it into a big killing zone, didn't they?'

'The Shermans dropped every kind of ordnance on those dumb fuckers and they went driving off the road, looking for cover – straight into minefields – more fucking carnage – and the task fell to 32 Armoured Engineer Regiment to clean the whole thing up for them. There must have been a thousand knocked-out wagons on that ridge, and hundreds of dead people. The CO was nancing up and down with his fucking shooting stick shouting, "good work boys!" egging us on. We were knocking the Iraqi wagons off the road with CETs but of course it fell to my luckless fucking squadron to dig the holes for those barbecued Iraqis.'

'Right,' Lee said, almost inaudibly. Bill was in his stride.

'We dug these fucking things with the bulldozer blades on the front of the CETs. We dug eight of these pits and we put eighty Iraqis into each one. They fucking stank, these boys, they were well ripe. Well, within hours of filling in every one of these pits we find a stiff in one of the wagons on the side of the road. This Iraqi is, like, a fucking black skeleton sitting at the wheel. We'd have left him, but the dogs were loitering. Then we find another fucker in the back of some APC. And so on. Well, the blokes on the squadron didn't fancy digging another big pit, so we just dug, like, a shell-scrape and threw these extra bodies in and covered them with a few inches of sand. Well, of course, the following day, we went back after some kip. Well, the fucking dogs had been at them: there was fucking bits of charred Iraqi all over the area . . .' Bill shook his head forlornly. 'And I stood there as our lads gathered up the scraps and I thought: "Is this it?" Eighteen years of soldiering, eighteen years of preparing to fight – the best sodding training that money can buy – and my role in this whole thing is to clear up the fucking mess that the Americans have left—'

'The Shermans had left,' Lee butted in, reimposing the argot which had bound them years earlier.

'The Shermans, right. A week later, I was in Jubayl on the way back and I run into this ex-pat Brit out there in a hotel. He's off his fucking head on Sid – the local home brew – and he says to me: "The Saudis sub-contract the Filipinos to clean the streets and the Koreans to build things. They just sub-contracted the British Army to fight their war for them." And I realised this cunt was right. We're no better than the choggis now, Lee. These Arabs hired us like we hired the Gurkhas to defend the Empire.'

Lee had hoped that getting Bill to tell a few stories might cheer him up a bit, but he doubted his wisdom. 'Bill,' he said eventually, 'I've had some problems myself, in the work line, and I was wondering if I could tap you for a few quid, just for a while; you know?'

Jessop stood up and walked to a leather jacket he had hung on the back of the sitting room door. He pulled a manilla envelope out of the inside pocket.

'I've been prattling on for so long, Lee.' Bill handed over the package. 'There's two hundred quid, I got it out of the Abbey National for you. I knew you would come.'

'You knew?'

'It's been in the paper that you were missing – one of the lads in the mess showed me. Then this fucking joker of a detective comes down here last week. He says he's looking up everyone who you might turn to; says they know you're short of money. He asked me to ring him if you appeared. Some chance! What a cunt!'

'Thanks, mate.'

'You don't have to give it back, Lee. You don't have to tell me what the problem is, but I can guess you're in danger, so you should know that I'll always be here for you, if there's anything you need.'

'I don't want to get you in trouble with the head shed, Bill.'

'They've been pushing me to take early redundancy. I don't feel any loyalty to them.' Without further explanation, Bill walked across the room a little unsteadily and went out into the kitchen. Lee heard a crash of pots and pans as Bill rummaged around under the sink. Then he re-emerged with a small dark grey holdall – Lee had seen RAF people carry them.

'This is something I picked up on the Mutla Ridge,' said Bill, as he let the holdall fall to the floor with a thump.

Lee opened it gingerly and saw the compact, dark lines of an MP-5 sub-machine gun.

'Nobody's ever going to trace that piece,' Bill said, looking down at the gun with some pride. 'I took the rounds from training stocks. There's sixty in there, three mags of twenty. I was going to use it to go and finish off Dee and her fancyman.'

'Well, I'm glad you didn't do that with it. She may be a rotten cook but I think your reaction's a little over the top.' Both men laughed as the tension eased away.

Lee glanced at his watch: they had been talking for two hours. He needed to make a call.

'Shall I pop out and get us an Indian take-away?'

'OK,' Bill said, slightly mystified.

'I noticed that Tandoori place on the way up here, is that all right?'

'Yeah, I hear it's fine.'

After they had phoned through the order, Lee set off for the take-away and the phone box he had noticed just outside it. He had decided not to use the phone in Bill's house. For one moment he had caught himself wondering whether Bill was setting him up with the gun. Then he felt ashamed of himself for doubting the friend who had just given him £200. It saddened him: this business was causing him to doubt his oldest mates. If the police or MI5 had been to see him, though, it was quite probable that they were intercepting Bill's phone.

At the box, he dialled the Manchester number from memory.

'Elaine?'

'Yeah.'

'It's Lee, you not out on the town tonight?'

'I've just come in from the gym, I'm going out later.'

Lee wasn't sure whether to believe her. 'Found anything?'

'I found some good things in the same place as when you first called me, remember?'

Lee knew she meant the B Branch database – MI5's personnel records.

'Yes,' he replied.

'He worked his last day yesterday; he's retired.'

'Shit!'

'I'll give you an address. Standing by?'

Lee juggled the phone, pressing it against his ear with his shoulder as he pulled out a notebook and biro. 'Fire away.'

'It's PO Box number 6989, Malaga, Spain. All pension transfers are routed through to a bank in Malaga too.'

Lee wondered where Denton would be. If the dollars in that deposit box had been his pension plan, he might not have made it further than South London.

'Thanks, Elaine, you're too good to me.'

'I am, considering . . .' She giggled.

Lee rang off and immediately redialled Denton's flat in Blackheath. It carried on ringing out. He repeated this several times. Had he gone already?

At about the same time Lee set off back for Bill Jessop's, the removal van which had taken Denton's belongings arrived at a small warehouse near Winchester. After the goods had been unloaded and the removers driven into the night, two men in coveralls began loading Denton's possessions into an incinerator. As the CDs crackled inside the oven, one of the men began breaking up an antique table with an axe, stopping momentarily to search each piece for any hidden objects before tossing them into the flames.

Lee suspected that Bill had been weeping while he was out. His eyes bore the signs of uncontrolled sorrow. As they ate they reminisced a little before Lee, seeing it was already 9 p.m., could no longer suppress his desire to find out about Denton.

'Bill, mate. I've got to go soon. I can't stay tonight, I'm sorry.'

'Don't you want to throw up in the spare room before you go?' They both laughed. 'Listen, Lee, it's been brilliant seeing you. You turned up in the nick of time to stop me doing something fucking daft. It's been great talking.'

They hadn't really talked about the substance of Bill's differences with Dee, but Lee decided that his old friend meant this. He had borne witness to Bill's outpouring, allowed him his catharsis, and that was enough.

'Be careful with that gun, mate. They can hurt people, you know!' Bill said as Lee stood to leave.

'I'll always remember what you did for me, mate,' Lee swallowed hard. 'Anyway, what are you going to be doing for the next couple of days?'

'I thought I might go up north. I've got some compassionate leave. I'll see the parents in Manchester, then maybe go up to the Lakes for a few days.'

'Oh yeah, I know a girl you might get on with up there, let me give you her number.'

Chapter Thirty-Five

It was not even midnight before Johnson cruised into Blackheath in his Escort – a quick journey from Chatham. In the world of Bill Jessop, which he had left barely an hour before, there was the first sign of dawn, an end to the long night of self-pity which had enveloped him since his return from the Gulf and his estrangement from Dee. In South London there was the usual Saturday night quota of youngsters staggering about the worse from Mexican lager or Nigerian stout – whatever crap the blades with white socks drank these days. He drove along the heath, in front of the building where Denton had his flat, checking it out, making sure there weren't hordes of cops or Watchers at hand. There was little activity. A few snogging couples on benches on the heath: teenagers with nowhere else to go.

Johnson drove around to the nearest point to the back of Denton's flat. As he was nearing it, he parked the car. He took the MP-5 in the holdall from the boot. As he shinned over a garden fence, hidden in the murky shadows of a footpath, the screwdrivers in his pocket jabbed into his side. He knew he was at the rear of Denton's house as he was close to the hide he had constructed in the garden to keep the old boy under observation. Johnson looked across to the basement flat windows – no lights. He then strolled across the back garden in what would have been full view, had any of the neighbours been looking. Johnson's training and experience in Ulster had taught him that behaving naturally, looking as if you own the place and know exactly where you're going, will deflect people's curiosity in the most incriminating of circumstances. After climbing the roof of the rear extension, it was easy to prise open the window of Denton's bathroom.

Within seconds of stepping over the tub, Johnson could see that the old man had cleared out. There were no toiletries on the shelf over the sink; no paper on the loo-roll holder. Johnson had taken the precaution of donning dark blue washing-up gloves – sweaty, but offering more sensitivity than leather ones – and he carried a maglight torch, a heavy black cylinder which could double as a club if anybody surprised him. He walked through the rooms, scanning the surfaces and corners with the beam from the light. As he entered the bedroom doorway the light picked out the shrunken figure lying under a sleeping bag on a single bed. At the base of the bed was a single suitcase. Johnson wondered if Denton might be armed. He removed the MP5 from his bag and eased off the safety before going into the room. Denton opened his eyes into the torchlight and blinked rapidly. 'Who . . . ?' was all he said at first. Johnson saw the old man was groggy, confused. His skin seemed lifeless; he looked much worse than during their last meeting. Perhaps his drowsiness was more the result of drugs than sleep.

'Wake up, we need to talk,' Johnson said softly, but all he received in reply was a few mumbled words. He realised Denton was incapable of talking to him. Johnson took an empty packing case from the next room, parked it in the corner and sat down. It was just after 3 a.m.

As Denton drifted in and out of consciousness he sometimes forgot Johnson's presence in the room and sometimes just thought it was some kind of vivid dream, like so many others he had experienced recently. Most of the time though he worried about the change of plan. A couple of hours elapsed in this state of half-waking anxiety before something in the sick man's body stirred and he emerged more fully from his sleep.

He recognised the man in his room, saw the gun, understood finally that it was no apparition and asked: 'Are you here to kill me?'

'Depends.'

'On what?' Denton asked as his mind raced to the meeting at Tower Bridge and how he was going to make it.

'Whether you help me. Your survival depends on mine, you might say.'

Denton had propped himself up slightly in his bed, so he could look Johnson in the eye. 'Surely you know that my life is very nearly over.'

'I know that, yes. I'd be sorry, only I'm more sorry for David MacFadyen and I'm angry too. Angry about Dave and about the goons you sent to attack me and my family.'

'What do you want?'

'Was it worth having people killed to protect that American paedophile? I'd just like to know.'

'A cornered dog is the most dangerous one, Mr Johnson.'

'I know that. But you've cornered me now and that's why I'm not going to let you go unless you get me out of this.'

'How can I do that?'

'I can think of several possibilities. You can come with me to a police station and give a full statement—'

'Don't be ridiculous!'

'The alternative is that I kill you, Mr Denton. Well . . . there is something else. You kept some of the surveillance material from the brothel, didn't you?' There was no reply. 'You had it in the Jiffy bag you recovered from Majestic. I want that material. I want the proof against the American.'

Denton did not say anything. Instead he thought through his options. Could he try and disarm Johnson? Not feasible. Could he remain silent and miss his rendezvous at Tower Bridge? Impossible. Should he simply accept death at this man's hands? The drugs let him flirt freely with the idea of accepting death, but he still wanted to live; he wanted to go home. Was he going home, though? Time and again he remembered the previous day's phone conversation, the change of plans, the place of safety. But he didn't want to reveal his doubts, so eventually he said: 'Perhaps you should get on with it and kill me then.'

Johnson thought Denton didn't mean it and that if he wanted a battle of wills, then that was what he would get. 'I'm not going to kill you now. I'm going to let you wait for it. I want you to go through what you put me and Dave through.' The old man had closed his eyes – in contemplation or sleep, Lee could not tell. The standoff was rudely shattered at 6 a.m., when Denton's alarm clock, an old-fashioned model with two bells on the top, sounded loudly. Johnson stood up and switched it off.

'Going somewhere today, Charles?'

'No—'

'It normally goes at 7.30 a.m. I've been watching you for days. You always appear in the back bathroom for your piss and shave just after 7.30 a.m. It's time for you to leave Britain, isn't it? I'm not going to let you though.'

'Please!'

'You give me that surveillance material and I'll let you go. You should know something. I followed you to your drop in Wimbledon a few days back, you know, outside the factory on the trading estate. That's when I understood that you were working for somebody else, not for blackmail.'

'So . . .' said Denton, deeply shocked that he had been followed.

'I wonder what kind of retirement plan they've got for you. It'll be poorer than you planned, won't it, what with you leaving all your money at the deposit box company. Still you'll never find out if you don't give me the stuff.'

Johnson had touched a raw nerve. Denton had waited all these years for the moment when he would leave behind his treacherous life in Blackheath but now he wondered whether his masters' change of plan involved a shallow grave for him. Perhaps he could use Johnson. He could think of no better way of ensuring that MI5 would know how great a spy he had really been: if his own people were not going to give him the glory he deserved, he had better get it for himself. After what had seemed to Lee like five minutes of contemplation, Denton finally said: 'Open the suitcase at the bottom of my bed.'

Johnson wondered whether it might be boobytrapped. Quickly, he dismissed the idea. Denton would not have known this was going to happen. Nevertheless, as he walked towards it he kept Denton covered with the gun, and he opened the two latches on the case gingerly and at arm's length. He opened the lid about half an inch and ran the tip of one of his screwdrivers around it, just in case of any tamper switch. Finally he lifted it fully.

'You will find that the top is false,' Denton guided him.

Johnson felt around the top of the case and began working at one of the corners with his screwdriver. Eventually he prised free a corner of the lining fabric, pulling it back with a loud ripping noise. The padded envelope fell out. Johnson picked it up, stood up and went near the window as he opened it. Inside was an audio tape, on it a sticker said 'No. 4786K3/71'. He put it in his pocket.

'We have a deal, Mr Johnson?' Denton asked.

'Yeah. One more question though. If you weren't doing all this for blackmail and you weren't doing it for MI5, who were you working for, all these years?'

'You're a cleverer man than I first gave you credit for, but I can't tell you. Just leave me be now.' He said nothing for a few moments, then opened his eyes to see Johnson had already gone. It was only as he stared at the empty room that he realised that he had actually wanted Johnson to know who he really was and what he had done.

Dodge had gone to Panther's offices in Croydon that Sunday

morning to find Pinchman pacing around, saying little to the two goons who had been on the abortive snatch job to the Isle of Wight. As soon as Dodge, clutching his rolled-up copy of the *Sunday Sport*, was through the door, Pinchman ushered him into a separate office.

'I was trying to get you all day yesterday,' Pinchman said in a vaguely irritated way. Dodge didn't reply. 'We've had a tip from Ryan at MI5 that Johnson is going to RV with his wife and kid at Turnham Green this afternoon.'

'Very nice,' Dodge replied.

'Odds are that he'll drive there and she'll come by public transport, so the tube station is the hot favourite for the meet. We've got to lift them.'

'And then?'

'And then top them. The clients obviously don't want us doing it on the streets of West London. But if we have to, they want it done then and there.'

'This job is turning into something of a bloodbath,' Dodge remarked in a tone of voice which bore no sign of trepidation.

'I've never regretted taking on anything as much as I do this, I can tell you. I just want it all finished. The American has promised us more dosh, but frankly I don't care.'

'It'll be a tricky job to lift them in a crowded street. Are you sure our two friends—' Dodge nodded towards the other ex-soldiers sitting in the main office 'are up to it?'

'Well, they'll have to be, won't they. We won't get another tip as good as this one. If we lift them, we can lose those two before you and I take the three Johnsons off to top them.'

'You're coming? You've decided to get your hands dirty?' Dodge said, his tone revealing his natural distrust of anybody placed in authority.

'Yes. I didn't think I could ask anybody to do this kind of job without being in the lead myself.'

Pinchman's clumsy desire to play the officer irritated Dodge even more. 'I thought you were going to draw the line at doing the kid?' he taunted.

'I don't need your fucking sarcasm right now, Martin. We've got to clean up this mess and today's probably our only chance.'

'And if it goes wrong?'

Pinchman lifted an Adidas sports bag onto the table, pulling it open for effect.

'Silenced Sterling sub-machine gun,' Dodge said appreciatively. 'Nice bit of kit for slotting somebody without disturbing the Sunday peace too much.'

'It goes without saying that if we're caught nobody will say they ever knew us.'

'So we're pawns. The money's good. I can't believe CIA and MI5 are going to let us spill the beans on this one,' Dodge said with confidence.

'There's something you should know.' Pinchman looked across at the other two men and then lowered his voice. 'The house in Jubilee Road was raided yesterday – I think. I was driving up there when I saw that van we've noticed around the area was outside and there was a gang of plainclothes blokes entering the house. Obviously I did a U-turn and left the area.'

The listening post which they had set up weeks before to monitor Johnson's conversations was compromised. Tim Ashman and his assistant Ted had inspected the trunk which housed the receivers and recording equipment and inserted a device of their own which would alert them when somebody came to the flat to change the tapes. Now, Pinchman had abandoned the idea of ever going back.

'Are you sure?' Dodge countered.

'I'm as sure as I can be. We're not going back to Jubilee Road to find out, that's for sure. It does beg questions though.'

'Like?'

'Like does this "Ryan" really work for MI5?'

'That could have been any bunch of clowns yesterday,' Dodge said, his voice betraying a certain irritation with the details. 'In any case, he always made it clear that the op was so secret other people in the organisation didn't know about it.'

'I don't know what kind of shit we've got ourselves drawn into, Martin,' Pinchman said, 'but when we go out there this afternoon our arses are on the line – we might as well face it that if it goes wrong we're spending the rest of our lives in the nick and nobody's going to help us.'

For Gunter Mandelmann, the pale yellow light of that Sunday morning brought the happiest day of his recent life. As he sat looking across the rooftops of Berlin from his flat, he could at last live free of the fear of imprisonment. Two days before, the trial of Colonel Gunter Mandelmann of the Ministry of State Security of the German Democratic Republic had collapsed when the Federal Prosecutor's Office said it had no further case against him. Mandelmann, known in his fourteen years in charge of the Stasi's department of illegals as 'The Lynx', had walked out of the court a free man. Of course, there had been little hope of a conviction following the verdicts on his superior, Wolf, the head of the foreign intelligence branch. Mandelmann had run Wolf's most secret department, the one which dealt with East Germans who had assumed secret lives as spies abroad.

Mandelmann studied the press cuttings of his trial intently. He underlined errors in the reporters' copy with a red biro. He found it extraordinary how many mistakes they made. Three different newspapers had given him three different ages, one the wrong middle name. He felt complete contempt for them, although he took comfort from the fact that few of the journalists even seemed to understand what an 'illegal' was.

The phone rang. Although he had hidden behind his

answerphone for weeks, he was in a good enough mood to answer it. Anyway, he thought, even those reptiles in the press wouldn't ring on a Sunday.

'Yes,' he replied coldly as he lifted the receiver.

'Herr Oberst, it's Esslin from *Der Spiegel*.'

'Do you know what day it is?'

'I'm sorry, I'm under a lot of pressure from my boss to complete a piece on your trial for the next issue.'

Mandelmann didn't mind Hans Esslin as much as other journalists. He had spoken to Esslin in his time, but he really had no further use for him. 'I'm afraid I've nothing to say to you.'

'I just had one question, Herr Oberst . . .' Esslin pleaded.

'So, ask it. I can't promise an answer.'

'When I interviewed you in 1991, shortly before charges were filed against you, you said it would suit the Federal Republic better to use what you could tell them, rather than to prosecute you.'

The Lynx knew exactly what he had meant when he said this to Esslin but replied: 'I don't remember, I'll take your word for it.'

'My question,' Esslin spoke carefully, choosing exactly the right words, 'is did you hand over to the Federal Intelligence Service your remaining illegals in order to secure a deal which would save you from prosecution?'

'Don't be absurd!'

'Somebody in the . . . I can't say where,' Esslin reined himself in, 'told me that the case against you was allowed to fail. There's been a lot of talk about some of the Stasi illegals still being in place abroad. Are these things connected?'

Mandelmann didn't like Esslin's persistence. 'Listen, young man. Shall we talk off the record for a moment?'

'Sure.'

'There are one or two very low-grade people still abroad. They have not been active in any intelligence sense for years;

they have just been allowed to remain where they are because their roots have gone so deep in these countries that they don't want to come home. Of course, in our time we had some very successful illegals – some of whom will probably never be exposed. But I can assure you that none of my agents remain abroad in any active sense.'

'Uh-huh,' Esslin replied, still scribbling. Mandelmann had torpedoed his pet theory. It was about as clear a denial as one could expect.

'If that's all?' said Mandelmann. Their conversation was at an end.

Chapter Thirty-Six

Later that morning a cab collected Denton and took him towards his rendezvous. He turned to admire the elegant lines of his home as the car pulled away from the kerb. Shortly after setting off Denton asked the cabby: 'Could you just pull in here for a moment. I have to post a letter.'

He climbed slowly out of the door, surveyed the scene briefly and tucked a single white envelope into the box.

Lee had chosen Turnham Green carefully as the place to meet his wife and daughter. The entrance to the tube station faces the green and is obscured from one side by the bridge which carries District Line trains thundering overhead. There are no buildings offering good observation points overlooking the entrance. Anybody who wishes to do so must stand opposite on the other side of the road in front of the small area of open space.

Going so near to his old CID stomping ground was a calculated risk. Lee accepted that he might be recognised, but he felt that his knowledge of the road layout and of some of the characters and businesses in the area would help him to spot any surveillance at the scene.

He parked the Escort in a road across the Green in a road which led under the railway bridge but was blocked to traffic at one end. Lee decided that this could work to their advantage if they had to flee the scene suddenly. He considered leaving the sub-machine gun in the boot, but decided to carry it, inside the grip.

Tim Ashman, Sam Boswell and a couple of people who ran the A4 Watchers had gone into a room at the 182 Hotel half an hour earlier, just after 2 p.m. The room did not overlook the station entrance, it was on the same side of the road and the railway bridge blocked its field of view. Bill, the A1 housebreaker, joined them a little later. They sat in the cheaply furnished room watching the kettle boil and wondering which of them would use the two mugs provided by the hotel. The A4 men had set up a radio and the voices of the Watchers scattered around the area occasionally crackled over its speaker. Boswell had not seen Ashman since the discovery of the radio receivers at Jubilee Road.

'It was competently done, nice workmanship.'

'Any prints on the trunk?'

'We haven't checked yet. The scanners were commercially available types, but it might be possible to trace the purchaser.'

'What about the landlady?'

'She said it was a bunch of builders rented the flat, always paid cash. Gave us some names but they don't ring any bells.'

As Boswell was sitting pondering the meeting, he suddenly remembered that Gerald Porton was due to return from his foreign holiday that morning. 'May I use the phone?' he asked nobody in particular. Nobody objected as he dialled the Cambridge number.

'Mr Porton?'

The answer crackled.

'Professor Porton, I beg your pardon. My name is Sam Boswell. I'm a civil servant at the Ministry of Defence and we're making some inquiries into a Charles Denton. I understand you were schoolmates—' Boswell was cut short as the professor gave him an unwanted lecture on the nature of his relationship with the eighteen-year-old Charles Denton. 'Anyway, I wanted to have a chat with you, show you some recent pictures of him—'

This time, Porton's reaction caught Boswell truly off guard.

'Zero, this is Mike Four,' a voice burst in from the radio.

'Send, over.' Harrison the A4 commander hunched forward over his microphone.

'I've got somebody who I believe is Target One approaching across the Green.'

There was a burst of activity in the room. 'Off the phone, please!' Harrison barked.

'I'm sorry, professor, I'm being called away. Can I ring you back a little later?'

Boswell rang off, said 'fuck', took out a notebook and started scribbling. An A4 man went to a camera with a long lens which poked through the room's drawn curtains.

'Which is mike four?' Boswell asked.

'He's in the van directly outside here – Mobile Four,' Harrison said, and then waved his hand at Boswell to silence him. 'Mike Three, go to your alternative location one, Mike Two go to road junction Alpha, Sierra One and Sierra Two move now to your alternative locations.'

One by one the surveillance operators on the ground responded.

'He's an hour and a half early!' Harrison said, glancing at his watch nervously to underline the point. 'I can move people around but he's going to rumble them sooner or later.' Harrison was in his late thirties, a clean-cut, conventionally handsome but slightly nondescript-looking man, one of the Service's best Watchers. His anonymity was a clue to his success. Harrison lit up a cigarette and crossed off his list of callsigns one by one as they confirmed they had heard his orders to redeploy.

'I've got him,' the Watcher at the window said, as his Nikon motor-drive powered into life. 'It's him; it's Johnson . . . he's got some kind of bag with him.'

Lee walked down the broad path which led to the road. He noticed the red van parked beside the road, a man at the wheel reading the *People*. There were seven or eight other people in his field of view. A mum and two small children, tick them off, safe. An elderly couple, look too unsteady on their feet to give chase, safe too. He reached the road and turned left, under the railway bridge and out of the field of view of the Watcher in the hotel room. He noticed another dozen or so around the entrance to the tube station.

'Who's on him now?' Boswell asked.

'Quiet for a minute!' Harrison scolded.

'Sierra Six, Target One has turned right, right, and is crossing towards the entrance.' Sierra Six was a woman in her fifties who was sitting on a bench in part of the Green which overlooked the entrance. 'He's watching people quite carefully, he's –' she broke off for a moment, which Harrison knew from experience meant that Johnson was looking towards her – 'he's buying some sweets at the station kiosk.'

Lee's own counter-surveillance instincts taught him that arriving somewhere a long time before a meet would give him a good opportunity to notice the vehicles which kept reappearing, the people who stayed put for too long. He stood in the tube entrance pretending to do the crossword on a newspaper somebody had dropped. In fact he wrote down notes – 'woman red jacket, 30s', or 'Blue Montego B583MUK' – if something attracted his suspicions. If he was going to stand there for an hour and a half there would be far more than he could remember. From time to time, he moved across the road, or in a position to observe people on the 182 Hotel side of the bridge. He noticed that there were two phone boxes on the Green side of the road, opposite the hotel, and wondered whether Elaine was home.

Within fifteen minutes Harrison had ordered Mike Four – his man in the red van parked outside – to move to a different location, and moved a different mobile, Mike One, into position, observing the station entrance. Mike One consisted of a man and a woman in their thirties sitting in a Toyota saloon.

Just after 3.30 p.m., Lee decided to go across to the phone booths and ring Elaine. He dialled her number from memory.

'Hi! I didn't think you'd be in.'

In the upstairs of the 182 Hotel there was a sudden flurry of activity.

'Tim, have you got that number intercepted?' Boswell asked.

'The phone box?'

'Yes, the phone box!' Boswell replied with obvious impatience.

'No, but it won't take Special Support a moment.' Ashman dialled the number on his mobile phone. 'Peter, this is Tim, we need an intercept PDQ on a box in Turnham Green Drive, West 11. There's a pair of them and the target's in the cash box.'

'The company you asked me about, BG Plastics in south Wimbledon,' Elaine said.

'Yes.'

'I didn't mention this before, because it didn't chime in with the Spanish addresses, but two of the directors have got lawyers' addresses in Munich listed.'

'That squares,' Lee replied, taking down the details.

'There's something else,' she said. 'The Watchers have left

this part of the world; one came through the office on Friday. They said they were gearing up for a big operation today, West London.'

Johnson felt a cool surge through his body, the hairs on the back of his neck prickle. 'Thanks. I'll be in touch, take care.' He replaced the receiver as quickly as he could, scanned every passing face with renewed anxiety. He wanted his wife and baby to be there now, so they could get away as soon as possible.

'He's finished the call!' Boswell said.

'Fuck! I'll get onto Peter.' Ashman pressed the redial button on his phone. He took out a pen and notebook and listened as the techical support people told him they had only been across the line in time to hear Johnson's last few words. He turned to Boswell. 'They got nothing of consequence on the conversation itself, Sam.'

'Brilliant!'

'But they checked the party he was talking to. Johnson just rang the home number of a detective sergeant in the Greater Manchester Police Special Branch.'

This revelation caused everybody to turn towards Boswell in anticipation.

'He's got somebody in the SB tipping him off?'

Harrison stubbed his sixth cigarette into the ashtray and swivelled on his chair to face Boswell. 'Are my operators compromised?'

'No reason to think they are,' Boswell said, but inwardly his faith in the operation was crumbling.

Lee had noticed the middle-aged woman on the park bench overlooking the station entrance. She was high on his list of possible surveillance operatives. He was so absorbed with the idea he almost didn't notice Jane and Gemma emerging from the station entrance. His glance met Jane's, then his eyes flicked down at his watch – 3.43 – then at the woman again. Then a gust of wind blew her hair and Lee saw the earpiece of her radio.

'Daddy!' it was Gemma's voice, breaking into his anxiety.

He turned and ran across the road to meet them.

'Tim!' Boswell prompted. 'Let's go!' The two men went pounding out of the room and down the stairs of the 182 Hotel.

'She's fucking early!' Pinchman shouted from his front seat in the white Transit van, as he, Dodge and the others made their way up Turnham Green Terrace. From behind he heard the sound of Dodge cocking his sub-machine gun.

Pinchman turned and saw Dodge opening the side door of the van. 'Wait! We're going to lift them!'

'Fuck you, Pinchman! We'll do it my way or I'll kill you too!'

Johnson, Jane and Gemma were walking briskly under the railway bridge as the Transit came across the oncoming lane of traffic and roared onto the pavment. Jane jumped clear, but as Lee picked up Gemma the van's front wing caught his legs, knocking him hard to the ground and stunning him into semi-consciousness.

'Zero, this is Mike One, there's something going on. A van just ran into Target One!'

As the van pulled off the pavement and travelled a short way up the road, Jane Johnson pulled the automatic pistol from her handbag. She looked down at Lee, whose eyes seemed to be rolling into consciousness again.

'Lee, can you walk?' she shouted.

'I'm OK, I'm OK . . .' But as he tried to stand, his left leg seemed to have no feeling or strength. Lee could see two men running towards them on the pavement.

The Transit had turned for a second pass. This time, Dodge could see Johnson and his wife from his open door on the side of the van. She had dropped to a semi-crouching firing position with her pistol. Dodge squeezed the trigger on his Sterling, sending a shower of bullets towards her. She heard no shots, but the crashing of glass as the 9mm rounds hit a shopfront behind her told Lee that they were under fire. Jane took aim at the driver and squeezed the trigger. There was a click but no shot. Ashman, who by then was only a few feet away knew exactly why. She tried again and again as the van picked up speed.

Lee had raised himself onto his right leg and was propping himself up against the door of the Seven Stars take-away. He pulled the MP5 out of the grip; he did not seem to hear or feel the impacts in the wall beside him as Dodge's second burst hit. With calm and concentration he extended the weapon's stock, cocked it, brought it to his shoulder to aim and let loose his first three rounds. His gun was far louder than the silenced Sterling and as his rounds shattered the front windscreen of the Transit, he could just hear people screaming.

'Zero, this is Mike One, all hell's breaking loose down here!' Harrison and the others tore open the curtains to the room and opened the window – desperate to see the drama unfold below.

Lee thought he had fired two bursts of three, but had actually sent eighteen rounds into the front of the van when he turned to Jane and shouted: 'Take Gems and run towards those phone boxes! Get into cover on the other side of the bridge!' He fired at the van again. Out of ammunition, he threw the clip aside and drew a full one from the bag. The van was hardly moving now. Johnson had put three 9mm rounds into the chest of its driver and killed Pinchman instantly with a shot through the forehead. As he turned to watch Jane's progress he came eye to eye with two men almost behind him. He snapped the MP-5 to his shoulder. 'WATCHERS, I'LL FUCKING KILL YOU!' he yelled, and Ashman and Boswell both raised their hands instinctively.

'It's OK, Lee! It's OK, take it easy!' Boswell said.

Then Johnson heard a sound like somebody slapping his thigh twice in quick succession. He knew it was bullets going into flesh and he saw the top of Ashman's head disappear, his twitching body crumpling to the pavement.

Johnson turned to see two men with silenced Sterlings walking up the road towards them. One was as tall as him, the other very short – he knew immediately who that was. For a moment he felt a strange thrill. 'Now I'll have you,' he thought.

He pushed past Boswell, who was crouching speechless over Ashman, dabbing pathetically with a blood-soaked handkerchief at his shattered head. He hobbled up the road as quickly as he could, then turned and fired a couple of bursts. He thought he could see the tall one drop.

As he crossed the road, he noticed a middle-aged woman still in one of the phone boxes, chattering away with her back to the drama – everywhere else people were cowering. As he passed he heard her saying: 'Well, I shall see Audrey next Tuesday.'

'Get going, straight up the path!' Lee shouted at Jane, glad for a moment or two that the railway viaduct would give him cover from fire. He looked down at his left leg: blood was seeping through his jeans. He could not find any bullet wounds as he hobbled up the path and turned to drop down behind one of the trees which ran up each side of it.

He spotted Dodge peering around the side of the viaduct's brickwork and fired a burst at him. He then ran off to find a second firing position. Dodge exploited the moment and left cover, running foward with a burst towards Johnson.

Lee turned and fired again, seeing Dodge drop forward by the phone boxes. He could see Jane and Gemma some way up the path, and looked back towards Dodge: he had dropped his gun but still seemed conscious. Lee turned back and began limping towards Dodge. As he got closer he could see the woman in the phone box slumped like a bag of old clothing, the receiver dangled by her motionless head with a voice repeating: 'Hello! Hello!' When Johnson was no further than five or six feet from Dodge, the little man looked up and their eyes met. With agonising slowness, Dodge's hand began to move towards the pocket of his combat jacket.

'Don't move!' Johnson shouted.

'You haven't got the bottle, you cunt!' Dodge replied, as his fingers found the familiar contours of a grenade.

Lee gave him two rounds in the head.

Within minutes, he had got his wife and child to the car and they had sped away. He saw no sign that they were being followed. There was a sound of sirens, but as they joined the M4 he was sure they had escaped clean.

In Cedar Falls, Virginia, Hal Canning and his wife Jean had yet to welcome their first guests for brunch. Her suspicions were aroused when Hal disappeared for almost thirty minutes. After looking around upstairs she realised he must be in the guest cloakroom near the front door. She did not call his name, but as she approached the closed door she heard a strange noise from within – a strangled sobbing.

'Honey, are you OK?'

The noise seemed to stop; it was followed by some sniffing. After what seemed like a few minutes, he unlocked the door and Jean saw his reddened eyes and sagging mouth. She had never seem him look quite so low.

'Honey?' Her own voice betrayed anxiety.

'It's all over,' he said.

She led him by the hand and they sat at the bottom of the stairs. In her own mind she was sure that her husband had received some terrible news about his health. 'What's the matter?' she asked.

'I feel like I just can't go on any more.'

Her mind turned from health to their marriage.

'There have been some things at the Agency . . .' he started. 'I can't go into detail, but I don't think it can go on much longer.'

Jean could feel only relief. 'Is it so serious?'

'It's something that will destroy me utterly if it ever comes out.' His eyes were moist again.

'I'll stand by you.'

'I know you will.' The tears began to stream down again as his head slumped against her shoulder. 'I know you will . . . I don't deserve you.'

Boswell remained sitting on the pavement with Ashman's body until the Scenes of Crime officer arrived and began combing the whole area. He hardly spoke to anybody. As he finally climbed to his aching legs, having spotted Travis arriving at the scene, Boswell realised that there was something he had not told anybody. As he approached Travis, the Legal Adviser looked ashen. 'What happened?'

'I don't know whose idea this marvellous operation was, but your technical officer is dead, Mr Travis.' Boswell struggled to muffle the emotion and anger in his voice. 'That little bastard over there under the white sheet by the phone boxes killed him – came within an inch or two of topping me and the Johnsons.'

'You did terrifically well, Sam—' Travis said lamely.

'There's something else you need to know.'

'Yes?'

'I spoke to Gerald Porton – the bloke who was at school with Denton. I don't know who the hell's been working for the Service for the last twenty-five years, but Charles Denton was killed in a car crash when he was nineteen.'

Travis could say nothing.

'If that's all, I'm going home to drink until I can't remember another thing about this sodding day!' Boswell put his mac over his shoulder and walked past the Legal Adviser, picking his way through the chaos of blue flashing lights which clogged Turnham Green Terrace.

Chapter Thirty-Seven

Hal Canning took the lift to the seventh floor at Langley. He did not want to be there. Since he heard that Vincent Dubois had been sniffing around the accounting system a few days before, his composure had begun to crack. Now he hated the building, its people, the Agency with all his will. His mind raced around different schemes: could he take one of the false identities he had acquired in his career and a great deal of money and simply disappear? Should he use information he had hoarded for years about Parker's slush funds in Southeast Asia to launch a pre-emptive strike against him?

The time for speculation, though, was at an end. As Canning walked into his outer office he found Parker standing there and his secretary said: 'DDO here to see you urgently, Mr Canning.'

'Hi Jim,' Canning said, shaking his hand.

'Hal, good morning,' Parker replied and the two men walked into Canning's office together.

'What can I do for you, Jim?' Canning asked, but he glanced downwards, then at his papers – everywhere except at Parker.

It was only 9 a.m., but Parker had already loosened his tie and rolled up his shirtsleeves. He did not reply immediately, instead waiting for Canning to meet his glance. 'Can you guess?'

'No, I can't.' Canning broke eye contact again.

'I'm here because I'd like to ask you about Mountain Resources, Crusader Systems and some little operation you've been running in UK.' Parker was deliberate but calm.

'I'm not familiar with what you're talking about.'

'Bullshit!'

'If you're going to take that tone—'

'Shut the fuck up.' Parker was moving around the room now. Canning remained seated behind his desk, glancing at his accuser uneasily from time to time. 'Do you know what happened in London yesterday?'

'No?'

'Well you should do.' Parker pulled a telex from his shirt pocket. 'Sitrep from London Station.' His eyes scanned the preamble. 'During a shootout in the Turnham Green neighbourhood of West London at least three men were killed yesterday. British news media have named the dead as Peter Francis Pinchman, Martin Dodge and Timothy Gerald Ashman. Ashman has been referred to by British newsmedia as a civil servant, but Station believes him to have been a member of the UK Security Service.'

Canning did not react.

'Vince has done some digging this morning and tells me that Pinchman ran Panther, to which you transferred something in the region of two million of Uncle Sam's dollars. I'm afraid Vince has also taken the trouble to look at your phone bill and boy, guess what – you've been phoning Pinchman at home!' Parker cracked a big smile.

'I knew him, that's true,' Canning said defensively.

'When I was last in London, I found my ass being chewed by the Chief of MI6. He thinks your Panther people killed two other Brits – some hooker and a cop. I told him nobody from this Agency would be so goddamn stupid as to run that kind of dumb-fuck operation in Britain. Then guess what? I get back here and start digging and, hey presto, I find something different: there is somebody that stupid in this agency, and if the Hill gets a sniff of this, that stupid sonofabitch is taking the rest of us down with him.'

Canning's head was reeling. He could not understand why British intelligence would have told Parker this – why would they blow their own source?

'You've been running some chickenshit operation, Hal.' Parker was in his stride now – talking, moving with increased urgency and emphasis. 'You can have your fun from time to time running little bullshit operations but I draw the line at killing people. What you been playing at, son?'

'I've done nothing wrong; if Pinchman has been committing crimes, I have nothing to do with it.'

'You just been paying him the money because you like him?'

'No—'

'No what? What's your story?'

Canning looked long at the beast of a man pacing his room. 'I'm not saying anything else until I have an attorney present.'

'Attorney? The fuck you will! You've been out there killing Brits, you've been misusing Agency funds by the million. When this hits the fan the Agency's going to be hurting so bad we'll all go down. I don't want anybody outside this room to find out what you've been doing.'

'You want to protect the Agency, eh, Jim?'

'That's right, protect it from a motherfucker like you.'

'Sure you don't just want to finish my chances of being Director?'

'Your chances? You're beneath contempt. I'll give you twenty-four hours to go to the Director and tell him what you've done, otherwise I'm making a full report.'

'All I've been doing is helping the Brits,' Canning said.

Parker's tone softened. 'Hal, whatever you've done is between you and your God, but I don't know how you ever thought you could go this far out on a limb and not come crashing down. If you've got any feelings for this Agency, you'll do the honourable thing.' He turned and walked out.

Canning sat at his desk and opened a drawer in which he had a .45 automatic pistol. Once or twice he lifted it and placed its frigid muzzle to his temple. He could not bring himself to squeeze the trigger; he shivered with fear at the thought of it. More and more he was becoming convinced that, whatever game Denton was playing, he could not have been playing him for the Brits. Suddenly he began to make sense of so many of the things which MI6 headmen had said to him over the years but which he had never understood. Certainly these people did not seem to think that they were running him. It had always been his nightmare that Denton was not what he seemed.

'Mr Canning, sir, there's a lady on the phone from London and she's most insistent that she wants to speak to you.' His secretary's voice sounded on the intercom speaker. 'She says her name is Jane Johnson and that she knows all about Nicola Dawson?'

'Put her through,' Canning replied.

'Mr Canning?' A nervous voice on the line inquired.

'Yes, Canning speaking.'

'It's Jane Johnson here, do you know who I am?'

'I think so. How can I help you, Mrs Johnson?'

'I've been reading the documents about your visit to a house in Kandahar Road in Bermondsey in 1971.'

'Yes?' Canning's voice seemed an almost lifeless monotone now.

'You should know that my husband and I have all the evidence we need against you.'

Canning heard the click as Jane Johnson turned on a tape recorder. 'You're hurting me, stop!' It was Nicola Dawson's voice recorded in 1971. Then he heard his own voice. 'Oh yes, yes . . . come on, honey, don't quit on me!' and then the grunts of his noisy ecstasy.

'A lot of people have died to protect your dirty secret, Mr Canning. You should know that I'm taking everything I know to somebody I can trust in the event of any harm coming to me or my family.'

'You'll not come to any harm,' Canning said, his eyes resting on the .45 in front of him. 'As for me, I was simply hoping to help your country.'

'MI5 wasn't blackmailing you, Canning. It was Denton, and he was working for someone else. I'd like to read you something, Mr Canning – hold on a minute . . .' Jane pulled out one of the photocopies from the folder in front of her. 'On the bottom of one of the papers reporting what happened with you, the head of the Security Service wrote: "Action: destroy all audio tapes and photographic material relating to this operation. Unlike my predecessor, I cannot foresee a circumstance in which we would use this kind of material to compromise an intelligence officer of so close an ally." That was written in 1972, Mr Canning.'

There was no response from Canning.

'Hello?' Jane asked after a moment.

'Thanks for reading me that, Mrs Johnson. It answers a lot of questions. I'm sorry . . . I'm sorry for everything,' Canning said, replacing the receiver.

Canning's secretary jumped as the .45 went off, and a river of spilt coffee ran across her desk as her boss's bloody head hit the floor.

Jane Johnson and John Middlebrook were met at the Members' Entrance by the Right Honourable Sir Dennis Poulter's secretary. They arrived in his office to find Donald Travis and Monica Davies already sitting there.

'Thank you, Polly,' Poulter said and nodded in the direction of the door. 'Mrs Johnson, I hope you don't mind two people from the Security Service being here?'

Middlebrook was about to speak, but Jane cut him off. 'No, not at all.'

Poulter had served Thatcher in the early years of her government as Home Secretary; he had left after a public row over prison budgets in 1983 and become a backbench critic of her government. He had hoped to renew his ministerial career after her fall, but the call had never come. The party still remembered his disloyalty. Jane could tell from his complexion that Poulter liked a drink. He seemed a good deal seedier in life than during his frequent television appearances and this worried her momentarily. She buried her doubts – it was too late for that now.

'You know why we're here, Mr Travis,' Middlebrook began, running his hand nervously across his bearded chin. 'We'd like guarantees, written guarantees of the Johnson family's security.'

'I'm sorry, that's simply out of the question. I won't put anything in writing,' Travis said briskly.

There was a pause. Middlebrook had understood that his strategy was probably unrealistic but had felt obliged to try it.

'I've got copies of the papers you want here with me now,' Jane began. 'I want your guarantee that no harm will come to my husband or my daughter and me.'

'You have it,' Travis replied emphatically.

'Marvellous!' Poulter exclaimed in an upper-class drawl. 'Can we all go home now?'

'Can you guarantee that there was no connection between you and the people who tried to harm the Johnsons?' Middlebrook asked, an angry rasp in his voice.

'Of course there was none,' Monica Davies replied.

'You understand that one of our officers died yesterday, don't you? He died because he was trying to speak to Lee

Johnson,' Travis said, bouncing Middlebrook's hostility back towards him.

Middlebrook and Jane looked at one another. 'I'm sorry,' she said.

'We understand a little bit more about who was trying to kill your husband, Mrs Johnson. It was a low-rent freelance mob; there's an international dimension. I think the people primarily responsible for trying to kill him died in Turnham Green as well yesterday.'

'So it's over?' Jane asked.

'It's over from our point of view,' Travis replied.

'Meaning?' Middlebrook looked hard at the MI5 Legal Adviser.

'Your husband killed two men yesterday, Mrs Johnson. He shot one in the head as he was lying helpless on the pavement. The police may wish to charge him for it.'

'They were trying to kill us.' Her tone was suddenly less calm. 'I was there – just talk to any of your people who were there, there were bullets flying around like confetti, I have never been so terrified in my life.' Jane was glad Lee had not come to the meeting, going to ground instead in one of his hiding places.

'They were trying to kill him, that's true,' Travis replied. 'Of course the same can't be said for that forty-four-year-old spinster he shot in the phone box.'

Jane was silent. Middlebrook replied. 'Who?'

'He put a bullet into a woman who was in a phone box – her condition is serious,' Monica Davies explained.

'That's the kind of thing that happens when you start spraying a machine gun around on a suburban street, Mrs Johnson,' Travis added.

'He was responding in the way the Army taught him – "the first to shoot lives", "don't take a chance with an injured man". These are the things they drummed into him. He used to repeat them to me again and again,' Jane replied.

'If he'd done it in Ulster you would have called him a hero!' Middlebrook couldn't contain his contempt any more.

'Leftie lawyer stands up for CID man with illegally-held gun who mows people down on a Sunday afternoon,' Monica Davies retaliated with undisguised hostility: 'Very novel!'

'Ladies, gentlemen!' Sir Dennis Poulter felt the time was right for him to step in as mediator. 'It seems to me that it would not be in the interests of either side for this whole affair to be put to a trial.'

'We can't stop the police, Sir Dennis,' Travis answered. 'They've got three murders on their books; they'll want to clear them up. That's all we're saying.'

'Try,' Jane Johnson replied, 'then I'll try to keep it out of the papers, and of course I'll give you back the tape your people recorded in that brothel in 1971.'

'Here we go again!' Sir Dennis wailed. 'Now it strikes me that you and me between us –' he nodded at Travis – 'can square this thing with the Attorney General on the grounds that this all relates to a highly sensitive matter of national security: prosecution is clearly not in the public interest.'

'Possibly,' Travis conceded.

'In return our two friends promise never to co-operate with the press on this whole matter. Is that agreeable?'

'It is,' Jane replied. Middlebrook leant across, obviously concerned, and whispered in her ear. 'It is,' she repeated, handing over a file with photocopies of the Operation RACE-TRACK documents and a cassette of the surveillance tape. The MI5 man saw immediately that the tape was a recent copy, but he was too proud to get Jane to confirm his suspicion that the Johnsons had kept the original of a recording Service records said had been destroyed years ago. Jane interrupted his thoughts, looking him in the eye. 'Hal Canning says he's very sorry about the whole affair.'

'Who?' Monica Davies allowed curiosity to get the better of her professionalism.

336

'I'll tell you later,' Travis said briskly to his number two. At that moment, he felt more awkward than he had ever done in his job before and he hated Jane Johnson for it. Poulter ignored this mysterious reference, taking satisfaction instead from the apparent deal. 'It would seem your husband is clear to put his head above the parapet, Mrs Johnson.'

'I'll tell him as soon as I can. By the way, he spoke to Charles Denton yesterday,' said Jane.

'Really?' said Travis, his hatred of Jane suddenly boosted beyond what he thought was feasible, but desperately keen to know.

Jane decided she wouldn't give them the satisfaction of saying any more. Instead she and Middlebrook thanked Sir Dennis for his good offices and left without another word to the two MI5 officers.

Poulter surveyed them coolly. 'A very clever lady, that Mrs Johnson. It strikes me that you're very lucky she was amenable to a deal.'

'Really?' Monica Davies replied.

'Yes. It's fairly obvious that you people have had a rather unfortunate experience, and if she's willing not to do the dirty, I would have thought it was in your interest to honour this bargain we've made here today to the letter.'

'We'll honour it,' Travis replied, buttoning his blazer and picking up his briefcase. 'Of that I have no doubt.'

Chapter Thirty-Eight

The usual gaggle of detectives, barristers and court reporters had gathered at the Central Criminal Court. Four men were to be tried for a range of serious offences including attempted murder, kidnap and grievous bodily harm. As the trial opened, the defence lawyers for 'Sancho' Doherty and his three accomplices learned that the Crown Prosecution Service did not intend to bring any charges relating to the robbery of the Majestic safe deposit company itself, but only to the events at Frithville Gardens. The prosecution advised the court that, due to 'events beyond our control', it would be impossible for them to bring a full case on the other charges. It was true that the murder of Detective Constable David MacFadyen and the disappearance of his partner meant there were no actual witnesses to tie the gang to the events at the safe deposit box centre. Sancho's lawyers had assumed that the recovery of several sacks full of property stolen from the boxes would be enough to bolt his client firmly to the robbery and the raft of charges that went with it – still, the CPS moved in mysterious ways. They contented themselves that their client might only go down for ten to fifteen years.

One person left the court as soon as the shorter-than-expected list of charges had been read to the men in the dock. Having made his way through the corridors and out onto the street, Donald Travis spotted his driver and was sped by Daimler back to the haven of Gower Street.

He took a number of calls from journalists that week.

Among the Legal Adviser's many tasks was liaison with the press. The tabloids had been quick to pick up the rumours that Tim Ashman, victim of the spectacular machine-gun shootout in Turnham Green, was a spook. Travis's line, deep background of course, was that Ashman had been one of their men but it was no more than a tragic coincidence that he was there at the time that some underworld types chose to slug it out. He told the one or two hacks who kept pushing that actually, Ashman had been a clerical type and it was sheer fantasy to suppose that he would have been involved in this kind of gun battle. Travis took satisfaction from the fact that none of the callers connected events with Lee Johnson – or, thank God, with the reports from Washington that the CIA's Deputy Director for Intelligence had committed suicide. But the Legal Adviser's confident tone with the press hid the state of near panic at Gower Street following the revelation that the Charles Denton who had served them for so many years was not the man they believed him to be.

The Director General thanked Travis for his good work, and told him a new investigation of a different order of sensitivity had begun. Messengers had begun to arrive with boxes full of documents from the Registry's deep storage archive outside London. Van after van drove into the underground car park, bringing mountains of paper: everything that Charles Denton had ever seen in his years at the Service. The Service's top molehunter, the Director of Counter-Espionage – perhaps the natural figure to investigate the possibility of penetration – was unacceptable. He, after all, had been Denton's boss for the last three years, writing him glowing personal reports. Instead the Deputy Director General for Operations – the number two officer – had taken control. As his boss looked down from her office onto the gridlock of Euston Road, she began to grope for the words that she would inevitably have to find to warn the Home Secretary of the possibility that an agent of an enemy state had